FURY

FURY

JOHN COYNE

WARNER BOOKS

A Warner Communications Company

Warner Books, Inc., 666 Fifth Avenue, New York, NY 10103

W A Warner Communications Company

Printed in the United States of America

First Printing: October 1989

10 9 8 7 6 5 4 3 2 1

Library of Congress Cataloging-in-Publication Data
Coyne, John.
    Fury / John Coyne.
    p. cm.
    ISBN 0-446-51420-9
    I. Title.
PS3553.096F8 1989   89-40036
813'.54—dc20   CIP

Book Design by Nick Mazzella

For Nansey Neiman,
who asked, ''What if . . . ?''

FURY

BOOK ONE

I wasn't unhappy or disturbed by what I was learning. Not in the least. As a matter of fact, it was a kind of liberation of understanding to realize that my life today was a result of the lives that had preceded it, that I was the product of many lives and would be again. It made sense. There was a harmony to that—a purpose—a kind of cosmic justice which served to explain everything in life—both positive and negative.

—Shirley MacLaine

I became aware that I was losing contact with myself. At each step of the descent a new person was disclosed within me of whose name I was no longer sure and who no longer obeyed me. And when I had to stop my exploration because the path faded beneath my steps, I found a bottomless abyss at my feet, and out of it comes—arising I know not from where—the current which I dare to call my life.

—Pierre Teilhard de Chardin

1

"MS. WINTERS," THE HOTEL receptionist said, "I believe we have a message for you." The small black man moved down the counter to the computer terminal and typed in a command, then waited for the response on the screen.

Jennifer glanced around the lobby of the Washington, D.C., hotel and spotted a printed sign that read:

MEET KATHY DART, CHANNELER OF HABASHA.
JOIN THE NEW AGE!
CHANGE YOUR PERSPECTIVE ON
LIFE, WORK, RELATIONSHIPS.

That's what she needed, Jennifer thought wryly, a change, especially in her love life.

"Yes, here it is," the reception clerk said. " 'Room twenty-three fourteen. Jenny, I have a two o'clock appointment. See you at four.' And it's signed, 'T.' " The reception clerk looked up. "Would you like a copy?"

"No, thank you. Room twenty-three fourteen, yes?"

"That's right. I'll delete this message?"

"Yes, please." She bent down and picked up her briefcase.

"And I'll have your luggage sent up," the clerk added, handing her a computer card. "Your room won't be ready for another twenty minutes, at two o'clock."

Jennifer took a deep breath. It was Tom who had also made sure his Justice Department meetings were scheduled for this Thursday so that they could spend the night together in the Washington hotel. She had not seen Tom in three days; they had not made love in a week. She wanted to make love to him so much now, she could taste it. Sometimes it seemed to her that all they had in common was good sex. They certainly did know how to make that work.

Turning away from the reception counter, she caught her reflection in the lobby mirrors and was pleased and surprised to see how thin she looked in her new Calvin Klein suit. The French blue color was right, she saw. It favored her fair complexion and her honey blond hair. But she wasn't happy with her lip gloss. The shade was too orange and exaggerated her lips. Her mouth was big enough as it was.

"Jenny! Jennifer Winters!" A woman's high, sharp voice stopped her. Jennifer glanced around and spotted Eileen Gorman waving to her from deep in the lounge. "Jennifer, is that really you!" the woman said, rushing toward her.

Jennifer grinned and went to her. "Eileen, I can't believe it's you!" She wrapped her arms around the smaller woman and briefly hugged her. "It's so good to see you! What a surprise!"

"Are you here for the conference?" Eileen asked.

"Yes, the foundation conference. Who are you with, Eileen?"

"Foundation, no. I'm here for Kathy Dart. She's going to channel Habasha."

"Who? What?" Jennifer let go of Eileen's hand and set down her briefcase.

"You don't know who Kathy Dart is?" Eileen asked, her green eyes widening.

She still looks like a cheerleader, Jennifer thought, smiling at her old friend. "Eileen, you look wonderful! Do you live here in Washington?"

"No, I'm still living on Long Island." She took a deep breath and sighed, then, still grinning, said, "What a wonderful surprise! It's so good to see you, Jenny." She reached over and again embraced Jennifer. "You look beautiful. Now, what do you do? Where do you live?" she asked.

"In the city. New York. Brooklyn Heights, really. I've been there since law school."

"I had heard you moved to California. Anita told me. You remember Anita?"

"Yes, of course. Yes, I did move to L.A., but . . ."

"Some guy?"

Jennifer nodded, then turned her thumb down.

Eileen laughed and asked, glancing at Jennifer's left hand, "Married?"

"No, just . . . well, involved." She shrugged her shoulders. "You know how it is."

"Tell me!" Eileen sighed, still smiling at Jennifer. Then she said, "It's so good to see you, Jennifer. What is it that you do exactly?"

"I'm a lawyer with the James Thompson Foundation. We give money to good causes—civil rights outfits, that sort of liberal thing. I came down for a meeting. Now, who is this Kathy Dart?"

"Oh, you must see Kathy. She's just wonderful!" Eileen's voice rose, and she beamed at Jennifer. "She's a channeler. A wonderful channeler!"

"What?" Jennifer asked, laughing.

"You know what a channeler is, don't you?"

Jennifer shook her head, suddenly feeling foolish. "I'm sorry, but I—"

"Channeling was written up in *People* magazine. There was a story about Kathy's psychic powers. Kathy receives information from this prehistoric human called Habasha who has returned to help us with our lives today."

"Are you into that stuff?" Jennifer asked.

"This is one of her few East Coast appearances this winter," Eileen went on.

"Appearance? Does she do seances?" Jennifer kept smiling at Eileen, amused by her overwhelming enthusiasm.

"No! She's a channeler." Eileen opened a pink folder. "It's a special session called 'A Weekend with Habasha'!"

"Who?" Jennifer laughed out loud, and then touched Eileen's arm and said, "I'm sorry to be so flippant."

"That's all right," Eileen answered. "I can't blame you. I was the same way until I heard him."

"Him?"

"Habasha. I know it's confusing, but Kathy Dart is only the channel, you see. Habasha uses her body to speak to us. It's sort of like possession, but isn't. She 'channels' him. He speaks to us through her body. What she does—Kathy that is—is to allow herself to set aside her waking consciousness to allow knowledge—Habasha's knowledge—that lies beyond conscious awareness to flow into her mind and through her ability to speak."

"A medium, you mean?"

"Yes, that, but more, Jennifer. You'll see."

"I'll see?"

"Yes, come with me to hear Kathy. She's about to have an introductory session. It's for, you know, spouses, friends. C'mon with me, Jenny, and then we can have a cup of coffee and talk, or maybe dinner. Are you busy tonight?"

"Eileen, I can't. . . ."

"Do you have plans?"

"No, but the foundation meeting opens tomorrow."

"It's just a half hour," she said enthusiastically.

"Okay, why not?" It might be fun, Jennifer thought, and also she'd have time to talk more with Eileen. "Are you sure it will only take thirty minutes?"

"It will take your whole life, once you hear him," Eileen answered, linking her arm through Jennifer's. "It's so good to see you. How long has it been? Graduation, right?"

Jennifer nodded. "I think so. It seems like an age. I mean, so much has happened in my life."

"You're telling me?"

They reached a bank of elevators, and Eileen pressed the down button. "It's set to start in five minutes," she said. "Kathy and Habasha are . . . is . . . never late."

"Who is she, he, . . . or it?" Jennifer asked, really confused now.

"He's prehistoric. A Cro-Magnon man."

"What!" Jennifer exclaimed, backing off.

Eileen laughed. "I know, I know. It all sounds silly and strange, but really it isn't. Just wait! Keep an open mind. I was the same way until I heard Kathy Dart speak. You'll see."

When the elevator door opened, they stepped out into the lower lobby of the hotel. Through a set of open doors, Jennifer saw a crowd of people already gathered on at least a hundred metal folding chairs. It looked like any other hotel conference session she had ever attended.

But at the far end of the room was a winged green satin armchair placed upon a small platform. The chair was surrounded with flowers, bouquets of bright spring blossoms, and Jennifer was stuck by how incongruous it all seemed. Directly behind the armchair, a beautiful crystal pyramid was suspended from the ceiling, though it seemed to hang in midair like a halo. Of course, she thought, remembering now some of the things she had read about the New Age movement. Quartz crystals were considered a source of psychic energy.

"They're all women," Jennifer said, scanning the crowd.

"Well, yes, mostly. I really hadn't noticed," Eileen answered as they stepped into an aisle and sat down in two of the folding chairs.

Jennifer saw that the majority of women were like her. They were mostly in their late twenties, well dressed, and many were wearing business suits and carrying briefcases, as if they had just come from the office. The few men in the audience were similarly well dressed and well groomed. This was not, she realized, a way-out group of people.

"One reason I feel comfortable going to one of these conferences," Eileen whispered to Jennifer, "everyone looks like me. See, we can't all be crazy." She smiled at Jennifer. "Oh, I'm so glad I ran into you. It's so exciting." Before Jennifer could respond, Eileen said quickly, "There she is."

Jennifer turned toward the door. Kathy Dart had appeared at the entrance, and the roomful of people immediately fell silent. Jennifer looked away for a moment and suppressed a smile. It would be impolite to laugh, she knew, but the flowers, the small throne, and all the pomp and circumstance were embarrassing. And now around her, Jennifer saw, people were smiling, and some had tears in their eyes as Kathy Dart entered the room.

The channeler came up the center aisle and smiled down at her audience. The palms of her hands were turned up, and as she moved toward the stage, she reached out to caress the cheek of one woman, to touch another's hand, to make physical contact with her followers.

She was beautiful, Jennifer saw. Beautiful in a delicate and fragile way. Very tall and thin, with sloping shoulders that concealed her height. She wore no makeup, and her very long and straight black hair set off her pure white skin. She looked like a woman who needed to be protected, who was too fragile for the world. Yet when she stepped into the room, she immediately overwhelmed it with her presence.

As Kathy Dart passed their chairs, her eyes swept down the row and then caught Jennifer's face, and she stopped walking. For a moment, her eyes were riveted on Jennifer, and the sweet smile slipped from her angelic face. Kathy Dart looked startled, as if she had been found out in some way. And Jennifer, at that moment, felt a surge of heat and pain sweep through her body, leaving her flesh aflame.

Kathy Dart broke off her gaze and turned abruptly away to find another face. She smiled warmly at the next person, as if she were trying to quickly reestablish herself with the crowd. Jennifer fell back into her chair, trembling from the silent exchange.

"She's almost thirty-three," Eileen whispered. "Don't you think that's interesting? You know, the same age as Jesus Christ?"

Jennifer could not catch her breath. The eye contact with Kathy Dart had surprised her, and seeing the disturbed look on the woman's face had frightened her. She turned to ask Eileen if she had seen the way Kathy Dart looked at her, but at that moment there emerged from the assemblage a soft humming. It swept across the crowded room, as if dozens of mothers were gently humming their infants to sleep.

Kathy Dart had reached the flower-decked platform, and the humming increased to a rushing crescendo. Kathy Dart faced the audience with uplifted arms. She was dressed in a long white gown trimmed in light blue. Around her neck she wore a gold chain that held a small quartz crystal.

The room lights dimmed and a small spotlight focused on Kathy Dart. She lifted her right hand, and as she slowly lowered it, the humming faded away.

"Thank you," she whispered, "for giving us some of your present time, for welcoming us into your life." She spoke slowly, smiling constantly at the audience, her bright blue eyes flashing in the spotlight.

It's going to be one of those talks, Jennifer realized at once. She was always uneasy around people who gushed with deeply felt emotions. Jennifer glanced at her watch. It was now 2:20. She had hoped to be through with her afternoon jog before Tom returned to the hotel. She would give this another twenty minutes, she decided, and then she'd leave.

"I'm sure you all know something—a little something perhaps—of channeling, of who I am, and of how this new man came into my life," Kathy Dart began, and the audience laughed.

She certainly had a nice easy delivery, Jennifer noted, coolly appraising her.

"My Old Man, I call him. God knows he's old enough," she said quickly, raising her voice in mock seriousness. "He's at least twenty-three million years old, give or take a few hundred years. Of course, I think he might be telling a few white lies about that age of his," she added, raising her eyebrows. Then she threw up both hands. "But who's counting!" The audience broke into quick applause.

Beside her, Eileen beamed up at Kathy Dart.

"Many of you, however, don't know about Habasha, and that is why I have these little talks early in the weekend, to give you and your friends a chance to meet my lover, my mentor, my best friend. I am sure some of you know that Habasha was once my warrior lover; in another time we were both pirates off the Barbary Coast, and in yet another time and another place he was my son. That is the wonderful nature of reincarnation. The wonderful nature of our spirits, ourselves, our souls. With the help of Habasha, I have regressed to my distant past, have tracked all my previous lives."

She paused and looked around the room, taking in the audience. Her large, shiny, saucer blue eyes caught and held everyone's attention.

"Reincarnation is such a wonderful, strange, and also beautiful aspect of our existence. It is a basic tenet of many religions. We are reincarnated! I know. And you know in your heart of hearts, too, that somehow, someway, you have lived before, have been another person, suffered perhaps and died, and then lived again.

"We know this from the religions of our childhood. I myself was raised a Roman Catholic, and within the teachings of my very first catechism, I learned how the saints of the early Christian faith came back from death to tell us about heaven as well as hell. I learned that all of us someday will join our Maker in eternity."

She had softened her voice, Jennifer realized, to draw people closer, to force them to be more attentive. Even she was leaning forward and paying more attention to Kathy Dart.

"I mention reincarnation because some people are made nervous by the idea that they are somehow born again in another person, in another time." Kathy laughed. "I guess if I thought I'd be reborn again with these big feet of mine, I'd be upset, too, but I have hope and faith that it won't happen the next time."

The audience broke into laughter. Jennifer leaned over to Eileen and whispered, "She does have a nice way about her, doesn't she?"

"She's wonderful," Eileen answered, her eyes moist with tears.

"But how do we know that we lived before?" Kathy Dart went on. "That we might have been—as I was—a Barbary Coast pirate? Or as Shirley MacLaine has said she was once, a hardworking woman of the night.

"We know," Kathy Dart whispered. "We know." She paused and swept her blue eyes across the room as she gently tapped her heart with her small closed hand. "We know in our hearts, don't we? We know we have lived before," she whispered, nodding to the crowd. Then her voice grew stronger and more confident. "We know because we have had that wonderful experience of turning the corner in some foreign country or looking at a photograph in a mossy old book and realizing, yes, we were there; we walked through those ancient streets, lived in those times. We, too, might have been a mistress of King George, a Christian tossed to the lions in the Colosseum, or perhaps a Cherokee princess, or an American housewife living the hard life on our western frontier. I mention those people in particular because they were some of my many former lives. I have lived and passed on. Lived and passed on again and again and again. We never die. Our spirits don't die. We all know that, regardless of our religious faith. Our spirits, ourselves, our egos, you might call it, have always been, will always be."

She paused and took in the audience. She had clasped her hands together as if in prayer.

"We know all this ourselves," she went on slowly. "It is a secret that has been locked away in our subconscious, but how do we know? That's the question."

"Exactly," Jennifer said out loud.

"Shhhh." Eileen nudged her. Eileen was sitting on the edge of her metal chair. Everyone was leaning forward, Jennifer saw; they were all on the edges of their chairs, straining to hear every word.

"Let me tell you how I know," Kathy offered. Her voice brightened and the audience stirred. They were going to hear a secret, Kathy's secret. Jennifer recognized the anticipation. Despite her cynicism, she, too, wanted to hear the secret of Kathy Dart's past lives.

Kathy Dart turned to the green satin chair and sat down. Even seated, she seemed to pull the audience close to her. She took her time straightening her long white cotton skirt, letting the audience adjust to her new position on the platform.

Jennifer glanced at her watch. She had been there for nearly twenty minutes. She should leave now, she thought, while there was a lull in the room, but the thought of standing up, of having everyone stare at her, kept her in her seat. It had been a mistake to let Eileen Gorman talk her into coming to this silliness. Jennifer glanced over and saw that Eileen was wearing a ring, and remembered that Eileen had married right after high school and hadn't gone on to college. It had surprised everyone at the time. There had been some talk, back then, that Eileen Gorman had to get married.

"I was, I guess, like any one of you," Kathy Dart began again, "just going along with my life, living it day by day, trying to get by, to be happy, to find someone to love.

"I'm sure you have heard something about the power of quartz crystals. It certainly has been in the newspapers. Shirley MacLaine, in her wonderful books, talks about crystals and pyramids and how they have been important to her in reestablishing her past lives.

"I didn't know it at the time of my first encounter with Habasha, but throughout history mediums have used crystals to align themselves with spirits, to capture the energy of past lives." She paused.

"I was a freshman at the time—this was in 1974—studying English at the College of St. Catherine in St. Paul, Minnesota, and my older sister, Mary Sue, who was in Ethiopia with the Peace Corps, had sent me a piece of quartz crystal. She had found it along the Hadar River, a tributary of the Awash River in southern Ethiopia.

"Some of you may remember that in 1974 Don Johanson, a paleoanthropologist working in East Africa with the famous Leakey family, found an early hominid and named her Lucy after the Beatles' song 'Lucy in the Sky with Diamonds.'

"Lucy stood three and a half feet tall, lived at the edge of the shallow lake, and died sometime in her early twenties.

"This all happened some 3.3 million years ago. But Lucy is very important in our lives—in my life especially—because she and her friends, all who camped and lived together on the banks of that Ethiopian river, proved that men and women had begun to bond, to share, to work together, to experience what we call human feelings.

"I didn't know any of this, of course. I was just eighteen years old; I had a paper due on Jane Austen the next morning and was secretly praying that the gorgeous boy I had met at Sunday afternoon's mixer would call and ask me out. You know how it is!" She said, shaking her head ruefully. The women laughed delightedly.

Jennifer smiled, too, remembering her own adolescence.

"Anyway, I was trying to work on my Jane Austen paper and in the mail came this small quartz crystal from my sister," Kathy Dart went on, fingering the clear quartz that hung around her neck. "I held it in my fingers, rubbing it slightly—out of nervousness, I guess—while I sat at my dorm desk.

"It was a typical fall day in St. Paul. My window was open and

I could hear kids on the lawn outside, and I was feeling sad that I was inside working on my paper when everyone else was having a good time—and then I heard a whooshing sound in the hallway. I glanced up and saw a brilliant blue-white light in the open doorway.

"I raised my hand to shield my eyes, and it was then, in the midst of this beautiful white light, that I heard Habasha speak to me."

She paused and looked down at her hands and the small quartz crystal. The room was silent. Jennifer realized she was holding her breath, waiting for Kathy Dart to continue.

"He spoke to me then," Kathy said softly, her head still down. "I can't say whether it was really words that he spoke, or if he just telepathically let himself be understood. But I did understand him. He said simply, 'Are you ready to receive me?'

"I remember shaking my head. I was too frightened to speak. And he went on, 'I'll come again when you are ready.' That was all. Gradually the blue-white faded. Again I heard the voices of students on the campus lawn. Habasha was gone. I didn't know his name, of course. I didn't know why he had chosen me, but I knew something wonderful had happened to me."

She paused to look searchingly at her audience. "I didn't see him again for ten years. He was waiting. Waiting for me to grow up and prepare myself to be his host in this world. He was waiting for me to agree to be his channel.

"I once asked Habasha why he had waited, instead of choosing someone else, and he explained that I had been ordained as his earthly host. Habasha and I are like runners in an endless race—passing each other and then stopping off somewhere, as it were, to spend a lifetime—and then in death flowing again in the endless cycles of the universe.

"And that is how Kathy Dart, of Rush Creek, Minnesota, the daughter of a dairy farmer, the youngest of eight children, came to be the channel for Habasha, who was first on earth at the dawn of civilization, living on the banks of the Hadar River, in southern Ethiopia.

"Habasha was killed on a sunny afternoon when a man rose up in anger and felled him with a blow of his club. His physical body died in a land we now know as Ethiopia, where my sister found a small piece of quartz crystal and sent it home to me. This piece of Africa that had once been part of Habasha's world, that was linked to his spirit, his time as a man, was now connected to me.

"When I touched the crystal that day at my dormitory, I pulled his spirit back to me through time. But I wasn't ready then. I wasn't open enough to receive him.

"In 1984 I was married, living in Glendora, California, and the mother of a darling little girl, Aurora. I woke one summer morning and realized that I no longer loved my husband, that I hated my life, and that I had to do something to save myself.

"I got out of bed before dawn and walked into the living room and over to the picture windows that looked out on our quiet suburban street. It was getting light outside. I could see the long line of palm trees that marked our cul-de-sac, and when I sat down in the window seat, I noticed my African crystal. Aurora had taken it out of my jewelry box to play with, and I picked it up and began to gently rub my fingers across its smooth clear surface. I was crying. I remember seeing my tears splash against my skin, and when I looked up again through the picture window, I saw him. He walked down the empty street, coming to me, and this time I knew I was ready, knew that I had suffered enough to be worthy of him. I knew then that I was going to be his channel.

"I live now with my daughter and a few close friends on my family's old farm in eastern Minnesota. It is there that we produce the tapes and books that reveal the wisdom of Habasha. It is from there that I travel to conduct these weekend sessions with Habasha.

"Now for all of you who wish to hear Habasha speak, we will have a trance-channel session this evening, and I hope you will join us. I know it will change your life. And now I must go, but to use the words of Habasha, 'I leave only for the joy of returning.' "

She stepped off the platform, taking the hand of a tall, thin, beautiful twelve-year-old girl who looked just like her, and walked out of the meeting room by the side exit. The audience rose and started to applaud. At the door, Kathy Dart paused, waved good-bye, and then dramatically disappeared.

"Oh, Jennifer, isn't she wonderful?" Eileen said quickly, as the applause faded.

Jennifer hesitated. She had to admit that Kathy Dart had affected her, but she wasn't ready to say how. "Well, it certainly was different!" She took a deep breath.

"She's just marvelous!" Eileen declared, standing.

"Yes. Well. I think . . ." Jennifer stood. The woman's presentation had dazed her. "I guess I don't know what to think." She turned to leave; she wanted fresh air.

"Are you coming tonight? To the channeling session?"

"I don't think so. I mean, I have to prepare for my meeting. What does the word *Habasha* mean, anyway?" she asked, to change the subject. They had reached the lobby of the hotel.

"*Habasha?* That's his name. Kathy told us it meant 'burnt face,' which is the name for Ethiopians. He took it himself, because when he was reincarnated as the female Lucy, speech hadn't yet been developed in the hominids."

"But Kathy Dart said he's at least twenty-three million years old. I don't understand. Lucy is only four million years old."

"Yes, I know." Eileen nodded. "What Kathy said was that Habasha's spirit appeared on earth 'in human form' four million years ago, at the dawn of man itself. Then, later, he has had other lives, other reincarnations. Just like us. But his spirit, or soul, is older than that."

Jennifer shook her head. The spell was broken. She no longer felt unnerved by Kathy Dart. She had been briefly swept away, but now she was all right. Jennifer was not like Eileen Gorman. She was not so overwhelmed that she had lost sight of what was reality.

"Well, I don't know who I once was, but I know for sure that I've never been a hominid, protohominid, or whatever they were called."

"But you don't know, Jenny. You don't know what you once were. And that's what's makes it all so exciting."

"Makes what so exciting?"

"Channeling! Habasha will tell you who you once were."

Jennifer was shaking her head before Eileen stopped talking.

"Not me. I've got enough bad memories just in this life. I don't need to learn about more lives."

"Oh, Jenny, come on, give it a try. Come see Kathy Dart channel Habasha, and you'll learn who you were in past lives."

Jennifer remembered the look on Kathy Dart's face when the channeler spotted her, remembered how her body had flamed up with pain and passion.

"No," she said firmly. "I don't want to know." And she meant it. She did not want to know, nor did she want to encounter Kathy Dart again.

"Excuse me," a young man said, approaching them.

Jennifer and Eileen both stopped talking and glanced up at him.

The young man smiled. He looked like a college student, Jennifer thought at once. A graduate student, perhaps. She noticed his eyes immediately. They were gray and almond shaped, like her brother's.

"My name is Kirk Callahan," he went on quickly, as if he were afraid they would bolt away. "I'm doing an article on Kathy Dart for *Hippocrates* magazine. And I was wondering if I might have a few minutes to talk with you about her, you know, and your experiences with channeling?" He kept smiling and had now focused his full attention on Jennifer, who was shaking her head before he finished talking.

"Not me!" she said defensively, and then laughed. "Perhaps my friend will talk to you. I don't know anything about any of this stuff." She glanced at Eileen and said quickly as the elevator arrived, "I'll call you later. 'Bye!" And then she stepped into the elevator before the doors closed, happy to be away from all these New Age people.

2

JENNIFER LEFT THE HOTEL by the side door, jogged down the sloping lawn to the bottom of Rock Creek Park, and picked up the bicycle path that she knew was good for running. She turned right and followed the level path under Massachusetts Avenue, heading for Georgetown and the C & O Canal. There was some snow on the ground, but the path was clear and dry.

The hour with Kathy Dart had made her uneasy, and she knew that being outside running would make her feel immensely better. It always did.

There were only a few joggers on the path, and Jennifer easily picked up speed. She hadn't run in several days, and she was surprised that her muscles were this loose. She unzipped the front of her blue Gore-Tex jacket and lengthened her stride.

The C & O Canal was the best place to run in Washington. There was always room for both runners and bikers, and as she moved easily past other joggers, she held close to the narrow gauge of muddy water on her left. The path she was on was once the towpath used to help barges up and down the river as far away as West Virginia, but now it went only thirteen miles into Maryland.

Jennifer knew she couldn't run that far. She had never run farther than three miles in her life. She had first taken up the sport because it was important to Tom, and it gave her another way to be with him. Now she ran because she loved the feeling it gave her, of being in shape and in control of her life.

She sped past a biker bent low over his front wheel. He was dressed in a tight black biking suit, with gloves and a black crash helmet. She caught his look of surprise as she swept past him, her feet now barely touching the hard-packed earth. He was breathing hard, gasping, and as she floated by, he rose up off the seat and pumped hard. She smiled and picked up her speed. For a few yards, she could hear him behind her, breathing deeply, and the slick sound of wheels on the hard earth, but gradually the sounds faded, and when she glanced back, she saw that the biker was disappearing from sight.

As she ran, she tried to establish a smooth easy stride, as Tom had taught her. "Run within yourself," he always urged. Jennifer had never been strong enough to run with his ease and speed. But Kathy Dart had upset her, and she wanted to burn off her anxiety.

She kept up the pace. She was well beyond Georgetown, running alongside the Parkway, and had outrun the other joggers on the path and even several dozen bikers.

She should go back to the hotel, she finally decided; it was getting dark, and she wasn't familiar with the canal this far beyond Georgetown. She slowed her pace and gradually eased to a walk on the running path. Now she felt the pain, and when she saw the marker beside the running path, she leaned over to read it:

13 MILES

Jennifer glanced at her watch. It was after five. She had been running for an hour and a half.

"What did you do then?" Tom asked. He turned on his side in the bed to look at Jennifer.

"Well, I tried to run back, but I couldn't, I was in too much pain. I came up out of the canal—there was a tollgate there—and I went onto the Parkway and hitched a ride from some woman. She took me here to the hotel. She was terrific. I mean, not like a New Yorker." With a groan, Jennifer moved to face Tom.

"I can't believe you jogged that far," Tom said. He had pulled himself up on his elbows. "You've never run more than three miles, right?"

Jennifer nodded. "I just felt like running, I guess, and also I was so tensed up by that channel woman."

"What?"

"You don't want to hear about her." Jennifer moved again with great effort, favoring her sore right leg, and stretched out on her stomach. "I thought making love was supposed to relax you."

"It does. But you've got to do it repeatedly." He nuzzled down next to her.

"Easy," she said.

"It's your legs that are sore, darling."

"Everything's sore." She cuddled close, wanting to be held.

He had been waiting for her when she came back from the long run, and they had taken a shower together and then made love standing under the spray, their bodies lathered with soap. She had wanted to wait until they were in bed, but he couldn't wait, wouldn't wait, and she let him have his way.

He came at once, before she was ready for him, and then he picked her up, and she slipped her arms around his neck and her legs around his waist. He carried her back to the wide bed, where they soaked the sheets and blankets with their wet bodies and made love again, and this time she did come, a long rolling orgasm that drained all the strength from her limbs. The intensity made her cry, and when he came, she had a second climax just as violent and wrenching as the first, and she wouldn't let him slip out of her. She held him tight, as if he were a secret prize she wanted to keep hidden forever inside her.

They had fallen asleep then, still wrapped in each other's arms, and when she woke, Jennifer felt the pain in her legs and thighs and told Tom what had happened.

"What do you want to do?" he asked, whispering in her ear.

"I don't want to do anything. I just want to lie in your arms for the rest of my life." And she meant it. She didn't ever want to move. She felt happy when she was in Tom's arms, when he was holding her and she had nowhere to go and nothing to do. But she sensed the reason for his question. Tom never asked anything directly; he was always trying to position her so that he could do what he wanted.

"I've got a dinner meeting," he told her.

"Damnit!" She moved to look at him directly. His dark eyes, intense even in the dim light of the room, had always affected Jennifer strongly. She could not see his face. "Now tell me again," she said.

"Honey, I didn't know myself until forty minutes ago. I had a message waiting when I got back to the hotel. The DA wants me to interview a new person down here who they're thinking of hiring. Look, it's only dinner. I'll be free by nine, and we can come back and do some more of this." He moved against her so she could feel his erection.

"Don't," she asked, but she knew there was no authority in her objection, and she knew that he wouldn't stop. She, too, wanted to make love. She couldn't get enough of him this afternoon, and her desire pleased her. In New York they were always in a hurry, rushing to make love in the brief moments that they could spare from their work.

"Turn over," he told her, and when she heard the edge in his voice, her nipples grew hard. "This way," he said, instructing her, and she let him pull her up by the waist. He was already kneeling on the bed.

"No, honey, that hurts."

Tom didn't answer her. His hands had seized her waist, and when she tried to pull away, he wouldn't let her. Jennifer never liked it when he entered from behind so she couldn't see his face, and it was only because he was so demanding that she let him.

"Honey," she whispered, but he didn't answer. She knew he wouldn't; he never spoke when they made love. She wondered then if all men were the same. Did they all have sex like animals, silent and purposeful, without words of endearment? Or was it her? Did she somehow make men behave in a certain way?

She gasped. He was inside her, and she fell forward onto the wet sheets of the hotel bed. Her face was pressed against the hard mattress, and she grabbed its edges as he came, driving her down. It was not the way she wanted, but as he seized her by the shoulders, drove deep into her, she felt her own orgasm in a dizzying rush. It grew and grew, took her breath away, and she gasped with pain as her body shook and quaked, and then she came again and again, in wave after wave of sweet pleasure.

She awoke in the silence of the big house and heard the rooms speak to her, whispering. Her teddy bear and Raggedy Ann listened, too, and kept her safe. She pulled them both close to her and slipped farther down beneath the warm blankets. Through the window she could see the moon, and the moon's shadow, as ghostly as her dreams, seeping across the rug.

She loved her room. It was safe and cozy, and full of her toys, and she spent hour after hour in it, playing with Barbara Ann, and Sally, and all her dolls. She would make tea and sandwiches and have parties, just herself and her doll friends. And she'd have parties for Sam when he came home from boarding school. They would lock the door, and she would sit on his lap and pretend that there was no war in Europe, pretend that they were all alone in the big house, with Mommy and Daddy far, far away.

But at night, after everyone went to bed, she was afraid to be alone. Afraid of the ghosts and goblins, bats and little lizards that lived in the corners of her room. They waited for her beneath the stairs, too, and in the rafters of the attic and behind the sofa in the living room, and they darted from sight whenever anyone entered, and they came out at night to hunt down all the humans. Sam told her as much, whispering in her ear, and she didn't want to believe it, but she knew it was true, and she wanted to be held by Sam in his arms, protected by his embrace.

Sam had first told her about the flying lizards and the ghosts when they spent a warm summer afternoon up in the attic, lying together in piles of their mother's old clothes. Sam was looking for his football pads. That was the summer he turned fourteen, and he wanted to take them with him to prep school. They had rummaged together through the trunks, and Sam had told her to take off her white skirt and summer shorts and try on Mommy's clothes. Okay, she had grinned. She liked the idea of taking off her clothes. It was hot in the attic, with the sun pouring through the small windows, and Sam had seen her without clothes before, wrapped up in a towel after her bath. But it was different now. She had breasts, tiny little breasts, and her mommy had already told her she'd need a brassiere before school started.

So she had taken off her skirt and shorts and tried on clothes for a while, posing for Sam, preening in the mirror propped against the attic wall. He searched for and found the farmyard set, then assembled it in a box to carry downstairs. But they didn't want to leave the attic, and she got bored with trying on old clothes, so she lay down in the soft pile of discarded dresses. It was warm, and she liked the way her brother looked at her, so she didn't put on her clothes again. As she lay there, in the pile of velvety dresses, she fell asleep, and when she moved again, Sam was lying next to her, holding her, touching her. He told her that he missed her, that he missed not being home with her all year, that he hated going to boarding school. Then he began to cry, and she kissed his soft cheek and held him and told him she would write him every day. Then he started to kiss her on the mouth like they did in the movies. She told him to stop, that they would both get in trouble, but he said it was okay, that he wouldn't tell. And he asked her if she would, and she shook her head, too frightened and excited even to speak. Something was happening between them, and she didn't know what or why, but she knew she couldn't stop, nor did she want to stop, and she waited and watched for her brother to do whatever he was going to do.

He took off her panties then and tossed them away, and then he took off his own trousers, and she began to giggle. But she loved the way her body suddenly felt, all tingling, and then Sam showed her what boys did and what girls did, and it was wonderful. It hurt a little, but he said that was okay, that it wouldn't hurt again, not the next time. She was so happy that he told her that; she knew she wanted to do it again.

Afterward, they lay quietly together in the warm, musty attic, and he told her that he loved her, and she told him that she loved him, too. He said that they couldn't tell their parents, and she nodded. She didn't want to tell them. She wanted it to be their secret forever.

Later, when they were getting dressed, he put his hands on her breasts and then he put his arms around her and hugged her, and they kissed like in the movies. She asked if they could do it again, and he said yes, at night, when Mommy was asleep and the house was quiet. He would come into her bedroom, and they would sleep together every night until he went away to school. She smiled. She would never again be so happy in her life.

After he left for school, she had written almost every day. But the next time he came home, he was different. He had begun to smoke, and their mother had yelled at him. Here they were paying two thousand dollars a year for his education, she had said, and he looked like one of those young toughs who hung around on city streets.

She had thought he looked neat, but when she hugged him, he acted funny, as if he didn't like her anymore, and her feelings were hurt. Later, in bed, she had cried into her pillow, muffling the sound so he wouldn't hear.

Now she wondered if she should creep down the hall to see him, but she was afraid to leave her bedroom. It was always safer in her bed, he had explained, because it was at the end of the hallway, farther away from their mother's bedroom at the top of the stairs.

She tossed off the blanket and went over to stand against the window-pane, feeling the cold air seep in from outside, staring at the snow on the lawn. Tomorrow they could make a snowman, she thought. She and Sam could make a big snowman all by themselves. She hoped the snow was good for packing.

Maybe he had a girlfriend. She knew there was a girls' school across from his. The thought made her jealous.

She heard a sound in the doorway, and when she looked up, she saw Sam slip into the room. He closed the door.

"Sam!" she whispered, bounding onto her bed.

"Shhh, for chrissake!"

"They won't hear us!" she insisted. "Come here, please. I've been waiting for you."

He sat down slowly on the bed and immediately she wrapped her thin arms around his neck and kissed him on the mouth.

"Don't." He pushed her away and wouldn't look at her.

"What's the matter?" She sat back, near tears.

He was sitting on the edge of the bed, leaning forward so that his long hair fell over his face and she couldn't see him. He had lost weight since he left for school.

"Are you mad at me?" she asked in a small voice.

He shook his head, then looked up and tossed his hair back. "No," he admitted. "I'm not mad at you."

"I've missed you."

"I've missed you, too, sweetheart."

"I thought you were coming home for Thanksgiving."

Sam shrugged. "I couldn't. I got sick. Mom told you, didn't she?" He stretched out on the bed and put his head on the pillow.

"But I thought you'd come home to see me." She curled down next to her big brother and embraced him. "I've missed you," she told him again.

He just nodded.

"Did you miss me?" she asked.

"Sure I missed you, dopey." He turned around and tickled her.

"Don't!" she laughed, struggling, trying to keep his hands off her body.

He stopped then, and they lay together, smiling, staring at each other. Then she asked, "Do you have a girlfriend or something at school?"

"No, dopey, you're my only girlfriend." He hugged her, and she kissed his neck.

"Can I come up to school and see you sometime? I mean, I asked Mom and she said it was okay."

"I don't know. Where would you stay?"

"Couldn't I just stay with you in your room?"

"No, you can't stay with me, for chrissake." He turned away from her and stared up at the ceiling.

"What's the matter, Sam?" She curled closer to him, and wrapped one leg over his.

"Nothing's the matter." He pulled loose from her and sat up again on the edge of the bed.

"Where are you going?"

"Hey, look, Nora, we can't do this anymore."

"Sam, I didn't tell Mom."

"Jesus, you're just a kid. You don't know what you're talking about. It's not right, you know." He stood up and walked to the window, and his face was silhouetted in the pale moonlight.

"But I love you, Sam. Besides, it makes me feel good." She got out of bed then and scampered across to the window to wrap her arms around him. He had grown since he went back to school.

He slipped his arm around her thin shoulders and hugged her. She turned her face into his chest and kissed the cotton top of his pajamas. She loved the way he smelled. After he had left for school, she went through his dresser drawers, took one of his summer shirts, and slept in it all fall. When her mother discovered it in her room, she only smiled and shook her head, then kissed her daughter on the forehead. She had been pleased that the two of them were such good friends.

"But don't you like me, Sam?" she asked, looking up.

He shrugged. "You're only thirteen. You know I could get put in jail or something."

"They can't put you in jail, Sam. You're sixteen. They don't put sixteen-year-old kids in jail. And I'll be thirteen years old next month. I read in a book that girls in Europe because of the war are getting married when they're thirteen."

"Not to their brothers, they aren't." He pulled himself from her arms and stretched out again on the bed.

She followed him onto the bed. "And I'm not your real sister, anyway. I'm only your half sister. We could get married, I bet. I have to ask Mom if we could."

"Don't you say anything!" Sam grabbed her arm.

"I wouldn't. Sam, let me go. That hurts!" Her eyes filled with tears and she pulled loose from him. "I didn't say anything to Mom, you jerk!"

"Shhhh," Sam whispered, putting his hand over her mouth.

Both of them listened hard.

"I don't hear anything," she whispered, slipping down into bed and tucking her teddy bear and doll into their corners by the pillow.

Sam listened for a few more minutes, turning his head so he could catch any noise from the hallway, and then he relaxed and lay down beside her with a sigh. "I'm tired. I want to go to sleep."

"With me, please," she begged, edging closer to him, but he didn't say anything, just lay beside her with his eyes closed. "We could just sleep together in my bed," she said. "We don't have to do anything. Please?"

He didn't answer. He just pulled the blanket down, slipped his long legs underneath it, and then pulled it up over them both. Pleased, she turned on her side and snuggled down close to him, then took his arm and wrapped it around her body.

He touched her then, and she opened her eyes and stared across the room at the moonlight coming through the window. She did not move. She let him find his own way. He had begun to breathe harder, deeper, and then she began to match his ragged breath. He had put his hand beneath her long woolen nightgown and slipped it up to touch her breasts. His hand was cold for a moment on her flesh.

He was struggling now to get closer to her, to slip his other arm between her legs, and he was breathing hard, as if he had run a long way to reach her. She told him to wait, jumped out of bed, and quickly reached down to pull the nightgown over her head.

She felt a sudden draft of cold air between her legs, then the lights flipped on. With her nightgown caught in her arms, high above her head, and her brother lying there beneath the blankets, she turned to see her mother standing in the doorway.

3

WHEN JENNIFER AWOKE, TOM was gone and the room was dark. She had been conscious for only a few minutes when the phone rang. Clearing her throat, she said "hello" out loud a few times before answering so that her voice wouldn't betray that she had been asleep so early in the evening.

"Jennifer? It's me. Eileen. Did I wake you?"

"Of course not. I was reviewing some reports. They always makes me sound sleepy." Jennifer sat up. "Thanks for telephoning. I needed a break." She tried to sound alert and businesslike.

"Well, I don't want to bother you. I know you're here on business. . . ."

Jennifer smiled. She was suddenly glad that Eileen had called.

"I thought if you weren't busy . . . I mean, if you didn't have a meeting, we might have dinner together."

"I'd like that, but don't you have a meeting yourself with Kathy Dart and her friends?"

"Not till nine-thirty. Jennifer, if you're busy, or whatever, I mean, I understand."

"Eileen, I'd like to. What time is it, anyway?" She reached for her watch.

"Seven-twenty."

"That's all? My body feels like it must be eleven. I went jogging this afternoon."

"Jennifer, you jog? That's a new you!"

"Yes, well, I guess there's a lot new about both of us." Fully awake, she realized she was hungry. "Eileen, I've got to change clothes. Can you give me twenty minutes?"

"Of course. Why don't we meet downstairs at eight?"

"Sure."

"See you in the lounge, then," Eileen said, and quickly added,

"Oh, if you have the time, maybe you'd like to come to this evening's session with Kathy Dart and Habasha. I have an extra ticket."

Jennifer laughed. "Thanks, but no thanks. One session with your guru. But I do have some questions about her. See you at eight. 'Bye."

Eileen Gorman, of all people, she thought, hanging up the telephone receiver. Slowly she got out of bed and walked naked to the shower, still bruised from the long run and from Tom's fierce lovemaking.

"I first heard Kathy eight months ago," Eileen said. They were both looking over the restaurant menu as they talked about the meeting earlier that day. Jennifer asked how Eileen had first heard about the channeler.

"As soon as I saw Kathy trance-channeling Habasha, I knew that was what I was looking for in my life."

"What do you mean, looking for?"

Eileen set down the large menu and sighed. She sat directly across from Jennifer, but she looked off across the room and into space. "I was lost. I mean, I had my marriage, but Todd has his work, you know, and what did I have? Bridge? A tennis game? Shopping? I mean, I was living out there on Long Island. I had— I have—everything that I could possibly want. I'm lucky, I admit, and I had no reason to feel at a loss for anything, but I did. I did feel lost. Lonely. I'd go to the malls and just wander around, do endless, useless shopping, and it didn't bring me any satisfaction. I don't wear most of the stuff I have jammed into our closets. I started to have affairs, you know, just to do something, to bring some sort of meaning into my life, or whatever."

"Eileen, I thought—"

"Listen, Jennifer, I'm not the only one. Half the women on Long Island are like me. I mean, you're lucky. You have this wonderful career. You have a life of your own, interesting friends."

"Eileen, so could you! You're attractive, you're intelligent. You were our valedictorian!"

Eileen was shaking her head, cutting off Jennifer's reply.

"You know I got married right after school. The truth was, we had to get married. There was this guy, Tim Murphy—I met him at Jones Beach. We were both lifeguards. Well, I got pregnant." She shrugged her shoulders, looked over at Jennifer, and grimaced, as if to say that was it, her life was over, a fait accompli. But her eyes were glistening. Then she leaned forward and smiled. "But it doesn't matter. I was meant to have that sort of life. It was my karma."

Jennifer frowned. "Eileen, we make our own lives. We're in control. Why do you think women fought so hard for equal status?" What do you think the ERA is all about?"

"This is not a woman's thing, Jennifer. It's beyond the here and now, beyond all these daily problems."

"Eileen, the feminist movement wasn't—isn't—a little daily problem."

"Jennifer, you're not listening to me. You're not hearing what I'm trying to say."

"I'm sorry, but—"

Eileen cut her off. "Kathy Dart is the most remarkable woman I have ever met. Maybe the most remarkable woman alive today."

"Eileen, please." Jennifer looked down at her menu.

"I mean it! You don't know. You haven't been exposed." Her voice had picked up, and there was anger in her tone.

"I'm sorry," Jennifer soothed. "You're right. I asked about Kathy Dart, and I haven't given you a chance to explain. Here's the waitress. Let's order and then I'll be quiet. Promise." She smiled at Eileen and for a moment tried to concentrate on her oversized menu but found she was too anxious. When the waitress arrived, she asked for the special of the evening.

"I saw her on television, the first time," Eileen began. "It was the 'This Morning' show, and they had three or four people, mediums, psychics. I had never thought about any of that stuff in my life. But I had the TV on, and I was sitting at the counter in the kitchen watching . . . killing time, you know, and trying to decide what to cook for dinner. It was September seventh, I remember, and it was rainy and cold, and I couldn't play tennis, but I was thinking maybe I should go to the club anyway. Then Kathy came on and I sort of started to listen, and it was as if she were talking just to me. She was telling me her life story, and what had happened to her as a child, and I found myself crying as I listened. I mean, she was talking about me, the mess I'd made of life, my feelings of being out of it, left behind, in the wrong crowd."

"But, Eileen, you weren't! You were the smartest person in our class. Brighter than Mark Simon, even! And you were captain of the basketball team."

Eileen started to laugh, "Jennifer, I can't believe you still remember all that stuff."

"I was jealous of you, that's why."

"Oh, don't be silly. You were going out with Andy Porterfield, and everyone on Long Island wanted to marry him."

"Well, thank God I didn't. He's on his second wife, I'm told."

"His third. We see him all the time at the club. But what I'm trying to say is that in high school you were having a good time. I wasn't, and the only reason I even played basketball was because Mr. Donaldson put me on the team after I tried to commit suicide."

"Suicide?" Jennifer whispered, remembering now the long-ago rumors about Eileen.

"I'm sorry. Of course, you didn't know." She reached over and touched Jennifer's arm. "I was jealous of you, Jennifer. You were the great social one. You had all the friends. My teenage years were a tormented time in my life, and Kathy Dart, or really, Habasha, has explained to me why I was so unhappy, why my body was out of sync with my spirit life. So I went to her. There was a conference like this being held in San Francisco, and I flew out for it."

"Flew all the way to California just to see her?"

Eileen nodded. "I had to know," she said thoughtfully, pausing and looking off across the room.

Jennifer stopped eating and watched Eileen. How rested the woman looked, how satisfied, as if all her responsibilities had been lifted off her shoulders.

"I've never been a religious person. I mean, I was raised a Unitarian, which isn't much of a religion, but when Kathy began to speak as Habasha . . ."

"He's not Kathy Dart."

Eileen nodded. "They are connected, as Kathy said. He was once her warrior lover. And they were pirates together. Kathy also told me that she once had his child in another lifetime. They are soul mates, from the same oversoul. And he speaks through her."

"So he doesn't sleep with her; he uses her body, instead."

"Okay, be a smart ass," Eileen replied with an indulgent smile. "If you'd only give Habasha a chance, you'd see."

"See what?"

"See that he can help you," Eileen said softly, not looking up from her plate.

"I didn't realize I needed help," Jennifer answered, annoyed.

"We all need help, Jennifer," Eileen replied without raising her voice. "And I think if you gave Kathy Dart and Habasha a chance, they might explain to you why you two had such a strong attraction to each other at the session this afternoon."

"What are you talking about? What do you mean?" Jennifer sat back and stared at Eileen.

"Kathy Dart asked about you," she explained.

"Yes? What do you mean, asked about me?" Her voice rose and she felt her hands begin to tremble.

"She spoke to me after this afternoon's session. She said she had a profound reaction from seeing you." Eileen was watching Jennifer as she spoke.

Jennifer nodded.

"What did it mean?" she asked.

"Kathy asked me to tell you that she senses that she knows you, from a past life, of course, and that she thinks you should speak directly to Habasha."

"Don't be silly," Jennifer answered at once.

"Kathy said to tell you that you are capable of a great deal in this life, and to tell you also that you are involved in a romantic situation that is not spiritually good for you."

"What!" Jennifer was outraged, and also frightened of what Eileen might know.

Eileen shook her head. "I'm only telling you what Kathy said. She wanted me to invite you specially to her session this evening." Eileen paused. "And she said to tell you that Danny is fine. That he has another life now, a happy life, and that he didn't suffer."

Jennifer threw down her napkin. She couldn't eat. "I don't want to hear any more of this silliness. I'm not interested in your seances and spirit entities." She was furious at Eileen for mentioning her dead brother. They had been in junior high school when Danny was killed in Vietnam.

Her sudden rage made her dizzy. She tried to find the waitress to pay the check but couldn't. As she glanced around the room, a glowing ball of brilliant light caught her eye. It was outside the windows; she leaned closer to the cold glass and squinted into the darkness.

Someone—something—was walking round the swimming pool. It was a man—a small, short-limbed man, moving clumsily, like a Cro-Magnon.

"Look!" Jennifer blurted out. "What's that?"

"What's what?" Eileen asked.

Jennifer looked back and nothing was there. The light must have been playing tricks on her.

Jennifer stood, dropping her napkin into her chair. "Excuse me, I can't take any more of this metaphysical crap." She glanced back out the window. The glowing light was gone from the terrace.

"Don't be afraid," Eileen said softly. "It will all work out. Kathy said it would." She smiled up at Jennifer, looking conspiratorial.

"I'm not afraid," Jennifer answered back. She opened her purse and withdrew a twenty-dollar bill. "The waitress can keep the change," she said, throwing it down.

"Jennifer, you're getting yourself upset over nothing. I'm sorry I frightened you."

"You haven't upset me, Eileen. I'm just sorry you've gotten yourself all tied up with these people. I always thought you were too smart for such . . . bullshit." She spun about and strode from the restaurant.

She walked through the lobby and stopped at the desk for her messages. Tom would have called, she knew, to let her know when he would be back at the hotel.

" 'Having drinks after dinner with Yale buddies. Back late. T.,' " the clerk read, then looked up at Jennifer. "Would you like a copy?"

"No. No thank you," Jennifer told him, and turning away from the counter, she went up to her hotel room alone.

4

JENNIFER LIFTED THE *New York Times* off the mat and stepped back inside her apartment. It was Saturday morning, the day after she returned from Washington. Closing the door, she flipped the paper open to the second section and scanned the page as she walked down the hall and into the kitchen.

It was not yet eight o'clock, and the building was silent. Tom was still asleep. She had just spread the newspaper on the kitchen counter when she spotted a headline:

SPIRITUAL GUIDE FOR YUPPIES

Jennifer stopped to read the first couple of paragraphs.

Channeling, a metaphysical quest for truth and wisdom that sprang to life in California, has found its way east. Ms. Phoebe Fisher, who holds a doctorate from the Metaphysics University of San Jose, is currently dispensing metaphysical truths from her West Side apartment.

According to Ms. Fisher, the "truth giver" is a spirit named Dance, who is a "sixth-density entity from Dorran, the seventh star of the seventh sister within the Pleiades system. He lives eight hundred years in our own future," according to the blond and beautiful Ms. Fisher.

Jennifer perched on the counter stool and pulled her robe closer. It was cold in the kitchen, and she wanted her morning coffee, but first she had to read this article.

Recently, a poll by the University of Chicago's National Opinion Research Council indicated that 67 percent of Americans believe they have had a psychic experience.

Many of these people are calling on the spirit world for solace and advice, using mediums, or channelers, who have established contact with "entities" from the past. Sometimes these "entities" beam down from outer space, such as Ms. Fisher's "sixth-density entity," Dance.

"I was walking through the Sheep Meadow in Central Park on a hot Sunday afternoon last August," recalls Ms. Fisher. "When I looked up into the western sky, I saw this tall, elegant figure wrapped in a glow of brilliant light. I stopped in my tracks, right in the middle of the Sheep Meadow, with people sunbathing all around me, and I said out loud, 'Yes.' Yes, for I knew he was coming for me.

"And he said to me from across the meadow, 'Phoebe, you are beautiful. You are a beautiful person.' I felt this enormous rush of cold air push against me. I was nearly knocked over, but I managed to nod. I couldn't speak. But I knew he or she—they don't have gender in the Pleiades system—wanted to use my body. He wanted me to bring the message of peace and love to our world, and I agreed to lend him my human form. We didn't have to speak. I knew telepathically. And then I felt another rush of air, but this time it was blazing hot. Later, I realized he had settled himself into my home, my physical body."

Jennifer shook her head, smiling to herself. She'd clip the article and send it to Eileen Gorman, she decided. Since storming out of the restaurant on Thursday night, Jennifer had been feeling guilty. This would make a nice peace offering, she decided, and a way of getting back in touch with her old friend. She slipped off the stool and went to the stove to boil water for coffee. She heard Tom then in the other room, padding across the floor to the bathroom. She glanced at the clock. It was only eight o'clock. Why was he up so early on a Saturday? He seldom told her his plans, and in the first days of their relationship had tried to make a joke of his secrecy, saying he would let her know "on a need-to-know basis." She had thought that funny then. But not anymore.

She put the kettle on the stove and then scooped several spoonfuls of fresh coffee beans into the grinder. The little machine roared in the silent kitchen, and it was only after she had dumped the finely ground beans into the coffee filter that she realized Tom had entered the room. He was standing at the counter, glancing through the paper. When he didn't look up or acknowledge her, she said coolly, "And good morning to you."

"Good morning," he answered. "Sorry. I was just checking to see if Giuliani made any statements. There was a rumor in the building yesterday that he was going to announce for the Senate." He smiled across at her, trying to make amends.

"Well, it would be nice if you just said hello, that's all." She poured boiling water onto the filter.

"You know I never have much to say in the morning."

"I wouldn't think a simple 'good morning' is too much for a big assistant attorney general like yourself." She added more water.

"Did you see this piece about the new yuppie fad?" Tom asked, as if to change the subject.

"Be careful what you say about yuppies. They're us." She glanced over at him. He was wearing only the bottoms of his pajamas and was standing at the counter scratching the thick dark hair on his chest.

"You may be, but I'm not." He looked up from the newspaper. "Any coffee?"

"In a moment, sire."

"Just asking, Jennifer. Just asking." He grabbed the sports section of the *Times* and went over to the breakfast table, sitting down in the soft wash of pale winter sun to concentrate on the basketball scores.

Jennifer finished making coffee, poured Tom a cup, and added a splash of half-and-half. She carried his cup to the table and placed it down next to him.

"Thanks," he said.

Jennifer slid down across from him at the table, satisfied for the moment with the taste of coffee and the slight warmth of the winter sun. She studied Tom while he read. She could see only his right profile—his better side, as he liked to say, because when he was still in prep school, his nose had been broken in a lacrosse game and badly reset. This morning his better side was shadowed with an overnight growth of beard. His long black hair tumbled over his forehead and into his eyes; it curled around his ear lobes. He looked like an unmade bed, she thought fondly.

She sipped her coffee and looked out the window at the snow-bound Brooklyn Heights street where a few early risers were trudging through the snow. She wondered if this was the right time to tell Tom she wanted either to get married or break off the relationship. Her friend, Margit, had warned her about men like Tom who were afraid of commitment. She knew she couldn't keep on living half a life with him. And besides, she knew she wanted to have children before it was too late.

"Are you okay?" he asked, glancing up. His cool gray eyes stared at her with the same compassion he might give the train schedule.

"I have no idea," she answered truthfully, staring at the snow that covered the street like the hard frosting of a day-old wedding cake.

"Your job?" he asked.

Jennifer shook her head. "My life."

"Your life, huh?" He nodded to the *Times* column. "Maybe you could use some spiritual guidance, one of these whatever-they-are."

"Please, Tom, I'm being serious." She looked straight at him. She was never any good at fooling people.

"You mean, us?"

"Yes, and more."

"What do you mean, 'more'?" There was an edge to his voice. At least she had his full attention, which gave her some satisfaction.

"I mean us, my stupid job at the foundation, and this!" She waved at the frozen street. All of it. The neighborhood, Brooklyn Heights, New York City. It hadn't struck her until that very moment that she was sick of New York, sick of her daily life.

Tom pushed the paper away from him. It was a gesture he always made when he was upset, as if he was clearing his deck for a new problem.

She was afraid now. She was always afraid when she got Tom angry. That was one of the underlying problems in their relationship. She wasn't honest enough with Tom, for in her heart of hearts she was afraid of losing him, of being without anyone at all.

"Well, what brought this on, this disgust about your life?"

"You know what."

"For chrissake, Jennifer, I slept with that woman once, and I was a goddamn stupid fool to tell you."

"You weren't telling me, Tom, you were bragging. You were showing off, you were being a jerk, and just so you could appear as a stud in front of your stupid friends," she answered back.

"Don't go back over that bullshit," he said softly, turning to his coffee.

"Bullshit yourself!" Jennifer looked away again, out the window at the cold day. She was surprised that she wasn't crying. She had gotten tougher in the last few years, she realized.

At the Justice Department Christmas party, Tom had gotten drunk and boasted to the other males that he had slept with Helen Taubman, the television anchorwoman, that fall, just when Jennifer had begun dating him seriously.

Jennifer had become dizzy, trying to reach the ladies' room in the crowded restaurant before she became sick. She had blamed it on the champagne, on the excitement and the warm restaurant, but of course all his friends knew she was lying. Tom's admission had shocked them all.

"You want to talk about this, Jennifer?" Tom asked. He was focusing his full attention on her, but then she saw him glance at the kitchen clock.

"Are you in a hurry?" she asked, trying to pin him down. "Are you going into the office? What is it? Why the glances at the clock?"

"Jesus, remind me not to cross you again early in the morning." He spun around and stood up.

"Tom! Listen to me!" He set his coffee cup on the counter and kept walking. She waited until he had reached the doorway before she called after him. "I think we should take a break from each other for a while."

That got his attention. She saw the way his shoulder muscles tensed, and he halted in the doorway. She watched him make a slow and dramatic turn. He was stalling for time, giving himself a chance to think of a response. She knew all his gestures and habits as if they were her own.

"Are you sleeping with someone else?" he asked.

Jennifer recognized the tactic. He was putting her on the defensive. She stared back at him, refusing to rise to the bait. When he came slowly back into the kitchen, holding her eyes with his, she began to tense. Her fingers tightened around the warm coffee cup.

"Right? Is this what all this oblique talk is about?" He had reached the table, but he didn't sit down. She knew he liked to hover over people.

"Our relationship isn't going anywhere," she told him.

"Don't give me that shit! Who is it? One of those assholes from the foundation? Handingham, right?"

"David?" She looked up at Tom, startled by his guess. "You think I'd be interested in David?" Now she was offended.

"He's your boss, isn't he? He's got the power around that place."

"Oh, for God's sake. You think I'd have an affair with David Handingham just because he's the president of the board?"

"You wouldn't be the first woman to fuck her way up the ladder."

"Tom, that's disgusting! I can't believe you'd think that. Sometimes I don't think you know me at all."

"Sometimes I think you're right." He sat down across from her.

She realized he was upset, and that pleased her. She looked away again, back through the kitchen window. It was suddenly much brighter. The sun had reached the street and was shining off the frozen snow, and Jennifer stared hard at the gleaming surface until her eyes hurt.

"Okay, let's talk about this later." He glanced at the clock, then over at Jennifer. "I'll call you later, okay?"

She wanted to say no, but that would be unfair to Tom, and unfair to herself. She had already invested over six months in their relationship.

"I'll be here," she told him.

Tom nodded, then sighed. "Okay," he said, tapping the table and pulling himself up. "I'll call before four. We're having dinner, right?" When she nodded yes, he said quickly, "I'll make the reservations."

Jennifer knew this was an effort to appease her. She was always the one who made their dinner reservations, who wrote the thank-you notes, who did all the little housewifely chores.

Tom walked into the bedroom to dress. She got more coffee and sat by the windows and watched the winter sun grow brighter.

When Tom came back into the kitchen, he was dressed in the clothes he had left in her closet—the blue cords, his thick walking shoes, the beautiful red sweater she had given him for his thirtieth birthday. He was wearing his parka and carried a briefcase full of files. When he kissed her cheek, she could smell his aftershave lotion, his hair shampoo, and she wanted to make love to him there on the kitchen floor but didn't have the courage to tell him so.

She didn't move. She sat perfectly still at the kitchen table and watched the sun and the snow. She didn't have the strength to get up and get dressed.

She would go back to bed, she thought. She would curl down deep into the blankets and sleep. She would stay there safe and warm in the dark shadows until she discovered what was going wrong in her life.

5

JENNIFER LOOKED AT THE elephants, the herd of mammoths that dominated the museum's African Hill, as she waited for Tom. It was Tom who insisted that they meet for a drink in such an out of the way place. These days his job consisted mostly of prosecuting drug dealers, and shortly before they began to date, someone had tried to kill him. Now he carried a gun and didn't like being seen with her. It was silly of him to worry, she thought. If drug dealers wanted to blow him or her away, they would. They controlled the city as far as she could see.

Jennifer stopped at the Gemsbok display and studied the pattern-faced Kalahari Desert animals. In the Museum of Natural History's magnificent diorama, they looked almost real. Then she thought: they were real once, roaming the great savannahs. She almost felt as if she could step behind the thick glass and walk through the long grass and acacia trees into the heat and heart of Africa. She wished she were in Africa. She wished she were anywhere but in New York City on a cold, snowy Friday afternoon waiting for her tardy lover.

She stepped up to another diorama, this one a cluster of hippopotamuses, sitatunga, and waterbucks, and saw that the sign said the animals were all gathered at the edge of one of the small rivers that formed the network of the Nile. The animals were standing in the thick grass and umbrella sedge. Jennifer stared at the posed figures; although she'd never studied anything about Africa, she felt something was wrong with the scene. Then she caught a glimpse of her own reflection in the bubbled glass. She had come directly from work and was wearing her corporate uniform: a tailored, heavy gray suit with a white silk blouse and the string of pearls Tom had given her for Christmas, their first Christmas together. She raised her hand to touch the pearls and felt a warm tear on her cheek. This was wrong. Why was she crying? She quickly brushed it away, thinking, I can't look like this. I can't be crying when he arrives.

Turning from the Nile River diorama to go find the women's room, she found herself in Tom's arms.

"Hi, sweetheart, sorry I'm late. It's snowing. The whole damn city is gridlocked." He stood shaking wet snow off his shoulders and from his thick black hair.

"That's all right," she said, relieved that he didn't seem to notice her tears. "I just arrived myself."

"Well, you look great!" He turned his full attention on her, stepping closer to kiss her on her cheek. "Look, it's freezing outside. Is there someplace here where we can get a drink? Or at least some coffee?"

"Yes, there's a bar under the great blue whale on the first floor. But come with me first; let's look around. I haven't been in this museum in ages."

"Where do you want to go?"

"Oh, let's just wander. We'll take the elevator to the third floor, then walk down." Directing their tour gave her the sense of being in control. That was her problem with Tom. When she was with him, she always felt manipulated. Now she just wanted to make him do what she said, to prove to herself that she could control him when she needed to.

On the top floor, they stepped off the elevator and saw a sign for a new exhibition.

" 'Bright Dreams, Bright Vision,' " Tom read. "What's that?"

"I have no idea," Jennifer answered. They pushed through the glass gallery door and stepped into the dark interior.

"Oh, great," he said, reading the first exhibit sign. " 'Prehistoric Man.' Just what I thought when I woke up this morning: 'I wish I knew a lot more about prehistoric man.' "

"I want to see this exhibition, Tom!" Her voice rose sharply.

"Okay," he whispered, "okay." He touched her arm. "Easy."

Jennifer turned away, embarrassed by her outburst, but the gallery was nearly deserted. She noticed an older woman with a cane, a few mothers with babies in strollers, and two female guards in blue uniforms standing together at the entrance.

"Hey, look!" Tom pointed at the display in the center of the room.

The focus of the diorama was the model of a prehistoric hut, built of mammoth bone, tusks, and leather. The jawbones of the mammoths were turned upside down and fitted into each other like a puzzle to form a twelve-foot circle. The arching roof was made with dozens of huge, curving tusks, over which animal skins were tied to form a cover.

"It's a model of one of their huts," Tom said, reading from the printed information plaque, "from the Ukraine."

"It's wrong," she stated in a whisper, staring at the diorama.

"What, sweetheart?" Tom asked, moving around the model to peer inside.

"It's wrong. It's all wrong! That's Nari's hut. I know it is!" Her voice rose, startling everyone.

"Honey, what the hell are talking about?"

"I don't know."

Tom started to laugh, then stopped, startled by the look in her eyes. "Jennifer?"

She was trembling. He put his hand on her arm, but she slapped his fingers away.

"Damnit, Jennifer. That hurt!" He shook his hand.

Jennifer caught sight of a guard. She was moving around the diorama and coming toward her.

"Let's get out of here," she said. Only when she was in the brightly lit reptile gallery again did she take a deep breath and slow herself down.

"Jennifer, what in hell is wrong with you?"

She shook her head and kept walking. Her heels snapped on the marble floor.

"What was that bullshit about the hut?" He lengthened his stride. They reached the hallway and started down the stairs.

"I don't know."

"You hurt my hand."

"Please, Tom, enough! I'm upset, that's all. I'm upset about us." They reached the first floor and kept walking, past the Theodore Roosevelt Memorial and into the Invertebrates Gallery.

"Well, do something about it, damnit!"

"I intend to."

"What?" His voice hardened. "You're going to do what?"

"I'm going to have a drink." She walked into the Ocean Life Room, where a massive blue whale hung from the ceiling and dominated the two floors of the gallery. "Here's the bar."

Jennifer walked into the lower floor, where a few white-clothed tables were set up to create a small cocktail lounge. The room was dimly lit to suggest the ocean floor, and the huge, plastic blue whale hovered above them, swamping the room with its size. It was not a place where people went for a drink on Friday night after work. Anyone here would be from out of town, a tourist.

She let Tom order at the bar while she picked a table away from the others. When he came back, he sat down close to her, but she shifted her body to keep some distance.

"Are you feeling better?"

"I'll tell you in a minute." She took a quick sip of the scotch and water, then sat back and nodded.

"What was that all about?" He took off his topcoat and settled into the chair.

Jennifer shook her head. She was still trembling. "I don't know," she whispered. "I just had this weird feeling that I had once been there inside that diorama. All of it was vividly real to me." She took a quick gulp of her drink.

"You were saying something, mumbling." Tom shook his head. "Maybe you saw the model in a book or something." He glanced around then, checking out the room.

"Yes, maybe," Jennifer whispered.

"It was like you were having a temper tantrum or something." He stirred his scotch.

"I was having something." She shrugged, feeling chilled. How she had behaved in the exhibition frightened her. "I don't want to talk about it," she announced.

"Okay, what do you want to talk about?"

"Don't be so prosecutorial."

He started at her. "Is it going to be one of those nights?"

She took another sip to bolster herself. Tom hadn't asked her what drink she wanted, but had gone ahead and ordered a scotch and soda. It was like being married, she thought.

"Tom, I can't keep doing this. I can't keep seeing you. I mean, we're not getting anywhere, are we?"

He looked away. "I'm still married, Jennifer."

"Then do something about it. You've been separated for three years. You told me when we met that you were getting a divorce." Her voice grew stronger as she spoke. "You shouldn't have started up with me if you still were in love with your wife."

"I'm not in love with Carol." He was angry now.

"Then get a divorce! You don't have children. What's stopping you? Tom, I deserve some answers and I deserve some respect."

He glanced away again, and she began to cry, as quietly as possible, afraid of attracting attention. She bent forward and sobbed into her hands, using the fur of her winter coat to muffle the tears.

When she had calmed down, Tom leaned across the small table and whispered, "Jennifer, I love you. I want to take care of you. I want to marry you. I want to be in your life forever. Okay? Just give me some time. This case has dragged on longer than I thought. I don't want to risk anything—any danger to you—by going public and having these greaseballs know you exist. You understand that, don't you?"

"Do you love me, Tom?" she asked. The tears were gone.

"Yes, I love you. Of course I do." He looked at her, and this time his gray eyes did show his feelings.

Jennifer shrugged. "I'm not afraid. I want to be part of your life, Tom. I want to take the risks you're taking."

He was shaking his head before she finished.

"I won't let you."

"I have something to say about that, too, you know."

"Honey, you don't know. These are crazy Colombians. They kill each other. They kill cops. They kill each other's families. You read about it in the papers. A mother and child found shot in the face while their car is parked at a stoplight." He shook his head as he spoke. "I won't do it. I won't expose you to that violence. Honey, we're almost done. We'll have the rest of that scum in jail by the end of the winter."

"Bullshit! By the end of the winter there'll be another case. If they want to kill me, they will. Don't give me that crap, Tom. It's nonsense."

For a moment they both were silent. Jennifer blew her nose and wiped away her tears. Several of the tourists were staring at them, and Jennifer moved her chair to block their view.

"I'm sorry," she said quietly. "I guess I've caused a scene."

"Fuck 'em," Tom answered. He was leaning back, balancing himself on the two rear legs of the metal chair.

When he got mad, he acted tough. She had always found that exciting. She liked the way he brought her close to the edge of his anger, but she was afraid that someday things might get out of hand.

Still, she couldn't deny her attraction to his toughness, especially in bed.

"Okay, what do you want to do?" he asked, as if summing up a business meeting.

"I'm going go to Margit and David's for dinner," she said, not looking up from her drink.

"Fine! You go ahead and do that!" He shoved the chair back and stood. He didn't even try to lower his voice.

They were like characters in a cheap drama, she thought, listening to his retreating footsteps on the marble floor. She was afraid to look up, afraid that the tourists were again staring at her. She felt exposed and defenseless. Then, slowly, the voices of the other patrons grew louder. She waited a few minutes more, until she was sure Tom had left, and then she fled the museum.

Outside on Seventy-seventh Street, the snow had deepened, and Jennifer, walking west, knew she'd have trouble getting a taxi. Putting her head down against the sharp wind, she headed for West End Avenue, her feet plowing through the wet snow. She began to cry, but this time she let the tears flow, let herself sob out her heartache.

She crossed Columbus Avenue, stopped outside the Museum Café, and looked up Seventy-seventh Street. Already the street was blocked with snow, and both sidewalks were deserted. Jennifer had lived on the Upper West Side when she was going to Columbia Law School, and she prided herself on knowing how to be careful in the city. She had even taken self-defense classes at the YWCA to boost her confidence, but once she left school and moved to Brooklyn Heights, she had become increasingly paranoid about being alone on the West Side. It was foolish, she realized, especially now that the neighborhood was so fashionable. Still, she couldn't keep herself from being wary.

She stood a moment longer on Columbus and looked for an available yellow taxi, but the few cabs moving slowly downtown were either filled or on call.

"Damn!" she said, feeling sorry for herself. Everything, it seemed, was going wrong in her life. Defiantly she pushed forward up the deserted side street, thinking guiltily that she should have asked Tom to walk with her as far as Broadway. That was the trouble with her. She fought so hard to be independent, but whenever she felt afraid, she wanted a man around. That realization made her furious. She looked up and purposely exposed her face to the cold, as if trying to freeze the pain she felt in her heart.

Then she felt the hand on her shoulder and was stopped in her tracks.

Tom must have come after her. She twisted away and turned to him. But it wasn't Tom.

This man was taller, bigger. He seemed to block the entire street. She could barely see his face, hidden in the dark cave of a jacket hood, but she knew he was dangerous.

"Get away!" she shouted. She tried to step back and run, but her boots didn't grip in the slippery snow and she stumbled just as the man swung at her.

"You bitch," he swore, then lunging at her, knocked them both into the gutter between parked cars.

He was on top of her, pushing through her coat and grabbing at her body. His hands were on her breasts, his thick lips on her face. He kept swearing, calling her filthy names, and then he jabbed his blunt, wet tongue into her mouth.

It was when he ripped away the front of her white silk blouse that she went for him. Reaching up with both hands, she raked her nails down his cheeks. She wanted to hurt him, and hearing him cry out gave her courage. She hadn't hit anyone since she was a little girl in the playground, and the pleasure it gave her to strike back was gratifying.

With the ferocity of a cornered dog, she grabbed his throat and curled her fingernails into his neck. She felt the skin pop as her nails broke his flesh and his warm blood ran down her fingers.

He swung at her blindly, and she ducked the blow. Then, moving like an animal, she attacked, catching him in the groin with her knee. He stumbled forward, groping for his testicles, and fell face-forward into the deep snow.

She did not run to the corner, where the snowbound traffic honked along Columbus Avenue. Instead, she licked the corners of her bleeding mouth and tasted the blood with pleasure. He grabbed the front bumper of the parked car and pulled himself up. She hit him hard in the back of the neck with the heel of her right hand, swinging at him as if she were chopping a block of wood. His big body slumped forward, skidding off the car's metal grill, and dropped into the gutter.

She couldn't let him go. She wouldn't. She grabbed him by his hair and, with her foot jammed against the shoulder blades, jerked back his head until she heard his neck snap.

Jennifer stayed on her knees beside the body for a moment, gasping for air. She cupped a handful of snow into her palm and, using it like soap, wiped her face clean of blood. Calmer, she moved close and saw that the predator was dead. She had killed him. She smiled.

Her name was Shih Hsui-mei. She was Chinese, the wife of Cheng-k'uan, and he was a young man then, living in the town of Silver Hill. It was during the boom years of mining, and he had come west with his father from St. Louis to settle claims for the government.

He delivered goods to Cheng-k'uan from his uncle's store and would see Shih Hsui-mei sitting on the porch facing the Yellowjacket Mountains, combing her hair. She was his age—sixteen, perhaps seventeen—and had come from China to be old Cheng-k'uan's bride.

She had long black hair, very long, very black, and she would comb it slowly, time after time, until it fanned across one side of her perfect round face like a blackbird's wing.

She would then take a paste made of rhubarb and comb it through the hair until it lay straight and still, like a fan, and then she would tie it out of sight.

She never wore Western clothing but dressed always in silk trousers and tight, beautifully embroidered jackets and small silver slippers. She had such tiny feet. When she walked across the boards of Cheng-k'uan's mountain shack, she never made a sound. He would see her one moment, then she would be gone, like a tropical bird.

He could never see enough of her. He went again and again to China-town just to catch a glimpse of the young Shih Hsui-mei, for she never came across the creek to the white side of town.

In the opium dives, he saw her tend to the men, bring them fresh pipes of opium. The men stayed for days, lost to the world, hidden away in their private hells.

The boy's hell was Shih Hsui-mei. He wanted her. Her old husband used to laugh at him as he sat watching her comb her hair in the bright morning sun. The old man made fun of the boy and spoke rapidly in Chinese to Shih Hsui-mei, asking her if she wanted to feel the white man's prick.

The boy went to the opium dives and paid to smoke in the cells. He went because she would come to him then and give him a pipe full of the sweet-smelling drug. She would look at him with her wet black eyes and her round, perfect face, and he would stare wordlessly at her.

Then she would pass away into the den, and he would smoke the sweet opium and cough into the filthy blankets. In time he would forget her, forget his pain, and in the dimness of his consciousness, she would appear again, and he would not know if she were alive or simply in his dreams.

He had her then as he always wanted her—in a place where they could be alone together, away from the world. Even if it was only a dream, she was with him, and he would smile and see her smiling, beckoning him farther and farther into the world of opium and dreams.

When he woke, into the fierce pain of daylight and consciousness, he did not want to live. He wanted only more opium, more dreams of her passing him in the den, hearing her silk trousers, seeing her lovely small body. But he would have to leave the den, stumbling down the snowy path, crossing the cold river on the narrow log bridge. Sometimes he'd be sick there, falling off the bridge, tumbling into the rocky creek, puking the night's anguish of opium onto the slippery river rocks.

His father threw him out of his shack. He was no good to him, no good at work. The opium had destroyed his mind. He could not write down a simple claim in a government ledger or help his uncle. He wanted only Shih Hsui-mei. And now he had no money to buy opium, to spend the night watching her slip through the dense fog in her silk trousers, tending to the worthless lot of Chinese miners, or himself, a hopeless pale-faced white boy.

He stole his father's long-barreled pistol, the one he had been issued in the war, and went to get Shih Hsui-mei. He had a plan. A crazy plan. He would take her away from old Cheng-k'uan. The old man had no rights. He was a miserable Chink. The Chinese were killed by the dozens in the mines of Idaho. He would steal a horse and take Shih Hsui-mei with him across the Salmon River and into Oregon, where he had family, cousins of his mother.

When he went to Cheng-k'uan and told him what he intended, the old man laughed and spit in his face.

He shot the Chinaman in the head. The bullet made a small, neat black hole in the yellow man's forehead and splashed blood and bone and brain on the whitewashed wall. The old man turned in a tight circle, dancing on his thin legs like a chicken when it's axed.

He ran into the side wall before he stopped moving and slid down, smearing the whitewash with his blood. The boy had to step over him to get at Shih Hsui-mei. She was screaming. He had never before heard a Chinese woman scream.

He couldn't get her to be silent. His hands tore her lovely embroidered silk jacket. He kept telling her to hush, talking to her as if she were a baby, but she wouldn't stop screaming. He tore her silk blouse, and her breasts were so small and lovely he was suddenly dazed by the sight of them.

There were Chinese coming from the mines, running up through the mud of late spring, through the snow still frozen under shack porches. He had never seen so many Chinese.

He grabbed Shih Hsui-mei, this time with his arm around her waist. He would carry her all the way to the Snake River, he thought. But they made it only to the little creek below Cheng-k'uan's shack. He ran through the cold water, slipping on the smooth stones, thinking that if he crossed the creek into the white part of town, he would be safe. No white man would harm him for killing a Chink.

Her people caught him at the river. There were too many of them. They pulled little Shih Hsui-mei from his arms, and one slit his throat as he might draw a blade across a squealing pig.

His gushing blood turned the cold creek water purple. He stumbled on the smooth rock and fell forward, grabbing his throat, and died faster than Cheng-k'uan.

The whites came running down from town. They found him cold and stiff and bloodless. There was not a mark on his body, except for the fine, thin slice across the length of his throat. His blue eyes held a steady, unflinching gaze, as if here in death, he had finally found the answer to his young life.

6

"OH MY GOD," MARGIT exclaimed, seeing Jennifer. "What on earth has happened?" She reached out and pulled Jennifer into an embrace.

"I was mugged," Jennifer stated, and in the comfort and safety of Margit Engle's arms, she began to cry.

"David!" Margit shouted over Jennifer's shoulder. "David, come quick! Jennifer's been mugged."

Jennifer pulled herself from her friend's arms and wiped the tears from her eyes. She felt her bruised cheekbone.

"Jennifer, are you all right?" David asked. He handed his wife his drink as he approached Jennifer. "What happened?"

"She was mugged, David!" Margit's voice betrayed her anxiety. "We have to call the police."

"No. Don't call anyone!" Jennifer blurted out. She caught sight of herself in the living room mirror and began to cry again, but this time she let the tears flow. David guided her to the sofa and arranged a pillow behind her head.

"I'll get my bag and we'll take care of these bruises. You're okay, Jennifer, don't be afraid."

Jennifer nodded, but moving her head drove a piercing wedge of pain between her eyes, and she reached up with her hand to feel the raw flesh on her forehead. It would be days, she guessed, before the bruises would be gone, and that made her start crying again.

"I still think we should call the police," Margit declared. She was standing in the middle of the living room, nervously twisting her fingers.

"No!" Jennifer said. She tried to sit up but couldn't gather her strength.

"Jennifer is right," David said, returning. "Jennifer has had enough trouble. And what are the police going to find anyway? Whoever did this is already long gone." He knelt beside the sofa.

"Get me towels and warm water," he told his wife. "I want to clean up these bruises."

"Thank you, David," Jennifer whispered, but her lips had swollen and she was having difficulty forming words.

"Shhhhh," David whispered, smiling down at her. "No need to say anything, just rest. Close your eyes. You're all right."

Jennifer did close her eyes, thankful that she had made it to West End Avenue and that Margit and David were taking care of her. She did fall asleep, knowing she was safe from everyone out on those city streets. But still she was frightened of herself, of what she had done.

When she awoke she could hear their muffled voices from the other room. She turned her head carefully on the pillow, trying to avoid the wedges of pain every time she moved, and saw through bruised eyelids that they had closed the door to the dining room. The lights were off in the living room, where she still lay, now covered with a heavy quilt. Her shoes had been removed and her skirt loosened.

She wondered if she should get up to tell them that she was all right, but even as she wondered, she knew she didn't have the strength. How could she tell them what had really happened, how she had killed the man? She couldn't tell anyone the truth, ever, and when she closed her eyes again, she wished that she wouldn't wake up, that she would never have to face the nightmare of what she had done.

She woke crying, struggling to free herself from the hand on her shoulders. It was a moment before she realized she was being held by David. "You're having a nightmare, Jennifer. That's all," he was whispering.

One lamp was lit, and she saw David above her and Margit at the foot of the sofa, both looking pained and upset. Jennifer relaxed and slipped down into the soft pillows.

"I'm sorry," she mumbled.

"Don't be sorry. You just had a nightmare."

"I'm sorry I'm causing you all this trouble. I really should go home." Jennifer started to rise, but David placed his hand on her shoulder.

"You're going nowhere. Stay with us tonight, and I'll take you home tomorrow, if you're up to it. Otherwise, you'll be our guest for a few days."

"Thank you, but I can't. I have to go to Boston for a meeting."

"Well, we can talk about that tomorrow. You listen to me; I'm the doc here." He kept smiling, comforting her with his gentle manner.

"Thank you, David," Jennifer whispered. She was relieved by his insistence. The thought of being by herself was frightening.

"What about something to eat? A clear soup?" Margit asked.

Jennifer tried to smile and said, "That would be wonderful, Margit. I'm famished."

When Margit left the room, David asked, "Jennifer, nothing else happened to you besides being struck, am I correct?"

"What do you mean?"

"You weren't raped, were you?"

"Oh, no." Jennifer sighed, terrified that David might guess the truth. "I managed to get away."

"Would you like to talk about it?" he asked.

Jennifer shook her head. "I'm sorry," she said. "I feel so stupid, getting mugged. I mean, I should know better." She had her eyes closed and her head back. In her mind's eye, she saw the man again, saw him lunge at her, saw rage and hunger on his face, and then she hit him, attacked him like an animal, with her bare hands.

"You'll feel better tomorrow," David said reassuringly.

Jennifer nodded, but she knew that in the morning she would feel worse, not because of her bruises, but for what she had done.

"Here we are," Margit announced, coming back into the living room with a bowl of soup, a place mat and cloth napkin tucked under her arm.

Jennifer tried to sit up and again felt the wedge of pain between her eyes.

"Easy," David cautioned. He had taken hold of her elbow.

"Maybe we shouldn't try this," Margit suggested.

"No, I think getting something warm into Jennifer will do wonders. You can sit up, right? Otherwise, Margit will just feed you."

"No, I want to sit up, please." Jennifer forced herself to swing her legs off the deep sofa. She marveled to herself that she did suddenly have the strength to overcome the stabbing pain between her eyes. Something had happened to her. She was different, somehow. She was another kind of person. She had never been able to stand pain.

Margit stood hovering over Jennifer, her hands clasped together. "Would you like some Italian bread to go into the broth?" she asked.

"Let's give Jennifer room to breathe," David suggested, moving away from the sofa and sitting down across from the coffee table. Margit stayed on the sofa next to Jennifer.

"I'm not sure I'm going to be able to do this. I can't feel my lips."

"You look as if you just did a couple of rounds with Tyson."

"And I feel it." Jennifer picked up the soup spoon and realized she was no longer trembling. She smiled weakly at Margit and David.

"Well, that's better," Margit said, sighing, and she reached out to touch Jennifer's leg. "Would you like to talk about what happened?" she said softly.

"Margit, leave Jenny alone." He stood and went to the liquor cabinet.

"I just think it's better if Jennifer has the opportunity to talk it out, that's all," she answered back.

"I know what you want," David said, lowering his voice as he bent to retrieve the scotch bottle from the bottom of the breakfront. "You want all the gruesome details. And I think Jenny deserves to have her privacy."

They kept talking past her, as if she were a child.

"There are no gruesome details," Jennifer spoke up, "and I don't mind talking about it." She turned to Margit and tried to force her bruised face into a smile. "I didn't lose my purse. He didn't really hurt me. I mean, except for the obvious. I ran away, that's all."

"Well, where did it happen? Right here on West End Avenue?" Margit leaned closer, her eyes widening.

"No, it wasn't here. It was over by—" Jennifer caught herself before she said Columbus Avenue. "It was over on Broadway."

"Broadway? But it's so busy. There are always people on Broadway. Didn't anyone come to help you out? My God, this city!" She glared at her husband as if he were in some way responsible.

"There's no one out tonight, Margit," Jennifer said, returning to her soup. Eating made her feel better.

"That's right. It's been snowing all evening," agreed David.

"I still think we should call the police," Margit said again.

"Why? You heard Jenny. She wasn't robbed. She got banged up a couple times, sure, but in this city, that's not even considered a misdemeanor."

"We can't just let him get away with it." Margit glanced back and forth, upset with Jennifer as well as her husband. "A woman isn't safe."

"Margit was attacked herself last week, Jenny," David volunteered, "and she's still edgy."

"I'm not edgy, and I wasn't attacked. Someone—a little black kid—tried to take my purse at Food City, that's all. The guard grabbed him. But everywhere you turn, it seems, the great unwashed, all the homeless, the poor, are coming out of their holes, or wherever they sleep at night, and attacking us. It's the mayor's fault, him and all these liberals."

"You were once one yourself, dear," David remarked coolly. "And the mayor certainly isn't one anymore, either."

Margit stood and began to pace the long living room.

"Margit, why don't you go to bed?" David suggested, speaking softly. "Jenny would probably like to get some sleep, too."

"I'm not going to sleep. I'm too upset." Margit kept pacing.

"Darling, it was Jenny who was mugged, not you."

"I know that," she replied, biting off the words, "but it could have been me. I'm on Broadway all the time."

"Oh, if you're going to start talking like that, then you might as well move out of the city."

"I'm not moving alone," Margit snapped.

David glanced at Jennifer and smiled apologetically. "We're sorry about all this, but you caught us in the middle of a long argument. Margit has had it with the city, wants to leave, move up the Hudson somewhere—"

"Or New Jersey."

"—and I don't. I'm not going to start commuting, not at my age." He drained his scotch.

"I don't blame you, Margit. Getting attacked like this is terrifying." Jennifer finished the soup and tried to wipe her mouth, but when she touched her face with the cloth napkin, she winced. "I'm going to feel terrible tomorrow," she moaned. "And I have to go to Boston."

"Well, thank God nothing serious happened." David stood up. "Margit, have you finished pacing? Ready to turn in?" He smiled over Jennifer's head at his wife. He was a big, sloppy, overweight man, but when he smiled, he looked like a giant, lovable panda.

He had been Jennifer's doctor since she was in law school, and then she had met and become good friends with Margit. Jennifer always felt that Margit treated her like the daughter she never had.

Margit seemed calmer. "Jennifer, I've made up Derek's room. You can sleep there tonight. The boys are away at school."

"Oh, Margit, thanks, I'm really sorry I'm causing so much trouble." She limped out from behind the coffee table, knowing that she couldn't walk to their son's room by herself.

"If you wish, Jennifer, I'll give you a sedative. It might help you sleep."

"Thanks, David. I think I do need something. My whole body hurts."

"Go with Margit. I'll get you the pill."

When he left, Margit whispered to Jennifer, "I'm sorry we carried on so. We're going through a bad patch, David and I."

"Margit, it's okay, I understand." She tried again to smile.

"No, I'm not sure you do," Margit answered back. "It's not what you think. We're not fighting over where to live. David . . . well, David has found himself someone else, someone younger, and . . ." Margit began to cry. She was holding on to Jennifer as they walked to the bedroom.

"Oh, Margit, I'm so . . . I didn't . . ."

"Of course. Of course. Why would you? He just told me." Margit straightened up to turn on the light in Derek's room. It was still littered with his teenage belongings, and a huge poster of Madonna posing half naked was pinned to the wall.

"Do you think you can sleep with her staring at you?" Margit asked, trying to laugh.

"I'll keep the lights off." Jennifer eased herself down on the narrow bed.

"Here you are, Jenny," David said, returning with the pill and a glass of water. "You can take it when you want. It will give you at least six good hours." He leaned over and kissed the top of her head. "Good night. In the morning I'll have another look at those bruises."

"Thank you, David. Thank you for everything." She smiled up at him.

When he left them alone again, Margit said, "I shouldn't bother you with my concerns. You've had enough for one night. How's Tom? Do you want me to telephone him?"

Jennifer shook her head. She looked up at Margit, her eyes filled with tears. "I don't know. It's not, you know, working out."

Margit nodded. "It hardly ever does, does it?" She sighed.

"Margit, you're going to be okay. . . . We both are."

"I had the best husband in the world for twenty-three years, and now he tells me he's in love with a thirty-six-year-old woman —one of his patients, I might add—who's an investment banker on Wall Street and makes more money than he does. She's madly in love with him, he says. Now, how do you think that makes me feel?" She shook her head. "No wonder I hate this city. You know, Jennifer, I wish it had been me and not you that got mugged. I would have let that man kill me."

"Margit, I won't let you talk like that! I won't let you believe—"

"Believe it, Jennifer. It might happen to you. Once you're over forty, they put you out to pasture." The small woman's voice rose with anger. "Well, if he leaves me, I'll make him pay."

"Margit, I'm going to cry. Please."

"I'm sorry. Please go to sleep. Don't worry about tomorrow. I'll take you back to Brooklyn Heights. David said he has to go into the office, or at least that's the excuse he's giving me." She stood up and forced herself to smile. "Sleep tight, dear," she said, and pulled the door closed, leaving Jennifer alone.

Jennifer sat very still, holding the glass of water in one hand and the sleeping pill in the other. She forgot about her own problems for a moment and thought of Margit and David: a lifetime together, two children, a long and happy life, and now David had found another woman. She hated him at that moment, even though David was her doctor.

She felt her hatred pump through her body. It began in her fingers and raged like a forest fire in hot wind. Her breath came quick and hard, and in an effort to try to control herself, she took the pill, washing it down with a gulp of water. Yet still she raged. She stood up, forgetting her pain. She wanted him. She wanted to hurt David.

She opened the door and stepped into the hallway. The lights were out and the apartment was quiet. With her feet silent on the thick carpet, she moved toward the light that seeped out from under their bedroom door.

Jennifer realized they were sleeping separately when she saw the light under Matthew's bedroom door. That he had left Margit alone in their bed enraged Jennifer more. At that moment she felt a draft of cold air and shivered. A surge of blood pumped through her veins.

With a violent push, Jennifer swung the bedroom door open.

David was in the bathroom. He was wearing just his pajama bottoms, and his heavy white flesh sagged over the drawstring. He was brushing his teeth and his eyes bulged when he saw her. He looked old and useless.

"Jenny," he mumbled, his mouth foamed with the white toothpaste.

"You!" She came at him with her hands extended, fingers reaching to clutch his throat. She knew how she would kill him—with her fingernails ripping into the flesh of his neck. But suddenly her vision swam; she felt lightheaded and stumbled forward. He caught her before she fell to the floor.

"It's all right, Jenny. You're all right." He lowered her to the carpet and called for his wife.

"What happened?" Margit asked, rushing from the other bedroom.

"She passed out from the medicine. It was too large a dose, I'm afraid. I forgot to ask her if she'd had something to drink earlier. She'll be all right, though. Give me a hand."

"She's not hurt?" Margit asked.

"No, but she's going to have a hell of a headache in the morning."

"Damnit, David, why weren't you more careful?"

"I was careful. She shouldn't have had this serious a reaction. Something must be wrong with her metabolism."

They had her in the hallway, carrying her between them like a sack of potatoes.

"What was she doing in there, anyway?" Margit asked as she struggled with Jennifer's legs.

"I don't know. I looked up and saw her in the mirror. She was coming straight for me," David said, puzzled. "I was brushing my teeth. I didn't have my glasses on. She looked wild, as if she were out of her head. I couldn't tell whether she was just wandering, or whether she had—I don't know—come to get me."

"Get you?" Margit looked over at her husband. "What do you mean?"

"She looked like she wanted to kill me," David replied, setting Jennifer gently on the bed.

7

JENNIFER STOPPED WALKING AND let the other Wednesday morning commuters rush by her. She stood staring at the bold headline of the *New York Post*:

APE KILLER MAKES MANHATTAN JUNGLE

Several people bumped against her in the crowded corridor, and she moved out of the steady stream of pedestrians, then closer to the newsstand to read the smaller print:

MAN FOUND WITH BONES CRUSHED. DOC SAYS, "ANIMAL DID IT."

Jennifer walked over to the newsstand and stealthily purchased the newspaper, as if she thought she might be watched. She took it to a relatively quiet corner and flipped through the pages for the story. There was a photograph of the street and an arrow indicating where the body had been found, wedged between the parked cars.

As she rode from Brooklyn to Manhattan, she scanned the story for details that might link her to the death. No one had seen the murder. A neighbor had found the victim on Monday while walking his dog. It had snowed hard all weekend, and by then the body had been buried beneath twelve inches of snow, but the dog had sniffed out the blood. One foot of the murder victim had been sticking out, like a raised flag, the neighbor explained. And so he had called the cops. There was a close-up photo of the man's battered old shoe.

"Inhuman," the neighbor with the dog was quoted as telling the *Post*. "The killer must have been some kind of King Kong. What's this city coming to?"

There was a description of how the man's neck was broken, and the article speculated on the size of the assailant. "Two hundred and fifty plus pounds," estimated Detective Coles Phinizy, "and maybe six feet six or seven. We're looking for a man the size of a defensive back, someone who'd give Hulk Hogan a match." The victim's identity was being withheld until his nearest relatives were located, but anyone with information about the murder was asked to call the Twentieth Precinct.

She glanced around carefully and then tore out the article and tossed away the newspaper. Her fear had returned—not that it had really left her, but she had been able to suppress it.

She had taken Tuesday off from work and, with the help of another sleeping pill, had slept most of the night. When she did wake, she remembered the attack but had begun to believe that she had simply overreacted. It hadn't been as brutal as she remembered. She hadn't killed anyone, she finally convinced herself.

Taking a shower that morning, she had studied herself in the mirror, searching for some telltale signs, a new growth of hair, a change in the size of her muscles, but there were no marks on her body, no signs that her body had changed on her.

Now her fear flooded her body. It wasn't fear of being arrested for murder. The police would not be looking for a blond white woman, five foot seven and 126 pounds.

Her fear was much more terrifying and secret. She had killed someone with the strength of her own hands, and she had no idea where it had come from.

She rushed through Penn Station, up to the street, and out into the cold New York morning. She was on her way to a meeting with the members of a nearby Catholic church that wanted funds for a homeless shelter. But as she hurried to the street, Jennifer knew she couldn't sit through any meeting. Instead of going to the church, she'd take a taxi to her office and have Joan telephone and reschedule.

The snow had been cleared from the streets and pushed into the gutter to form a high ridge, already blackened with soot and broken down at places where pedestrians had beaten an icy path into the street. A taxi stopped ahead of her and a man with a suitcase jumped out, over the ridge of snow, and went toward Penn Station. Jennifer bolted immediately for the cab. Out of the corner of her eye she saw that another man had spotted the taxi and begun to run. Jennifer picked up her pace, found an opening in the ridge of snow, and ran into the street. She came at the taxi from behind, from the blind side.

She had it, she told herself, breathing hard as she raced through the slush. She had forgotten about her situation, the murdered man, forgotten her own fear. She needed that cab.

The other man, sprinting down the street, had reached the front of the cab. When he saw her, he began to shout. "Hey, lady, this is mine!"

Jennifer opened the back door, slid inside, and slammed the door.

"Broadway and Fifty-eighth," she told the driver, leaning forward so she'd be heard through the glass. She heard the man shouting at her through the side window. She reached out and locked the door, then sank back into the seat with relief as the taxi pulled into traffic. She never looked at the man as he slammed his fist on the side of the departing taxi.

The driver swore, glancing around.

"Don't stop!" Jennifer asked. She was trembling.

"Animals!" the driver shouted. "Goddamn animals!" He accelerated his taxi, still swearing, complaining now about the traffic.

Jennifer glanced at the name and picture on his hack license. It was unpronounceable, full of consonants. Now she stared out the side window, as if by looking away she could avoid any more confrontations.

"Animals!" the driver exclaimed again.

"Yes," Jennifer whispered. "I think I am."

"Oh my God, what happened to you?" Joan exclaimed, seeing Jennifer's bruised face.

"I'm okay. I'm okay," Jennifer assured her secretary. "Joan, follow me. I need you to cancel an appointment." Jennifer walked through the foundation's outer rooms and into her own small office that looked north. The sun reflected brilliantly on the hard-packed frozen snow.

"Would you like a cup of coffee?" Joan asked, as she followed after her.

"Yes!" Jennifer called back, shedding her wool coat and dropping it on her office sofa. "And get Dale Forster on the phone. I'm going to have to break our squash date." Jennifer slid into her chair. She didn't look up, but she knew her secretary had followed her into the room with coffee. "I want you to call Father Merrill and tell him I'm sorry, but I can't make this morning's meeting. Also,

I want you to clear my schedule for this afternoon." She pulled her calendar across the wide desk and glanced down at Wednesday. "What do we have?"

"You have the eleven o'clock meeting with David Meyer on his film project. That's set up in the conference room. He wants to show you his film on Sun Valley. And he's already here. Then you have lunch with Evan Konechy upstairs in the dining room. Unless you want to have me make reservations elsewhere. This afternoon, there's a slide presentation for the St. Louis project, remember?" The secretary carefully set down the coffee cup, then perched on the edge of a chair at the corner of the desk. She had her pad out, ready to take notes.

"Damnit! I forgot about St. Louis." Jennifer fell back into her high-backed leather chair, the one David and Margit had bought for her when she started to work for the foundation.

"Jennifer, are you all right?" Joan asked. "Tell me what happened."

"Yes, I'm all right now." When she'd called in sick the day before, she'd said nothing about the assault. Now she was trying to make light of the incident. "I got mugged outside my apartment, that's all."

"Oh, you poor thing! You didn't tell me! Are you okay? Did you have to go to the hospital?"

"No, I just have to go see the . . . police," she lied, avoiding Joan's eyes.

"And look at mug shots?" Joan asked. "Janet Chan—you know, the one who just took over the Woman's World Foundation—was robbed last fall, and she had to look at mugshots. That was in Scarsdale."

"Well, I don't know about mugshots. I never saw the man." Jennifer reached for the cup of coffee, thankful that her hands had stopped trembling.

"Was he a black person?" Joan whispered, still leaning across the desk.

"I don't know. I told you, I never saw him." Jennifer opened her leather briefcase and took out her files in an attempt to stave off other questions. "Any calls?"

"Yes, several. . . . Tom called . . . twice." Joan did not look up as she glanced through the yellow phone messages. "And the president's office phoned. Dr. Handingham wants to speak with you about the talk he's to give at the Silbersack luncheon on Monday."

Jennifer suddenly felt overwhelmed by her work. On her desk were several bulky files, projects that needed attention. And there were all her meetings today. But she couldn't concentrate. She couldn't take her mind off what had happened.

"Jennifer, are you all right?" Joan asked again.

"Yes, I'm just tired, that's all." She gestured at the stack of files. "I've got to get some work done. Can you keep everyone away from me for a little while?" She smiled across at Joan, blinking away tears.

"Don't worry about a thing, dear." Joan Corboy stood. "Drink your coffee, and I'll close the door and let you have some peace and quiet."

"Thank you, Joan, for taking care of me." She smiled after her secretary, and when her office door closed, Jennifer reached for the telephone and dialed Tom at work.

"Is Tom Oliver available?" she asked his secretary.

"May I ask who is calling?"

"Ms. Winters." Jennifer fingered the telephone cord as she waited, and spun her leather chair around to look out the window. She could see a long thin slice of the park from her windows and up Central Park West as far north as the museum. She focused on the massive Romanesque museum as she waited for Tom to come to the phone. She could not see Columbus Avenue, where she had killed the man.

It hadn't happened, she told herself. It couldn't have happened. But she knew now that was not true. She had gone over the murder a thousand times. In her mind, she had killed him a thousand times.

"Jennifer!"

"Tom, yes," she whispered into the phone.

"Where have you been?"

"I need to see you."

"I need to see you, darling." He sighed into the phone. "God, I've been calling you. But your machine—"

"Tom," she interrupted, "I have to talk to you." She had cupped her hand over the mouthpiece of the phone.

"What? Honey, I can't hear you."

"I need to talk to you!"

"Okay! Okay! When? Where?"

"Can you meet me for lunch?"

"Sweetheart, I can't. I've got to be downtown."

"All right!" She spun around and studied her calendar. "Are you free later, after four?"

"I will be. Where do you want to meet?"

"Come to Brooklyn, please."

There was silence for a moment, as he decided. "Okay, but don't be late. I don't want to have to hang around on the street."

"You have a key."

"Not with me."

"I'll be home early. Tom, I need your help. Something has happened." She was crying, and she reached over to pluck a tissue from the box on her desk.

"What are you talking about?"

"It's not what you think. I'm okay." She knew he was constantly worried that she'd get pregnant. "Don't say anything. I mean, don't tell anyone in the office you're meeting me."

"I never do, honey, you know that."

"I'm serious, Tom, this is important!"

"So's my case."

"What I need to talk to you about involves just me. Me alone."

"Honey, I just don't get you."

"Did you see the *Post* this morning?"

"Of course not!"

"Take a look at the headline."

"Come on, what gives? I've got a hearing in fifteen minutes."

"The headline says, 'Ape Killer Makes Manhattan Jungle.' "

"Yeah . . . so?"

"I need to talk to you about this 'ape killer.' I know who it is!" Then, unable to say more, she slammed down the phone. What had happened to her? She stood and came around the desk as her office door opened. Joan was holding a bright red file.

"It's for your eleven o'clock with Meyer," she said, handing the thick file to Jennifer.

"Call this number for me, please," Jennifer said as she strode from the office. "Eileen Gorman. See if she can have lunch with me today in the city. Tell her it's very important. And call Evan Konechy and tell her I have to cancel."

Joan followed Jennifer out of the suite of offices and stood with her in front of the bank of elevators. "Jennifer, are you sure you're all right?" She peered over her glasses at her boss.

Jennifer stared at her reflection in the polished bronze doors of the elevators. In the contours of the metal, she looked gross and deformed, and she turned away from the image.

"I'm not sure," she whispered. And then the doors opened and she stepped into an empty elevator. Turning, she pressed the button for the conference room floor, then glanced at Joan, who was still watching her, her face knit with concern.

"You can tell me," Joan offered.

Jennifer managed to fake a smile. "I wish to God I could," she whispered to herself as the doors slid smoothly closed, locking her briefly in the safety of the descending car.

8

JENNIFER COULD NOT EAT lunch. Instead, she sat across from Eileen Gorman and listened to the woman talk. Jennifer had wanted to see Eileen as soon as possible, once she realized that everything about her had started to go wrong after she met Eileen in Washington. She and Kathy Dart had exchanged a strange look, and then she had run thirteen miles. All of it, she guessed, was somehow connected to Eileen Gorman.

She had also wanted to tell Eileen what she had done, how she had killed the man who attacked her, but now she couldn't tell her high school friend. In her heart, Jennifer still believed that she wasn't capable of doing such a horrendous act.

So she spent lunch listening to Eileen tell her about the New Age philosophy, channeling, psychic auras, all of the metaphysical beliefs that Eileen followed. Something told Jennifer that she had to learn more about this new form of spiritualism if she was going to find out what was wrong with her body.

"I didn't believe in meditation or est, or anything having to do with pyramids and quartz crystals, either," Eileen went on, "not at first, certainly. But then I began to notice how my life—what was happening in my life—had a pattern. I started to read, to investigate everything, you know, the unexplained. And that is what finally led me to the teachings of Kathy Dart and Habasha."

Jennifer waited for her to go on, to explain what she meant.

"I just decided I had been reincarnated." Eileen shrugged. "I mean, reincarnation was the only thing that made sense about my life. Anyone's life." She waved her hand in the air. "None of our lives make any sense, unless there is some reason."

"There is a reason," said Jennifer. "Some people call it heaven and hell. Others call it evolution." She could not yet accept what Eileen was telling her, but could she dismiss Eileen's reasoning, either?

"Look, I don't have your law degree," Eileen said, leaning forward, "and I didn't graduate from the University of Chicago like you did. I really haven't studied at all, not since high school. But I've learned a lot on my own just from reading the New Age material. It's incredible, really, once you see the connections, the links between lives. The plan of what we are doing here on earth."

Jennifer raised her eyebrows.

"Listen, there's something about me I never told you. You know I married that lifeguard, Tim Murphy. Well, we had a baby. A little premie. A girl. We called her Adara, and she lived just a week."

"Eileen, I didn't know."

"Of course not. You were away at college." Eileen continued, "It was a forceps delivery, and the poor little thing had these deep gashes on her forehead."

"Oh, no," Jennifer whispered.

"No, that didn't kill her. She was just too young. Her lungs hadn't developed. Perhaps today with all the advancements in medicine . . . but she didn't live. And because of that, plus a lot of other things, naturally, Timmy and I just drifted apart. I mean, we really had nothing in common except Jones Beach.

"I went a little wild after we split up," she said with a grimace. "I got kind of heavy into drugs and playing around. Some mornings I woke up and didn't know where I was, who I was with. It was that awful. I was trying to kill myself, I guess." Eileen shrugged. "And I would have if I hadn't met Todd. He was just getting over this terrible divorce, and we sort of found each other—saved each other.

"Here he was, this big, successful New York City insurance executive, with this great house in Old Westbury. I mean, I couldn't believe how lucky I was. And he loved me, too. I actually knelt down one night by the side of my bed and said my prayers, as if I was a little kid again, and thanked God for sending Todd into my life. But it wasn't God who had given me Todd. I was simply fulfilling my karma.

"Anyway, we were married on the fourteenth of September, and our son, Michael, was born the same day, two years later. It was exactly five years before that day that I had lost my little Adara.

"Michael had a perfectly fine delivery, no forceps. Yet when I saw him, when the doctor laid him on my chest, he had two marks on each side of his forehead, just like Adara. And I knew. I knew."

"Eileen, please."

Eileen nodded. "Yes, I'm certain of it, Jennifer. Michael and

Adara are the same soul. That's not so strange, either. There's a psychiatrist in Boston, Dr. Susan Zawalich, who has been collecting information on just such occurrences.

"And I read about one case. It happened in Ireland. Two boys, eleven and six, were killed in an IRA bombing. Right after that, their mother got pregnant, but this time with twins. Two girls were born, and they had marks on their bodies that were exactly like the marks their older, dead brothers had had. The same kinds of marks, in the same places, the same color eyes, the same expressions, everything."

"Eileen, you're letting your imagination run away with you."

"You mean my guilt?" Eileen suggested.

"Well, maybe," Jennifer answered, caught short by Eileen's self-awareness.

"I thought about that—that I might just be projecting onto Michael what Adara had looked like. So I did some checking. I went back into the drawer where we kept all her papers, all the hospital papers, and found that little first footprint they do of all newborns. I took Adara's and I got Michael's, and I gave them to a friend of Todd's who is deputy sheriff over in Garden City, and asked him to compare the prints." She paused dramatically. "They're the same, Jennifer. My two children have identical footprints. They are the same soul."

Jennifer looked away. She didn't believe it, but perhaps Eileen needed to believe something like that. It would give her a way to justify what had happened to her firstborn.

"The unexplained, Jennifer, is just that. It is beyond our so-called rational thinking. We were brought up, taught, to have rational explanations for all actions. Well, the truth is that there are some phenomena that just don't allow themselves to be easily explained. There is always a reason, but it is sometimes beyond our comprehension. And some people, like Kathy Dart and other channelers, they have a gift—a gift from God. There's nothing satanic about any of this. Their gift is to show us that there's a logic in the randomness of events, but it's the logic of a superior power."

"You sound like a TV evangelist," Jennifer replied.

"I'm not religious, I told you that. We don't attend church, Todd or I. But I believe in God, and I believe that we're all part of a plan, a system of life. Here, let me give you one example." She leaned on the table excitedly, ticking off the references on her fingers as she talked.

"Two of our presidents who were assassinated knew they were

going to be killed. Lincoln had a dream where he saw himself wrapped in funeral vestments. This was only a day or two before he was killed. And Kennedy told Jackie that if someone wanted to shoot him from a window with a rifle, then no one could stop him. But there is more than just that. Both of them died on Friday. They were both shot in the back of the head while sitting next to their wives. Both of the killers had three-part names—John Wilkes Booth and Lee Harvey Oswald. The two killers were born exactly one hundred years apart, and both were murdered before they came to trial.

"Booth shot Lincoln in a theater and fled into a warehouse. Oswald shot Kennedy from a warehouse and ran into a theater. Kennedy had a secretary called Lincoln. Lincoln had one called Kennedy. Lincoln was in Ford's Theater when he was shot. Kennedy was riding in a Lincoln, made by Ford. And both presidents were succeeded by southerners named Johnson." Eileen sat back. "This isn't just chance, Jennifer. There's a plan. A divine plan. And I'm not alone in thinking that Lincoln and Kennedy were the same soul, reincarnated."

For a moment they were both silent, tired from the long afternoon of talking. Jennifer could hear muffled traffic from the street, and the rattle of dishes and pans deep in the restaurant. It was past time to go back to the office. She glanced at her watch.

"I don't believe in reincarnation," Jennifer announced.

"I don't see why not. All religions do, in one way or another. What's life after death but reincarnation? All of nature is cyclical. The raindrop that falls from the sky into the ocean, first came from the ocean. It's the same raindrop. It's the same soul. We only come into existence once and are reborn throughout time. Our soul is the home of our good, our unselfish and noble aspirations. When we seek to aid the homeless, to stop suffering, to go to the aid of our neighbor, that is our soul at work."

Jennifer thought of the man she had beaten to death. To stop herself from being overwhelmed with the image, she asked, "Well, where does this karma of yours come into it?"

"Karma is the law of consequences—of merit and demerit, as the Buddhists say. It is a sort of justice that is measured out to us —so much good, so much bad—in our next life in accordance with what we did in this lifetime. In a sense we're condemned to pay for what we did in our past lives, to keep reliving our lives until all our bad karma has been replaced by good karma."

"What happens then?"

"Then we gain what our souls came into life for in the first place: eternal peace and happiness. At least that's what Kathy, or really, Habasha, tells us."

Jennifer nodded. She knew just enough about occult teaching and the paranormal to follow Eileen's argument, but what had suddenly happened to her behind the museum? Why there? Why then?

"I have to get back to the office," she announced, too weary to continue.

"All right, but, Jennifer, I'm at home, you know, whenever you need to talk." She smiled, and Jennifer marveled again at the peacefulness of Eileen's face. Jennifer saw none of the tension that stared back at her each morning from her own bathroom mirror. Perhaps she should buy the whole bag of nonsense just for that look of contentment. It would be worth it, she thought fervently, to get a good night's sleep.

"It's snowing," Eileen said with surprise when they stepped outside the restaurant. Jennifer walked with Eileen to where she had parked her car.

"I'm sorry you drove into town, Eileen. The expressway home will be a nightmare."

"I never worry about things like that, not anymore," Eileen answered. "Before I got connected with Kathy and Habasha, little things like driving in snow, making dinner for guests, meeting new people, why I'd go half out of my mind with worrying. Not now!" She shook her head, smiling confidently.

"How? How do you stop worrying, driving yourself crazy?" Jennifer stopped walking and turned to Eileen. "I want to know," Jennifer insisted. She was tired of all the general talk of love, of getting in touch with one's feelings, of meditating and using a quartz crystal for guidance and wisdom. She wanted answers and results. "Tell me how to live in this city without losing your humanity, and then I'll believe in your African man."

"It's not that simple, Jennifer. I mean, you have to be receptive."

"I'm receptive. Believe me, I'm receptive."

"Try, Jennifer. Try. Open yourself up." Eileen smiled and her eyes glistened from the cold. "Here!" she said, pulling a quartz crystal from her pocket. "Take this, carry it with you. The crystal will take care of you until you've had a chance to talk to Kathy or some other channeler. Just think about it, about having it in your pocket." She leaned forward and kissed Jennifer lightly on the cheek. "Be caring," she whispered, and then added, *"Tiru no."*

"What?" Jennifer pulled away, frowning.

"It's Habasha's saying, meaning, 'It is good.' You are good. We are good." She waved good-bye and went into the entrance of the parking lot to pick up her car.

Jennifer kept walking east toward her office. It was snowing harder, and ahead of her the traffic stalled as cars tried to negotiate the wet city streets. Eileen would never get home, she thought guiltily.

She crossed the street, making her way between gridlocked cars, and reached into the pocket of her fur coat to feel the quartz. It was warm in her pocket, like a small heater, and having it with her did, for some odd reason, make her feel better. She wondered why.

Once in the building, Jennifer took the elevator to her floor, and went toward the ladies' room. Out of the corner of her eye, she spotted a woman waiting at the elevator, and when she unlocked the bathroom door, the woman turned abruptly and followed after her. Jennifer stopped at the entrance, suddenly apprehensive. It was a small thin white woman that she had never seen in the building, but then she realized she could take care of herself and continued into the bathroom.

There was a black maintenance woman cleaning the toilets. Jennifer stepped to the sinks, set her purse on the ledge below the mirror, and began to apply fresh makeup. She only glanced at the heavyset woman when she came out of the stall. She moved slowly, with the roll of a big ship anchored in a harbor.

"Snowing out there, ma'am?" she asked.

"Yes, it is, I'm afraid," Jennifer answered, as she applied her lipstick.

"Oh, I hates the snow. Nothing but trouble, winter." She stuck her mop in the bucket of soapy water and came toward Jennifer. Her bulk, Jennifer realized at once, had blocked her in the corner.

"Okay, honey," the black woman said softly, almost as if she were whispering to a child, "why don't you just dump that purse out on the counter?" Her melodic voice sang sweetly in the silent room.

Jennifer stepped away from the mirror and backed up against the tile wall. Now she realized what was happening and was unable to speak, to even think of what she might do to escape. When the door of the first stall opened, she thought at once, Thank God, it was the other woman who had followed her from the elevator, but then Jennifer saw the thin woman's eyes fix on her leather bag.

"No!" Jennifer moved as the thin woman grabbed at the bag. "Please, don't," she begged.

"Get back, you white bitch!" The heavyset woman hit Jennifer on the shoulder, tossed her off balance, then seized the purse and dumped the contents into the wash basin. Her chubby short fingers sifted through the contents.

Jennifer saw herself react. She saw herself push off the gray tile wall and jump the big woman. She seized her by the throat. She held up the woman with one hand for a moment, as if she were a lioness in Africa showing off her prize. Then she banged open the metal stall door and, still with one hand, shoved the black woman's face in the toilet bowl. The water splashed from the bowl as the heavy woman thrashed under her hands, but Jennifer leaned over, pressed her full weight on the woman's shoulder, and flushed the toilet with her foot. She kept flushing until the woman stopped struggling. Then Jennifer wedged the woman's bulky body against the back wall of the stall and left her facedown in the blue toilet water.

Jennifer backed off, calming herself with deep breaths, turned to the counter and picked up the contents of her purse, slipping them into her large leather bag. She looked up into the mirror and caught a glimpse of her flushed face and blazing eyes, but then she saw the other woman, the thin white woman, had not run. She had stayed and now was coming at Jennifer with a club in her hand.

Without pausing, without a rational thought, Jennifer lunged forward and hit the woman. She caught her squarely on the bridge of the nose. Jennifer felt the bone crumble beneath her hand and saw a flash of pain in the woman's dull eyes before her blood spurted out of both nostrils in thick red jets. Jennifer tapped her on the forehead, and the dead woman slid silently to the wet tile of the bathroom floor.

Jennifer stepped over her, straightened her suit skirt, and walked out of the bathroom. She turned away from the conference room toward the bank of elevators and hit the down button. Fright swept through her, leaving her trembling. She leaned against the wall, praying for the elevator to come, praying that no one would discover that she had killed again.

She dug her hands deep into the pockets of her fur coat and felt Eileen's crystal. Slipping her fingers around the quartz, she felt its strange warmth and at once felt better. Jennifer closed her eyes and concentrated on the quartz crystal, letting its strange calming vibrations smooth her troubled soul.

$100 REWARD

RAN AWAY from my plantation, in Calhoun County, Alabama, a Negro woman named Sarah, aged 17 years, 5 feet 3 or 4 inches high, copper colored, and very straight; her teeth are good and stand a little open; thin through the shoulders, good figure, tiny features. The girl has some scars on her back that show above her shoulder blades, caused by the whip; smart for a Negro, with a pleasing smile. She was pursued into Williamsburg County, South Carolina, and there fled. I will give the above reward for her confinement by a soul driver.

Charles B. Smythe
Norfolk Times
October 6, 1851

He stood away from the dusty dock, away from the crowds, and watched the slave speculators loading the runaways. He stood out of the wind, on the wooden porch of a riverside bar, and watched for women, but there were few of them being shipped south, and those that he saw, he did not want. They were old and beaten down by age and hard labor. Still, he waited. He only wanted one; two would be more than a surprise. It would be a blessing, he thought, and smiled to himself.

On the cold December day, the few slave women he saw wore thin dresses, little underwear or petticoats, and all were barefooted. Small ice balls hung from the hems of their clothes.

He took out a se-gar, struck a match against a post, and lit the corona while he kept scanning the busy river dock.

The slaves were already being led onto the steamer, so as to be safely in the holds before passengers like himself boarded. He watched a chain line of seventy Negroes, men, women, and children, each carrying a small bundle of their belongings, being whipped up the plank, the shouts of the soul drivers carrying clearly on the frosty morning. These slaves were runaways, being taken south to be sold at auction or returned for reward money.

The Negroes walked with their heads bent, making no protests as the whip cracked across their backs. Although he did notice in passing that several of the little ones were silently weeping, he guessed that was more from fatigue than fear. These little pickaninnies had no fear, he realized, because they did not know what waited for them in the Old South. Farther away, other slaves loading goods on the ferryboat began to sing, and their strong voices rose above the snap of whips and the shouts of the soul-drivers.

> Poor Ros-y, poor gal,
> Poor Ros-y, poor gal;
> Ros-y broke my poor heart,
> Heaven shall-a be my home.

He smiled, enjoying the spiritual. He had heard it before, sung by the slaves on Sea Island. There were no finer voices in the whole world, he guessed, than the simple voices of black people. God gives each of his creatures some meager gifts, he thought, even his blacks.

Then he saw the woman and he forgot about the spirituals. Standing up, he followed her progress as she approached the docked steamer. He had seen her once before, when he had spent a night at the major's plantation, and then she had been no more than seventeen. But it was her, he knew at once, and his heart quickened. She was in chains, and it appeared she was the sole possession of a slave driver. It was Sarah. She was headed for Calhoun County and Charles B. Smythe. But not, he told himself, if he could stop it.

The soul driver who had Sarah was a pinelander, he saw, poor white trash from Georgia. He was a small man with a yellow-mud complexion, straight features, and the simple dumb look of one baffled by his life. He appeared as if his head had been kicked by a mule. The pinelander would be no trouble, he thought with satisfaction, already feeling the flesh of the beautiful black woman naked in his arms. He moved off the porch and made his way across the crowded wharf to where the pinelander stood with his private bounty.

He'd buy her off the man for the stated reward money and save the man the trip to Calhoun County. If the pinelander questioned him, he'd simply say he was headed south to visit the major. But the soul driver wouldn't protest, he knew. Not with a hundred greenbacks in his pocket.

He'd have the soul driver deliver the woman to his cabin and chain her there to the furnishings. No one would be the wiser, nor would he be seen with the girl. His mouth watered, thinking of having her, and he picked up his gait, suddenly in a rush to buy his prize.

He waited until the steamer was underway before going down to his cabin, and then when he opened the door to his rooms, he did not see her. His heart quickened, thinking the pinelander might have tricked him, gone off with his money and the slave, but then he saw that she was chained to the bedpost and was sitting in the dark corner of the small room.

The candlelight from the passageway caught only the gleam of her brown eyes. He closed the door behind him and locked them both in the darkness of the cabin.

"Hello, Sarah," he said to calm her. "You are all right, girl. I won't beat you." He did not soften his words. He never treated slaves with kindness, for he had learned they always misunderstood intentions and later thought they had some claim on his affections. He treated all slaves the same, whether he had slept with them or not. "I will unshackle you from the bed, Sarah, and I want you to strip out of those filthy rags of yours, then use the bowl and water on the counter and wash yourself, especially your privates."

He spoke calmly, not allowing her to notice his excitement. It was best with slave women that they not understand the desire he had for them.

The girl was trembling, but he did not try to soothe her fear. She knew well enough what he wanted, and it did not matter to him how she felt.

In the darkness of the tiny cabin, he lit another corona and watched the girl. She went to the washbasin and splashed the cold water onto her face, washed her hands.

"Take off those rags," he ordered when she didn't rush to do so.

She pulled the thin cotton dress over her shoulders, doing it so as not to look at him.

"All of it," he added when she did not immediately slip out of her thin petticoat.

As she pushed off her petticoat, she began to cry.

"Stop it!" he told her, and in one quick motion, he sprang off the bunk bed and slapped her face.

Sarah slid to the floor, clutching his leg, still crying. He kicked out, but her arms were clutched around his leg, and he stumbled against the wall of the cabin.

Now he swore and, reaching down, seized her shoulders and lifted her to his face.

She weighed nothing. His massive hands held her easily off the floor. Her face was inches from his. He could smell her frightened breath, smell her flesh. Her kinky hair smelled of smoke, her body of the river musk, of her own animal sweat. He loved the smell of black women, even more than he loved their flesh.

He kissed her, forcing his mouth over hers, digging his tongue into her gasping mouth. She tried to struggle, and he quickly slipped his arms about her, pinning her naked body to him.

She cried out, but her small voice was muffled by the heavy beating of the paddleboat, the noise of the river.

"Scream," he told her, laughing, enjoying her helplessness. No one would hear her. Then he pushed Sarah away and studied her face.

She was almost as beautiful as a white woman, he thought, with the same thin features, the small mouth of an English woman, and wide, bright, chocolate brown eyes. Her skin was copper colored and smooth. There was white blood in this bitch, he thought next, and he felt her small breasts.

She gasped, and he laughed again, clinching the tiny corona in his teeth.

"You like that, huh?" he asked. "And this?" He grabbed her sex with his right hand and hoisted her up.

She screamed and went to hit him, but he struck first, knocking her across the small cabin.

"Get up, bitch!" he ordered, "and over here."

He turned to the small bed and took off his coat, then sat down and told her, "Pull these boots off, girl." He reached down and pulled his small pistol from the top of his right boot and tossed it on the soft bed covers. "Hurry, you!"

Wordless, she crept over to him, still crying from the beating, took hold of his right boot, and jerked it off.

"There," he said, "that's better."

He raised his left leg, and she pulled off the boot. She was still on the wood floor of the steamer cabin, and she carefully placed the boots together at the foot of the small bunk bed, then slowly, still in pain, she pulled herself up. She was so small and thin that her whole body did not take up any space in the tight room. He towered in it. He crowded her.

"Forget about your Major Smythe, Sarah. I have no plans to put you back in those cotton fields. I have better plans for you. Plans of my own, girl, if you have the right temperament. How would you like to visit New Orleans?"

He was pulling off his ruffled shirt, placing the pearl buttons on a tray, and then she suddenly reached, like a hungry child seizing food, and he saw she had grabbed the derringer.

"Bitch!" he shouted, reaching for her arm.

She fired at once, not looking, screaming and terrified. The single shot would have been wild, but he stumbled forward and was hit in his left eye. The bullet smashed the socket and drove up into his brain, and the blood splattered her naked body, and then the walls and ceilings of the tiny cabin as he turned and stumbled to his death, crashing against the washstand, spilling the water and breaking the large porcelain pitcher.

No one heard the shot. No one heard her cry out in fright, and she wasn't sure whether she was really crying or whether the rage and horror were only in her head. She sat for a while, trembling in the corner, watching him across the cabin. He no longer moved, and the blood spread like sewage around his body and across the floor, seeping into the wood.

Toward morning, the first song of the slaves rose from deep in the river steamer, and she awoke. The voices called to her, came to her through the vastness of the boat. It was a funeral song. Some slave had died in the hold of the steamer.

Oh, graveyard, oh, graveyard,
I'm walking through the graveyard,
Lay this body down.

Your soul and my soul
Will meet on that day,
Lay this body down.

Sarah stood and, moving so that she wouldn't see or come too close to the sprawling dead man, she retrieved her dress and petticoat and then dressed with her back to the man she had killed. She only looked at him once to be positive in her own mind that she didn't know him, and then she opened the cabin door, slipped out into the empty passageway.

On the deck she went at once to the back of the steamer, knowing that at any moment she would be seen, shouted at by the white men. But it was still early and quiet on the river. Sarah could see the green shores and the calm river. It would be a lovely day, she thought, reaching the paddlewheel.

Someone shouted, and she glanced around and saw a black man, one that had helped load the cargo of slaves. He was waving, motioning her away from the spinning wheel, and getting up off the deck to come to her. Sarah smiled, thinking that she was a free woman now, and that she loved her God in heaven, and that she was glad she had killed the white man before he violated her. Then she jumped—as any young girl might, full of life and energy—into the twisting of the giant paddlewheel and disappeared down into the foamy white and deadly-churning paddlewheel water.

9

"I THINK I KILLED them," Jennifer told Tom, holding the teacup in both trembling hands. The cup was warm and comforting. She sipped the tea slowly, letting it warm her whole body. She was in Tom's apartment, sitting in the corner of his leather couch. She had telephoned him to meet her at once at his place.

Tom was in a chair on the other side of a glass coffee table. He listened patiently as she described what had happened in the foundation bathroom. He kept interrupting with questions, and he scribbled notes on a legal pad while she talked, as if she were his client instead of his lover.

"Don't," she told him.

"Don't what?" He kept writing, using the gold Cross pen she had given him.

"Don't take notes. It makes me feel like a criminal."

"You're not a criminal unless you're convicted." He finished a note, then sat back in the soft, light brown leather chair and watched her for a moment. She knew what was coming. He was framing his statement, trying to make it sound less threatening, but before he could speak, she stood and walked to the windows of the apartment, staring out across the Hudson River at the bleak industrial shores of New Jersey. The day had cleared. It had stopped snowing, and a hard-edged blue sky had reappeared. "We're going to have to talk to the police," he said behind her, trying to sound casual.

"No!" She felt a wedge of panic and reached out to touch the windowpane with the palm of her hand, as if to let the cold glass calm her. "No," she whispered.

"We're looking at justifiable homicide," he went on, speaking in the same soft, measured tones.

She had first met him on a grand jury trial, and she remembered how she had been captivated by the way he cross-examined witnesses. He was like a bird of prey, a dark handsome falcon hovering, circling, closing in. Slowly, softly, without raising his voice or seem-ing to intrude, he had backed each poor witness into a corner, and then stripped him bare, exposing the lies.

"No!" Jennifer shouted, turning. "I won't."

"Honey. Jennifer, please," Tom said. "You just told me. There are two, maybe three people dead. We've got to get on top of this situation. What happened to you has got to be drug related—the Colombians are on to you. If it isn't, if we've got a simple mugging, you're still okay. I mean, you'll be viewed as a female Bernhard Goetz. No one is going to send you to jail. Look. We go to the police. We start a public relations campaign. No jury—"

"But I'm not Goetz!"

"Jennifer, you've admitted to me that you killed a person. And you may have just killed two others." He nodded toward uptown. "I'm an officer of the court, for God's sake. I can't—"

"Please! Please!" She went toward where she had dropped her coat on the chair. "I'm sorry I came to you. I'm sorry I compromised your goddamn position." She was crying as she grabbed for her coat.

Tom leapt to his feet, swearing, and seized her arm.

"You're going to sit down here, Jennifer, and we're going to prepare a defense. You're a wanted woman. I'm not going to let you damage your life and career." He pulled her away from the door, but she jerked loose from him.

"Leave me alone, Tom. I'll work this out myself."

"Jennifer, sweetie, you're not being rational." He moved toward her with his arms out, as if to embrace her.

She backed away. "Don't touch me."

The tone of her voice stopped him. She saw the sudden fear and apprehension in his eyes, and that pleased her.

"Please, Jennifer, you need help," he offered, but kept his distance.

Jennifer realized she was no longer in control of her own body. Her heart was pounding, and she felt a surge of strength in her limbs. My God, she thought. I am a monster.

She looked up, into the mirror behind Tom's couch, and stared at herself. Her own brown eyes looked frightened, not enraged. Her face was ashen, and what makeup she had put on that morning had worn off. Her hair needed to be combed. It frightened her to see how unkempt she looked, but her face wasn't disfigured. She didn't look like a monster. She took a deep breath.

"Jennifer, are you okay?" Tom whispered, alarmed at the expression on her face.

"I don't know," she confessed.

"What happened just then?"

"I don't know. I get angry, enraged, and then . . ." She started to cry, deep sobs, but this time Tom came over and wrapped his arms around her. She collapsed in his embrace and let herself be comforted.

"I've got to get you to bed," he finally said, after her sobs had abated. He leaned over and easily picked her up. After settling her into his bed, he pulled a heavy quilt up over her. "Are you warm enough?" he asked, arranging the quilt over her shoulders.

Jennifer nodded and pulled her legs up. She cuddled against his pillow and seized his hand in her fingers. "Don't leave me," she pleaded.

"I won't," he whispered, sitting on the edge of the bed.

She kissed his fingers, then laid her cheek against the warmth of his palm and fell asleep still holding on to her lover's hand.

When Jennifer woke, the room was dark and silent. She came awake slowly as if she were swimming to the surface of her life. Then she recognized her surroundings, realized she was in Tom's apartment, and immediately grew apprehensive. She sat up and swung her feet over the side of the bed.

She heard voices. Or at least one voice. Without her shoes, she moved quickly and quietly to the closed bedroom door and pressed her head against it to listen. Silence. Carefully, she opened the door. The empty living room was glowing like a Vermeer, with the clean yellow light of the winter sunset.

She noticed that Tom was in his office beyond the living room. She saw his shadow as he paced in the small room. He was probably on the phone. He always paced while talking on the telephone. She crossed the room, her feet silent on the hardwood parquet floor. At the office door, she paused and looked inside.

He was standing at his desk, looking out the window at the Hudson River. The sunset froze him in profile, softened the edges of his dark features. He was listening to someone, then whispering his replies. When he turned to pace back across the office, she stepped to one side of the door and stood in shadow. Her heart was in her throat.

He came to the threshold and stood looking across the long, darkening room to the doorway of his bedroom.

"No," he said to someone, "she is still asleep. Yes, I understand. Yes, I'm letting her rest." He stepped away from the open doorway. She heard the leather of his chair stretch as he sat down, and when she chanced a glimpse inside, she saw that he had swung his legs up over the edge of his desk and was leaning back in the chair, running his fingers through his hair. It was one nervous habit that always annoyed her. It left his hair standing up.

She moved stealthily from the dark corner to the other side of the living room, forcing herself to be calm. After picking up her fur coat and purse from the chair, she grabbed her boots from where she had left them by the front door. She moved quickly across the living room, through the swinging door, and into the dark kitchen.

She knew there was a service door off the kitchen, and behind it the back stairs and an elevator. She had used the exit before to do laundry in the basement.

Jennifer slipped off the chain lock and stepped into the lighted back stairwell. Her heart was racing. With trembling hands, she slowly pulled the door closed behind her. She kept imagining she heard Tom running after her, grabbing her before she could escape. She pressed the elevator button and then, too frightened to stand and wait for it, took off down the back stairs, her stockinged feet slipping on the concrete steps.

She reached the lobby level and stopped in the stairwell to slip on her coat and shoes. Then she opened the heavy steel door and looked out at the empty lobby. She saw the doorman outside under the entrance awning, helping a woman out of a taxi. Jennifer stepped far enough into the lobby to see that the front elevators were closed. Tom had not yet discovered that she was gone. Running to the entrance, she grabbed the now empty taxi and, brushing past the old woman and the doorman, slid into the backseat and slammed the door. "Uptown!" she shouted.

"Where, lady?" He picked up his clipboard to note the address.

"Uptown. Hurry, please." She glanced at the entrance of the building, half expecting Tom to come barreling out after her.

"West Side or East, lady?" the driver asked, still waiting and watching her in the mirror.

"Uptown! The East Side." Jennifer was trembling. "Hurry!" She glanced around again. The doorman and the old woman were moving slowly toward the glass door. She didn't see Tom.

The taxi finally moved. The driver steered with one hand as he put aside the clipboard.

"You got to tell me, lady. The East Side is a big place." He laughed, trying to make a joke of her indecision. The car bounced out of the apartment building's cul-de-sac and turned onto the side street.

Jennifer sank into the seat, exhausted by her fear. She was thankful that she had gotten away from Tom, but she didn't know what to tell the taxi driver. Where in New York City would "a wanted woman" be safe?

She opened her purse to take out a tissue and wipe her eyes, and there, stuffed into the cluttered purse, she saw the newspaper clipping she had meant to give Eileen, the one about Phoebe Fisher, the channeler. She pulled it from her purse and scanned it, looking for an address, then leaned forward and spoke to the driver.

"I've changed my mind. Take me up to the West Side." Now she knew where to go and who might help her.

10

AT SEVENTY-NINTH AND Broadway Jennifer got out of the cab and called information for Dr. Fisher's telephone number. Then, standing at the pay phone, with the wind from the river blowing across the avenue, she called her. As the wind sliced into her, cutting between muscle and bone, she stamped her feet on the packed snow, trying to keep them warm.

It was only six o'clock, and the sidewalks were crowded, but still, Jennifer felt vulnerable. When a police car halted at the traffic light, she turned her face into the booth, but she was convinced they had spotted her, that the composite photo was already out and the cops were searching for a blond white woman, five foot seven, wearing a full-length fur coat, wool jacket and skirt, and a wool turtleneck. She pulled the collar of her coat up around her face and listened to the phone ring.

"Please, dear God, please let her be home," she said out loud. When a woman did say hello after a half-dozen rings, Jennifer spoke rapidly. She explained about reading the article, about having the strange reaction to the Ice Age display. She told her about seeing Kathy Dart, and about the thirteen-mile run out along the C & O Canal. She stopped herself before she mentioned her attack on the mugger near the museum, and the women at the foundation.

When she stopped talking, she was out of breath, and crying. She couldn't stop her tears, couldn't keep herself from sobbing into the phone.

"Come see me at once," the woman said, giving Jennifer her address.

"Thank you," Jennifer whispered, wiping the tears from her face. "I'm coming." When she finally hung up the phone, the traffic light had changed, and the police car was gone. Jennifer ran out into the street, and turned north toward Eighty-second Street and the home of Phoebe Fisher.

* * *

"Welcome," a small woman said, pushing open the iron gate that guarded the basement apartment. "You were very close to me when you telephoned. I could feel your presence. I am Dr. Fisher." She stepped back, and Jennifer saw that Phoebe Fisher was lame, that she used a thin, silver cane to support herself.

"I ran," Jennifer replied, still gasping for breath as she followed the woman into the warm apartment.

Phoebe Fisher was dressed like a teenager in a tight black leotard and a wrap-around black skirt, with a bright red scarf knotted around her long thin neck. She was very small and very beautiful, with coarse black hair already streaked with gray. Her pure, white skin was the color of bisque pottery. Jennifer felt large and ungainly beside her in the low-ceilinged apartment.

"You have a fireplace!" she exclaimed as she entered the living room. The blazing fire made her feel immensely better.

"Yes, and I'll make you a cup of tea, and we'll talk." Phoebe Fisher smiled at Jennifer. Her sculpted lips were neatly sketched into her tiny face. And when she smiled, her mouth widened and made her seem even younger. Jennifer liked her at once. She felt safe here. Maybe Phoebe Fisher would be able to help her. The fear that had been building and spreading through her body all afternoon eased away, leaving her suddenly lightheaded and very tired.

"Here," Phoebe directed, touching the deeply cushioned chair close to the fireplace, "come sit down and get comfortable. We can get to know each other a bit while I make us a fresh pot of tea. Would herbal be all right? I'm afraid I don't have anything else."

"Thank you. Anything. I'm just fine, thankful to be here." Her declarations surprised her. She was never this open with strangers, but now she felt the need to share her emotions, to tell this woman everything.

"Now, Jennifer, how did you meet Kathy Dart?" Phoebe asked, standing behind the kitchen counter that divided the rooms as she made the pot of tea. "And what were your feelings about her?"

Jennifer told the whole story as Phoebe made tea, then came back to sit beside her in front of the fire. Jennifer told her about Eileen Gorman and their chance meeting, about her jog along the C & O Canal and what had happened to her in the museum. She explained that she had known, really known, when that hut in the Ukraine had been built.

"What is wrong with me?" Jennifer asked, crying.

"There is nothing wrong with you, Jennifer. Nothing. You are a very fortunate person. A gifted person. It's your electromagnetic frequency, that's all." Phoebe was smiling. "We share it, my dear. We are both gifted that way." She reached out and touched Jennifer's knee.

"I don't understand," Jennifer whispered.

"Of course you don't. I didn't either when it first happened. None of us know, really, but we learn. You are experiencing the first flashes of mediumship. To put it in academic terms, you have already gone through what is termed the first stage, conceptualization, and now you are in stage two. Preparation." Phoebe paused for a moment, staring thoughtfully up at Jennifer. "Welcome to the gang." Her soft brown eyes widened and glowed.

"Well, what is this gang? I feel like my body has been taken over or something."

"You're right. It has," Phoebe said, "but you're joining people like Emperor Wu, from the Han dynasty in China, and the Greek Dionysian cults of the sixth century B.C., the Celtic bards in the British Isles, not to mention Jesus Christ and his disciples. You're in good company, Jennifer." When she saw the uncomprehending look on Jennifer's face, she asked, "Would you like me to try and explain how it all comes about? Why this is suddenly happening to you now, here in New York City in 1987?"

Jennifer nodded emphatically.

"Most of what we call mediumship, or channeling, is the product of an arrangement that is made between two bodiless entities—the person who is going to be the channel and the entity or consciousness that is going to be channeled. After that, one entity is incarnated in a body and begins life without even remembering the agreement. Life continues normally until the person gets to a place where he or she does remember. It's called an encounter, and it's different for everyone."

"But I didn't go through any encounter," Jennifer protested. "I was just going on with my life, and then, wham, this!"

"I don't know yet what happened, Jennifer. I don't know enough about you yet, but later perhaps, if you are comfortable, I might try to channel to see what we can learn. I'm sure you were experiencing, or suffering, something. . . . And then your frequency connected somehow."

"How did it happen to you? What was your encounter?" She

slipped out of her chair and sat down beside Phoebe on the small rug. "This is a Dessie rug, isn't it?" she heard herself saying.

"Yes, it is. But how did you know about them? They're from Ethiopia and very rare." Phoebe laughed. "But of course you know. That is the wonder of being a medium."

"No, I don't know." Jennifer was shaking her head, afraid again. "I mean, I know this is a Dessie rug, but I don't know why I know it."

Phoebe shrugged. "That's it. You've always known. You learned it in another life, and you have carried that bit of information tucked away in your subconsciousness, from one age to the next."

"Oh God, I can't believe this." Jennifer dropped her head into her open palms, held herself for a moment, then threw back her head, rubbing away her tears with her hands. It was very warm near the fire, but she didn't want to move. For some reason she didn't want to be away from Phoebe Fisher, who was silently watching her, smiling sweetly as if she had all the time in the world.

"Okay, how?" Jennifer asked. "Tell me what happened with you. That might help me understand what's going on with me."

"Well, about three years ago, at two different times within a two-month span, I had very close physical sightings of Dance's spaceship here over New York City. What I didn't understand then was that that was his way of signaling me, sort of tapping my subconscious memory. But it wasn't until my experience in Central Park—the one that was written about in the *Times*—that I really began to investigate. I did all sorts of research into metaphysical theories, and eventually I came across ideas on mediumship.

"Then I met several mediums, and one of the entities who came to those meetings offered to teach anyone who was interested how to channel. Even then I didn't think I would devote my life to channeling. I was working as an editor at *Redbook* magazine. I had a career. I had a boyfriend who I was living with, and who I thought I loved. I was happy. Or thought I was.

"But it was in that class, in a receptive state, under the guidance of the other entity, that Dance made the telepathic connection. And as soon as he did, the memory of that previous agreement came back to me: who he was, who I was, what the ship sightings and the experience in Central Park had meant. All of this that had been blocked out of my consciousness came back to me."

She smiled over at Jennifer. Now it was dark in the room, and the firelight cast their shadows against the far wall of the apartment.

"When I saw you in the doorway, I knew," Phoebe went on softly. "I knew that you had had a similar experience. The only difference is that the entity you're channeling is from the past, and Dance is from the future."

"You mean he tells you what's going to happen a hundred years from now?"

Phoebe shook her head. "Dance isn't of this planet—he's an extraterrestrial, which makes him different. Most channels—like Kathy Dart—allow discarded consciousnesses, which have been alive and no longer are, to come into their bodies. Those consciousnesses have no physical entity, but Dance does—it's just not like ours. His is an extraterrestrial consciousness, and he and I are linked telepathically."

"Why is he here? Why is he doing this to you?"

Phoebe shrugged. "I'm not sure, really. I think he is coming through now to assist us in learning that we have the answers we need, to live the lives we want to live.

"He does not appear physically, because he wants us to focus on the message rather than the messenger, which is where we'd focus, of course, if we saw this little green man walking around." She laughed. "Dance is channeling through me so the message will stand on its own. And we can decide whether the message works for us or not.

"What he has to share in no way implies that he thinks his world is better than ours, just that he—they!—are different from us. They recognize that we are learning a lot, that we are beginning to explore things that are relatively new to our society."

"Is his name really Dance?"

"No, they don't have names in their society because they are telepathic. I call him Dance because that was what he seemed to be doing when I first saw him hovering over Central Park. He seemed to be dancing before my eyes."

"But I'm not like you. No one is trying to speak through me. I just have these feelings, these weird, frightening experiences, and suddenly—"

"Because, Jennifer," Phoebe continued, "you have been trapped inside your own logical, organized, institutional world, and your so-called 'logic' has kept you from the great wealth of knowledge within what we call the spiritual world.

"There's nothing strange about psychic ability. It's simply survival. It's how our minds work to keep us functioning in the world.

The reason we can see is so that we don't fall off a cliff. The reason we can taste is so that we don't ingest poison. All of our senses are keyed to survival, including the psychic sense.

"However, we know our physical senses. The mystical is what we do not know. We have to surrender to this experience and enter into it."

"I guess that's my problem. I'm afraid to surrender to the mystical world," Jennifer admitted.

Phoebe nodded. "You know, Einstein used to get up every morning and say that he didn't know anything. He believed that everything he knew could be disproven at any time. He wanted to treat his mind like a piece of blank paper. Let me experience! Let me learn all over again! That's what the New Age philosophy is all about."

Phoebe sat up straight. One leg was pulled up underneath herself, the other sticking straight out. Using her long, thin fingers to tick off the names, she listed the great mediums from history.

"Joan of Arc heard voices telling her to go to the king of France. She was then thirteen years old. Joseph Karo, a fifteenth-century Talmudic scholar, channeled a source called 'maggid.' Saint Teresa of Avila and Saint John of the Cross, both Christian mystics, were channelers. Joseph Smith channeled an angel named Moroni and, based on what the angel said, took his people to the promised land and founded the Mormon church. The list is endless."

"But I can't—"

"And didn't you just tell me you were suddenly able to run thirteen miles after you saw Kathy Dart?"

"Oh, I don't know." Jennifer shook her head and stared into the blazing fire. "I don't know anything," she whispered.

"Yes, you do. You know everything, and now you're getting a glimpse of what the world as a whole has to offer. It's frightening to realize your true potential. No one can blame you for not going forward, for saying: That's enough. I'm comfortable. I'm happy. But are you really happy with the limits of rational thought? Jennifer, give yourself a chance at least to experience life."

"How do I know it's true? How do I know you're to be trusted?"

"Begin with yourself. Trust yourself first. Ask yourself why you are feeling these emotions."

"I don't want to do this!" Jennifer interrupted. "Don't you understand? I don't want to be a channel! I don't want anyone, or anything, to take me over, to use my body. I want it to stop!" Again

Jennifer kept herself from saying more, from telling Phoebe how she killed, once she was seized with the brutal power.

Phoebe kept silent. She picked up one of the fire irons and poked at the burning logs till the dry wood sparked and hissed into a burst of sudden flame.

"What is it?" Jennifer asked, realizing the woman had more to say.

"I'm not sure there is anything you can do," Phoebe said softly, then looked up at Jennifer. The sweet smile was gone from her face. "This entity wants to be heard. He, or she, wants to be channeled through your body, and I'm afraid there's nothing you can do to stop it. Just as I could not stop Dance from coming to this world to teach, you cannot stop your entity. The spirit's time has come, Jennifer, and you have been selected to serve its needs in this lifetime."

Jennifer looked away and stared at the fire. Okay, she thought, but Phoebe's Dance had come to teach. Her entity, Jennifer now realized, had come to kill.

11

JENNIFER FLUNG HER ARM out and hit the bedside lamp, knocking it to the floor. The phone was ringing. As she reached for it, she knocked the receiver off the hook. The illuminated dial of her digital clock read 5:24 A.M.

She picked the phone up from the floor and said angrily into the receiver, "This better be good." But the line went dead.

"Shit!" She slammed down the receiver. Fully awake now, she sat on the edge of the bed and rubbed her eyes. The heat was coming on in the building, and the steam pipes clanged. She knew she wouldn't be able to get back to sleep. Telephone calls in the middle of the night always made her think someone was watching from an apartment across the street or from a darkened phone booth at the corner.

She pulled on soft slippers and shuffled across the dark room. As she passed the mirror on the back of the closet door, she glanced at herself. As a child, she had been afraid of the dark, and the only way she could calm herself was to rush to a mirror. Her shrink had later told her that she'd had a low self-image. No, she had answered back, she was just afraid of the dark.

She went into the kitchen, turning on lights as she walked. Well, she told herself, if she was up, she was up. As she filled the kettle with cold water for coffee, she reached over and turned on the small Sony on the kitchen counter. Maybe she would make pancakes, she told herself, and cook sausages. She'd have a big breakfast and forget about running and staying in shape for one morning in her life.

She had opened the refrigerator and was pulling out butter and milk and eggs, only half listening to the all-night cable channel she was tuned into when she realized she was hearing Kathy Dart's voice.

Jennifer stood up and turned toward the set. Kathy Dart was

sitting cross-legged, facing the camera. She was not channeling, but talking to the group of people who also sat cross-legged, in a tight circle.

"It seems to me," she was saying, sweeping her gaze around the circle of people, "that there are two generally accepted views of why we are all on earth.

"One view I'll call the religious. It tells us that we are creations of God, and damaged creations at that; that we are born into the world with sin and must spend our lives proving our value to God so that at death we can be accepted into heaven.

"The second notion about life is the modern view. It explains that we are here today because of a series of chance occurrences in space. The big bang. The small bang. The survival of the fittest. Whatever you want to call it! Every few years we are given a new explanation.

"The trouble with these two views of life is that they exclude a lot. They cheat us out of all the possibilities of our wonderful minds."

Kathy Dart paused and looked around the circle. Watching her, Jennifer noticed again how beautiful she was. It wasn't really her looks, but the calmness of her face. No wonder Eileen responded to her, Jennifer thought. Kathy Dart had such a trusting face.

"We must remember that the mind and the brain are not the same thing," Kathy Dart said next. "The brain is a physical organ, while the mind is simply energy that flows through this organ. As human beings, as bodies, we cannot be everywhere. But the mind can travel, relocate, be somewhere else, as when we have an out-of-body experience. For example, we all know how it is possible for the body to be on the operating table while the mind is up on the ceiling, looking down, watching the surgeon operate."

"Yes," Jennifer said aloud. She stopped breaking eggs into a plastic bowl and turned her full attention to the screen. "Yes," she said again.

"We do have other levels of reality. We daydream, hallucinate, sleep, dream, and all have some sort of mystical, or psychic, communication with others." She leaned forward. "I will tell you a true story. It has happened to each of you. You are in a restaurant, you are on the street, you think of someone, perhaps a friend, someone you once knew in another place and at another time. His name pops suddenly into your mind, and then within moments, you see him. He suddenly appears, as if out of nowhere!"

She leaned back and smiled knowingly, and then the camera panned the small circle of people, and they, too, were smiling, in recognition of what Kathy Dart was saying.

Jennifer set the eggs aside and pulled the small kitchen stool up close to the television set. Opening up the pad she used to jot down her shopping list, she waited for the woman to continue.

"Perhaps the best way to understand what is happening to us," Kathy Dart went on, "is to think of our psyches, our minds, as houses with many rooms. In our everyday lives, we use only one or two of those rooms, but we do not inhabit the attic or basement, we do not know what is happening at night down the long dark hallways."

She motioned to the group, gesturing back and forth with one hand. "We speak to each other on one level, but that is a limitation. It forces us to see our world as having only one level, one reality.

"When I go into a trance, it is as if I am moving to another room in my psychic house. There it is possible for me to have a different state of consciousness, a different persona, different knowledge. It is possible for me to speak directly to Habasha, and to have him communicate directly with you. We came naked into this world, but our psyches, our spirits, came with the collected wisdom and knowledge of all time. Plato said that the soul has been 'born again many times, and having seen all things that exist, whether in this world or in the world below, has knowledge of them all.' "

Then, as the camera closed in on her face, Kathy Dart grimaced and added wryly, "So why, you might ask, aren't we rich?"

Her audience laughed.

"We're not rich," Kathy said, "because we have in our present life only a certain amount of all the knowledge we possess, knowledge that Plato says we are remembering. Nothing is new under the sun, as the saying goes. We are only remembering what we already know but have forgotten.

"Artists tells us that they create by intuition, by bursts of creativity. What is creativity?" She paused to study the circle of students. "The act of creation is drawing from within, from our heart of hearts, from the knowledge we already know. We create what we have already created."

The kitchen telephone rang, startling Jennifer. She looked at it for a moment, puzzled by its ringing. It was not yet six-thirty.

"Jenny?" The man's voice was soft and far away.

"David? Is that you? What is it? What's wrong?" She suddenly felt cold and shivered in her wool nightgown. A window had opened, she thought. Or a door.

"Oh, Jenny," David whispered. He began to cry.

"What is it, David? Has something happened?" Even as she spoke, Jennifer knew.

"She's gone, Jenny. She's gone. I found her a few minutes ago. I had gotten up to go to the bathroom . . . there was a light under her bedroom door." He was crying, stumbling over his words. "She had taken an overdose of Valium. It was my prescription. She had said she was having trouble sleeping. I had no idea." He kept explaining, telling Jennifer the suicide was all his fault.

"It's not your fault, David," Jennifer said, raising her voice so he would hear her through his tears. "Stop blaming yourself! I understand! Have you called the police?"

"Yes, yes, I've done all that." He was suddenly angry. "They're here. I have a cop in my goddamn living room. They won't remove the body until the coroner comes and signs the death certificate."

"What can I do? I don't want you to be alone."

"You can't take the subway at this hour."

"I'll call a car service. Don't worry."

He started to cry again. "Why, Jenny, why in God's name would she do this?"

"We'll talk about it when I get there. Hang up so I can get dressed and call a car. 'Bye, David. Oh God, I'm so sorry."

"Thank you, Jenny. Thank God for you," David whispered. He sounded like a little boy.

When Jennifer hung up the receiver, her hand was trembling. She felt the cold again, a swift rush of wind, and from the dark hallway of the apartment, she could see across the living room, through the front windows and into the street. Dawn was breaking, and the very pale light of early morning was filling the dark corners.

Then she saw Margit in the room. She was standing by the door to the kitchen, smiling, motioning that everything was all right, that she was all right. She looked a dozen years younger, and beautiful in a way that Jennifer had never seen her. She moved through the dark apartment, her body a silver envelope of light. She was wearing a white dress, a long white dress that flowed around her and spread across the floor and furniture.

"Margit?" Jennifer asked, terrified by the sight of her friend.

"Hello, Jennifer," Margit said, but she did not speak. Yet Jennifer knew just what she was saying, knew what she wanted.

"Let me hold you, please," Jennifer asked, stepping toward her.

Margit shook her head. "I'm sorry, Jenny, but you can't, not now."

"Margit, what happened?"

"David . . . David poisoned me."

"Oh no. Oh God, no!"

"It's all right, Jennifer. It's all right." She kept smiling.

"But why? Because of that woman?"

"It was more than that. I had money. My family's money, and he wanted it. Jenny, he's a very unhappy man."

"Margit, this isn't possible. I'm not seeing you. I can't be." She tried to turn away but was frightened now to look away from the misty figure of Margit Engle.

"I've seen your brother Danny, Jenny. We've talked, and he wants you to know he loves you very much and that you can't blame yourself for what happened to him. He is very happy."

"You saw Danny?" Jennifer exclaimed. She began to smile. "Let me talk to him, please. Let me come close to you, Margit."

"It's not time, not yet. But I've come to warn you. . . ."

"Warn me?"

"Be careful, Jenny. Someone wants to hurt you."

"Who?"

"A woman. She was once your friend, Jenny. In another time, she was once your friend."

"Who, Margit?" Jennifer whispered.

Margit shook her head, whispered that she couldn't, and then her image began to fade from sight. Jennifer did not cry out to hold her on earth. She watched the image dissolve and then disappear. And then Jennifer realized it was daylight, and she was standing in the bright sun. Margit was gone.

She turned from the window and walked back into her bedroom. The sun filled that room, too, spreading light across the unmade bed. Jennifer glanced at the digital clock. It read 11:47. She had been talking to Margit for over five hours.

BOOK TWO

Each of us is responsible for everything to everyone else.
—Fyodor Dostoevski

". . . It is absolutely necessary that the soul should be healed and purified, and if this does not take place during its life on earth, it must be accomplished in future lives."
—Saint Gregory I

12

TOM GRABBED JENNIFER WHEN she came up out of the subway at Columbus Circle.

"We've got to talk," he told her, seizing her wrist.

"You've heard?" she asked.

"About Margit? Yes. David phoned me yesterday. Where were you? I've been calling."

"At home."

"You didn't pick up. I went to Brooklyn; you didn't answer."

"I didn't want to talk to you."

"Jesus Christ, Jenny, what's happening? Why did you sneak out of my place?"

They were standing at the top of the subway escalator and morning-rush-hour commuters were pushing past, glancing at the obviously angry couple but keeping their distance.

"You were calling the police when you thought I was asleep."

"I was not," he said outraged. "I was calling your office. Talking to What's-his-name . . . Handingham."

"Come on," Jennifer said, taking his hand. "Let's get a cup of coffee."

"Margit and I talked for over five hours," Jennifer explained to Tom, "and when I called David back, it was almost noon. The police were still there. Margit's body was on the floor of her bedroom, where she told me she had died, and everyone was waiting for the coroner to come. Tom, I'm telling you: David killed her!"

Tom put down his pastry and stared at her.

"Jennifer, she died of an overdose. The coroner found evidence in her body. David told me. Besides, she died at approximately five o'clock yesterday morning. How could you have seen her? What are you talking about anyway?"

"She had traces of Valium in her stomach. Of course! David

got that for her, but he wasn't stupid enough to poison her with it. He's a doctor; he's smarter than that."

"Well then, how did he kill her? How did Margit say she died?" He was treating her as if she were a child who needed to be humored. She kept her voice slow and steady. "He killed Margit with lidocaine. It's used in emergency situations to slow down the heartbeat where there's been a coronary seizure."

"I know what lidocaine is. But how do you know?"

"I don't. I don't know any of this. But Margit does—or did. She was a nurse before she married David. That's how they met. She told me about the lidocaine." Jennifer leaned over the restaurant table and continued in a whisper: "It comes in a disposable syringe called a Flex-O-Jet. There's one gram of lidocaine in twenty-five cc's of fluid. When a person has a seizure in a hospital, they inject it directly into a bag of sugar and water that the patient is getting intravenously. You never inject lidocaine directly into the vein in a concentrated form. But that's what David did. She had fallen asleep in bed, and David came into the bedroom, injected the lidocaine, and then pulled her onto the floor, so it would look as if she was trying to reach the door."

"And Margit told you all this?"

Jennifer nodded. "When we talked, she was in her afterlife—that's a nonphysical reality we all enter following death. All souls or spirits go there between incarnations."

The waiter returned to refill their coffee cups, and they both fell silent until he stepped away. Then Tom spoke without looking up. "I think maybe you should talk to someone, Jennifer."

"I agree." Jennifer sighed, feeling relieved. "Do you know the detective on the case? What precinct is it, anyway?"

"Jen, I'm not talking about cops. I'm talking about a doctor. A shrink."

Jennifer stared at him. "Tom, we're talking about a murderer."

"Sure—who was also her husband, and your doctor, and a physician on the staff of New York Hospital. Honey, you've been under a lot of stress. And I haven't helped matters with my behavior about getting married. I was thinking that maybe we should fly down to the Caribbean for a few days and let all this blow over. My case against the dealers will go down soon. I'll have time off. And you can get a long rest." He spoke as if he had decided to take over her life.

Jennifer stopped listening. Tom didn't believe her, but how could he? She had been on an immense journey in the last few days, and she had left him far behind. She could barely believe it all herself—but when she doubted, she remembered Margit and the envelope of light around her, and she believed again.

Tom was watching her. "Jenny, you're not well," he said softly. "You have to understand that. It's not a sign of weakness. I know you. I know how you never want to be caught with your guard down, but all of us have some bad patches. You're going to be okay."

"I'm okay!"

"No, Jenny, you're not," he answered patiently. "You're going through something, I don't know what. I wish to God I did, but, honey, I love you, and I'm going to take care of you, regardless of what you say. Okay?" He smiled, trying to dull the hard edge of his pronouncement.

Jennifer nodded. She had learned in the last few weeks that it was never any good to argue with Tom; it was better to go around him.

"So you'll come to the Caribbean with me?"

She nodded. "But I have to go back to my office. You go downtown; I'll come and meet you as soon as I make my arrangements with Handingham."

"I've already talked to him about it," Tom said.

"You did?" She pulled away, looking surprised.

"Yes, that's what I called him about the day you thought I was on the phone to the police. I said you'd been under some stress, and he agreed you could have some medical leave. It's no big deal, honey, your job will be there when you return."

"Well," she said, controlling her anger, "then you can also call the coroner and ask him to go over the autopsy results again."

He shook his head. "Darling, I love you. I think you're wonderful, but there's no case there. I can't do anything. You can't do anything. I know you're upset, but I'm telling you, your mind is playing tricks on you. Lidocaine stays in the blood, in the skin tissues. If it was there, they would have picked up traces in the autopsy."

"Sure, if they were like the doctors on TV. But they're not. Why is the mayor always firing coroners if they're so good?"

Tom was being rational, but she no longer trusted his cool logic, his faith in the system, in the rational world. She thought of what

Phoebe Fisher had told her, how people were trapped inside their logical world and couldn't accept the mystical. But she wasn't. Not any longer. She had seen Margit in her living room, and she realized there was only one person now in New York City who would listen to her story and believe what she had to say.

ECCLESIASTICAL INVESTIGATION
RELATING TO THE VISIONS AND
MIRACULOUS CLAIMS OF VERONICA BORROMEO
MISCELLANEA MEDICEA 413
THE YEAR 1621
STATE ARCHIVE OF FLORENCE

Account of the visions, miraculous claims, and sins of the flesh as related by the Abbess Veronica Borromeo to the Papal Nuncio, Giuseppe Bonomo, Bishop of Siena, on the thirteenth day of September, 1621.

On the First Friday of Lent of the year 1620, while in bed between the fourth and sixth hours of the night, I contemplated the sufferings of Our Lord the Most Holy Jesus Christ, and our Master appeared to me in the flesh, holding in His bleeding hands His most Holy Cross. Our Saviour was alive, and he asked me if I would suffer His own crucifixion and death.

I made the sign of the Cross, thinking that the Devil had come upon me, but our Lord said to me that He was God and he wished me to suffer His death. He instructed me to get out of my cot and lay upon the stones in the form of the cross, as He wished to implant the wounds of the crucifixion upon my body.

When I followed as He had told me, I felt great pains in my limbs and breast and saw that blood was oozing from my flesh, but afterward, I felt only peace and contentment.

During the following week, from day to day, each morning, I studied my limbs and saw nothing, no marks or signs, but on the Friday next, from twelve until three, the hours that our Lord hung upon the cross, I, too, bled from my hands and feet, and from the right side of my breast, and the nuns of the convent came and ministered to me, and I begged them, beseeched them in our Lord's name not to tell the laity of what had occurred to me here within our monastery walls.

Each Friday I joyfully suffered as our Lord had suffered, and then on Easter Sunday, after our Saviour had risen and ascended into Heaven, I was praying in the cloister garden when suddenly there appeared to me an angel dressed in a blue garment. He had long white and gilded wings, and he said to me, "Our Lord is well pleased by your sufferings, and He wishes you to surrender your body to him again, living on in this world the life of a saint, and suffering, as the saints have, for the greater glory of God."

Afraid that I was being sorely tempted by the Devil himself, I fell upon my knees and begged for God's guidance. The white angel took me to our church, to our humble priest, Father Giovannetto, who told me on behalf of Jesus Christ that I was not being deceived by the Devil, and I knelt before him and received the Holy Eucharist. The angel revealed himself to me again and said that his name was Gabriel, the archangel Gabriel, who brought great joy to the Blessed Virgin Mary, and that he would stay with me now in my hours and days of great need.

From that day forth I suffered many travails, as I had wished. I was visited by the Devil in the form of a handsome young man who sought to corrupt my body and soul. In my vigils in our chapel, the stones beneath my bare feet were set ablaze by the Devil and his minions, but still I kept the name of Jesus on my lips and prayed incessantly for the strength to keep my faith.

And then our Lord came upon me another time, and said I was to be His bride.

I opened my arms to him, then, and Jesus raised his golden sword and cut away my simple heart and took it to his own, and said to me, "Lovely lady, I give you my heart, as any bridegroom must," and slipped his heart into my breast, where it lodged, too large and glorious for my body, and then he took my left hand in his and slipped upon my finger a wedding ring, and in all my life I have never felt such great contentment.

Account of the visions, miraculous claims, and sins of the flesh of the Abbess Veronica Borromeo as related by Sister Maria Sinistrari to the Papal Nuncio, Giuseppe Bonomo, Bishop of Siena, on the second day of October, 1621.

I saw her open her arms and then kiss the fourth finger of her right hand and mumble her thanks to God, saying over and over again, "I am not worthy, O Lord. I am not worthy, O Lord." Then I heard her say, "I want to have her sit on that first chair and to explain her life," and she quickly went to where our Lord sat. And she told me the candles she had lit symbolized the thirty-three years that Jesus lived in this world, and the three largest ones were the three years closest to his death.

Next she spoke of how Christ had taken her heart and given her the wounds of His crucifixion. Then she said many things which I cannot remember, and I knew she was not herself. Her voice did not sound like her own. Then she prayed for several hours. We knelt together on the cold stones and prayed together.

When she was finished, we shut out the lights and left the choir and retired to our cells. She was in great pain, and I would go to her cell at night and sit beside her. She kept telling me that a dagger was striking her body, bleeding her heart, and she would take my hand and press it against her breast so I might feel her great pain.

She would tell me, "Hold me," and as soon as I touched her heart, it would quiet her. I asked her what was causing the great pain, and she said it was Jesus testing her virtue.

And then she began to call me often to her bed. It was always after my disrobing, and when I came to her, she would force me down into her bed and kiss me, as if she were a man, and then she would stir on top of me, like a man, so that we were both corrupted.

She would do this in the most solemn of hours. She would pretend that she had a need, a great pain, and call me to her cell and then take me by force to sin with her.

And to gain greater sinful pleasure, she would put her face between my breasts and kiss them. And she would put her finger in my genitals and hold it there as she corrupted herself. And she would kiss me by force and then put my finger into her genitals, and I would corrupt her.

She would always seem in a trance when she did such corruption, and call herself the angel Michael, and speak like a man. She would wear a white robe with gold-embroidered sleeves and a gold chain around her neck. She let her hair loose, and it curled at her thin neck, and she crowned her own head with a wreath of flowers taken from the convent's garden.

And as the angel Michael, she told me not to confess what we did together, for it was no sin in God's eyes. And when we were corrupted together, she would make the sign of the cross over my naked body and tell me to give myself to her with my whole heart and soul and then let her do as she wished. "If you do this," she said, speaking in a man's voice, "I will give you as much pleasure as you would ever want."

DIARY OF SISTER ANGELA MELLINI

April 4, 1622: Veronica Borromeo was purified at age eighteen. She was brought before the Grand Inquisitor and High Priest and her sins were read out to her, and then she was burned, as was the young sister, Maria Sinistrari, until dead. Once dead, the Abbess Veronica Borromeo and Sister Maria Sinistrari were brought into the chapel as is the custom of our sisters. The bodies were then buried beyond the convent walls, in a secret place, and at night, so that the laity might not defame the remains and take the bodies of the dead women and cast them out to the wolves of the forest.

13

JOAN WAS NOT AT her desk when Jennifer arrived at the foundation. She wanted to give her secretary work to do before she went to see Phoebe Fisher. Jennifer took a stack of telephone messages off Joan's desk and walked into her office, closing the door behind her. She flipped through the pink memo slips. There were a half-dozen calls concerning foundation matters, and the others were personal. Janet Chan had phoned to cancel their lunch on Thursday. Her dentist, Dr. Weiss, had called to remind her about her appointment. David Engle had called. He wanted her to phone him at home as soon as possible. And there was a long-distance call from Kathy Dart in Minnesota.

Jennifer stared at the slips, her hands trembling. She was too frightened to call David. She didn't know what to say to him, not now. On impulse, she dialed Kathy Dart in Minnesota.

"Hello, *Tenayistilligan*," a man's voice answered.

"Hello?" Jennifer said.

"*Tenayistilligan*," the man said again, "this is the Habasha Commune. Simon speaking."

"Oh, hello." Jennifer remembered now. Eileen had explained that Kathy Dart's believers used Amharic expressions and gave themselves Ethiopian names in honor of Habasha. "My name is Jennifer Winters. Kathy Dart telephoned me earlier. I'm returning her call."

"Just a moment."

Jennifer waited for a moment. Soon she heard Kathy Dart's clear and crisp midwestern voice. "Oh, Jennifer, I am so pleased that you've called. I telephoned Eileen Gorman earlier to get your phone number. Are you all right?"

"Why, yes, I think so," Jennifer answered.

"Well, I spoke to Eileen a few days ago and she told me you have been experiencing some difficult feelings. . . ."

"Yes?" Jennifer tensed up.

"This morning when I woke, Habasha was waiting for me, waiting for me to awaken, and he mentioned your name. He said you were in trouble."

Jennifer took a deep breath.

"Yes. Well, I'm in trouble, that's for sure." She laughed, but now she was frightened. How could Kathy Dart know?

"This happens," Kathy Dart said softly, anticipating Jennifer's anxiety. "The spirit knows. We have all had premonitions. Habasha, of course, is attuned not only to my life, but to others as well. It is obvious now to me that you and I are somehow related in the same group."

"I'm not sure what you mean, what sort of group. A spiritual grouping?"

"Spiritual is the right term. You and I—and Habasha, of course—and others are all part of what is called the oversoul. I thought so when I first saw you sitting with Eileen at my introductory seminar in Washington. We have shared some previous life experience, which, naturally, isn't that unusual, as we are all part of the Mind of God."

"What did Habasha say? I mean, what's going to happen to me?"

"You have had some terrifying experiences."

"Did Habasha tell you?"

"No, but I have experienced several troubled nights, and when I spoke with Eileen, she told me that you were troubled and were also inquiring about New Age beliefs."

"Yes, I did ask her." Jennifer grew cold suddenly, and she glanced up to see if her office door had opened. She didn't want anyone to hear what she was saying to Kathy Dart. "I do have a lot of questions now about all this . . . stuff. I am trying to understand . . . you know, channeling and everything." She was talking very rapidly, realized she was perspiring.

"The channeling experience is normally a cooperative experience," Kathy Dart went on calmly. "I have accepted Habasha. I had no questions or qualms about acting as his channel, his connection with this life."

"I remember your talk. I remember how he came to you out of a California morning. But I think something else is happening to me. I have had—" She caught herself then. She could not tell this stranger about the killings. Instead, she said quickly, "I was at the

Museum of Natural History the other day, and I had this weird sensation."

She told Kathy Dart about the Ice Age exhibition and her reactions to the model, how she knew she had been there once herself, had walked down the path, had slept under the bones and tusks and dried skins of the Ice Age mammoth. She knew it all, but of course it was not possible for her to have such knowledge.

"But it does make sense, Jennifer," Kathy insisted. "This place, these people were once part of your life—in another time, of course, in this prehistoric period."

"Kathy, excuse me, but I have to say something." Jennifer walked to the windows and stood there, staring out at the cold day as she went on. "I am having a difficult time, you know, accepting all of this. I have a friend, and he's—"

"That's Tom, isn't it?"

"Yes, you know . . . ?"

"Well, no, but Eileen mentioned you were seeing someone. I have asked Habasha about Tom. I have asked him to see if Tom is the right person for you."

"And what has Habasha said?"

"Oh, he takes his own sweet time about such requests. Basically he finds them annoyances. He'll tell me one of these times when I am channeling. But please go on. I've interrupted you."

"Well, none of this makes sense to him, either. Rational sense, do you understand?"

"Of course I understand," Kathy Dart replied calmly. "I had many of the same questions and apprehensions I know you are experiencing. For all of us it is an uncharted journey, a leap of faith, but also, and this was true for me, we realize that there is something missing—something out of whack, let's say—with our lives. For me, Habasha has been able to put this life into perspective.

"Look, Jennifer, this isn't terribly new or strange or weird, all this reincarnation talk. We were raised on a belief in an afterlife, in heaven and hell, but at the same time we are caught in a cultural reality that says there can't be any such thing as reincarnation, or premonitions, or ghosts! But nevertheless, man has throughout history known about our connection with the other side, with the voices from beyond."

"But that still doesn't explain why I—"

"Why you were selected? Chosen?"

"Yes! Why me?"

"Because, Jennifer, you are ready. It is as simple as that. I wasn't ready when I was a seventeen-year-old in college, but when I had children of my own, after many life experiences, I was finally prepared to handle the responsibility of channeling Habasha. Someone, some person, is preparing you to channel his or her entity. Why else would you have such sudden strength to run that far in Washington? Jennifer, I know you are being prepared for channeling some spirit."

"Oh God," Jennifer whispered, her legs weakening. She leaned forward and pressed her forehead against the cold glass. Across Fifty-ninth Street, dozens of floors below her, was the entrance of the park, where a half-dozen men stood loitering, standing out in the cold day. They were selling drugs, she knew, calling out to people as they passed by on their way to the subway.

Kathy Dart broke into her thoughts. "I think it would be good if we could talk in person," she said.

Jennifer nodded. She was crying again, and finally she managed to say "I would love to talk to you." She turned away from the window and went to her desk to pull out a handful of tissues. Kathy Dart was still speaking, telling her how difficult it was to have this special gift, to be open to such communication, to be sensitive to altered lives.

"But I'm not that kind of person, Kathy," Jennifer finally protested. "I never played with an Ouija board or did automatic writing."

"What kind of person, Jennifer?" Kathy Dart said quietly. "Do you believe in God?"

"Yes, of course. I guess so. I mean, I did once."

"And angels? And the devil? And miracles? Of course you do. Or did. And you believed in life after death, too. It's a tenet of Western culture. We were all raised to believe in a God or some Supreme Being that established order in our universe. Even the Big Bang theory is a stab at trying to explain ourselves, why we are here on earth, the meaning of our lives." Kathy Dart sighed. They had been talking for over twenty minutes and both were getting tired. "Listen, after all of this, I still haven't told you why I really called, or what upset Habasha this morning."

Jennifer waited. She had returned to her leather chair and was sitting behind her wide desk. The telephone console was flashing, and she was sure that Joan had returned to her desk and was in the outer office taking her calls.

"Habasha was disturbed about you. He is painfully vague about much of his information but said you were in danger."

Jennifer did not answer. She thought of the *New York Post* headlines and realized again that the police were still searching for her.

"There is a man . . . I have only a name . . . a first name." Kathy Dart was speaking slowly, as if she were still trying to decide how much to tell her.

"Yes?" Jennifer asked quickly, raising her voice.

"David. Do you know a man named David?"

"Of course I do," Jennifer whispered. She suddenly lost all her strength. "David Engle. He's the husband of my friend Margit. She just committed suicide."

"Be careful, Jennifer. I am sorry to have so little to tell you. Usually I do not like to do this—give people bits and pieces of information—but I am taking a chance with you. I feel you are someone special. Special to me, to all of us."

"Thank you," Jennifer whispered gratefully. "I'm not afraid," she added, surprising even herself.

"Good! Remember, you are not alone. You have your guides with you always. Your guardian angels, as we used to call them in Catholic school. And you have me. Please call me. We must keep in touch. I feel—I know—we are important in each other's lives."

When Jennifer finally hung up the phone, she sat very still at her desk and watched the lights of her phone flash. Then, impulsively, she pushed down one of the buttons and reached out to pick up the receiver.

"Hello?"

"Jenny?"

Jennifer recognized the voice at once. "Yes?"

"Is that you, Jenny? I'm so used to getting that secretary who guards your palace door."

"Yes, David, it's me." Jennifer knew her voice sounded stiff and distant, but she couldn't bring any warmth to her words.

"I'm calling to ask if you can come by later today for a drink. I have some things I need to talk to you about."

"I'm sorry, David. I have to meet Tom right after work," Jennifer said. The last person she wanted to see was David Engle.

"Jenny, please. I really need someone to talk to."

"I understand, David, but I can't. I—" Jennifer suddenly stopped talking.

"Jenny? Are you there?"

"Yes, David. All right, I'll come about four." Now Jennifer was smiling. There, in the far corner of her office, in front of the wall of bookshelves, Margit Engle sat on the leather sofa and nodded to Jennifer, encouraging her to accept the invitation from her husband.

14

JENNIFER LISTENED TO DAVID Engle lie to her. He was telling her about Margit's death—how she had said good night, gone to her bedroom, closed the door, and swallowed a dozen Valium. And how he had found her later, on the floor at the foot of the bed. He started to cry as he spoke. Jennifer guessed that he had been drinking most of the day.

Jennifer sat on the sofa and sipped her white wine, watching him. Now he was talking about their sons. They were both home from school and handling the funeral details.

"I couldn't face it," he confessed to Jennifer, coming back to where she was sitting on the sofa.

Jennifer realized how worn down he was. He couldn't be more than fifty, but he had aged since she had spent the night at the apartment. His whole body sagged, his face was gray. Gray from beard bristles. Gray from the long winter without sun. He looked like a corpse.

"Margit was a much better parent than I was," David said. He told her how when the boys had pneumonia, she had slept for a week on the floor in their bedroom. "And I was the goddamn doctor," he swore, sobbing again.

Jennifer didn't go to him. She was crying, too, but her tears were for Margit, the mother of his children, his wife for twenty-three years, the woman whom he had murdered in her sleep.

"I made friends with people easily," he said next, pulling himself together, "but it was Margit whom they came to love." He leaned forward in the chair, gesturing with one hand and spilling his drink. "Like you! Like you! You were my friend, too, but Margit took you away from me."

"David, please!"

He waved off her protest. "Don't you tell me about Margit. I knew her. I knew what she was like." He was crying, and he kept rambling on, claiming that Margit had stolen all his friends, turned them against him.

Jennifer set her drink down on the coffee table.

"David, I'm going to have to go," she said softly, reaching for her coat.

David did not respond. He was still leaning forward, staring at the rug.

"Go?" he said finally, looking up, blinking into the light. Jennifer was now standing.

"I'll telephone the boys later to find out about the service. I would like to say something, if you don't mind. I'll speak to Derek about it." She walked past him but did not bend over to kiss him on the cheek as once she would have. He would turn on her next, she knew. His self-pity was engulfing everyone he knew.

"You were my friend first, Jennifer, or have you forgotten?" The ringing phone startled him, and he stood staring at it. After a moment, Jennifer stepped around him and picked up the receiver. "Hello, the Engle residence," she said calmly.

"Hello, is . . . Jenny, is that you?"

"Yes, Tom. Hello."

"What in God's name are you doing there? Is David with you?"

Jennifer sighed and closed her eyes. She was tired of men shouting at her.

"Yes. What is it?" She glanced over at David. He was standing in the middle of the foyer, staring at her. His eyes were glassy.

"Get out of there," Tom whispered, "get out of that apartment and away from him. What in the world possessed you to go see him? Jenny, the son of a bitch is a killer. You were right! I called the coroner's office when I got back downtown. I was doing it just as a favor, you know, so at least if you asked again, I'd have the facts, and the tests on Margit's skin had come back. There was lidocaine in the tissue. He did it, Jenny. Like you said."

Jennifer looked into the small foyer mirror and saw her own startled eyes. Behind her, still standing at the entrance, David clutched his empty glass and watched her. She was right. She wasn't some crazy person, having dreams and seeing ghosts. It was all true. Margit had come to her after her death.

"Is that Tom?" David asked.

Jennifer nodded into the mirror. She was listening to Tom

explain that a warrant had been issued for David's arrest. "Now get the hell out of there, Jennifer. I don't want you involved. I don't want David to get an idea of what's gone down."

"There's no need to worry, Tom," Jennifer answered coolly. She was angry with him for not believing her at first, and now angry again that he was telling her what to do. "I can take care of myself."

"Jesus, Jenny, let's not try and prove anything, okay? I was wrong. I admit it. Now get out of there."

"I'm going home, Tom. To Brooklyn. Come over later and we'll have dinner. I have more to tell you. Kathy Dart called me at the office."

She hung up the receiver and turned around to David, who had stepped closer to her, but only so that he could lean against the wall to steady himself.

"That was Tom," Jennifer said quietly, pulling on her leather gloves. "He told me that he spoke to the coroner and that the tests came back on Margit's skin tissue. They found evidence of the lidocaine, David. I guess the police have a warrant for your arrest." She spoke without raising her voice.

"You knew?" David asked weakly.

"Yes, I knew."

"How, goddamnit?"

Jennifer went to the apartment door and paused there with her hand on the knob.

"Margit told me on the morning after her death. We talked."

"She couldn't!" David protested, stumbling forward.

"She loved you, David. She loved you all her life. She kept your home and raised your sons. She never wanted anything but your love and respect, and what did you do in return? You turned her out for another woman, a younger woman who was—what did you tell Margit—'more interesting'? And then you just didn't settle for a divorce. No, you had to kill her for her money."

He threw his glass at her. With the speed and deftness she was only beginning to realize she possessed, Jennifer grabbed the glass out of the air before it hit her, and set it down on the small hallway table. She managed to smile curtly at him, and then she went for him. It suddenly seemed so natural and so right. She would use her powers to settle the score. He had taken her dear friend's life, and now she would take his.

Jennifer grabbed David by the throat and jerked him off the floor. Holding him at arm's length, she smiled at him while he gasped for breath and tried to break her grip. Then with one motion, as if she were flicking off a fly, she tossed him away. He flew across the living room and hit the wall, then crashed to the rug.

She moved closer, knowing she had to finish him off, that she couldn't let him live, when she heard the doorbell. The sharp ring snapped her concentration, broke her desire to kill, and she turned away from him, leaving him choking up blood. She walked toward the front door, and in desperation he lunged at her, tried to grab her leg. Jennifer kicked him in the face, knocking him away, and opened the apartment door.

"You're looking for David Engle?" she asked the two men at once.

They nodded, startled by her question, and then by the sight of David behind her on the living room floor. He was trying to pull himself up onto his knees.

Jennifer gestured toward David, who had recovered enough to begin to cry. "Well, you've found him."

Then she moved quickly to the elevator doors and caught them before they closed. She looked back and saw the two men reach down to help David Engle off the floor. They were already reading him his rights.

15

JENNIFER COULDN'T FOCUS ON her surroundings. She was thinking of Margit, of David, and of herself. She was thinking how she had gone after David and would have killed him if the police hadn't come. She was trembling, frightened again, as she realized they could have arrested her, too, there in David's apartment. She was mad, she thought, trying to kill David. She was losing her mind. In her confusion, she found herself walking along Riverside Park.

Plowing through the snow tired her, and she decided to turn left at the next corner, cross over to Broadway, and catch the subway home. Two men were ahead of her. They had come out of a park entrance, turned and walked off. Jennifer felt her heart race. She glanced around to see another man trailing her by fifty yards, and she knew instantly what they were planning. She should have crossed the street in the middle of the block and walked into one of the co-op buildings as if she lived there. The doorman there would call her a cab. Then she spotted another man on the other side of the street, tramping through the snow with his head down, his hands deep in his pockets. She should cross, she knew. Cross immediately, right there in the middle of the block. But she didn't.

She kept plowing ahead, with her own head down, as if she were consumed with her own thoughts. What was she doing? she asked herself. Why was she behaving this way?

The two men had hesitated at the corner, as if waiting for the light to change, but she knew they were waiting for her. She knew, too, that they would come back toward her as the third man approached, and then they'd surround her and pull her off into the park. A dozen yards and she'd be completely out of sight in the winter afternoon darkness. There were no joggers in this weather, no one walking dogs. She was the perfect prey. They knew it. She knew it. And the thought made her smile. She felt her blood pumping, as her body warmed to the encounter.

The men were turning toward her, and from far behind, she heard the third man pick up his pace and start to run. She watched the men approach. They had spread out on the sidewalk, as if to give her room to pass. Both had long wool scarves wrapped about their necks, and stocking hats pulled down over their eyes.

They were close enough now for her to see that they were Hispanic, teenagers who weren't more than kids, really. As they passed her, they said something in Spanish and lunged at her, grabbing her between them, lifting her slight body easily, and pulling her off the sidewalk.

Jennifer looked up to see the third one waiting. He had raised his fist and was holding a club in his hand, a short piece of pipe wrapped in electrical tape.

She waited for the surge of strength, her wild power, to consume her, and at that moment, as the small one raised the clumsy club, she thought, It won't happen, I'm defenseless. Then it hit— the rising rage of her primitive self.

She felt the sudden shudder of cold through her body, felt her heart pump, as if it had a life of its own, then her blood surged through her limbs and, using the two men who held her as posts, she suddenly lifted her body up and swung her legs. The heel of her right cowboy boot caught the short man in the mouth, driving his teeth up into the soft roof of his mouth. He couldn't even scream when she kicked him away.

The two others swore, furious, and one of them freed his left arm and swung at her head. She ducked the blow, slipping down onto the snowy path and pulling both of the men with her as she fell. She seized their thin necks with both her hands and heard them gasp and gargle for breath as she squeezed the life from them. She realized, holding them both aloft, that she was smiling at her own strength, at her own revenge.

She smelled their breath, the odor of their bodies. She smelled the beer they had drunk that day, the tacos they had eaten somewhere in Spanish Harlem, the women they had slept with. She slapped her hands together, banging their skulls.

The force of the blow, the smashing of flesh and bone and brain, sounded hollow, like pumpkins squashed by a car. There were no other sounds, no cries of pain. Their bodies sagged in her arms. She flipped them away then, into the bushes beyond the footpath, where they fell together in a lump of legs and arms, all bent out of shape.

She went for the third one next, knowing, as no animal would, that she couldn't let him escape to tell the police. The small man had recovered enough to stumble away from her and was spitting out blood and bits of teeth while he tried to run deeper into the park.

She loped down the hillside as he dashed frantically for the bushes that framed a children's playground. She grabbed him in full gallop by the scuff of his neck and, without losing speed, threw him like a human javelin into the high iron-mesh fence that surrounded the children's park.

The force of the impact bent the thick iron webbing. And when his body slipped down, the jagged points caught his clothes so he hung there on the wire like a wet, dirty rag blown up against the fence.

Jennifer stopped to pull her racing heart under control. She could smell herself, her own sweat, and the musky scent pleased her. When she looked up again at the dead man, at what she had done to him, she marveled once more at her speed and strength.

Jennifer took the subway home. She had only stopped at the park fountain to wash their blood off her hands and face. She knew her wild look would keep anyone from sitting beside her.

At home, she started a log fire and burned all her clothes, even her underwear. She got rid of her brown boots, stuffing them in a trash bag to go out with the garbage. Then she took a long hot shower and shampooed her hair, and finally she filled the tub with steaming hot water and scented bath bubbles, opened a bottle of white wine, and took glasses and an ice bucket back to the bathroom. Stretched out in the tub, she listened to WQXR playing Mozart and waited for Tom to arrive.

Tom had his own keys, and though she was drowsy from the hot water and the wine, she heard him closing the front door, dropping his attaché case, and calling for her.

She listened to his voice grow louder and nearer. She smiled and moved her arm slowly in the hot water. The bath had made her weak, and she was tired, too, from what she had done. She thought back on the murders as if they were something she'd just seen in a movie or in a late-night news clip. None of it had any connection to her life, to who she really was.

"Jenny, there you are," he said softly, appearing in the doorway. "Why didn't you call out, tell me where you were?" He came into the bathroom and sat down on the toilet seat. He had already shed his suit coat and tie, and now he carefully rolled up the sleeves of his blue Oxford shirt.

His body always excited her, and she was absurdly pleased by her own arousal. It was such a simple emotion, and so gratifying. Slowly, gracefully, she stroked her breast with the sudsy water.

"David confessed," he said. "I spoke to the detective uptown." He sighed and slumped down on the seat. "Well, why are you smiling?"

She shrugged, and when she did, her pink, flushed nipples broke the surface of the hot water. She watched him focus on her breasts, watched him catch his breath.

"Do you want me?" she asked.

He nodded. His eyes were canvassing the length of her, and she obliged him, arching her back so that the wet web of her sex, foamy with bubbles, surfaced like a pale buoy. Then she settled back in the scented, soapy water.

As Tom shed his clothes, she moved in the tub to make room for him. The water whooshed, and large drops dripped from her arms and breasts as she sat up.

"How do you want me?" she whispered. She could feel her throat tighten, and her fingers, as they always did, trembled with excitement.

"Hurry," she told him. Tom stepped gingerly into the tub, and she reached out for him, gently nipping his penis with her teeth.

"Easy, honey," he said, "that hurts." He couldn't move. She had total contol of his body, holding him by his genitals. "Don't," he demanded. He tried to ease himself down into the water, but she wouldn't release her hold on him. "Jenny!" He was becoming angry.

She kept at him, ignoring his protests. Whenever they made love, he was the one who dictated the terms, and now she wouldn't give up her advantage. A part of her wanted only to relax, to let him have his way, but right now she couldn't stop herself from playing with him, from making him do what she wanted.

She grabbed his waist and tugged him down, her teeth still clenched around his penis. As his erection began to fade, Jennifer gently caressed the inside of his thigh with her warm hand and then abruptly shoved her index finger into his rectum.

He came in her mouth.

She gulped, trying to swallow the flood, then choked and pulled away as he showered her face and hair with jetting semen.

When she could breathe again, she laughed at her own foolishness.

"What are you trying to do, kill me?" Tom said, lifting her into his arms. "Trying to bite off my cock, are you?" He grinned. "Well, I know how to shoot back."

"It feels like sticky molasses in my hair," Jennifer complained, and immediately turned on the shower, drenching them both in hot water.

"More S and M," Tom shouted over the water, but his voice was happy and excited. Both of his arms were wrapped about her body, with his fingers grabbing her taut bottom.

Jennifer spread her legs and, hooking her arms around his neck, she clung to him as he slipped inside her, and rode him a moment with her face turned into the hot spray. Then she concentrated on coming, moving against him as he drove up against her. She jabbed her nails into the flesh of his shoulders, wanting to draw blood, and her breath came in a quick series of gasps. They were splashing water all over, soaking the towels, but she didn't care. All she wanted was to sustain the driving, escalating force which gained and gained, until she was breathless and in wonderful, excruciating pain. She was gasping, trying to consume his life, trying to suck the breath from Tom as she drove her tongue into his mouth, reaching for the very soul of him, and then the orgasm slammed through her, leaving her limp, out of breath, and clinging to him for safety. She ached with pleasure.

"Oh God," she whispered, and licked the damp hairy mat of his chest.

Tom was not done with her. He seized her buttocks again in both his hands and hoisted her up. She still was impaled, and he turned her to the wall, centering them both under the driving shower. He had her pinned to the wall, and braced his feet against the corner of the tub as he drove into her.

He hit her bottom once, slapped it hard, and she gasped with delight. He slapped her again, and she grabbed his head, slipped her long fingers into his thick black hair, then stuck her tongue in his ear, licked him, and snapped at his right earlobe. He slapped her again, harder and harder.

He had spanked her before when they made love, and she had liked the tingling sensation as she came, the naughty notion of being beaten. He had never hurt her, and always he had been gentle with her later, kissing her flesh, soothing her bottom.

Now he did not stop and she did not want him to stop, and he slapped her harder and she fought back, growling at him, digging her fingers into his shoulders. He swore at her and pumped harder, kept her jammed back into the corner of the tub.

She lashed out at him, hitting him ineffectually on the neck and shoulders with her fists, but her fingers were slippery, wet with water and the blood that she now saw was discoloring the water. She did not want to hurt him, but she did want to resist; she wanted him to ravish her, and she did not know why.

He came. He stopped fighting her. He squeezed her body and shuddered. His face was turned against her; her ear was in his mouth, and her head was pinned to the corner of the shower stall. She was momentarily thrilled at her success, at having made him come with such violence.

When he stopped gasping for breath and kissed her gently on her neck, they slid down together into the deep water and forced another tide of it onto the bathroom floor. Tom reached to shut off the shower, and Jennifer was briefly stunned by the silence. She shook her head to clear the water from her ears, then she lay resting against Tom's wet chest.

"Well," he said, laughing, "that's one for the record books."

"Are you still bleeding?"

"I don't think so." He strained his head to look at his shoulders. "I hope I don't have to explain this to some doctor."

"I'm sorry," she whispered and sat up. "I don't know why I tried to hurt you."

"You didn't hurt me, darling." Tom pulled her again into his arms. "That was fun. You surprised me, that's all. Where are you learning all these new tricks?"

"I don't know any new tricks! What do you mean?" She turned to him. She was wedged between his raised legs in the tub, which now seemed too small for both of them.

"Honey, you came on to me like some goddamn animal."

"Don't say that!"

"Well, it's true!"

"Don't say that! Don't ever say that!" She pulled herself out of the tub, wrapped her terry-cloth robe around her, and went at once to the sink, where she wiped the palm of her hand across the foggy mirror. Seeing herself reflected there made her feel immediately better. She had begun to have a terrifying premonition that she'd look into a mirror one morning and see some sort of she-ape grinning back.

Behind her, Tom splashed out of the water and grabbed a towel to dry off his hair.

"I'm sorry I upset you," he said, his voice muffled by the thick blue bath towel. "What's the matter?"

She watched his face in the bathroom mirror.

"You make me feel like I'm weird, the way I make love."

"I love the way you make love." He kissed her earlobes.

"I don't do tricks."

"Okay, I'm sorry. What's the matter? Why are you so edgy?" His face darkened, as it always did when he was upset.

"Oh, great. You insult me, then call me 'edgy' because I don't just sit back and take it."

"You've been edgy for weeks, since Washington, really." He stepped up behind her and began to dry her wet hair. "I think that thirteen-mile run drove too much blood into your brain."

"Damnit, Tom, stop making comments like that." Jennifer took the towel from him, threw it on the floor and walked out of the bathroom, making large wet footprints on the hall rug.

He caught up with her in the kitchen. She had taken out a carton of milk and a packet of gingersnaps and was dipping each cookie into the milk before she took a bite.

"What do you want me to do, Jennifer?" he asked, standing in the doorway and tucking the large blue bath towel around his waist. "Tell me, what in the world do you want?"

"I want you to take my kitchen knife and plunge it into your heart," she answered back, biting a gingersnap cookie in half.

"Jenny, please." He stepped into the narrow kitchen.

"Don't touch me!"

"I'm not going to touch you. I just want a gingersnap before you devour them all." He grabbed one and stepped away, then chanted plaintively, "I'm sorry. I'm sorry. I'm sorry."

"No, you're not." Jennifer reached up into the overhead cabinet and took down another large tumbler. "Would you like a glass of milk?"

"Yes, please." He grinned and stepped closer.

"Don't touch me," she ordered again.

"I'm not!" His hands shot into the air. "I'm just trying to get along here, you know. Get through the next few minutes, that's all."

"It's not something to joke about. I don't want to be jollied out of my mood. Okay?" She turned around and looked at him. "I want you to take me seriously, that's all."

"I do."

"This morning over coffee you told me I needed to see a shrink—but wasn't I right about David?"

Tom nodded, munching on the cookie.

"Look, I don't understand what's going on with me any more than you, but I need your help. I need you to support me. Is that too much to ask?" She looked up at him, tears beginning to form in her eyes.

"Of course not, darling. Of course not," he whispered, and wrapped his arms around her.

Jennifer let herself be held by Tom, taking comfort in being held and cuddled. For the moment neither one of them spoke. She wrapped her arms around him and squeezed, then used his hairy chest to wipe away her tears.

"Stop it! No!" Tom laughed, edging away. "That tickles."

"Good!" She nibbled his right nipple, then licked his breast.

"See!" he said at once, "you're doing it again. I mean, don't get me wrong, I think it's wonderful, but you're much more—"

"Careful, Tom," she said, stepping away and opening the refrigerator door to put away the milk.

"I'm just telling you how much I like it, that's all." He tried to recapture her in his arms, but she moved his hands away and walked back to the bedroom, where she stripped out of the bathrobe and stood naked for a moment in the shadowy light of the room.

Tom came to the bedroom door and watched her while he finished his glass of milk. Jennifer crossed to her bed and pulled back the quilt.

"God, you're beautiful," he said from the doorway.

"Thank you." She knew she was. She felt beautiful. Having sex always made her feel beautiful, and she was aware, too, that the shadowy light on her body aroused Tom. She turned toward him, and beckoned him toward her. He was right; she was behaving out of character. She felt as if she were watching herself on film.

"Jenny?" Tom whispered, approaching her. He sounded slightly nervous.

She smiled, inviting him closer with the coy downward slant of her lips, enjoying her control over the pace of their lovemaking.

"It's all right," she whispered, and she reached for him, slipped her arms around his shoulders and brought his face close to her breasts. "Here," she told him, "they want you," and then she slowly, softly tumbled him over onto the bed and made love to Tom again.

O boy with the slim limbs,
I seek you but you do not listen,
for you see not me, nor know
you are the charioteer of my soul.

Anakreon set down his split-reed pen and his papyrus, then leaned back against the cool wall of the palestra. The boys had come into the center of the gymnasium and were stripping off their clothes and lathering their young bodies with olive oil, and his eromenos was among them. His heart tugged at his throat, spotting the lean youth. He could not take his eyes off Phidias, who now, among the other boys, was laughing at some remark, enjoying himself. Anakreon smiled with pleasure, simply enjoying the sight of him. He had waited there in the shade of the colonnade for just the chance of seeing him.

"Ah, there you are, Anakreon," a voice said from down the hallway.

Anakreon reached out and rolled up his piece of papyrus, hiding his poem from his friend Xenophanes, another of Athens' aristocrats.

"Writing to the Gods, huh, Anakreon?" the man asked, folding his cloak beneath him and sitting down next to Anakreon on the bench. He was a large, fleshy man who was already sweating beneath his white cloak in the hot Athenian morning. "And which of these lads has your fancy this season, my friend?" He watched the pupils as he spoke, squinting his eyes against the bright sun.

"The finest of fair," mumbled Anakreon, pulling himself up on the bench.

"They're all fair at the age of puberty," whispered Xenophanes, still keeping his eyes on the courtyard.

"True, Xenophanes, but my soul sings for young Phidias, the son of Ptolemy, there!" He nodded toward the courtyard where a red-cloaked instructor had divided the boys into wrestling teams, setting an older pupil to instruct the younger ones.

"Do you remember our days here, Anakreon?" Xenophanes asked, glancing at his friend, who still watched the courtyard and his young eromenos. When Anakreon did not respond, Xenophanes asked, "Have you coupled with the boy?"

Anakreon shook his head and sighed. "I have showered him with gifts, told him of my love. His family knows, of course." He redraped his blue cloak and glanced at Xenophanes, adding, "Life was simpler, my friend, when we were the loved objects, not the lovers. The boy drives me mad with his cleverness."

"His coyness, you mean," Xenophanes answered, laughing.

"True. True. I would not have him be a prostitute, but by Zeus, his passivity drives me mad. He'd rather be with his friends, at his games, instead of walking about the city with me. There is much I could teach the boy."

"I'm sure there is, Anakreon," Xenophanes commented, glancing at his friend, "but your time will come. It always does, doesn't it?" Xenophanes whispered, leaning closer. "You have had your way with many of these palestra boys."

"It is my poetry, I confess, Xenophanes, and not my gross flesh that keeps their interest. And yes, I have had my way with some. I know. Yet the wait is always maddening." Anakreon sighed. "And my loins ache."

"So meanwhile, you have your poems to keep you company, to sing your song: 'For my words the boys will all love me: I sing of grace, I know how to talk with grace.' "

Anakreon smiled, pleased by his friend's acclaim, then said in verse, " 'Again I am in love and not in love, I am mad and not mad.' " He nodded toward the boys. "So goes my life. I'd rather have one moment with his flesh than a room full of papyrus poems or an olive wreath at the Olympic games."

"The games! Come, come, your days of sports are over."

"I am not yet thirty, my dear Xenophanes."

"And they are not yet fifteen," Xenophanes commented, with a gesture toward the young sportsmen.

Flute music began and at once the athletes threw themselves into their wrestling matches. A chorus of shouts came from the courtyard, and the dust from their trampling feet rose in clouds, obscuring the men's view.

"We'd do better in the Agora, buying hares from Boeotia, than standing in this dust storm. Let us go to the baths. My skin is filthy. I spent the morning with a Sophist at the foot of the Acropolis, and even there, the dirt and dust from the Agora were awful."

"My loins sing for the boy," Anakreon answered, "that boy is my muse."

He glanced back at the courtyard. The instructor had called a halt to the wrestling matches and the dust had settled. Anakreon could see his young eromenos, wet with sweat and oil. He stood with his hands on his bare hips, panting in the bright sun. The fine gray dust of the courtyard clung to his lean frame, glistened in the daylight. Then the boy looked up, saw Anakreon standing there beyond the colonnade, and smiled. His white teeth flashed in his face, his bright blue eyes gleamed.

Anakreon's heart soared. Tentatively he waved back and then went gladly with Xenophanes, swelling now with joy, for he had been noticed. In time he would plan to visit the family again, shower the lad with gifts, and someday soon, soon . . . His heart ached with anticipation and he said to Xenophanes, buoyant with his good fortune, "Come, my friend, let us go drink some wine at the baths, and I'll write a poem about you, sing of your long-gone days of glory at the games."

"It was only for you, Anakreon, that I wanted to win," Xenophanes said, pausing to look at the poet.

Anakreon stopped walking. The two men were in the narrow street outside of the gymnasium. Below them lay the wide expanse of the Agora, the Athenian market square, above them was the Scambonidai, where all the wealthy of Athens lived in two-story stone houses with wide porticos and courtyards, and gynaecea, rooms for the women.

"I never knew," he said seriously.

Xenophanes nodded. "Ah, my dear friend, we, too, suffer who do not have Apollo's gift for poetry." He tightened his cloak on his shoulder, smiling sadly at Anakreon. His round, fat face was losing its shiny glow. He seemed suddenly older in the fierce Aegean sun.

His abrupt confession had stunned and silenced Anakreon, and the poet reached out and touched Xenophanes's arm, whispering, "I will go to Delphi and sacrifice a goat to Apollo, so that he will send me the muse to write a poem in your honor, Xenophanes. Soon, you will be known throughout the world, the great Xenophanes. Schoolboys and students at the academy will recite my poem of your heroic deeds."

"I have no heroic deeds, Anakreon, except for the number of kraters I can consume at a banquet." He was smiling, trying to shake the moment of melancholy, and the two men turned again to walk to the baths.

Together on the narrow street, jockeyed as they were by the press of people and animals going also toward the center of the city, Anakreon reached over and gently touched his old friend, saying, "We have had more than one moment of bliss, my dear Xenophanes. We have had a lifetime of shared brotherly pleasures. We heard Aeschylus together at the theater and saw Alkaios win the stadion at the Olympics."

"I'd give it all up to have had you once look at me the way you gazed on young Phidias."

"I didn't know, Xenophanes. I did not know."

"Ah, the pity of it, as you poets would say."

Anakreon looked up, and in the distance he could see the sea, blue and calm to the edge of the horizon. He thought of his current quest, the young Phidias, and recalled the look of his lean limbs, his bright eyes, that wonderful innocent smile, and Anakreon's heart tugged in his chest. Then the lumbering Xenophanes brushed against him on the rocky street, and Anakreon felt the weight of the big man, felt his sweat and gross flesh, and he, too, whispered, "Ah, the pity of it." Then he fell silent and the two aristocrats walked in silence down the steep Athens hill to their drinking club.

16

"I THINK IT'S TIME for us to try to discover who you really are," Phoebe Fisher said, after she had listened to Jennifer's account of her recent behavior. It was the first time that Jennifer had seen the channeler since she killed her attackers. It was early in the afternoon and the midwinter sun filled the rooms and reflected off the waxed hardwood floor. Again Jennifer thought how lovely and charming the apartment looked. She wished that she could bring this kind of warmth to her own Brooklyn Heights place. It was all the wall hangings, the fabrics and the exotic plants, she decided, that gave the living room its special quality.

Jennifer had not told Phoebe about the killings but did allude to the change in her behavior with Tom, how she was becoming increasingly more aggressive in her lovemaking.

"And was he upset?"

"No, I guess not," Jennifer answered, laughing. "But I was! I mean, it makes me nervous to be that . . . way."

"There's no need not to enjoy your new intenseness. You are just experiencing what is truly you. Your essence."

"I'm afraid I'm going to frighten him away," she told Phoebe, as if to make a joke of her fierceness in bed.

"Do you want to talk to Dance?" Phoebe asked next.

"Oh God, I don't know. That's scary." She sat back in the oversized mission rocker.

"Good!" Phoebe said, smiling. "Being frightened is good. It clears out the pores, makes us more aware of our surroundings." She lifted up her teacup and took a sip.

Jennifer looked again toward the flames of the fire. Phoebe was giving her time to decide. She wasn't rushing her, but that only made her more nervous.

"How do I talk to him? I've never done anything like this."

"Well, when I go into a trance," Phoebe explained, "and he

comes through, he usually says something that shows he understands your problem, and then he'll say something like, 'How may I help you?' That's his signal. Then you may ask anything, talk about anything, whatever. There is no such thing as a stupid question. Out of the most mundane questions have come answers and information for all of us. To him nothing is boring, everything is for the first time. This is what he has been sent to do for our society. If he feels a reluctance on your part to talk about something, he will not volunteer information. If he feels you want to get the ball rolling, he will go as far and as fast as you want to take it. He reflects whatever energy you put out."

"But can he help me understand what is happening?"

"Jennifer, I don't know. I think he might be able to point you in the right direction. He might even have some specific answers. He might be able to look into your spirit life and see where you have been, in what ways you have been reincarnated."

"How will I know that Dance is here? Do you tell me or what?"

"Well, when the connection is made you'll see my body go through a few little reactions. Nothing about this is painful to me, you should know. The experience is very energizing and very valuable. For me it is like a very deep dream. I really don't hear the words because consciousness is not focused in that way. I am aware that there is an interaction going on, and I feel the emotions, I feel the energy, but that's all. I don't listen to your conversation. Dance and I are having our own conversation."

"Does he speak English?"

"They don't use language at all in his world. His mind sends thought, and because my consciousness is diffused, it allows his mind to sort of imprint its vibration on mine. So basically my energy is being used as a translator box for him. Whatever language I'm programmed in, that is the language in which his thoughts will emerge from my mouth. That's what you hear. He is not actually speaking at all."

She paused a moment. "Are you ready?" she asked.

"I don't know. I guess," she laughed nervously.

"All right, then, help me prepare myself to be receptive. Let's meditate for a few minutes." Phoebe drew herself up and crossed her legs. "Let's close our eyes. After the meditation, when I'm in my trance, you can drink tea, whatever, but at the beginning let us be quiet and keep our eyes closed. Get comfortable yourself and try to breathe as fluidly as you can."

Jennifer did not close her eyes. She was afraid of the darkness, afraid of not knowing what Phoebe Fisher was doing.

The small woman linked her legs together and laid her arms loosely in her lap. Her eyes were closed and her head was bent forward as she softly spoke.

"I ask the salamanders to put a ring of fire around us tonight, to protect us during this session, and Dance, I ask you that you only bring the spirits for our highest good to us."

For a moment Phoebe was silent, meditating. She had lit small candles in the room, and in the gathering darkness and the dying fire, they glowed like distant vigil lights.

"I want you to see yourself surrounded by a big ball of blue," Phoebe said, whispering now. "A very bright, vibrant blue color. All around you. It covers you from head to foot like a big cocoon. It goes through you, permeating you. This beautiful blue brings peace and serenity and spiritual awareness. In front of you, behind you, over your head, through you. Now clothe and purify us. I want to bring down one white light through both of us. See it entering through the top of your head, gently coming into every part of your body. Don't block it, Jennifer. Let it gently wash through you from head to foot. See it entering every cell and every pore. This beautiful beam of white light."

Jennifer closed her eyes and tried to concentrate on the beam of light.

"Now, Jennifer, I am going to say a few words. Let your mind freely associate with these words in a positive way. This is an exercise in raising your vibrations so we invoke only the higher entities.

"Love."

Jennifer thought of Tom, of the first time she had seen him striding into a courtroom, and how he seemed to overwhelm everyone else with his presence and authority.

"Joy," Phoebe whispered.

She thought of running across the meadows of the nature center at Planting Fields. She had been with Kathy Handley and Eileen. It was a wonderful warm spring day, and they were all skipping school.

"Peace."

She had made love to Tom and was lying in his sleeping arms. It was a quiet afternoon in the city, and she did not want to be anywhere else in the world, ever. And she had thought then that that was real peace.

"O Master of Creation," Phoebe went on, "Thou art the sky full of happiness that displays all the stars of the universe. I humbly ask to be a channel today to Jennifer, that I be out of the way, that I give up control of my body to the spirits so that they may come and speak to her. We want to thank all of you who are with us today for coming and giving us your time and your energies. God bless you all.

"Let us now return to the silence. Be very still and quiet in guiding the spirits to come and to speak."

Jennifer opened her eyes again. They had adjusted to the darkness, and she could see clearly. Phoebe was before her, still sitting in her yoga position. Her head was still bowed, but her body moved, as if she were unsettled and disturbed by a nightmare. Her small shoulders drew tight, and like a reflex, her arms jerked, then settled down again into her lap. She took several quick, deep breaths.

Jennifer's eyes widened. But then Phoebe settled down again, and from deep within her came a man's voice.

"I come in love and fellowship, to clear the blocks that are in your way so that you will become more enlightened about where you are going and how to get there. Now how may I help you?"

Jennifer, mesmerized, could see Phoebe's small body react, see her shake and jerk, as if the voice were tearing her apart with the force of its power.

"I see that you do not consider your feelings valid. When you were a child, your parents did not treat your feelings with respect."

"Yes," Jennifer whispered. She had never put the feeling into words for herself before, but she knew he spoke the truth.

"Your feelings, your emotions, were discarded, and now in your adulthood it is difficult for you to feel valued. You are questioning something. There is doubt. There is mistrust of yourself, and this reflects directly onto others. There is anger."

"I'm not angry," Jennifer whispered.

"Support yourself," Dance continued, not responding to Jennifer. "Begin to know yourself and your reactions. You are human just like everyone else, and your feelings are natural."

Dance stopped speaking, and Phoebe took several deep breaths. Her eyes were still closed, and her face was calm, showing no emotion.

Jennifer leaned forward in the dying light of the fireplace and peered closer, trying to see if Phoebe were truly in a trance. Then

Dance spoke up again, his voice loud and hard in the silence of the room.

"You have come with questions?" he asked. Phoebe lifted her head and her eyelids fluttered.

"Yes, I have some," Jennifer responded, surprised by her own courage. "I am told my body is carried forward. What part is carried forward?"

"Just your spirit, that is all."

Jennifer thought a moment. "Like if I see someone I think I know from before, but there is no way I could know him or her?. . ."

"That is an energy recognition. Everyone vibrates a certain way. Other spirits will recognize your energy. That is what soul mates are all about. The flesh body is just what you have chosen. Some people choose to be crippled in this lifetime to balance a karma from a previous lifetime, perhaps one in which they were abusing their flesh."

"How far back do I go? I mean, how far back do my lives go?"

"To the very beginning, where everyone was created equal. All souls are the same age. Now, some people are called 'old souls' because they have been through many reincarnations. Other souls have chosen to return only once or twice. Some have never been reincarnated."

"We ourselves choose to be reincarnated?"

"Yes, but only a part of you is reincarnated each time. There is a highly evolved part of yourself—part of your total soul group —that is called the higher self. Only the parts of your soul that needed to experience this incarnation are here today. Part of you has already gone through a more highly evolved development and is now above you, guiding you."

"What about my other incarnations?" Jennifer asked. "What was I in past lives?"

Dance stopped speaking for a moment, and Phoebe's head jerked back.

"I see one lifetime. You were a nun in Italy, and a sinner."

"Was I evil?" Jennifer thought of her murders. Maybe she had always been evil; maybe that was her destiny.

"All souls—or spirits, as you call them—are given the opportunity to be the creator as well as the created. Some spirits create bad in their lifetimes, and some, good. There was an upheaval at the source of the universe—all our universes—and that was the beginning of karma."

"When did that happen, in time?"

"Time is not relevant. There is no real time; we don't measure. There are none of your words to explain it. Some of the karma lessons are painful, but they are always for the good of the soul. I wish you could see—with my mind—how far you have come."

"What will happen to me in this life?"

Phoebe Fisher shook her head. "I know, but I wish not to tell you, Jennifer," Dance replied. "This life you must live. Yet do not fear. You are not alone. You have spirits around you, parts of your soul group, your teachers and mentors, and they will guide you, as they always have. Listen to them."

"Are they always with me?"

"Yes and no. Spirits come and go. We don't own each other. If you seek them, if you enlighten yourself, they will come to you and aid you."

Jennifer watched Phoebe Fisher, wondering if it all was a game, playacting. And as soon as she had the thought, she dismissed it. The happiness she felt in Phoebe's presence was not something that could be faked.

"Do you have any more questions?" Dance asked.

"Yes, I do. Do you know what has been happening to me, what I've been doing to other people?"

"Tell me," Dance said, and Phoebe's body leaned forward to listen.

Jennifer told her story, told of the incidents and her violent reactions, and when she finished, she asked only, "How do I keep myself from doing this again? From hurting people?"

"I cannot help you," said Dance, as Phoebe rocked back and forth. "Someone from your past life—not your future lives—is trying to gain hold of your spirit. In the past, in the deep and hidden past of your soul, lies a secret and a tragedy. You must discover yourself what this secret is. And to discover this truth, you must return to your first breath of life. And there lies the mystery of your life.

"And now I must leave you. My dear Phoebe is tiring. I leave you with one warning. Do not fight this spirit who wishes to speak."

Jennifer nodded, then realized that Dance was slipping away, but before she could speak, Phoebe's shoulders shook. Her head rocked back, and her small body trembled. Then she looked up and smiled at Jennifer. "Well, he came, didn't he?" she asked in her own voice.

"Yes," Jennifer said. She had become so accustomed to Dance, she was shocked that Phoebe was herself again.

"And was he helpful?"

"You didn't hear?"

Phoebe shook her head, smiling apologetically. "Dance was helping me with some of my own questions."

"He told me I was once an Italian nun."

"Oh, how lovely! I was once a maid in the royal household of King James, as well as—briefly—his mistress. It's exciting, isn't it?" She smiled at Jennifer, looking more alert than she had seemed earlier.

"I don't know. I don't know what to believe," Jennifer said, sighing. "But at least he told me what I had to do. Learn to meditate." Jennifer smiled and stood up. "I must go. I'm exhausted." She began to collect her belongings.

"What else? Do you want to share with me what else he said?" Phoebe asked.

"You don't know, do you?" Jennifer said, staring at the smaller woman.

Phoebe shook her head. "No, really, I don't. I mean, it must seem silly, my talking to you, but I wasn't consciously there. I had turned over my body to Dance."

"Well, it seems there's someone struggling to get into my body. One of my past lives."

"Yes," said Phoebe, nodding. "As I said when we first met, I had this feeling, this emotion, that there was someone else—a trapped soul—who wanted to speak."

"Well, he's not speaking," Jennifer replied, then kept herself from saying more.

"Perhaps it is a she," Phoebe answered. "Gender isn't an issue in the spirit world." She hugged Jennifer as they said good night. "Good luck to you," she whispered. "And remember, I'm always here for you."

"Thank you," Jennifer said, with tears in her eyes. It had been a long time since she had felt this close to another woman. "Thank you for everything. For your understanding most of all."

"Yeah, that's my job." Phoebe laughed, then looked up into Jennifer's eyes. The smile was gone from her face.

"What's the matter?" Jennifer asked.

Phoebe shook her head. "I'm not sure. I felt something, that's all. I felt danger, I think. I mean, it was a new emotion for me. Be careful."

"I'm going right home."

"Good! I want you to promise you'll call if you want to have me channel Dance again."

"Thank you."

"And I think you need a crystal."

"Oh, I have one!" Jennifer answered. She produced the small piece of quartz from the pocket of her coat.

Phoebe frowned at it a moment. "Did you buy it for yourself?" she asked.

"No. A good friend who knows Kathy Dart gave it to me."

Phoebe shook her head and plucked the small crystal from Jennifer's palm.

"I think it is best," she said carefully, "if you have your own crystal." She slipped Jennifer's quartz into the deep pocket of her own wool skirt, then drew a pencil and pad from the same pocket. "Here is a name of a crystal store downtown," she said. "I know the owner. Please go see him as soon as you can. This afternoon if possible." She handed the slip of paper to Jennifer, and patted the pocket where she had hidden the quartz. "I'll see about 'deprogramming' this one. For the moment, I think you're safer without out a charged-up crystal that doesn't have your best interest in mind."

"What?" Jennifer stared at Phoebe, completely baffled.

"I'll explain everything in time." She gently pushed Jennifer out the door.

Jennifer nodded, too confused to respond. "Oh, I almost forgot," she said, reaching for her purse. "You have been so helpful to me. What is your fee?"

"Well, I usually charge fifty dollars for a thirty-minute session, but . . ." She was looking away, as if embarrassed to be talking about money, "But yours is such an unusual case, and you are clearly a sympathetic soul. Let's say twenty-five dollars, shall we?" She looked up at Jennifer with a smile.

Jennifer pressed the twenty-five dollars into Phoebe's hand and pushed open the heavy iron gate. It had started to snow again, and she realized she wasn't going home to Brooklyn Heights until she had a crystal to protect her.

"I'll call you," she said, turning to Phoebe.

"Yes," Phoebe replied, "I know you will." Smiling still, the channeler closed the iron gate of her basement apartment and stepped back into the dark interior of her home.

17

JENNIFER TOOK THE SUBWAY to the Village. It was not rush hour, so the train was half deserted. Instead of burying her head in a book as she usually did on the subway, she glanced around, checking for transit police. When she saw one, she slipped down into her fur coat and hid her face.

The store was located off Fourteenth Street. It was a tiny sliver of a place, with steel bars drawn across the showcase window. Not open, she thought, disappointed that she wouldn't be able to buy a crystal. But then, behind the counter, she saw a man, and she stepped up the snowy front steps and opened the door.

"I thought you were closed," she said.

The man smiled. "We keep the bars around the windows all the time because of the location. You never know what people will do."

"I'd like to buy a crystal," Jennifer said, embarrassed to be saying it out loud.

"Well, let's hope so!" The man smiled. He held a quartz crystal in his hands and wiped it lovingly with a piece of soft cloth. "Is it for you, or are you buying someone a gift?"

"Does it matter?"

"Oh, yes." The man slipped the crystal back into the case, then gave Jennifer his full attention. "If you're buying one for yourself, then I'd want you to hold it in your hands. To see if you feel anything." He gestured at the hundreds of crystals on display. "One of these is right for you. You'll see. The crystal will choose you, not the other way around."

Jennifer liked the man, liked his soft blue eyes. "Well," she confessed, "I want to buy a crystal for myself."

"Fine. Take your time, look around."

"I want a small one," Jennifer said quickly. "One I can carry around with me. In my pocket." Jennifer stepped closer to the small glass case. Dozens of clear quartz crystals were displayed on blue velvet trays.

"This is your first crystal?"

"Yes, I guess. I mean, a friend did give me one, but . . ."

"Do you know why you want a crystal?" he asked next, reaching into the case and pulling out two trays.

"Do I have to have a reason?" Jennifer realized she sounded defensive. "I mean, a friend suggested it. And I thought it might be fun." Her voice had risen.

The salesman looked over at her questioningly. His blue eyes were even softer and kinder up close. Jennifer felt foolish for having raised her voice.

"Well, what I meant is that people buy crystals for different reasons. Besides, the crystals are themselves different. Now this is a lovely single-terminal quartz crystal. As you see, it has just this single point. And this smokey quartz here is helpful if you're seeking to calm yourself down, gain control of your feelings. Or this amethyst. Amethysts are very protective crystals; they're used by many people to raise spiritual powers." He paused to look at Jennifer for a moment. "You don't know much about crystals, do you?" he asked. "I mean, the power of crystals and why we use them?"

Jennifer shook her head, feeling foolish.

The salesman lifted a small crystal off the tray and held it out to her. "Hold this in your hand, why don't you, while we talk. My name, by the way, is Jeff."

Jennifer nodded. "Hello. I'm Jennifer."

"Okay, Jennifer, here comes Crystals 101." He, too, was holding a crystal in his fingers as he talked. "Crystals hold the four elements of our world within their very being. Earth, fire, water, and air. They are also beautiful, as you can see, in their pure, clear symmetry. So when you hold your crystal, you are holding the world within your fingers. You are holding creation itself.

"Some crystals are meant for you, others are not, which is why I wanted to know if you were buying the crystal for yourself. It's important to be in tune with the crystal from the first. Here, why don't you hold another." He gave her a second crystal, and as soon as Jennifer slipped her right hand around it, she felt a charge of warmth through her fingers.

"This one feels better," she said.

"Good! We're getting closer. Now you have to program your little friend."

"Program?"

Jeff smiled. "Yes, you need to tell a crystal what you want. Crystals contain energy; you have to direct it."

"How?"

"Hold it in your hands. Think of what you want to have happen or what you wish to do. Visualize. Say it's a health problem. Someone you love is suffering from cancer. You visualize that person active again and place the image of this healthy person in the crystal." He leaned back from the counter. "You don't believe in the power of crystals?" he asked.

"I'm not sure," Jennifer said slowly. "I'm afraid that, you know, it's all so faddish. It's so much the yuppie thing to believe in."

"It's not really, you know," Jeff said. He returned one tray of crystals to the display case and took out two large pieces of smoky quartz. "Some people, I guess, think that crystals are just part of the New Age movement, but primitive societies all over the world have used them throughout time to heal, and to predict the future. There's nothing new about crystals or crystal lore."

"Well, yes, I know," Jennifer said quickly. "It's just that I know it's all tied up with channeling and everything."

The salesman seemed at the moment not to be listening to her. He had picked up the smoky quartz and was turning it in his hands, and then she noticed that he had focused the point at her. "What are you doing?" she asked.

"Smoky quartz has the power to calm. To soothe nerves."

"Please," Jennifer said, "don't point it at me." She backed away from the display case.

"You have nothing to fear," Jeff said, watching her. "Crystals are harmless. You bring to them your own energy, and they expand it, energize it, that's all."

"That's what I'm afraid of," Jennifer answered, trying to make a joke of her concern, but she was thinking, too, of what she had already done.

The man carefully returned the quartz to the blue pad.

"Why are you here?" he asked, frowning. "Why do you want to purchase a crystal? I'm not sure you're ready for one."

"Please," she said, stepping toward the counter. "I was told . . . that a crystal would help."

"It will help," he answered, "but you have to be ready to accept that help. I'd be more comfortable with myself if I didn't sell you one at this time. You can try elsewhere, of course."

"Oh, come on. Are you in business or not? What's the owner going to say?"

"I am the owner," he replied softly. He walked around to the other counter, as if he had already dismissed her from his store.

"I was told to come here. To buy a crystal from you."

"By whom?" He looked directly at Jennifer.

"By a channeler," Jennifer said carefully, not sure if she should give out the name.

"Who?"

"Kathy Dart," she lied.

The store owner flinched at the mention of Dart's name. "I must ask you to leave," he said.

"Why?"

"I don't want anything to do with that woman."

"She's a nationally known channeler. She has made video tapes and records."

"Please leave." The owner came out from behind his counter.

Jennifer began to back away from him. "Please," she said quickly, "I really need my own crystal."

"Out!" He was angry. "Kathy Dart is a charlatan, not a shaman."

"You may be right," Jennifer answered, noting the antique words he used.

"I am right."

He opened the front door. Snow was blowing into the store, but he stood there, grimly, waiting for her to leave. What has Kathy Dart done to this man? Jennifer wondered.

She stepped outside, thankful at least that she hadn't turned her rage on him.

"Would you tell me something else?" Jennifer asked, standing on the snowy sidewalk. "Do you know Phoebe Fisher?" He nodded. "Is she who she says she is?"

The question seemed to surprise him. He stared at her for a moment, as if deciding how to respond, and then he said simply, "Yes," and closed the door.

Jennifer turned and walked toward the subway. She had gone nearly a whole block before she realized her right hand was still clutched around the small, clear, single-terminated quartz crystal. It was small and warm in her hand, as if it were a tiny bird, lovely and alive. With her fingers nestled around it gently, she tucked it into the safety of her deep coat pocket. She should return it, she knew. She should walk back and give the man money for it, but she didn't. She continued on her way toward the subway. Later, she would send a check to the Crystal Connection. Now the crystal belonged to her. It felt warm and snug in her pocket, and for the first time in days, she felt secure.

As she walked the several snowy blocks to the station, lost in her own thoughts, she never saw the solitary hunter limping along behind her, never heard the steel-tipped cane digging deep into the snow as she was followed from the Crystal Connection.

This hunter had spotted her first in front of the Ice Age hut built of mammoth bones and tusks twenty thousand years ago.

The hunter rode the subway out to Brooklyn Heights, got off with Jennifer, and moving ahead when she stopped to buy a small bouquet of flowers, limped off into the gathering darkness of early evening to await her arrival home.

Jennifer never bought flowers at the small subway shop, but seeing the cluster of fresh bright bouquets near the newspaper stand, she had acted on impulse and paid an exorbitant five dollars and forty cents for a half-dozen carnations. It was something, she thought, to brighten up her spirits on a dreary day.

Out on the street, she thought briefly about buying some groceries before going home, but she was suddenly afraid again of being spotted, of somehow being recognized as the "ape killer," so instead, she buried her head in the deep collar of her fur coat and hurried home.

Also, Tom was coming over later, and she had so much to think about. He had come to accept her knowledge of David Engle's guilt as an instinct on her part; while he still didn't buy her story of seeing Margit, he was willing to believe that in some vaguely spiritual way, her close friendship with Margit had given her some special insight. But Jennifer wondered what he would do if she told him about Dance.

She was too tired to think about it. The fresh air was making her feel better, though. She was glad to be back in Brooklyn, and the thought of being safely inside her apartment made her smile in anticipation. She was away from the busy streets, going downhill toward the water, where the streets were darker and less congested.

She stepped between two parked cars and dug deep into her

pockets, hunting with her fingers for her apartment keys, and then she stopped and stared ahead at the empty sidewalk. There was no one approaching. The dark sidewalk was shadowy but deserted. She heard nothing but the cold wind. A car passed, its tires crunching in the new snow.

Something was wrong, but she did not know what. The feeling she had was vague and unfocused, like a tiny nag at her subconscious. She was being paranoid, she told herself. She stepped ahead, forced herself to continue down the street, still wary from her premonitions.

She walked slowly, edging away from the buildings, keeping some distance between herself and the dark front steps of the brownstones, with their small gated stoops. She kept away from the garbage cans, glanced to see that no one was crouched behind them, hiding until she got within reach.

She felt her fear. It pumped through her body, making her sweat under her layers of clothes. She loosened her fur collar and took a deep breath. She was damp under her arms, between her legs.

Then she smelled the hunter. She caught a scent in the swirling wind, and she raised her head and sniffed the air. Someone was here, somewhere in the darkness, behind a car perhaps, hidden in the shadows next to a building.

She spun around. Her primal rage swept through her, pumped rage and fear into her veins. In the gathering darkness, she dropped her fresh flowers and crouched down, growling and baring her teeth. She backed away from where she sensed the hunter was, hiding behind a cluster of metal garbage cans. She would not attack unless she was attacked. She kept moving backward, watching the dark corners of the buildings, the hidden doorways of basement apartments, the shadowy hedges. There were now, she knew by instinct, dozens of places where a person might hide from sight until ready to strike.

Snow blew against her face and blurred her vision, but she could see better now in the darkness, and she cocked her head, listening for sounds, the deep steady breathing of some animal waiting to pounce, the sudden motion of a hunter as he got her within range.

She heard the cane before it struck. She heard the thin walnut stick slice the winter air, caught a glimpse of the silver knob, and she tried to duck, but the hunter had surprised her, leaped down from the low branches of a sidewalk sycamore, and struck her in the back of the head. Jennifer was dead before her knees buckled and hit the ground.

When Amenhotep returned from Abu Simbel, Roudidit had already crossed to the other side. Amenhotep went immediately into mourning for his wife, spending the long days as custom required, in idleness, waiting for her body to be prepared for the tomb. He kept himself from thinking what the embalmers were doing to her beautiful body, how they were cutting out her brains and organs, wrapping them up in jars for burial, then filling the body with spices. It took all of three months before Roudidit was properly wrapped in bandages for burial and the funerary furniture was ready.

Amenhotep insisted on adorning her, though the first sight of her terrified him as nothing had ever frightened him in battle. Her beautiful face had shriveled and sunk, and her lips were wizened.

He stood looking down at his dear wife, wrapped in linen, with beeswax covering her eyes and ears, and whispered his farewell.

"I was a young man when I married you, and I spent my life with you. I rose to the highest rank but I never deserted you. I never caused you unhappiness. I never deserted you, from my youth to the time when I was holding all manner of important posts for Pharaoh. Nay, rather, I always said to myself, 'She has always been my companion.' Tell me now, what do I do?"

Amenhotep stood a moment longer, and then slowly, gently, he adorned the mummy. He covered the incision where they had removed her organs with a thick gold sheet inlaid with the oudja, the sacred eye with the power to heal wounds. Then he placed a copy of the Book of the Dead, the guide to the underworld, between her legs, and dressed her with necklaces and amulets, as well as finger stalls for each finger and toe, rings and sandals, all for her long journey to the other bank of life. All of this was new jewelry that he had had made after her death. He had a winged scarab with the goddesses Isis and Nephthys carved as the supporters, and then engraved the back with the words, "O my heart, heart of my mother, heart of my forms, set not thyself up to bear witness against me, speak not against me in the presence of the judges, cast not thy weight against me before the Lord of the Scales. Thou are my ka in my breast, the Khnoum which gives wholeness to my limb. Speak no falsehood against me in the presence of the god!" He added other engraved scarabs, not mounted, but with hearts of lapis lazuli, and all carrying his dead wife's name.

He had amulets and statuettes of the gods Anubis and Thoth, which he hung around her neck and attached to the pectoral. Besides the ornaments, he placed tiny reproductions of walking sticks, scepters, weapons, for he left nothing to chance in his wife's house of eternity. The next world, he knew, was no place of peace and quiet. It was full of hidden traps and dangers, and Roudidit must be prepared for her journey.

When he was done, he stepped back and let the embalmers wrap her again in linen bands and place a gold mask over her face. Then, turning to him, they nodded. She was ready for the cortège.

His servants went first, carrying cakes and flowers, pottery and stone vases. Behind them came the furniture: beds and chests, cupboards, and the chariot, everything that Roudidit would need in the other world. Behind them came his wife's jewelry, all Roudidit's necklaces and jewels, carved human-headed birds and other valuables, displayed on dishes so the crowds would see her wealth, the wealth he had given Roudidit and which would travel now with her to the other side.

The idlers watching the procession could not see Roudidit herself. The stone sarcophagus containing her body was hidden beneath a catafalque drawn by cows and men, all of it mounted on a boat and flanked by statues of Isis and Nephthys.

The women followed, his sisters and relatives, and all the hired mourners, who had smeared their faces with mud and bared their breasts as they wailed and rent their garments, lamenting Roudidit's departure.

At the Nile they were met by a priest with a panther's skin draped over his shoulders. He carried with him burning incense, and the bare-breasted mourners bowed and stood back, letting the boat bearing the catafalque be lowered into the water.

Amenhotep, too, stood aside, and watched in silence as the catafalque was launched into the Nile River. He stood thinking of his wife, of when they were young and first in love. She had been promised to an Ethiopian monarch, and he to Tamit, the daughter of Nenoferkaptak. He had beseeched Pharaoh, and the gods had said he could marry Roudidit if he won her in battle, if he defeated the Ethiopian and brought the kingdom of Kush as ransom. He had gone off to do battle with an army of Nubians fully armed with coats of mail, swords, and chariots. And when he reached Egypt again, he drafted the Nubians into his army, gave them command of the archers and leaders of their people, and branded them all slaves under the seal of his name. And Pharaoh, seeing the wealth he had gathered, gave him Roudidit to wed.

He had never loved another woman in his life, and he knew now he would never love another, though already he had been offered the young sister of his brother's wife. He was too old, Amenhotep knew, to let another come into his heart.

As the boat bearing the catafalque slipped away from shore, he and the mourners stepped into a second vessel to follow close behind, accompanied by two boats full of Roudidit's possessions. The women went at once to the roof of the cabin and continued to cry, sobbing in the direction of the catafalque. Their dirge carried across the wide river:

Let Roudidit go swiftly to the west, to the land of truth.
The women of the Byblite boat weep sorely, sorely.
In peace, in peace, O praised one, fare westward in peace.
If it please the god, when the day changes to eternity,
we shall see thee that goest now to the land where all men are one.

From the eastern shore came the reply from others, wishing their fare-wells, their voices carrying clearly over the calm Nile:

To the west, to the west, the land of the just.
The place thou didst love groans and laments.

Amenhotep stepped to the bow of the boat, into the hot Nile sun, and shouted in the direction of the catafalque, to where his lost wife lay wrapped in her scented linens:

O my sister, o my wife, o my friend!
Stay, rest in thy place,
leave not the place where thou dost abide.
Alas, thou goest hence to cross the Nile.
O you sailors, hasten not, let her be:
Ye shall return to your houses,
but Roudidit is going to the land of eternity.

When he had sung the dirge, he moved again into the shade of the cabin and out of the blazing sun. The cries and laments of the female mourners rose up, filling the air, but he turned toward the western shore and saw that a group had already gathered on the sandy bank. A number of little stalls had been set up to sell goods, food, and devotional objects.

Everyone profits from the crossing over, Amenhotep thought, everyone but myself. I am the one who has lost his world.

She had almost died once, in childbearing when they were first married, and he had prayed to the goddess Hathor, the Lady of Imaou and of the Sycamore, to save Roudidit's life and that of his newborn son. And then the baby had cried "Mbi" and turned his face to the earth, and Amenhotep knew then that nothing but evil would prevail. And he had taken his son out then, and without naming the boy, without entering it in the House of Life, killed the infant, before more harm could come to his family.

She had never given birth to another child.

The four boats were docked and unloaded, and the procession was gradually reformed. They moved up the bank and away from the booths, following behind the catafalque, which, across the flat, cultivated land, was being hauled on a sledge by two cows. Ahead of them all was the priest, sprinkling water from a ewer.

There was only the funeral procession now, all the elders had fallen away, left behind at the bank. Amenhotep moved ahead to greet the goddess Hathor, who, in the shape of a cow, emerged from a clump of papyrus at the entrance of the tomb.

The catafalque was brought to the entrance and the sarcophagus removed. He stepped to the sarcophagus and placed a scented cone on its head, as if greeting a guest in his own home. Behind him, the female mourners began again to weep and beat their heads in anguish. There were more priests now, coming forward with bread and jugs of beer, as well as an adze, the curved knife shaped like an ostrich feather, and a palette ending in two scrolls.

All these, he knew, were objects to empower the priests to counteract the effects of the embalming, to restore his dead wife on the other side so she could use her limbs and her missing organs, so she could see, could open her mouth and speak, could eat and move once again.

The long months of mourning, of suffering his losses, were over.

Amenhotep cried out, "O my sister, it is thy husband, Amenhotep, that speaks. Leave me not! Dost thou wish that I should be parted from thee? If I depart thou wilt be alone, and none will be left to follow thee. Though thou wast wont to be merry with me, now thou art silent and speakest not."

He turned away from the women and stepped down into the tomb, down to the square stone receptacle that had been carved out, and watched as his servants carried his wife and lowered her into place. He placed Roudidit's amulets beside her, then moved away so that the heavy stone lid could be set in place. The jars containing her organs had been put in a chest, and this chest was set down in the tomb by the priests; the funeral furniture had been arranged, and then boxes of oushebtiou, the small statuettes of all her loved ones, were placed in the vault.

He moved out of the tomb, back into the brilliant sunlight of midday. The priests came out, still sprinkling water, and the masons moved to wall up the entrance of the tomb.

Before him, in the sunlight, Amenhotep could see that food for the mourners had been placed out in the courtyard of the building that he had constructed, years before, above the tomb.

He walked through a small garden of sycamores and palm trees and sat in one of the newly decorated rooms of the building. He had always thought that Roudidit would be the one to sit there when he crossed over to the other world. He had never thought that he would be the one left behind on earth.

A harpist came forward from the entrance and thanked all of the mourners for coming, singing that Roudidit was happy in the world beyond. Another harpist picked up the melancholy strain, and sang:

Men's bodies have gone to the grave since the beginning of time
and a new generation taketh their place.
As long as Re shall rise in the morning and Atum shall set in the
west, man shall beget and woman conceive and breath shall be in
men's nostrils.
Yet each that is born returns at the last to his appointed place.

The song was not meant for Roudidit, Amenhotep knew, but for him.
The gods were telling him that he must go on with his life, that his lovely
wife was safe and happy in the land of the west, and that he must turn to
human concerns.

He smiled and motioned his servant to pour him wine, to bring him
food, and he noticed that his sisters smiled at his sudden enthusiasm. Then
he stood and raised his cup to his lips, and over the cool rim, he studied
one woman, a maidservant, who had come to beat her breast, rend her
garments, and mourn the passing over of his wife to the other side.

18

JENNIFER SAW HERSELF FLOATING above her body. She was dead, she realized, but the thought caused her no pain or fear. She felt only free and oddly happy. All her guilt was gone. She regretted nothing. She missed no one. Not Tom. She would have liked to have said good-bye, but that was all.

How wonderful death was. Why did people fear it? She watched the team of doctors hovering over her body, inserting tubes and needles. She felt nothing. She had always been so afraid of injections, but now she smiled, and her smile bubbled up into a laugh. It was as if she had drunk too much and was losing control. But now there was no control to lose.

The doctors were blocking the view of her face, and she moved into a different position. It seemed as if she were hang gliding, surrounded by the silence of the wind. Doctors and nurses were shouting to each other. She was aware of their urgency, but she didn't listen. The details they were discussing no longer mattered to her. It was so much easier to have died this way, without any pain, without any long illness, without having to see her life slip away year after year as she grew older. She had died young, that's all. It was no big deal.

And then she felt pain. A wedge of excruciating pain took her breath away. She saw her face on the table reflect it.

"It's not time, Jennifer," a voice said, a voice that she recognized although it had been years since she heard it.

"Danny! Danny! Where are you?" She looked around, but the world she floated in was gray with clouds.

"I'm here. I'm here."

She understood him, but there was no one speaking to her. Somehow, she just knew what he wanted to tell her.

"Let me see you, Danny," she begged, still scanning the grayness for a sign of life.

"You would not know me, Jennifer. I'm not as you knew me. That was another life, another time for me."

"Oh, Danny, I don't understand. I don't know what's happening to me. Please . . ." She sounded like a little girl, as desolate as the day Danny had disappeared from her life, gone off to die in Vietnam.

"You will, honey. You will. And I'll be there to help you."

"I love you, Danny. I love you, and I'm sorry you were killed."

"It had to happen, sweetie, and it's all right. You know that now. You know it means nothing to die."

"I don't want to live, not anymore. Let me stay with you."

"You can't, Jennifer. It's not your time. But we'll be together again in another time. Go and fulfill your destiny, what your soul chose for you."

"I thought I understood. . . ." Jennifer was weeping again. She had a piercing headache centered between her eyes.

"You will in time."

"I'm sorry you were killed. I didn't want you to die. I loved you, Danny. You've the only one I've really loved." She reached out for him, although she couldn't see him, then realized she was moving, falling, slipping away from the safe place of her death, down and down into her very own body. She struggled, she fought it, but the battle was over; she was slipping back again, into life.

"Okay, we've got her," one of the doctors shouted, eyeing the gauges of the life-support system, seeing that the flickering needle was responding. "We've got life here."

"Thank God," one of the nurses was whispering. "She was really gone."

"I know. I know," the doctor said, unsnapping a rubber cord from around Jennifer's right arm, "but we got lucky this time. Clean her up and take her upstairs." As he turned away, Jennifer fell asleep, feeling no more exhausted than if she had had a tough day at work, but she had been on the emergency-room table for over an hour.

When she woke, Tom was with her, dozing in the chair near the hospital window. She watched him while he slept. The sunlight was on his face, and he had not shaved. He had on his old blue Oxford button-down and gray cords. He had kicked off his Adirondack moccasin shoes and was wearing the pair of thick red wool socks she had bought him for Valentine's Day. She realized she wanted to hold him, but when she tried to sit up, she was too weak to move. Her wrist was taped and she was being fed intravenously.

"Tom," she whispered, and at the soft sound of her voice, he stirred and blinked his eyes open and quickly came to her, lifting her hand to press her soft palm against his cheek. She could feel the stubble of his dark whiskers. "Tom, I'm sorry," she told him.

"It's okay. Hey, you were mugged." He was smiling at her, his gray eyes cloudy with sleep, but soft, too, and tender. "You're going to be fine. Just fine." He kept smiling.

"I'm sorry for everything I've done to you." She began to choke on her tears, and he stood quickly and pressed the buzzer for the nurse.

"I spoke to the cops. I'm having this room guarded."

"Honey, it wasn't your drug dealers."

"Don't try to talk, sweetheart. Don't say anything," Tom said urgently. He glanced at the doorway, then called out "Nurse! Nurse!" in a loud, panicky voice.

"It's okay. I'm okay," she told him. "Come and sit by me." She wanted him close.

"You're fine, darling. Everything is going to be fine now. I love you. I do!" He leaned closer still to kiss her eyelids.

"I want you to listen. Please," she pleaded. "I saw Danny. I mean, I talked to Danny. And he's all right. He's happy."

Tom nodded, but his eyes were clouding over again.

"I'm okay, Tom, I'm not crazy."

"Of course you're not."

"I died. I left my body. I saw the doctors, everything. I wanted to stay dead. It was so wonderful, Tom. Then I saw Danny and he spoke to me, told me that it wasn't time yet, not yet the end of my lifetime."

Tom nodded. "Jennifer, you've got to sleep. Why don't you try to sleep."

Jennifer smiled. He didn't understand what she was talking about. Of course not. He hadn't died and come back to life. She closed her eyes. Yes, she should sleep. She needed to rest and regain her strength. She had so much more to do. It was time.

19

TOM WATCHED JENNIFER PACK. He had made himself another drink and now stood in the doorway of her bedroom as she went back and forth from the closet to her suitcase on the bed.

"Are you going to say anything at all, Thomas? Or are you just going to stare at me all evening?" Jennifer asked. She was holding up a white cotton blouse by the shoulders and deciding whether she should pack it for Minnesota.

"You know what I think," he answered back. The two double scotches he'd downed had put an edge on his voice. "You've just got out of the hospital. You need to rest, not take a goddamn trip out to the middle of nowhere!"

"I have to do this my way," she said.

Tom nodded and sipped the scotch. "It's going to be fucking cold out there," he said softly, as if to make amends. "Why does she live in Minnesota, anyway?"

"It's where she is from."

"She knows you're coming?"

"Yes, of course." Jennifer decided against the blouse. "Eileen telephoned her at the farm—that's what the center is called." She hung up the blouse and reached to the top shelf to pull down her heavy wool sweater, while she waited for his next question. It was as if they were playing tennis, lobbing responses at each other. Then she stepped away from the closet, turned, and faced him.

"Tom, I told you. I'm being driven nuts by this, too. I don't want to have 'out-of-body' experiences. I don't want to know that I can suddenly turn into some sort of caveman who can kill people with a blow of his fist. I don't want to think that every time I'm threatened, I'm going to turn into a freak."

"Jenny, you don't—"

"Yes, I do. Let's not gloss over it, okay? Maybe those people deserved to be killed. Maybe they were scum, or whatever you called them, but then so am I. I killed them. Maybe not me, but some part of me. A past-life person."

"Oh, for chrissake!"

"Give me a chance, Tom." She stared up at him. "Let me go find out what's wrong with me, okay?" Her eyes had swelled up with tears, and to keep herself from crying, she turned to the bed and continued to pack.

"I talked to a couple of shrinks," Tom said slowly, coming into the room.

"Of course," Jennifer replied.

"Of course, what?"

"Of course you would talk to someone. That's you." She glanced up to show she wasn't upset with him. "What did they say?" she asked, softening her voice.

"I spoke to Dr. Senese, the one I saw for a while after I broke up with Helen. I told him about this woman, Phoebe Fisher."

"And Kathy Dart."

"Yeah, about all this goddamn channeling shit."

"Tom, please!" She felt a wave of anger and immediately tried the exercise Phoebe had taught her, focusing her attention on the word *love*. Gradually she felt her body ease and the tension diminish. She glanced at Tom. He was sitting on the edge of the bed now, his drink still in his hand. She noticed that he had put on weight, that there was a new roll of fat around his middle, and that his shirt had grown tight at the neck. He was like an animal, she thought, who stored up fat for winter. Perhaps he had stopped jogging. She had not run since her Washington trip. She was afraid to run, afraid of what might happen to her body.

"Senese says that these channelers are suffering from personality dysfunctions. According to him, a fractionalized piece of their personality gains control. You've read about these multiple personality cases."

"Multiple personalities, Tom, happen within the same person. Habasha was a living person from another time period. Dance is from another galaxy. It's not the same thing."

"Oh, for chrissake."

"Tom, I'm not asking you to understand any of this, either. I just want you to have some faith in me, that's all. I want you to be at least as supportive as Eileen Gorman."

"That loony! I talked to her at the hospital when she came to see you. She's out of her fucking mind!"

"Tom! How dare you!" Jennifer threw down one of the sweaters and turned on him. "Eileen has been absolutely wonderful, coming to me when I need her, listening, understanding. How can you sit there and . . . and . . ." Jennifer felt a surge of rage sweep through her body. There was a pattern to her primitive urges. They sprang from the base of her neck, shot down across her chest, and poured strength through her body; the result was an overwhelming urge to attack. It was becoming worse, she knew. Each time the rage returned, it came in stronger waves, and sometimes she realized she wanted to sink her teeth into someone. She could feel the desire to satisfy that pleasure. It was like having sex—once she spun off into an orgasm, she never wanted it to stop. She wanted only to ride the waves. She took several deep breaths and brought herself under control.

"If you hadn't met her in Washington, then none of this nonsense would have started in the first place," Tom shouted back.

He was drunk, Jennifer realized, drunk and angry and threatened.

"It would have happened anyway, Tom," she answered. "It was meant to. These events aren't coincidences or happenstance." She looked across the bed at her lover. "Let me work this out my way," she told him.

Tom stood staring at her in the dumb way drunks do when trying to comprehend. She went back to packing but watched him out of the corner of her eye. She was leaving first thing in the morning; Eileen was coming in from Long Island to pick her up, and they were going to drive together to Minnesota.

She could send him home in a taxi, Jennifer thought, or let him sleep there tonight. He'd be sick in the morning.

"Tom, why don't you go into the living room and lie down on the sofa?" She encouraged him with a smile, but his eyes had glassed over, and he kept swaying against the bed. She went to him and took away his drink. "Come on into the living room, honey," she whispered.

"You're leaving me, I know," he mumbled, but let himself be led away. "You're leaving me because I didn't do anything about Helen."

"Darling, I'm not leaving you. I'm going to see Kathy Dart and talk to her about what is happening to me. I'll be coming home to you soon. And I'll be okay again." She spoke brightly as she eased him from her bedroom. Now his full weight was against her, and she had to struggle to keep him from toppling them both over. Where was her strength when she needed it, she thought, gasping for breath as she slid him down onto the sofa. When Tom dropped onto the cushions, Jennifer sank to her knees.

At least he would sleep until early morning. And he wouldn't hurt himself. She slipped off his shoes and pushed his legs up onto the sofa, then loosened his shirt and his belt. She peeled off his black socks and dropped them into his shoes, then went back into her room, took the extra quilt from the cedar closet, and tucked it around him.

He was already sleeping soundly. Jennifer knelt beside him and gently caressed his face. The deep sleep had swept away all the tension; he looked like a teenager, with nothing more on his mind them the pleasure of a wet dream. She leaned forward, kissed his cheek, and whispered, "I love you."

It was after midnight when she woke and sat up in bed. She was suddenly wide awake and quite clearly she heard the front door of the apartment being unlocked, heard the two tumblers turn. She jumped from the bed and rushed to the bedroom door. Tom was up and off the sofa. He had grabbed his pistol from his briefcase, and when he spotted her, he put his finger to his lips, motioned for her to be silent.

She watched as he carefully stepped around the sofa, moving silently in his bare feet. Then she heard the dog, heard his paws on the bare hardwood floors of the front entrance.

She started to move out of the bedroom, and frantically Tom signaled, waved her back into the room, motioning that she should close the door.

"What is it?" she whispered, and then she caught a glimpse of the dog in the dim light of the living room. It had run in from the front hall, and spotting Tom, it immediately growled and bared its teeth. It was a pit bull, Jennifer saw, watching the small blunt-faced beast.

"Get away, Jenny!" Tom ordered, raising his pistol. He fired as the dog leaped at him. The bullet missed the animal and shattered the glass in her breakfront beside the bedroom door.

Jennifer screamed.

The pit bull landed on the back of the sofa and then jumped at Tom. Backing off, Tom tripped over the coffee table and shot again. This time the bullet dug into the high ceiling.

The dog was on top of him now, had seized his forearm in his teeth. Tom swung the pistol around and shoved it against the pit bull's face and pulled the trigger. The automatic pistol jammed, and before he could get off the next shot, the dog ripped the flesh off his forearm. Now Tom screamed.

Jennifer went for the beast. She dove at the animal, grabbed his white slavering muzzle with her own bare hands and wrenched open his jaw with one smooth strong motion, as if she had been killing animals in the wild all of her life.

Then with her arms outstretched, she let the heavy beast twist and turn under her strong grip, let him struggle to get loose. She saw the anguish in the dog's yellow eyes as he gasped for breath, and then with a sudden jerk, she ripped open the beast's mouth and broke his jaw. The fresh blood from the soft white insides of his mouth sprayed her face and splattered the pale yellow rug of her living room. She dropped the prey.

Tom crawled away from the pit bull. Crawled away in pain. His arm was bleeding and his flesh hung loose from the muscle.

"Jenny!" he gasped, seeing what she had done to the dog.

He was frightened, she saw. Frightened now of her. But Tom wasn't her enemy. He did not want to harm her.

Jennifer smiled at her lover, and slowly, carefully, as any animal would, she wiped her lips clean with the tip of her tongue.

BOOK THREE

If we open to these sources of inspiration and creativity, we open a window to a universe that is going to be becoming better. Someone once asked me about which model of the universe I favored. I said, "To hell with the model, let's just channel the universe. Let's become one with it. That way we don't have to play little games."

—Channel Alan Vaughan

He [my guru] asked me to pray, but I could not pray. He replied that it did not matter, he and some others would pray and I had simply to go to the meeting . . . and wit and speech would come to me from some other source than the mind. [I did as I was told.]

The speech came as though it was dictated, and ever since, all speech, writing, thought and outward activity have so come to me from the same source.

—Sri Aurobindo

20

JENNIFER SLEPT AS THE car swept across New Jersey. When she woke, stretched out in a sleeping bag in the back of Eileen's station wagon, she saw they were on an interstate, passing through bleak farmland. The trees were bare, and icy snow covered the low, rolling hills. The sun, reflecting off the snow, blinded her for a moment, and she thought at once of how she had killed the pit bull, and to keep her mind off the frightening memory, she asked, "Where are we, Eileen?"

"Well, good morning, sleepyhead. According to the last sign-post, we're just beyond Lock Haven, Pennsylvania, heading west on 80. Do you want coffee?"

"Oh, no, just keep driving." Jennifer did not want to stop. She liked feeling that she was escaping from New York, driving away from danger.

"I have some with me. Here." Without taking her eyes off the road, Eileen handed back a thermos. "There are sandwiches packed, too, and sodas. Would you like to drive?"

Jennifer shook her head. "Not unless you want me to," she said. "I'm exhausted." When Eileen had picked her up that morning at the apartment, she was still trembling from the dog's attack. She was afraid that Tom wouldn't let her go, but he had wanted her to go then, thinking that she would be safer in Minnesota, far away from the drug dealers. But it wasn't drug dealers, Jennifer knew, who had sent the pit bull into her apartment.

"Well, you're okay now," Eileen told her, smiling into the rearview mirror.

"I don't know. I don't think I'll ever be all right again."

"Yes, you will. Kathy's going to help you."

Jennifer smiled, then reached over and tenderly squeezed Eileen's shoulder. She closed her eyes again but immediately conjured up the nightmare vision of the dog attacking. She saw the animal's

slobbering mouth, its bare white teeth. Jennifer opened her eyes
and blinked again at the brilliant winter sun.

"Tom thinks the dog was sent after him," she said. "By drug
dealers he's prosecuting."

"You don't believe that." It was a statement, not a question.
Eileen's eyes found Jennifer in the mirror.

"The dog was after me, Eileen," she said. "I just have this
feeling that whoever attacked me outside of my apartment is still
after me." Her own words frightened her. "I guess I'm trying to
warn you, Eileen, even if it's too late. I mean, here we are all alone
on the interstate in the middle of nowhere."

"We'll be careful," Eileen said reassuringly.

"I'm just sorry that you have to be involved."

"I want to be involved. Kathy Dart practically told me to hand-
deliver you to Minnesota."

"Oh?" Jennifer looked over at Eileen. From where she was
sitting, she could see her right profile.

"You know Kathy is concerned about you," Eileen said.

"Yes, I know. Is she this concerned about your well-being, too?"
Jennifer shifted around and rested her chin on the back of the driver's
seat.

"Yes, I think so. Habasha says that I was once in King Louis
the Fourteenth's cavalry. That must explain my love for horses.
Anyway, Kathy was my commanding officer and I saved her life.
That explains why she is linked to me. And look at us, you and I.
Why were we so close in high school? Why did we just—you
know—pick up afterwards? There's a reason. It's not coincidence.
We're totally different people. My parents weren't wealthy; yours
were. I was raised a Unitarian. You were what, nothing?"

"I wasn't nothing!" Jennifer answered back, laughing. "I was
raised a Lutheran. And Lutherans believe in God. I do!" she added
defensively. "So there!"

"So there yourself!" Eileen answered back.

They rode in silence for a moment, watching the highway ahead
of them. There was very little traffic, and Eileen was speeding in
the left lane, passing an occasional car. At that moment, Jennifer
felt happy and secure. She had turned her life over to Eileen and
Kathy Dart. They had answers about what was happening to her,
and that was more than she had herself.

"It's scary sometimes, I know," Eileen said softly. "I remember
one of the first sessions I went to with Kathy. A man there was

having trouble with his wife and teenage daughter. There was a great deal of bickering, he said, and he couldn't understand why. None of them could, really. Well, Kathy used acupuncture on the man to release his past. It was scary. I had never seen anyone being pierced with needles, but it didn't seem to hurt him, and then when Kathy began to lead the man back through time, he reached this point where he was an Indian living on the plains. In that lifetime the soul who's now his daughter was his wife. *That* was the problem. His wife today was jealous of their daughter because she was her husband's lover in America before Columbus landed here."

"It all seems so crazy," Jennifer whispered, doubting for a moment why she was going to see Kathy Dart, why she needed to see the channeler.

"It's not so crazy. Reincarnation is a part of every religious tradition."

"I'm just having such a hard time rationalizing it."

"That's the trouble. You shouldn't try to rationalize reincarnation. You'll see, once you speak with Habasha. Then you'll understand why you are on earth. And what the purpose is for all your heartaches and joys." Eileen was speaking urgently now, with conviction. "If you believe in reincarnation, all the coincidences have meaning."

"That's what I don't like," Jennifer spoke up. "I don't like thinking that all those coincidences are linked together. It seems too planned, too neatly worked out to be real."

"But it makes sense, Jenny. Your spirit is created by God, or whoever, and it passes through lifetime after lifetime. The spirit never dies, but it keeps changing. You're born a man. You're reborn as the same man's great granddaughter. It's wonderful when you step back, when you think of all the possibilities, and the wonderful art of it, really."

"Maybe it's not so wonderful," said Jennifer. "Maybe someboy's 'soul' has come back from another life to kill me."

"Easy, Jenny. We don't know that." Eileen shifted again into the left lane and passed a long distance trucker. As they sped by, the driver blasted his horn. The noise startled Jennifer, and she spun around and gave the finger to the truck driver.

"That wasn't such a great idea," Eileen said coolly.

"Why? I hate it when jerks like that think it's cute to harass women drivers."

"Yes, I know, but now every trucker on Route 80 is going to be watching for two women in a gold '87 Buick."

"How? What do you mean?"

"CBs, honey. They're all linked together."

"Damnit! You're right."

"It's a long trip, and these guys have nothing else to do but amuse themselves. Don't worry. We'll avoid their hangouts. It's okay."

"Thanks. I guess I'm like someone's obnoxious teenage daughter."

"Well, you might have been mine. . . ."

"Yes, I know. In another life."

They both laughed and then fell silent, watching the white lines flash beneath the car as they sped west, and listening to the hum of the tires and the wind whipping against the windows. It was cozy in the station wagon, and Jennifer slipped down into the sleeping bag and curled up in its warmth.

"Do you mind if I go back to sleep?"

"Please do. I'd like you to drive later, if you don't mind."

"Sure," mumbled Jennifer, already half asleep.

"Sweet dreams," Eileen said, glancing back. Jennifer had closed her eyes. She couldn't see that the smile was gone from Eileen's face. Her high-school friend's bright green eyes had glazed over and were as cold as crystal.

21

"WHAT DO YOU THINK, Jenny, are we ready to stop?"

Jennifer glanced at the dashboard clock. It was six o'clock, and Eileen had been driving in the dark for over an hour.

"Yes, I guess. I need a drink and an early evening. Have we covered enough territory?"

"Yes, you made good time on the second leg. We'll catch the turnpike first thing in the morning and be just south of Chicago by tomorrow evening." Eileen moved the station wagon to the right lane. "I've stayed at the Howard Johnson at this exit before," she explained as she exited Route 80.

Jennifer, now sitting in the front seat, watched Eileen's profile reflected in the windshield. They took the brightly lit exit, then turned right at the intersection and drove into the Howard Johnson parking lot. "What are you looking at, Jenny?" Eileen flushed under Jennifer's steady gaze.

"I was just thinking that you've been incredibly nice to me, that's all." Jennifer usually found it difficult to tell people how she felt, but she had always been able to talk to Eileen, ever since they first sat next to each other in their freshman home-room class.

"Oh, you'd do the same, if I needed help," Eileen said quickly.

Jennifer saw that her eyes were glimmering with tears. She reached out and squeezed her friend's arm as they pulled into a parking space. Then, as she reached to open the car door, she said, "Let's check in and then hit the bar." She stopped and turned back to Eileen. "Do you mind if we share a room? I mean . . ." Jennifer looked away, suddenly embarrassed. She saw several men opening the trunks of their cars and taking out luggage. "I mean, I'm still a little nervous. I'd feel safer with you sleeping in the same room."

"Sure, of course. I hate traveling alone, myself," Eileen answered quickly. "It's scary, all the weirdos out here. You never know."

"Listen!" Jennifer said, laughing. "The weirdos I can handle. I'm worried about Mr. Nice Guy." She lowered her voice as they entered the hotel lobby. "I'm afraid I might cut off his balls if he steps out of line."

"It would serve him right, cheating on his wife," Eileen replied.

The vodka on the rocks made Jennifer giddy. She was telling Eileen about Bobby Scott, a boy they had gone to school with, and how he had tried to kiss her underneath the stadium stands when they played Westbury for the division championship. "Here I was trying to go and take a pee. It was cold, remember? And he just wouldn't let go. I started to cry from pain."

"He was not too smart, Bobby."

"Whatever happened to him, anyway?" Jennifer stared down at her menu and tried to concentrate. Now that they were out of the car and in the warm hotel, she suddenly felt very hungry.

"Oh, he married Debby O'Brian. Do you remember her?"

"He married Debby? She was such a sweet girl, with that beautiful long red hair."

Eileen nodded. "He went to Queens College, then married her, and they had four kids quick as rabbits. She was a big Catholic. Anyway, now he works for Goldman Sachs. I hear he owns a brownstone and is worth millions."

"Well, good for Debby."

Eileen shook her head. "Oh, he dumped her for someone else, a real hotshot investor herself. I met them both a few years ago at a benefit. He was with his new wife, who bought junk bonds, or sold them, or something, and she and I talked. The men were working the room, you know, and here was this woman—Rita, that was her name. She was so unhappy she started to cry, right there in the Grand Ballroom of the Waldorf."

"With millions of dollars and a brownstone! Why?"

"Bobby beat her. She told me it was the only way he could get it up. Here we were two strangers, and she unloads this gruesome story on me." Eileen shrugged, then sipped her drink. "She had to tell someone. She was so pitiful and desperate, and I, at least, had known Scotty when he was a kid."

Jennifer sat back in her chair. She remembered Bobby Scott and how he hadn't known how to kiss her, or any girl. She remembered again the beer on his breath on that cold Friday night. She had kissed him back just to get rid of him. "Maybe it was my fault," she joked. "Maybe I shouldn't have played so hard to get."

"People choose what they want out of life, Jenny. That's one of the first things you learn from Habasha. People choose their parents. They choose their lovers and their friends. They choose because they need to fulfill whatever is unresolved from a past life." Eileen set down her menu. "I think I'm going to have chicken," she announced. "I never get anything too fancy when I'm eating on the road."

"Choice, and deciding for others, is all based on experiences from previous lives," Eileen continued after they had ordered.

"I don't get that. What do you mean?"

"Well, take us. Who was class president?"

"I was!"

"And I decided you should be."

"Eileen, don't be silly!" Jennifer leaned forward. She had had too much to drink and was trying to keep her voice down. "It was my clique, you know that."

"You're wrong."

"I don't believe this." Jennifer sighed, baffled. "I remember everything about high school. Everything! It was one of the happiest times in my life. I mean, why would I screw up something like that? I remember when I decided to run for class president. You were the newspaper editor; Karen was in charge of the yearbook. And if I could be president, then our clique—my clique!—would control the senior class and practically all of Shreiber High." Her voice had risen, and she saw out of the corner of her eye that she was attracting attention. Several diners looked up from their meals, and two men at the bar swung around to stare at them. Jennifer realized suddenly that she and Eileen were the only single women in the restaurant. She lowered her voice.

"Jenny," Eileen said slowly, "let me tell you a story and see if you recall it. Okay?"

Jennifer nodded. The two drinks had given her a slight headache. She reached over and took a sip of water and saw that her hand was trembling.

"Do you remember our junior year?" Eileen asked.

"Of course."

"Do you remember Sam Sam and when we went to Jones Beach?"

"Yes! Sam Sam!" Jennifer smiled. It was a name she had forgotten, the girl from Thailand who had been an exchange student at their school.

"Do you remember what happened to Sam Sam, Jenny?" Eileen asked. The waitress had returned with their food, and Eileen was calmly unfolding her napkin, watching Jennifer carefully.

Jennifer shook her head. She could picture Sam Sam, a small girl with beautiful long black hair, pretty brown eyes, and a wonderful smile.

"You don't remember those jerks from Bay Shore? Those three bikers on the dunes? You and I and Sam Sam were on the beach that Saturday, sunning?"

"Yes, I do!" Jennifer said, suddenly recalling. She remembered then the young hoods swaggering along the beach. They looked so weird coming through the sand in their tight jackets and their long hair. They had wandered down to the patch of sand where she and Eileen and Sam Sam were stretched out on blankets.

"And one of them called Sam Sam a nigger?"

"Yes," Jennifer whispered.

"See, Jennifer, you do block events, don't you? We all do."

"I was so afraid," Jennifer confessed.

"But do you remember what you did?"

Jennifer shook her head.

"You stood up to all of them, told them off, and told them you'd have them all arrested."

Jennifer nodded, smiling, pleased to recall the long ago incident. "I guess I did. I was so scared."

"And I was so proud of you. I remember Sam Sam thanking you. I decided then you should be class president. I told everyone what you had done."

There were tears in Jennifer's eyes. "She was really lovely. I wonder what happened to her."

"She was killed in an auto accident in Thailand when she was nineteen."

"Oh God! No! How do you . . . ?"

"We wrote once a year or so, and then her brother wrote saying she had been killed."

"I can't believe it. Little Sam Sam . . ."

"It's all right," Eileen said quickly. "She was reincarnated as a member of a royal family in Asia somwhere. Habasha told me. Within our lifetime she'll be a great leader of her people. We didn't lose Sam Sam. She simply went on to a better life, a more important and perfect life. It was her destiny. You must learn to accept this, Jenny. Let life happen to you. Know in your heart that all these events—good and bad—will pass, and that you, too, will pass into other existences, other worlds."

Jennifer sat back in her chair, shaking her head. "It's all so strange." She looked away from Eileen, glanced around the room, and saw that the men at the bar were watching them, whispering to each other.

"You're just not ready, that's all." Eileen reached over and seized Jennifer's wrist. "But you have great ability, Jennifer. Your electromagnetic frequency is much better than mine, more powerful, perhaps, than Kathy Dart's. She has said as much to me."

"I can't do anything," Jennifer whispered back across the table, "except kill people."

"You have only destroyed what needed to be destroyed. You have only rid this world of individuals who needed to be reincarnated as better, purer spirits."

"I can't channel. I don't know—"

"I understand." Eileen broke in. "You can't summon guiding spirits the way Kathy does. But you're gifted in a way that she isn't. You can 'see,' Jennifer."

"Then why didn't I see that guy with the club? The one that hit me?" Jennifer had raised her voice again, disturbed by Eileen's certitude.

"As I said, you weren't ready," Eileen answered calmly. "I have a feeling that soon we'll know why you've been singled out. There's a connection somewhere." Eileen, excited, was waving her hands and inadvertently summoned a busboy carrying a coffee pot. "I'm sorry." Eileen laughed. Both she and Jennifer began to giggle, exhausted by their long drive, their drinks, and the intensity of the conversation.

"Excuse us," Jennifer said, recovering, "would you please have the waitress bring us the check?" She smiled warmly at the young man, who stared blankly at both of them and then wordlessly walked away.

The waitress approached then with a tray of drinks. Jennifer looked up and shook her head. "We didn't order another round," she explained.

"The gentlemen at the bar asked if they might buy you all a drink," the waitress said, leaning over to set down the glasses.

Jennifer stopped her, saying quietly, "Please thank the gentle-men, but we don't accept drinks from strangers." Although she did not glance over at the men, she knew they were watching, and at once she felt her pulse quicken and her blood surge.

"Jenny, easy," Eileen whispered, "let's not—"

"It's okay, Eileen," she said calmly.

"Jennifer," Eileen whispered urgently. "Let's not have an incident with these jerks." She reached over to grab Jennifer's hand and immediately pulled away, her eyes widening, as she caught the look on Jennifer's face.

"Get me out of here," she told Eileen.

Eileen had her purse open and was dropping money onto the table. Jennifer stepped around the table and rushed for the door. She would be all right, she kept telling herself, if she could get outside, away from the two men at the bar. It was only a question of control. She had to control herself. Nervously she licked her lips.

"Hey, honey, what's the rush?" One of the men had come off his bar stool. He was a big man, the kind who had played football in school, and whose muscles had since turned to fat. He had no neck and a brick-shaped head.

Jennifer made it out of the restaurant and turned down the long, red-carpeted hallway that led to their room. But if he followed her, she realized, he'd know where to find them. She stepped abruptly out of the hallway and into the small alcove that had the ice and Coke machines.

"Hey, I've got some rum to go with that Coke of yours," the man said, turning the corner. He wore steel-rimmed glasses that pinched his face. He was grinning.

"Please, go away," she asked, refusing to look at him.

"Hey, honey, Pete and me, we just wanted to buy you and your girlfriend a drink. Jesus Christ, you could be a little sociable. I mean, we aren't out to rape you. Hey, here's my card." He flashed a small white card from his vest pocket. "The name's Buddy Rich. No relation, right? I'm the district salesman for Connect Computer." He seemed to swell before her. "We're the largest computer firm east of Illinois, servicing hospitals, universities, major companies." He had blocked her from the exit as he waved the card in her face. "Take it!" he ordered.

Jennifer took it from him.

"There! That's not so bad, right?"

She could smell the liquor on his breath, smell his sweat, and she was knew what was coming. She knew she could not stop herself, not without help.

"Please," she whispered.

"I think a couple of granddaddies and you'll be just fine. Whatcha say?" He was leaning close.

"Please?" she asked. By now she was backed up against the wall of the alcove. She concentrated on sounds—the humming of the giant Coke machine, the rumbling of the ice maker. Then he touched her.

Jennifer grabbed him by the throat before he took his hand off her shoulder. She looked up and saw his pale blue eyes bulge in his face. She smiled at him so he knew she was enjoying this.

She was holding him several inches above the cement floor with one outstretched arm, marveling at her own strength. Then she turned slowly around, spinning until she realized he had lost control of his bowels. Without pausing, she slammed his face against the ice machine. The blow broke his glasses and bloodied his face, and a bucket of small cubes tumbled from the machine and cracked against the concrete floor. Still holding him with one hand, she shoved his square head into the opening of the ice maker. His head was too big for the slot and she had to press harder, tearing the flesh off his forehead and the tips of his ears before she had successfully wedged him into place.

She left him there with his head jammed in the ice maker, kneeling in his own urine and excrement, and stepped into the dark hallway where Eileen stood, trembling and terrifed.

"I think we had better check out," Jennifer said, and walked down the long hallway to their room.

22

"STOP LOOKING BACK, JENNY! He's not following us."

"How can you be so sure?" Jennifer glanced again out the rear window of the station wagon but saw no cars or flashing police lights gaining on them. The road was blank. They were alone on the dark interstate, traveling west through Ohio. It had begun to snow slightly, and the high beams picked up the flakes blowing against the windows. Jennifer felt the car shake as it was buffeted by bursts of wind.

"He's not about to go to the police and tell them some woman shoved his fat face into an ice machine." Eileen started to giggle, remembering. "I don't think I've ever been so impressed in my life. Jenny, you beat the shit out of that guy! Like you were Rambo or someone!"

"More like Hulk Hogan," Jennifer answered. She was sitting in the backseat with a car blanket wrapped around her, shivering. The cold was something that came with her power. When she calmed down, she knew, she'd feel better, and her hands would stop trembling. She wondered if it was her fear that provoked the trembling, or simply the aftermath of her rage.

"We're okay, Jenny. I tell you, stop worrying."

"I wish I could." Jennifer buried her face in the thick blanket to smother her tears. She was so tired of crying. Her emotional swings, she thought, were as disturbing as her extraordinary strength. "Eileen, I don't think I can do this. I can't sit in this car all the way to Minnesota."

"We're not going to drive all the way. Right now, we're an hour from Akron. We can leave the car there and fly to St. Paul. I'll telephone Kathy, and she'll have someone meet us at the airport. If we make good connections, we'll be on the farm by tomorrow afternoon."

"Where is it, exactly?"

"About an hour north of St. Paul. It's beautiful country. You'll love it!"

"Who's there? Besides Kathy?" Jennifer pulled herself up in the backseat, realizing how little she knew about Kathy Dart. She would never have taken such a spontaneous trip if it weren't for Eileen. It was really Eileen Gorman whom she trusted.

"There's Aurora, Kathy's daughter. She's a beautiful child, so gifted, just like her mother."

"What about her father? Kathy's husband?" Jennifer asked. She had been so wrapped up in her own problems that she had never even considered the personal life of Kathy Dart.

In the car's dark interior Jennifer could see Eileen shaking her head.

"I really don't know that much. No one does. I mean, you heard what Kathy said in Washington, how she was living in California and unhappily married." Eileen shrugged. "That's about all any of us know. The outsiders, I mean."

"But there must be more. There's always more," Jennifer said. They drove in silence for a moment. Jennifer found she did not want to look out the window. She was afraid of the dark, afraid of everything that was new to her. And that fear made her angry. It was as if part of her life had been taken away from her.

"So besides Aurora, who's on the farm?" she asked next, breaking the silence.

"Let's see, I'm not really sure. People come and go. When Kathy isn't traveling, she holds sessions in the tukul. That's the main building, where they all have their meals and hang out. And it's the place for community meetings."

"Is it like that place out in Oregon—that Indian cult with free love?" Maybe she had taken too much on faith.

"No! It's nothing like that, Jennifer," Eileen soothed. "You're getting yourself all bent out of shape over nothing. I wouldn't do that to you. I wouldn't do that to myself!"

"I don't know what to think. But I do know I don't want to get mixed up in any sort of weird movement, with chanting and wearing red and having sex with guys who shave their heads. I just want to talk to Kathy Dart."

"And you will," Eileen answered, encouragingly. "People consult her all the time. When I was out in September, a group of corporate types—you know, chief executives, vice presidents— were taking this human-potential training that Kathy offers. She has a one-week session called Desta, which is Ethiopian for 'happy,' and during the week she channels Habasha.

"But there's other stuff, too: role-playing, confessions, meditation. Kathy says that it's helpful for people—especially managers—to discover their own self-defeating attitudes. And I tell you, Jenny, after a week out there, these guys were just flying! They were so excited. I remember thinking that if all Kathy Dart and Habasha ever do is bring such joy to a bunch of businessmen, well, then, channeling is worth it."

Jennifer smiled as she listened. She had forgotten how enthusiastically Eileen embraced the world.

"Okay, business guys, who else?" she asked, trying to envision what the farm was like.

Eileen shrugged. "People like you and me."

"That bad?"

"And worse, can you believe? Everyone has heard about Kathy, seen her on television."

Jennifer nodded. She remembered how she had seen Kathy Dart at five o'clock in the morning. "Where do we sleep?" she asked. "They don't have dorms, do they?"

"Oh, no. Everyone has his own room, with a single bed. Kathy believes that people need to be isolated, especially if they're meditating. Also, she believes that everyone needs their own personal space. Especially twin-souls."

"Twin-souls?"

"Yes. A twin-soul is someone with whom we may once have shared a lifetime. There is a tremendous attraction between twin-souls, but also great resentment. Elizabeth Taylor and Richard Burton were twin-souls. And Madonna and Sean Penn. Real twins often function like that in life. They love and hate each other simultaneously. Your problem might be because of some conflict with a twin-soul."

"What has happened to me—is still happening to me!—is more than just a love-hate relationship."

Eileen nodded. "I realize that, and I don't know the reason for these outbursts, but you seem to be suddenly attracting other souls who once shared a lifetime with you. Your past lives are coming together in this one."

"Why now?" Jennifer sat back, and for a moment they rode in silence. "I didn't ask for any of this," she finally said.

"I know," Eileen admitted. "Maybe I'm the cause. I exposed

you to Kathy." She kept her eyes fixed on the road. "But Kathy can save you, too. And if not Kathy, then Habasha."

Jennifer closed her eyes and was comforted with the thought that help was waiting for her in Minnesota. When she opened them again, she saw bright lights on the dark horizon. The sudden sweep of lights made her think of the movie *Close Encounters of the Third Kind*, when the sky lit up with the arrival of the spaceship.

"What's that?" she asked.

"I believe," said Eileen, easing her foot off the gas pedal, "that it's downtown Akron."

"What if there is no such thing as reincarnation?" Jennifer asked next, as Eileen pulled off the highway. "What if there are no twin-souls or collective lives or multiple personalities!"

Eileen did not take her eyes from the interstate as she answered. "Then I think you are in real trouble," she said quietly.

"Why?" Jennifer asked.

"Because it means you are a killer. A cold-blooded killer."

It was colder now during the day and the light of the sun disappeared before Bura and the others had time to gather wood from the valley.

Because Bura was older, having lived through thirteen winters, and strong, strong as any of the males, except for Nira, she carried a full load back along the length of the valley.

She paused on the grassy slope where they had lived as long as she could remember. As she looked into the deep caves that had been cut with flint axes into each ledge, she thought of what her mother's mother had told her. When her mother's mother was a girl, they had come to live in these limestone caves, spending the cold months huddled by the charcoal fires, wrapped in the skins of wolves. Only the men would go out during the few hours of sunlight to hunt, and when they returned with a beast, there would be a great feast for all their people.

Bura thought how wonderful it must have been to live in the cave. Her mother's mother had shown her where she slept on the cold ledge, hidden from the north winds, while the old men talked, and told Bura how she used to lie awake watching the flame dance against the rock walls, huddled there beside her sisters.

But now they lived in a round hut made of bones and bear skin, and now only children played in the caves during the warm months. Bura had bled from her womb, and her mother and her mother's mother had taken her to the cave of drawings, and there she had drunk of her own blood, and her face and breasts had been marked with thick dark smears, and the women had prayed to all the spirits that her womb would flower with offspring. Her mother had said that Bura would go to live with Nira's people, and she had gone that night to sleep in the thick warm skins with his sisters, and now it had been three days and three nights, and he had not come for her.

Bura knew that he would come that night. She had been told that the men never came to take their women on the first night, and that the longer they waited, the more powerful was their coupling. She was not afraid. She had seen her brothers coupling with their new women, heard the moans of pleasure and pain.

Bura was climbing up the cave path at dusk, bent forward to balance the driftwood on her back and shoulders, when they seized her. They had hidden themselves in the shadows of the ledge, kneeling out of sight and waiting for the women to climb up and out of the riverbed. One covered her mouth with his hand, slipped his arm around her naked waist. The second one pulled her legs out from under her, tumbling her over as if she were a thin-legged deer. They dragged her back into the forgotten caves, littered now with the bones of animals.

Bura bit the thick hand that covered her mouth and kicked out with her legs, but the two men had her between them. They had seized her skin covering and ripped it from her waist. She was naked now except for the shells she had strung around her neck, and one of the men seized them, twisting the thin cord of leather tight around her throat until she could not breathe.

They were trying to mate with her. Already she could feel the one who had her from behind, his arms wrapped around her stomach, shoving his organ into her. She twisted in his grasp until the leather cord grew even tighter around her neck. She broke one hand free and scraped her fingernails down the face of the man in front.

As the strip of leather around her neck loosened, Bura tumbled into the dirt, gasping for breath. She knelt on the ground, and when she had swallowed one long breath of air, she bolted from them, darting off like a rabbit caught in an open meadow.

They ran to catch her as she climbed up the steep limestone path. She was taller than both of them, and faster, and even in the dark, she knew the caves and ledges. If she reached the ridge, she would be all right.

Her breath was on fire in her throat, and there was a pain in her side. But if they caught her now, they would kill her. She could not see them behind her on the path, but she heard them, knew they were still after her.

She reached the top of the path, ran into the open meadow, and sighed with exhaustion and relief. She was safe. She saw the sparkling flames of the fires, twinkling like stars, and pushed forward for the safety of her mother's hut. She could even smell the meat burning on the flame as she lengthened her stride and ran into Nira's arms.

"Where were you?" he asked.

She tried to speak, to explain, but managed only to raise her arm, a signal that she was being followed.

He saw them at once, stumbling into the open meadow, and he leaped at them, hitting one of them at the base of the neck with his club. Bura heard the bones break, like a tree struck by sky light. She ran after Nira, jumping over the dead body of the fallen male, and followed him down the limestone path as he went after the other.

Swinging the short club with all his strength, Nira struck the other male once on the side of his face, killing him as the men of the plains killed the lynx that came down from the hills, and pushed him over the edge.

Bura ran to Nira and wrapped her arms tightly around his waist. She leaned forward to stare into the deep black pit. There was no sound, no echo that came back to them as it did when they tossed rocks off the high ridge.

She looked up at Nira and saw his black eyes studying her. She wanted him to take her into the private, forgotten caves and mate with her, but he didn't seem to hear her silent longing, so she took his hand and brought it up to touch her naked breast.

As she brushed her bare bottom against him and felt his organ swell, she heard his breathing grow rapid and hard.

"You!" Nira said. "You bred with the Yellow Eyes."

Bura shook her head. "No!" she said.

"Your opening is wet from them," he told Bura, pushing her away.

"Nira, they caught me, but I got away. I ran." She was frightened now. "I have mated with no one," she begged, dropping to her knees.

Nira swore at her and tried to kick her away, but she clung to him, knowing that if he left her, she would be banished by his family. No one was allowed to mate with outsiders and come back to the tribe.

"No, Nira! No!" she cried, grabbing his waist and pulling herself up. Her fear gave her surprising strength, and when he wrestled her, she fought back. Her naked body, slippery with sweat, made it harder for him to push her away, but then he seized her by the hair and drew the sharp edge of his quartz stone across her breasts, marking her body, branding her as one who had mated with Yellow Eyes.

Enraged, she kicked out, aiming for his organ. He moaned and doubled over. Unable to stop her rage, Bura hit him again, and this time she seized his thick black hair in her fingers and pulled him forward toward the sheer edge of the limestone cliff. He tried to stop her, but she ducked away, and with the strength gained from long days of gathering wood, she pushed him off the edge. Nira screamed as he tried to seize the thin air, and then he dropped into the dark gorge.

Bura fell onto the hard path and cried, reaching out over the edge as if to pull him from the abyss. Now she had no man, and she knew the elders of the tribe would learn what she had done and would take her life.

All was lost. Her life was over. Standing at the rim of the deep gully, she thought briefly of her mother, of how she had disappointed her own, and then she leaped soundlessly into the void, falling endlessly into black space.

In the morning, word reached the highland huts, and the bodies of Nira and Bura were carried up to the high ground. As the people of the highlands moved away from the limestone cliffs, to better hunting lands farther south, new tribes came into the great meadowland and cut up the earth for planting. The old people remembered the time they left the cliffs, and some talked of the death of the young people. No one remembered their names.

23

"YOU'RE SAFE NOW," KATHY DART said, pulling Jennifer into a gentle embrace. She was smiling, but it seemed to Jennifer that she was also close to tears. "You've had a long journey," she said softly, "but now you're home."

Kathy led her away from the front door and into the center of the living room. The house had once been a barn, and Kathy had stripped it back to its original log beams. The interior was quite grand, with stark, bare-wood walls that swept up to a cathedral ceiling.

The south end of the long room was filled with windows, and Jennifer glimpsed a lake below the house, and more buildings clustered together by a nearby evergreen grove. But her attention was quickly drawn back to the massive stone fireplace that dominated the room. Soft leather chairs and sofas were grouped around the open fireplace.

"This hour is scheduled as personal time. Everyone is off in meditation or sleeping or skating down on the lake. I'm channeling Habasha after dinner. Oh, I'm so glad you're here!" Kathy beamed as she took Jennifer's hands in hers.

She was much more beautiful than Jennifer had remembered, with a clear, perfect complexion. Kathy Dart must be a very happy woman, Jennifer thought.

"We'll have lots of time later to talk, Jennifer." She glanced at Eileen. "I've told Simon I wanted you both in the big house with me. That way we can get together easily to talk. So let's get you settled. You both must be exhausted." Kathy turned and led them across the room.

"Oh, is there somewhere I can make a call to New York?" Jennifer asked. "I should check in with my office." When they arrived in St. Paul, she had called and left a message for Tom that she had arrived safely.

Kathy paused at the entrance to the hallway. "Of course, Jennifer. But I should mention that one of our objectives here on the farm is to separate you from all worldly, everyday concerns. I've found—Habasha has found—that the channeling sessions go much more smoothly if you can concentrate on what is happening here, rather than thinking about outside problems. I'm sure you understand."

"Yes, of course," Jennifer said quickly, embarrassed.

Kathy kept smiling, and added, "When Simon comes in with the luggage, I'll have him show you to my office."

"Simon?" Jennifer asked. "Does he work for you?" She felt Eileen nudge her in the small of her back.

Kathy laughed. "Oh, I don't know if any of us work for each other. Although there are days, as I tell Habasha, when I think I spend my whole life in slave labor for him. No, Simon doesn't work for me." She opened the door leading to the east wing of the barn, where their rooms were located. "We're twin-souls and have been together in previous lifetimes. Now, I guess you'd say we're lovers."

Jennifer's room had a view of the shallow valley that stretched away from the farm. The sun was setting, and its northern light softened the harsh landscape with an orange glow. She stood very still, concentrating on the lovely winter scene.

And then she heard a soft knock on her bedroom door. Without turning her eyes from the scene, she said, "Come in."

"Your luggage," a man's voice replied. Jennifer turned. The man standing in the doorway was silhouetted by the hallway light. She could not see his face, but she knew that he must be Simon.

"Thank you."

He set the bags aside and came to her, pulling off his leather gloves as he approached. His presence filled the room, and she found herself unaccountably giving way to him.

"I'm Simon," he said, "Simon McCloud."

"Yes, I know," she said. "Kathy's friend."

He smiled.

"Don't I know you?" Jennifer asked, staring up at him.

"I don't know. Do you?" He was still smiling.

"I mean, your face is so familiar." He looked like a lumberjack, with a full beard, dark brows, and thick hair that curled out from under a wool cap.

"That's what they all say," he teased, slowly stuffing his gloves into the pockets of his jacket. "And you're . . . who?" he asked politely.

"Jennifer. Jennifer Winters." She could feel her face flush with embarrassment, but still she couldn't take her eyes from him. "I'm sorry I'm staring," she apologized, "but I keep thinking I'm going to remember. Did you go to school in Chicago?" She tried to imagine him on campus.

He laughed then, and his blue eyes sparkled. Jennifer laughed, too. He was so unlike a New Yorker, she thought, immediately friendly and open. So this was the Midwest. No one had a hostile edge.

"I've never been to Chicago. I've never been anywhere, really, except Duluth and St. Paul." He shrugged good-naturedly.

"Well, you just look so familiar," Jennifer replied. Finally able to break her gaze, she glanced out the window. "I was just enjoying the sunset," she explained.

The orange glow had disappeared from the hillside, and now in the fading light, Minnesota's winter landscape looked threatening. Simon came over and stood beside her, staring out at the disappearing day. She was acutely conscious of him near her, of his warmth, and as she watched his breath fog the windowpane, she realized how much he was affecting her.

He broke the stillness. "It does look bleak, doesn't it? Not a night to be outside. But later, after dinner, the moon will come up and the whole valley will be lit. We usually go skating by the lake, build a fire there on the bank, and make hot chocolate and hot buttered rum. Do you skate?" he asked.

"Well, I try."

"Good! I'll help. All of us Minnesotans are born with either skates or skis on our feet. He tapped the glass with his fingernails, making a sharp click. "It's going to be a cold one." Then he grinned and moved away. "I better deliver Eileen's luggage. Kathy said you had a long trip and you need to rest." At the doorway he paused and turned to her. Jennifer had not left the window. "Welcome to the farm, Jennifer. It's your first visit?"

Jennifer nodded. She was searching frantically for something to say that would keep Simon with her.

"It changed my life, coming here," he said. He paused. "I owe my life to Kathy." He looked over at Jennifer and smiled that warm, honest smile. "She'll save you, too. I know." And then he closed the bedroom door and disappeared.

Jennifer did not move. She held her breath in an effort to hold on to his presence, to hold the intimacy of their shared moment. Gradually, she returned to the present, heard distant sounds from the huge old building, heard footsteps and muffled sounds, and took a deep breath, all at once exhausted from the long trip and from the week of tensions. She sat down on the edge of the single bed and pulled off her boots. Then, standing again, she slid off her wool skirt, unhooked her bra, and still in sweater and panties, slid under the heavy blankets and surrendered herself to sleep.

Jennifer felt a hand on her shoulder. Not yet fully awake, she reached out and grabbed the intruder's wrist.

"Jenny, it's me!" Eileen cried. "Ouch!" She fell against the bed. "Wake up, Jenny. Wake up. You're okay. Everything is fine."

Jennifer let go and pulled herself up. "I'm sorry. I was so . . ."

"I know. I knocked, but you didn't answer. I'm sorry I had to disturb you."

"What time is it?" Jennifer asked, rubbing her eyes.

"Around six. You've been asleep for two hours."

"Oh God, I could sleep for a week." Jennifer fell back on her pillow. "It's pitch black out!" she said, staring out of the window.

"It's the country, Jenny. That's what it's like." Eileen moved from her perch on the bed and turned on the desk lamp. "Better?"

"Yes," Jennifer agreed. She sat up. "I guess I'll get dressed. After a shower, I'm sure I'll be okay. Where are the showers, anyway?"

"Down the hall. They're communal."

"Oh, great!" Jennifer yawned. "I won't take a shower at my health club, let alone here."

Eileen shrugged. "Oh, it's not that bad. There are private stalls, if you need them, but Kathy believes we're too culturally bound. This is one way to break down our inhibitions."

"Taking showers with strangers should do it."

"I'm sure you wouldn't mind taking a shower with Simon McCloud." Eileen smiled.

"Why? What do you mean?"

"Oh, I saw that he took his time to 'drop off' your bags."

"Eileen, come on." Jennifer tossed back the blankets and stood. She picked her wool skirt off the back of the chair and stepped into it.

"Well, what were you doing in here?"

"We were watching the sunset," Jennifer replied curtly.

"He's incredible, isn't he?"

"Incredible, how?" Jennifer waited, curious to know what Eileen thought of Simon.

Eileen shrugged. "I don't know. Incredibly 'country,' don't you think? I find it odd that Kathy, who's so sophisticated, would be involved with him. Don't you?"

Jennifer concentrated on unpacking. She pulled a terry-cloth robe from her suitcase.

"Don't you?" Eileen persisted.

"Getting involved with anyone that gorgeous can't be considered too odd," said Jennifer decisively, folding the robe over her arm. She knew she couldn't lie to Eileen about feeling an attraction. Better just to acknowledge it and forget it. "But I also know that he's involved with Kathy Dart, just like I'm involved with Tom. I'm not going to jump the poor guy in some dark corner. Or the shower." Eileen laughed as she walked out, heading for the bathroom.

The showers were empty. Jennifer sighed, thankful for small favors. She remembered how she and Tom had made love in the steamy bathroom back in Brooklyn, and the memory aroused her. To cool down, she turned on the faucet and doused herself with water.

When she came out of the shower room ten minutes later, she was wrapped in towels. She stood in the doorway of the bathroom and glanced down toward the living room to see if the coast was clear.

The door was open at the end of the hall and a shaft of light from the living room filled the entrance. She could hear voices from farther away in the house. There were several people talking and laughing among themselves. Perhaps it was the skaters having a drink before dinner.

Jennifer turned toward her room and saw a figure step into the hallway, coming from the living room. She stopped at once, startled by the sudden sight of the man, and took a deep breath. She wasn't driving herself crazy, she thought, and started to say hello when she realized it wasn't another guest.

The man's size alarmed her. He was immense, larger, it seemed, than the doorway itself, and he was moving slowly toward her, coming at her from the only exit. She backed off, terrified. She was immediately assailed by the odor of sweat and urine.

"Hello," she said, needing to hear her voice, and peered into

the dark hallway, hoping to see his face. But his features were hidden
in the rags he used to keep out the cold. Then she realized who it
was. This was the man she had killed outside of the museum.

He was not dead. He had come to get her, and now he had
her cornered in the hallway. She backed away from him and the
lighted living room, but he kept coming toward her. His body filled
the narrow hallway, squeezed out the light from the living room,
plugged up the exit as if he were a stopper. She was trapped.

"No," she whispered, clutching a towel to her breast. She tried
to scream, but no sound escaped her throat. She waited for the
inhuman rage to take over her body and turn her into a beast, but
this time there was no transformation. She felt no cold draft of air,
no pumping of her muscles. No rage.

Jennifer stumbled against the wall. She reached the end of the
hallway, glanced around for a door, but there was just a window,
sealed against the cold, and beyond it, the darkness of the rural
night. She slid sobbing to the carpet and waited for him to kill her.

"Jennifer, are you all right?" Kathy Dart's voice broke into her
consciousness. She was curled up, shrivering in the corner, and
barely felt Kathy Dart's comforting hands stroke her hair. "It's all
right, Jenny," Kathy whispered. "I am with you. Something frightened you, that's all. You're safe."

"I thought I saw something," she tried to explain, not looking
at Kathy Dart. Jennifer realized then that she had wet herself, and
humiliated, she struggled to a sitting position. She felt like a child.

"Yes?" Kathy waited patiently for an explanation. She knelt
beside Jennifer on the carpet. "Tell me. You saw someone from your
past? Was it Margit?"

Jennifer shook her head. "It was no one I knew. I mean, it
looked like a homeless man. Someone I . . ." She tried to concentrate. "It was weird. I thought it was the man . . ." Jennifer shook
her head, then began to sob. Kathy Dart pulled Jennifer into a
gentle embrace.

"I'm going crazy," Jennifer whispered. "I kill people. I have
conversations with dead people in my apartment. I hallucinate. Oh,
dear God, help me."

Jennifer pulled her head from Kathy's embrace, leaned back
against the wall, and closed her eyes. She felt Kathy reach out and
wipe away her tears. For a moment Jennifer let herself be comforted.

"In the next few days, Jennifer," Kathy said softly, "we will answer these questions and straighten out all the mystery. You are at the edge of great possibilities."

"I'm at the edge of an abyss."

"It is when we look into that abyss that we discover the truth. You are so close, Jennifer."

Jennifer looked up at Kathy Dart. Her eyes gleamed. Her smile emanated confidence and enthusiasm. Jennifer nodded. She would try. "Thank you," she whispered.

"Give yourself a chance," Kathy continued, "to become the great person that is your destiny. I believe there is someone seeking to use your body as a medium into this world. Someone wants to channel through you. Someone wants to 'get out,' and I find that terribly exciting."

"It has only been terrifying for me," Jennifer answered, pulling herself off the hallway floor. She needed another shower.

"I went through this myself, Jennifer," Kathy said calmly. "Habasha wasn't just someone I met by chance in an aisle at the A and P."

"I was happy the way I was," Jennifer answered.

"You only thought you were," Kathy Dart answered back.

"I would rather have been left alone."

"But don't you understand," Kathy said quietly, "this person who wishes to be channeled won't let you be your old self." And then, smiling, she leaned forward and kissed Jennifer softly on her cheek.

"When you're dressed, come into the living room, and we'll talk. There's so much to tell you." Then Kathy Dart nodded good-bye and walked back to the living room, blocking out the light at the end of the hallway as she disappeared from sight.

24

"HI, HOW'YA DOING?" Simon McCloud was suddenly at her side in the living room. "How 'bout a cup of tea?" he asked solicitously.

"Fine. I'm just fine," Jennifer answered, accepting the warm cup. Kathy Dart must have told him what happened in the hallway. "I think I'm finally adjusting to the frozen north," she added. She nodded toward the blazing fire. "That helps a lot. It looks so warm and inviting."

"It's actually a waste of energy." Simon shrugged. "We'd do better closing it down and putting in a wood stove, but Kathy's a great believer in the illusion of the fireplace . . . everyone sitting cozily around it." He smiled, as if amused by the deception.

"Well, I think it's lovely, illusion or not," Jennifer answered back. "Isn't there room for illusions in your life, Simon?" As she sipped her tea, she scanned the room for Eileen.

"Do you want to meet any of these people?" Simon asked, ignoring her question.

"No," Jennifer said truthfully, glancing around at the dozen other guests who were milling around the room. Many of them looked flushed, as if they had just come in from the cold. "Who are they?"

"International consultants. They work with Third World countries, telling their citizens how to act, teaching them to eat with knives and forks, and how to get along with Americans." He shrugged dismissively, then added coolly, "To tell you the truth, I don't pay that much attention to most of the people who come through here. There's a different group nearly every week. This place is like a bus station sometimes. I just stand at the front door, punch tickets, and take money." He reached over and set his cup of tea on an end table.

Jennifer was startled by his candor. "Is that how you consider me . . . and Eileen?"

"No, of course not," he replied. "You're not like these people. You're one of us."

"Us? What do you mean?"

"Us . . . you know." He shrugged. "You and Eileen, and Kathy, of course, and me. I mean, the four of us are linked. Hasn't Kathy told you about all of this?" Suddenly Simon looked worried, as if he had said too much.

Jennifer shook her head and kept her eyes on him.

"Kathy explained what happened to you," he went on. "She told me before you came that we . . . you and I . . . had this . . . connection. She said I'd have an emotional pull toward you." He was staring down at her, and Jennifer returned his gaze. She felt as if she could lose herself in his deep blue eyes.

"What exactly are you saying, Simon?" she found herself asking calmly, though she knew exactly.

They were both sitting now on the window seat at the far end of the room. Jennifer felt as if she and Simon were completely alone. Her heart was pounding.

"Kathy told me how you and I, and she, too, were all once— maybe more than once—connected in another life." He suddenly seemed embarrassed and he looked away.

"Why are you saying this, Simon? What are you suggesting?"

"I'm saying that the moment I saw you I knew I wanted you."

"I don't think Kathy would appreciate hearing that," Jennifer said.

"But she knows," Simon explained. "And she understands. Habasha told her. In a previous life, you and I were living in an Idaho mining town. You were Chinese and married to an old man. I was killed—"

Jennifer stood up. "I don't know anything about that," she said. She knew that she had to get away from Simon. Her desire for him was dizzying. She made an effort to move, but he seized her by the wrist. Jennifer felt faint.

Just then, she spotted Eileen approaching from the other end of the room. "Stop, Simon," she whispered. "Please."

He let go of her wrist.

"There you are! You didn't come and get me after your shower. Hello, Simon." Eileen's eyes took in Jennifer's guilty look, and she smiled.

"I'm sorry, Eileen. I forgot. After my shower, I ran into Kathy."

"It's my fault, Eileen," Simon interrupted. "We got to talking about our shared past lives."

Jennifer took a deep breath and stared into the blazing fire. Simon was smiling at Eileen, enveloping her with his charm. As he explained that he and Jennifer once lived together in an Idaho mining town, he slipped his arm around her in a brief embrace.

Jennifer felt her knees weaken, but she forced herself to recover, to pull away from Simon's embrace. This was crazy. Her emotions were totally out of control.

"And what about me?" Eileen made a face at Simon, fretting about her exclusion.

"Yes, you were with us. Kathy has told you that, hasn't she?" Simon cocked his head.

"Of course she has. I was just teasing." Eileen reached to touch Simon's arm.

But she wasn't teasing, Jennifer realized. Something was wrong. Eileen was upset. But before Jennifer could question her, Simon interrupted, nodding toward the center of the room.

"I think we're ready."

Jennifer turned to see Kathy Dart standing in front of the blazing fire. Many of the other guests had already settled into the leather chairs. Kathy looked up and smiled over to where they stood, and immediately Jennifer stepped away from Eileen and Simon and walked into the circle of chairs. Now she needed distance from everyone.

She squeezed herself between the others on the brown leather couch and turned her full attention to Kathy Dart.

"We have several new people with us this evening," Kathy began, as she introduced Jennifer and Eileen. "As some of you know," she went on, "I like to spend a few minutes each evening before dinner talking about various aspects of parapsychology. To remind everyone again, this is a relatively new discipline that studies extrasensory perception, or ESP; psychokinesis, or PK; and survival phenomena, which include channeling, reincarnation, afterlife evidence—you name it, the list goes on." She paused to smile at the group. "I know that many of you have questions about us and what we are all doing here at the farm. So, let's take a few minutes to answer some of your questions."

Kathy paced slowly back and forth before the small gathering. She was wearing stone-washed jeans and a white cashmere sweater. But despite the casual clothes, Jennifer noted, she was perfectly turned out with pearl earrings and makeup. Her long, glossy black hair was loose and tossed over her shoulder.

"Channeling, to give a definition developed by Jon Klimo in his wonderful book, is that 'process of receiving information from some level of reality other than the ordinary physical one. And this includes messages from any mental source that falls outside of one's own.' "

She paused and grinned down at the group. "Got it?" she asked with a laugh.

Jennifer found herself smiling. She had promised herself that she would be skeptical of everything she heard and saw. But she had to admit that Kathy's warmth and humor made her sound especially convincing.

"But who are the channelers of today?" Kathy went on. "And where are our oracles? Do you think I fit the mold?" She was laughing again.

"Actually, I think I'm a channeler because I'm such a lazy person. It's true, really. My spiritual guides say that lazy people make the best mediums because they don't have an agenda. They're not trying to hit home runs for God." She paced across the hearth and then nodded to one of the guests who had raised a hand.

"But, Kathy," the woman asked, "how did you know that you could channel? How does it actually happen?"

"It really began before I first saw Habasha, but I didn't understand what I was experiencing. I think I was always a channel. For example, I've never been afraid of ghosts or graveyards or horror movies. When I was a child, I wanted to have a ghost as a friend. Even back then, I began to have a sense that I could talk to the dead, and I was drawn to certain people because they seemed somehow to be connected to me.

"I began with automatic writing, which, by the way, is nothing more than doodling. I'd hold a pencil in my hand, usually during a boring college class, and without warning my hand would start moving.

"And I used the Ouija board, even though my priest denounced it as the devil's tool. And in a way he was right to warn people. Ouija boards are not toys. They have great power.

"Once you enter the world of the spiritual, you must tread carefully. I know this sounds a little medieval, but one has to use caution."

"Are all channels alike?" someone asked.

"No, they're not. Think of musical instruments. You can't play keyboard music on a flute, which plays only one note at a time. But you can play Bach on the flute; you can play Bach on the pipe organ. It's just that it sounds different on each instrument.

"Different mediums are like different instruments. Each one has an inherent limitation, but also a unique quality. The sound of a pipe organ, for example, is different than the sound of a piano or a harpsichord. Not better or worse, but different. It's like that with channels. Not all spirits can communicate or even want to communicate through all channels.

"Besides, not all mediums are verbal. Some channels have healing energy. Some sing. Some dance. Isadora Duncan, I believe, was a great channeler."

Jennifer glanced across the room and saw another raised hand. "What about these spirits that I hear talked about?" the woman asked. "Are they around us now? Do we need to worry about them or what?" She laughed nervously.

"No, you don't have to worry," Kathy reassured her. "They are very much like the rest of us. Some are between incarnations. Others will be spirits forever. They may be positive or negative. But they are all angelic forces. Manifestations of higher consciousness.

"And, of course, we have their polar opposites, the demonic forces—spirits consumed by unevolved energy that pulls everyone down. The Greeks summed it up when they talked about the harpies and the sirens. The sirens are the seductors who lure you into actions that are not in your best interest. The harpies shriek guilt and self-hatred into your ear. Both are very real."

"Are these spirits our personal angels?" someone asked.

"No, they're universal. No one owns a spirit. But spirits do befriend and work with certain people, and some of them may represent our spiritual brothers and sisters, or perhaps even higher aspects of ourselves."

"What about all this out-of-body stuff I keep reading about?" another guest asked.

"Very simple. You leave your body and go somewhere else. Where, precisely, we don't know. Remember that the mind is not a physical entity. When we lose consciousness, it is because our mind, or consciousness, is somewhere else."

"But where exactly?" Jennifer heard herself ask.

"We don't know, Jennifer," Kathy said, softening her voice. "The Russians have been studying this phenomenon. I guess they'd like to spy on us by sending people out of their bodies, to go through walls.

"But let's look at it from another angle," she went on. "Let's talk about dreams. Basically, dreams are out-of-body experiences. If you didn't sleep at night, you'd go crazy! The stress of being 'in body' is too great to maintain."

"And reincarnation?" a woman asked. Jennifer found herself nodding. Yes, what about it? she thought.

"Well, technically speaking, you're either in the body—'in carna'—or out of the body—'discarna.' Carna is, literally, the flesh. And death is the ultimate out-of-body experience. But, in fact, we leave our bodies all the time! Sometimes a person's mind is half in one place, half in another. The truth is, it can be in both locations at the same time. You see, the mind is not physical, and so doesn't need to follow the physical limitations of the body. When we talk about being out of body, we're talking about energy that travels.

"So the idea is this: the mind goes out of the body. The body dies, but the mind continues to exist. It is free to form a new relationship with physical matter. A relationship that is not necessarily confined to human form."

As Jennifer sat listening to Kathy Dart, she suddenly felt a curious spasm and saw a clear image of Phoebe Fisher, sitting by the fireplace in her apartment in New York. Phoebe was speaking to her, but Jennifer couldn't hear the words: she saw only that Phoebe was frowning, beckoning her away from the living room of Kathy Dart, telling Jennifer to flee. Jennifer raised her hand to reach for Phoebe's image, and then she felt the warmth of a soft palm, and she looked up to see Kathy Dart lean forward and smile down at her.

"Dinner, Jenny?" she asked.

"Oh, yes, sorry."

"There's no reason to be sorry. Were you trance-channeling?" Kathy teased, smiling.

"I don't know what I was doing," Jennifer admitted, chagrined by her behavior, and by what she thought she had just seen: Phoebe Fisher sitting next to Kathy and warning Jennifer to get away from her.

"Jennifer, I know you have been approached by Simon. I know you two were once lovers."

Jennifer glanced to the channeler, waved her hand and said, "It was a simple misunderstanding."

"It's all right, Jenny. Please, you're getting yourself upset. Of course you are attracted to Simon. He must have told you that we were all once together in a previous life. The physical attraction we have for each other is extremely powerful." Kathy flashed one of her bright, wide smiles and linked her arm into Jennifer's. "And if you two decide you want to make love, please follow your instincts. I don't own him, Jennifer. We're all free to act on our impulses and desires, especially here at the farm. I can't keep you two apart. I wouldn't if I could."

And then she grinned like a schoolgirl.

25

WHEN THEY RETURNED TO the living room after dinner, the furniture had been moved away from the fireplace. Kathy Dart was already sitting in an overstuffed chair in front of the windows on the other side of the room. She was wearing a long white gown and had combed out her black hair so that it fanned over her shoulders. Her only piece of jewelry was a gold chain and the crystal that rested between her breasts. It was the same crystal she had worn when Jennifer first saw her in Washington.

Jennifer slipped into a straight-backed chair away from the others, craning her neck to make sure she had a clear view of Kathy. She wanted to be able to see her when she went into her trance. Eileen had produced a small tape recorder from her purse; unable to find a chair close enough, she slipped to the floor at Kathy's feet.

From her angle against the side wall, Jennifer saw the whole room, and she watched the others as they found seats. Some of the young students who were on work/study programs at the farm came out of the kitchen still wearing aprons over their jeans and slid down as a group against the length of one wall.

Jennifer spotted one young man who looked familiar, and she studied him for a moment, trying to place where she had seen him. He looked like the other students, but with short hair, and the build of an athlete. He looked up at Eileen then and smiled, and Jennifer remembered where she had seen him. He had been the young reporter writing the article about Kathy Dart. They had met briefly outside the meeting room, and he had reminded her of her brother.

Simon stepped into the room, and Jennifer kept herself from looking at him. She was afraid he might walk over and sit beside her, and she did not want him near her, not when Kathy Dart was in her trance and Habasha was speaking.

Simon, however, was busy. He had brought a large pitcher of water and a glass from the kitchen, and he set them down on a small table beside Kathy, who glanced up and smiled briefly at him. When he leaned over and whispered something, she laughed, then he stepped away and took a seat by the fireplace. Kathy turned to the group and asked cheerfully, "Are we all here?"

She glanced around the room, smiling at everyone, and went on. "I'd like to explain to our new people a little of what happens when I do this trance-channel. So everyone who has been with me before please indulge us." She directed attention initially to the row of young students and then went on.

"I begin with a short prayer, and I ask that you join in with me. This enables us to come together as a group, as one being, so to speak. I'll lead the group in an African chant—one of Habasha's chants—that I find pulls Habasha closer to me and, of course, to you as well.

"After the chant, there will be a moment of meditation as I slip into the trance and allow Habasha to come forward. As many of you know, I am elsewhere during the trance; if it were not for these tape recordings, I wouldn't know what was actually said by Habasha."

"Where are you exactly?" someone asked.

"Sleeping, actually," Kathy responded, and they laughed. "I get a good nap while Habasha does all the work." Kathy glanced around the room again, caught Jennifer's eye, and smiled. Then she spoke again to the group. "Usually Habasha has something to say, perhaps a story from his own life, and he'll be prepared for questions. I know that many of you have things you'd like to ask, so please, don't be shy." She looked pointedly at Jennifer. "Oh, you should be aware that Habasha will often use African terms when he speaks," she added. "Later, if you wish, I will explain to you what he has said."

Jennifer felt as if her heart were freezing up inside her. She slipped down farther in the chair but did not take her eyes off Kathy.

"Also, I'd like to request that none of you cross your arms. We don't want to close ourselves off from each other, from the flow of energy in the room."

She smiled, then turned to Simon, who reached over and dimmed the overhead lights. A dozen blue candles had been lit throughout the room, and their small flames flickered in the darkness. "All right," Kathy said softly, "let us begin."

She moved forward to sit on the edge of her chair, lifted her arms, turned the palms of her hands up, and said clearly, "Spirit of light and truth unite us. Inspire our minds and fill our hearts with love. Heal and energize our bodies. Receive our thanks for the many gifts that have come to us. Guide us on the path that we may please and serve thee.

"Holy art Thou, Lord of the Universe. Holy art Thou, the Vast and the Mighty. Lord of the light and of the dark. O Jehovah! O Yahweh! O Abba! O Jesus! O Allah! O Brahma! Be with us today in our work."

Kathy bowed her head for a moment, and when she looked up again her eyes were closed and she chanted:

Ommmmmmmmmmmmmmmmmmmmmmmmmmmmmmmm.
Ommmmmmmmmmmmmmmmmmmmmmmmmmmmmmmm.
Ommmmmmmmmmmmmmmmmmmmmmmmmmmmmmmm.

She fell silent, rocking gently back and forth on the edge of the chair.

Then her own sweet voice was given over to the voice of Habasha, the ancient African, a strong, full voice that roared into the silent gathering.

"I am Habasha, the great one! How are my dear friends of America? *Tenayistilligan.*"

"*Tenayistilligan,*" a few replied. "*Tiru no.*"

"*Ameseghinallehu,*" Habasha answered.

Kathy turned her head slowly from left to right. Her eyes were open, and they seemed even larger than usual. So she was not going to channel with her eyes closed, as Phoebe Fisher had done.

"We are very well, Habasha. *Ameseghinallehu,*" Simon said quickly, and there were a few other soft, mumbled greetings from the students and from Eileen. But most of the audience sat silent, staring up at Kathy Dart.

"I am happy to be with you today," Habasha went on in his strong bass voice.

"I take pleasure to say that there is amongst you this evening one who has singular spiritual gifts, which, in due time, will manifest themselves to the benefit of your society. We are certain that all of you who have committed yourselves to the path of enlightenment shall know more and more with each day that comes, and you shall soon be in positions to shed much light, from the light which you possess, on where there is great darkness in this world.

"And, therefore, let us say that by taking care of your own need to know, you sooner will take care of others who need to know, for this light which you acquire for yourself will be the light that shines for others.

"For when you are illuminated you are like a light that shines. Wherever you go, if there is darkness, your own light will shine.

"You have come to the light, my dear friends, and you will go to another place. And we congratulate you for doing this goodness in our world.

"Let the truth be your essence. Let the truth lead you to your higher self. Know yourself and let that truth flow through your consciousness.

"As for those who will not understand, some prefer the darkness. Remember, my dear friends, that all those who walk in the shadows do so by their own choosing. We ask that you will not be followers. Neither let yourselves be leaders. For if you are a follower you are standing in someone else's shadow; if you are a leader, you are casting a shadow upon others.

"We commend to you this work and say: Do not hope for perfection. Do not seek a perfect heaven where all things will lead forever, without fault and without flaw, without need of further thought, or further exercise.

"All life, my dear friends, is an adventure. It is an adventure! Indeed, to know everything that was ever going to be, to have absolute and total knowledge—if you could have that knowledge, would it not deprive you of a great sense of adventure?

"If one knows everything, what more can one know? If one has done everything, what more can one do? We cannot know the end of knowledge, and that is the mystery of existence. How much power is in the universe? How much gold is in the mountain? How much love is in your soul? It is all there. The great adventure of life is to find out how much there is, and the only way you can find out is to start to use it, start to spend it. Truth is. It is all here, waiting for your adventure and your discovery."

Habasha suddenly fell silent and Kathy Dart rocked in the soft chair, then sat back, as if exhausted by the long discourse. She placed her arms on the chair's arms, raised her head and again in that strong voice asked, "If any of you have questions, I will try to answer them. Speak up!" Her eyes were now closed.

"What is the purpose of life, then?" came a voice from one of the front rows of chairs.

"*Woizerit*," Habasha answered, "the process of living is living."

"What about past lives?" Jennifer spoke up. "My past lives."

"You may have past lives, or not, *Woizerit*. You may still be living your past lives. People live different lives simultaneously."

"What about our spirit, then? I mean, how can our spirit, or our soul, whatever we call it, be everywhere at once?"

"Each of your lives is lived with but a part of your total soul," Habasha replied.

"But then how can we have good lives and bad lives?" Jennifer asked immediately.

"If those lives are beautiful and benign and contribute something to the lives they are living now, on this plane, then I think the answer is that you consider them gifted. If the lives they are living on other planes create conflict with what they are trying to do here, then we consider them to be mentally and emotionally disturbed. And they all are the result of lives you have lived before, in other lifetimes."

"What do you mean," one of the men asked. "Other planes?"

Kathy Dart slowly turned her face in the direction of the speaker and Habasha said, "Other planes are dimensions beyond our existence here. These planes, or dimensions, are not necessarily stacked upon each other. Different planes may exist in the same place. Heaven and hell exist in exactly the same place. People used to think that heaven was up, and hell was down. But two people can be sitting together on a sofa, and one can be in hell, the other in heaven."

"Who or what are extraterrestrials?" Jennifer asked, thinking of Phoebe Fisher's Dance.

"Extraterrestrials are bound by the specifics of a time and the physical laws that govern their particular planes, wherever they are, but once they transcend those planes, they may be bounded by other considerations, such as weightlessness.

"We are all bound by laws. In terms of time travel, you have to know that time stands still and matter moves through it. Time does not move. Time simply is. Because all things exist now, there is no other time but now in any direction or plane. Therefore, the phenomenon of time is better understood as the distance between nows."

"But if you have a past life," Jennifer asked, pushing the point, "how would that be? Would you have a past life now?"

"Where did you put your past life?" Habasha challenged. "Did you hide it under your bed? Where did it go? Does the past just dissolve? Does it disappear? Where is yesterday?"

"It's used up," Jennifer responded, anxious to hear where the argument might lead.

"You cannot destroy anything, only change it. Can you say that the whole of yesterday is just banished from the face of existence? And for that matter, what about tomorrow? Is it all being re-created for you to experience anew?"

Kathy Dart sat back again in the chair. She was nodding her head, as if Habasha had summed up the question.

"Is it tomorrow already?" the young reporter asked from the floor.

"Yes."

"I'm still confused," Jennifer interrupted. "If in a previous experience you lived completely in the past—as we usually understand the past—then are you simultaneously living that past life as you are living this present life?"

"Perhaps. Let's talk about the nature of existence. Is it physical or mental?"

"Both," Jennifer answered.

"How much of life does your physical body encounter?"

"Very little, I guess. I mean, just where I am. Who I am."

"And your mind embrace?"

"More."

"More! Indeed it does. Your body experiences only the physical now. So everything about the nature of your existence is a reality of the mind. It is a reality of the spirit."

Kathy Dart suddenly sat forward again and gestured with both arms, then Habasha said loudly to Jennifer, "Do you love anyone?" he asked abruptly. Kathy's head was tilted up, and her eyes were now closed, but still Jennifer tensed.

"Yes," she whispered, thinking immediately of Tom.

"But you don't at this moment have a physical relationship with that person, do you?

Jennifer shook her head.

"No, you only have that physical relationship when your bodies touch. The real nature of this love is spiritual. If you did not exist as a spirit, then that love would cease to exist the moment your bodies ceased to touch. If you have knowledge of the world, if you have a sense of the past or the future, if you have a sense of the meaning of things, the purpose of life, it is only because of spiritual awareness. That is the nature of existence.

"And what about that?" Habasha asked next. "If you remember your life, do you remember it chronologically?"

Jennifer shook her head.

"No! You remember the most important things first. The most important thing that ever happened to you might have occurred many years ago. It might be easier for you to remember something that happened when you were twenty than something that happened two weeks ago. Or yesterday.

"Indeed, something that happened to you as a child might be much more important than what you do now. And something that happened to you in ancient Egypt or Atlantis or Greece might be stronger in your consciousness now than what you do today, here on the farm."

"That's what I mean," Jennifer said quickly. "If I had another life in ancient Egypt, or whatever, and that feeling is very strong in me, does that means it is taking place right now, while I am also living this life?"

"It couldn't be very ancient if you're still thinking about it," Habasha said, and around them everyone laughed.

"No, it couldn't," Jennifer admitted, smiling.

"It's obviously contemporary, then."

"How do you explain history books," Jennifer went on, sensing that she had trapped Habasha in her argument.

"History deals with linear time."

"Chronological?"

"Yes. You must understand that what is called 'ancient Egypt' is only ancient because it is measured relative to this date in history. It seems ancient, but it did not end; it continues to exist in another time dimension, another part of the now, a part other than the physical plane you occupy at this moment."

"Habasha, why are you here?" one of the women students asked. "Why did you come to earth again?"

Jennifer glanced from the student back to Kathy Dart, who was slowly nodding before Habasha replied.

"Many have asked me that, *Woizerit*. Some say, 'Habasha, do you not have a better place to go than here on this planet, at this time? Is there no paradise that awaits you? Is there no heaven in which you would rather be? Why would you come here? Why?'

"Because," Habasha answered himself, "sometimes we see wonderful things happening. We cannot help the whole planet, but we can help some of the planet, and you seem more than willing to let us be a part of your lives. I am pleased. Pleased with what I hear, pleased with what I see.

"My message to you is go where you are wanted. My message to you is that there are some people on this planet who really want what you have to offer, and they will love you and thank you and work with you if you will look for them. We spirits look for those who are willing to work with us and to receive us, and that brings us pleasure because then what we have to share is meaningful.

"And I say, too, there are people on this planet, among your friends and acquaintances, who do not wish you well, who plot against you, and will cause you pain." Kathy Dart raised one hand, and Habasha whispered, "I warn you. I have come now to warn you."

"Who?" Jennifer asked at once.

"I believe, *Woizerit*, that you do know."

"Who is trying to harm me? I don't know!" she said, raising her voice.

"You are an unusual one, *Woizerit*," Habasha said. His voice had slowed its cadence. "I see spirits, good and evil, who surround your aura and fight to dominate your soul. Do not be afraid. You are in good hands. Here at the farm, the healing graces will conquer the evil that confronts your mind. Much is being asked of you, *Woizerit*. You have suffered. You must be careful." Kathy Dart raised her hand, cautioning her. Her head was cocked, as if still listening to a faraway voice.

"How do I protect myself, Habasha?" Jennifer asked, pulling his attention again in her direction. "From these evil spirits?"

"You want answers always, *Woizerit*. Answers are only part of the solution. What is more important are the questions." His voice had shifted. There was an edge of anger in his tone.

Jennifer felt it but kept pushing. "I need the answers," she insisted. "My life, this life, you say, is in danger." She caught herself from saying more. She glanced at Eileen and saw her friend furiously shaking her head.

"He who seeks danger receives it. He who looks for happiness finds it. Your unconscious has been responsible for getting you where you are. So you say that the unconscious part of you is somehow manipulating your affairs. Perhaps you are more responsible for your actions than you know. But how can you come to a place in life where you are able to take conscious control of your life and not be the victim?"

Habasha stopped speaking. Kathy Dart's eyes were open again, and they were blazing, as if blue candles were shining from the irises.

Habasha stopped speaking, and Kathy Dart suddenly stood and stepped away from the chair. Eileen and several of the young students pulled back to give her room, but Kathy moved with the assurance of a sleepwalker through the crowded room.

She had turned away from the sofa, turned toward the wall of students, and Jennifer knew at once that she was coming for her. She should have left when she had the chance, she told herself. Now she couldn't move. It seemed as if she were frozen to her chair.

Kathy Dart stepped to where Jennifer was seated and, clasping her hands together, raised them to her neck and carefully took off her crystal. Grasping the stone, she placed her hands gently on top of Jennifer's head. Jennifer closed her eyes, afraid of what was coming, afraid of all the faces watching her.

"O spirits of the past, spirits of our lives, leave this woman, my *Woizerit*. I implore you in the names of all our gods to seek peace with her. Rise up now and flee us. Rise up and flee us, I, Habasha, ancient of ancient, Dryopithecine, Cro-Magnon, warrior of Atlantis, poet of Greece, priest and lover, knight of the Round Table, Crusader for Christ, pioneer, and profiteer, command the evil spirits that possess this woman to flee this plane, these dimensions, this human body."

Habasha's voice had risen. It filled her mind and rang in her ears. She felt the pressure of Kathy's hands on her head, felt the weight of the crystal, and then she felt the fire. It started in the tips of her toes, seared the soles of her feet, then snaked up through her legs and thighs. It tore her flesh from her bones, flowing to the center of her body in a ball of flame.

She heard her own cries of pain as the fire consumed her body. Flames licked her breasts, rose up around her throat, and set her hair on fire.

Kathy Dart grabbed her then, before she fell, before she disappeared into the shock and pain.

Nada waited for the sun. She had made her paint from the reddish-brown clay by the river's edge and carried it back to the cave. Now, stacking the clay onto thick green palm leaves, she carried the paints to the wide back wall that faced south. Soon the sun would reach the entrance of the cave, and she would have only a few hours of sunlight in which to paint clearly the pictures that exploded like stars in her mind and filled her up. She could almost taste her desire to depict the scenes of battle that she'd heard as a child, the great battles between her people and the hunters from the north.

Ubba had called her to his side when he saw the pictures she had carved on the cave walls and told her to use her magic hands to paint the battle so that his sons, and the sons of his sons, would see what a warrior he was.

"No man among us will forget the day we battled and killed the Saavas," he whispered, "and they will remember me when my spirit leaves the earth and goes to sing with the birds."

Her mother's heart had swelled with pride, and she, too, had felt her heart fill. She knew she would never be hungry again or want for a warm bed, for Ubba would take her into his own cave and give her to his son, Ma-Ma.

But with the excitement was fear. If Ubba did not like the sketches on the wall, if something displeased him, then he would banish her from the clan. She knew of others who hid in the woods, who slept without fire, and stayed in trees to save themselves from the wild beasts. Sometimes she caught glimpses of their shadows, following the clan as it migrated with the sun, trekking north after the bears came out of the trees and the frozen north to slap at the fish in the swift waters of the Twin Rivers.

Stories were told in the depth of the caves, stories of Ma-Ta and her brother Ta-Ma. Stories told, too, of Zuua and Chaa and the sons of the old woman Arrr, who was killed by the Spirits, struck down with the fiery flash of lightning. Ubba had banished her male offspring to the forest, fearful that the Spirits would strike again with flaming sky-bolts.

As Nada got ready to begin, others of the clan left their fishing and came up from the river to sit hunched at the entrance of the cave. They sat and watched her with their large brown eyes, waiting for her magic on the wall. Nada paid them no mind, though she was aware of their silent looks. She felt proud, though she did not know the word for her feeling, and busied herself with her drawing tools, slivers of rock that she sharpened herself.

Ubba approached the hillside with the aid of a bone, helped, too, by the sons of his sons, who huddled around him and bayed for favors. One carried a stool cut from the trunk of a tree. A dozen men had labored with the tree stump and fashioned for him a round chair, smoothed with river water and the oil of pigs.

Now it took three of the sons of the sons to carry the chair up the hillside to the flat entrance of the new cave. Nada waited there, hunched beside the gray cave wall.

She waited for Ubba to begin his tale of fighting the Saavas. As he remembered his battles, he told of how he fought with blood dripping into his mouth. It was a tale Nada knew, a long story that she had first heard when she still sucked her mother's teat. Still, she listened, tried to find the pictures in her mind. She tried to summon up the images of Ubba's past, the evil dreams that had come to him, and followed him even now, many winters after the spear had sailed through the jungle trees and struck his throat, leaving him to whisper for the rest of his life. She listened with her eyes closed, still sitting on her haunches, thinking of him as a young man, fleet as the deer of the north.

Ubba stopped. The tale was told, and now the brown eyes of the clan all turned to her. She waited, pleased that she possessed the truth of his tale in her mind, held as she might hold a bird from a net in her fingers.

She lifted the slivers of rock crystal and went swiftly to work, dipping their sharp edges into the red clay. She drew and drew, dancing before the crowd of clansmen, as excited as she was by the painting. When she had filled the back wall with the story of battle, she stepped away from the pictures, exhausted and afraid of Ubba's judgment.

She sat again on the heels of her bare feet and rocked back, not daring to look up at the great man as he was lifted from his stool to peer up at the red clay drawings.

He paused at each figure, touching none, as he carefully walked the length of the south wall, seeing the story of his battle there in the pictures she had made of red clay. Then the old man stepped close to her and lifted her chin with his crippled hand.

"Nada, you tell the truth," he whispered. And he motioned to his eldest grandchild, the son of his daughter Noo, and said, "She is yours."

Nada fell to her knees in front of the warrior king and kissed his feet, as she had seen other females do when receiving a great honor from their leader. She was saved. Her mother and sister were saved. She let herself be lifted up by Ubba's grandson, and she glanced quickly at her mother as she was led away to his bed of skins. Nada's eyes sparkled with joy, for she had been saved by her magic fingers, and now the children she bore would someday be leaders of the people who lived beside the Twin Rivers.

26

KATHY WAS WAITING FOR Jennifer when she came into the dining room for breakfast the next morning. Several of the other guests were already serving themselves from the buffet table, but the house was still quiet. It was not yet seven o'clock.

"Why don't we have some quiet time for ourselves," Kathy whispered, coming up to Jennifer and kissing her lightly on the cheek. "How do you feel?"

Jennifer nodded, too distraught even to speak. She let Kathy direct her into a small area off the dining room.

"This used to be the hothouse when the farm was working," Kathy explained, "but I use it a lot during the cold months. It gets most of the winter sun."

The bright, sunny room had a vaulted ceiling, large windows, a tiled floor that Jennifer realized was also heated, thick Indian throw rugs, and oversized chairs.

"Sit here, please," she went on, motioning Jennifer to a deep chair next to a glass table. "Nanci will serve us."

Jennifer looked up to see a young woman who had been in the audience during the last channeling session.

"Jennifer, this is Nanci Stern. Nanci is teaching our New Age dance classes. That's something I wish you would try. She also is taking my course on the secrets of the shamans, learning how to bridge the communication gap between humans and other life forms. Aren't you, Nanci?"

The young woman nodded shyly as she placed a teapot on the glass-topped table.

"The shamans? Who are they?" Jennifer asked, unfolding a damask napkin on her lap.

"You've heard the term?"

"Yes, I guess I have," Jennifer admitted, shrugging. "I mean, somewhere in the recesses of my mind. I must have heard it in an anthropology class I took once." Again, she felt like a child in a room full of adults.

"Well, primitive cultures had a person whose role was to act as the intermediary between the spirit realm and the society. The shaman altered his or her condition by chanting, singing, or eating psychoactive plants. There have been shamanlike figures in cultures as diverse as Siberia and the West Indies. Voodoo is a good example that's close to home."

"And you," said Jennifer.

"Yes, of course. And other channelers like me. In a way, we're modern-day shamans. We interpret the other realm, the spirit world, for people." She nodded toward Nanci, who had gone into the other room. "She has a real gift," Kathy continued, her eyes shining. "I'm very proud of her. And she has a wonderful relationship with Simon."

Jennifer kept her eyes down as Kathy poured tea for both of them.

"They've been lovers now for about three weeks. It's wonderful to watch, to see their affection for each other grow and develop. Both of them have so much to give."

"I thought you said that you and Simon were . . ."

"Lovers?" Kathy glanced over at Jennifer as she set down the teapot.

"Yes." Jennifer tried to return Kathy's gaze, but the woman's steady, unblinking blue eyes unnerved her and she looked out the windows instead. Through the foggy glass she could see an edge of the frozen lake, and in the distance, farm fields, all bare and snow covered on the bright winter morning.

"We are, Jennifer, and so are Nanci and Simon. It isn't a secret, you know." Nanci returned with glasses of orange juice and plates of scrambled eggs, then retreated quickly.

"I'm sorry," Jennifer began. "I didn't mean to imply—"

"Nor are we promiscuous here on the farm."

Now Jennifer looked across at Kathy Dart and simply raised her eyebrows. "What about AIDS?"

"What about it?"

Jennifer shrugged. "I'm sorry," she said simply. "This is none of my business."

"But it is!" Kathy insisted, leaning across the table. She sat poised, holding her knife and fork above the heavy brown ceramic plate. "All of you, us, are connected. Nanci, Simon, you, me, and

Eileen. We are all part of the oversoul, and therefore, there's a natural attraction—a physical attraction—among us."

"Has Eileen slept with Simon?" Jennifer asked without thinking, then quickly added, "I'm sorry. That, too, isn't my concern." She stared down at her food.

"I don't know. I haven't asked her. It doesn't matter, does it?"

"Of course not." Jennifer lifted her fork and tried to eat. She wanted only to get through breakfast, but she realized she had suddenly lost her appetite.

"It is your business, Jennifer, and that is what I am trying to tell you. I know you're attracted to Simon. I know that he is attracted to you. I am simply saying that there is nothing wrong with that. It is normal! It is healthy! It is right!"

"I'm sorry, that's not the way I conduct my life." Jennifer poked at her eggs with her fork, feeling better now that she had answered back.

"Simon approached you last night, didn't he?"

"Yes. You know that."

"But I don't know what happened between you."

"Nothing."

"Perhaps not."

Jennifer glanced over at Kathy, furious now. "Nothing happened, Kathy," she insisted.

"It is not necessary for Simon to physically sleep with you, Jennifer, for something to happen."

Jennifer dropped her knife and fork and pushed back her chair.

"Don't run away from yourself, Jenny."

"I'm sorry. I'm sorry I came here. I will not be . . . I do not have to put up with this." She would pack and leave, she decided. If she had to, she'd walk to the airport, anything to get away from these people.

But Kathy seized her wrist and forced Jennifer back down into her chair.

"I'm sorry," she said firmly. "But I want you to carefully think about what you are planning to do."

"And what am I planning?" Jennifer shouted.

"You want to leave. You want to run away," Kathy calmly told her. "But you cannot escape. It doesn't do you any good to flee from here. You aren't going to escape your past—all those lives you have already lived, in other generations, at other times."

"I'm afraid of you," Jennifer told her.

Kathy nodded. "Of course you are. I would be afraid, too, if I were you. But it is only through fear and adversity that the soul is enriched. When we are totally happy, wrapped up in our own affairs, we float through life and nothing is impressed upon our souls. We do not gain in wisdom."

Fear swept through Jennifer's body. "You are going to hurt me," she said. "I know you are. I can feel it." Yet she continued to sit there, unmoving. She had the sudden revelation that no one could hurt her, that she had conquered this woman before, in her past.

"We have been connected, Jenny, I keep telling you this," Kathy Dart said patiently, but there was an edge now in her voice. "And the only way we are going to understand the connection, see what the problem is, is to go back in time and look at who you were and how we are all linked. What is the cosmic connection?" She smiled softly. "In a way, we have already begun. Habasha has cast out the negative spirits in your body. The pain and consuming fire you felt last night when Habasha touched you through my fingers was his way of expelling the evil spirits from your body."

"You admit that you're going to hurt me," Jennifer insisted again, staring at Kathy.

"The truth hurts, yes," Kathy agreed, nodding. "But it's also the only way that you can overcome this rage that is within you."

"Are you talking about acupuncture?" Jennifer asked. "Maybe that's how you're going to hurt me."

"It does hurt a little," Kathy said, nodding, "I won't lie to you. But the pain dissolves quickly once the needles are absorbed by the body. It's like a pin prick, nothing more."

"Then what happens?"

"I use what is called periosteal acupuncture, placing the needle deeper into the body. It is hardly more painful than the simple tip contact, and it goes only an inch into the skin. I use a collection of needles, either silver or gold, but I do not use as many needles as, say, a normal acupuncturist. I am seeking other answers.

"The body remembers, Jenny. You've been told this, I know. But it's true. Your spirit carries forward, from one generation to the next, the history of your lives on earth."

"You just put these needles into me and I start sputtering out past lives?"

Kathy Dart shook her head. "No, it's done much more subtly. I twist the needles as my spirit guides instruct me, and this in turn stimulates your recall. You'll 'see' what lives you have lived, as if you were watching a movie."

"Will you be watching the movie, too?"

"Well, I won't see your lives, but we can discuss the images, if you like. We are set up to record what is said in the sessions— you'll want to listen to yourself again afterward."

"It doesn't seem possible," Jennifer said.

"Yes, I know." Kathy Dart sank back in the chair and looked across the frozen landscape of Minnesota. Her customary confidence and poise had slipped away, and Jennifer thought she saw a flash of fear in those brilliant blue eyes. "The truth is," Kathy admitted, "that I don't understand my own ability, but I fear it. I never wanted it."

At that moment Kathy Dart looked lost, a slender, delicate young woman overwhelmed by her life. She was very beautiful, Jennifer noticed again, in a way that had nothing to do with style or fashion. She was blessed with pure white skin and fine small features, and ironically, her clarity of expression hid her very heart and soul. Jennifer knew she could never fathom what Kathy was really thinking.

"Once Habasha walked into my life," Kathy went on, "nothing stayed the same. I left my husband. I left my friends and my teaching career. When I moved back here with my daughter, who was just seven, I had no money, no plans of any kind, but Habasha told me to go home to Minnesota. I was to build a new life, here on the banks of the St. Croix River."

Kathy glanced over at Jennifer. "This is where I was born, you know," she explained. "My grandparents and parents farmed this land. Then my brother, Eric, took over and mortgaged all the five hundred acres and lost the place. I was able to buy just this old barn and the outbuildings at a public auction four years ago. I used all the money I had from my divorce settlement to buy back my home. I had to do it. Habasha told me I would only find real happiness by being close to my roots. In the spring I love to go outside when the fields are being plowed and smell the fresh earth as it turns. It's all so wonderful and right."

Kathy Dart stopped talking and Jennifer reached over and took hold of her hand.

"None of this is very easy, Jenny, I know. But we have to go where our hearts tell us. We have to listen to our own spirits and respond to their directions. We are not alone. That's what you, what

I, what we all have to remember. We have each other. You must know that. You came here to the farm in search of the truth."

"The truth can be very frightening. Sometimes, I guess, I'd rather turn my back on it, walk away."

"But you don't feel that way now, do you?" Kathy asked, searching Jennifer's face with her eyes.

Jennifer nodded. "I don't think I fully realized I couldn't hide from the truth until last night, until Habasha touched me. When I felt the burning—"

"His energy hurt you. He was casting off the evil guides that had surrounded your aura. Jennifer." Kathy squeezed Jennifer's hand. "He has set you free, Jenny!"

Jennifer stared back into Kathy's eyes and said firmly, resolve in her decision, "I'm ready, Kathy. I want to know who is trying to reach me. I want to end my misery. I want to know the truth, whatever it means for my life."

27

IN A SMALL, ENCLOSED room off the living room, Jennifer slipped behind a screen and took off her clothes, then draped herself in a warm flannel sheet.

"This used to be the birthing room on the farm," Kathy said. "When a mare or cow went into labor, she was brought into this section of the barn. It was always the warmest, because it was in the center."

She was carrying a small tray on which a dozen silver and gold needles floated in alcohol, next to a package of gauze. She set it down near the wide, padded massage table in the middle of the room.

"Would you prefer it if someone else were here?" she asked, as Jennifer emerged. "Eileen, for example?"

"Oh, no. I'd be too frightened."

Kathy laughed. "Well, some people are frightened to be alone when they go through the treatment."

"What's it going to be like?" Jennifer asked as she approached the table. There was very little furniture in the clinic: a few white steel cabinets, a wash basin, and open shelves filled with flannel and cotton sheets and stacks of white towels.

"It's a different experience for everyone. For me, it went very slowly. Each vision, each lifetime took several hours to view; it took me a month of past-life treatment to complete my history. For others—Eileen, for example—we went through centuries in a matter of minutes. She could only get a glimpse of herself, she said. Often, it was just a suggestion that she had been there somewhere—among the Romans, or the Irish." Kathy shrugged. "It depends. A man named Howard, who is doing research on the right side of the brain, has a thesis that the more creative you are, the more vivid your recollections will be.

"Also, you might not recall anything during this first session.

Your defenses may try to protect you, keep you from knowing. It might take several sessions before we break through the median points and reach what I call the Core Existence, the center of a past-life experience. Think of it this way, Jenny. Your past lives are like blisters. Once I prick a blister with my golden needle, you'll be able to 'see' the lifetime that you have already lived."

"How can you find the right blisters?"

"Oh, that's easy. My spirit guides will tell me where to place the needles. They know where your past lives are recorded in your body. Ready?" She smiled reassuringly at Jennifer. "I want to meditate before we begin."

"What will I feel?" Jennifer asked, delaying.

"It depends. If you feel, for example, a sudden rush of warmth, you're getting a negative reaction from hostile spirits. I call them the little devils." Kathy Dart smiled down at Jennifer. She had moved a tall stool closer to the massage table and was perched on its edge.

"What if we don't find anything?"

"Is that what's worrying you?" Kathy asked. "That you won't recall?"

Jennifer shrugged. "That there won't be anything, period! No past lives."

Kathy Dart nodded, then said thoughtfully. "It's never happened. I have never had a patient who didn't recall a previous existence. Some, of course, are much more vivid than others. Some are lives of great importance, but the majority, I'd say, are ordinary lives: farmers, serfs, one or two adventurous types, a bandit in one generation, a thief in another."

"Have you had any patients who share my experience?" Jennifer asked. "That strange rage and physical power?"

Kathy Dart picked up a silver needle from the white towel and replaced it carefully. "That's what frightens you, isn't it? That somehow I'll tap a certan cell in your body and you'll become—"

"A raging primitive, yes." She looked directly at Kathy Dart.

"That won't happen."

"How do you know?" Jennifer challenged.

"Because nothing like that has ever happened to me, or to anyone I have treated. You will 'see' your past, but you won't become it. No one ever has."

"No one else is me. I'm the one who has the out-of-the-blue surges."

"But they are not out of the blue. They only occur when you're threatened. Do you feel threatened now?"

Jennifer shook her head, remembering how she had even tried to summon up her rage in the dark hallway the previous evening.

"Perhaps what has happened is that you feel safe on the farm. You're not in a hostile environment, and your senses intuitively know that." Kathy shrugged. "It's really as simple as that."

Jennifer nodded. Perhaps that was it. She remembered the computer salesman at the motel. She would never have touched him if he hadn't threatened her.

"Look, you'll be fully conscious," Kathy explained. "If you begin to feel that you're losing control in any way, I'll stop." She hesitated. "Are you sure you wouldn't like Eileen to be with you?"

Jennifer shook her head. "No, thank you. I better go at this alone. Aren't you afraid my monster self will attack you?"

Kathy Dart laughed. "Not me! I've got Habasha, and he's king of the jungle. He told me so." She swung Jennifer's legs up onto the wide table. "Now, relax," she instructed.

"Are you kidding?"

"Try," Kathy Dart insisted. "I'll spend a moment in meditation and channel my spirits." She moved around to the end of the table and out of Jennifer's line of sight.

Jennifer closed her eyes and took long breaths. She would try, she told herself. She would try to surrender herself; maybe Kathy Dart could find out what was happening to her body.

"Try not to think," Kathy whispered. "Just let your mind flow. Be at peace."

Jennifer took another deep breath. She felt a wave of cold air cross her body, then a hot flash. She listened to Kathy sitting behind her at the head of the table and tried to match her steady breathing. Then her thoughts shifted, and Jennifer let herself go with them. She was listening to the house, but only occasionally did a muffled noise filter into the room. The acoustic tile on the walls told her the barn was soundproofed. She felt far away from the world, far away from time. And happy. So safe.

Kathy had moved around the table to her side.

"I am ready," she whispered to Jennifer, but her voice had changed, become more confident. "My guides have told me where to seek your lives." She reached up for the edge of the flannel sheet and pulled it off Jennifer's shoulder, then tucked it in at her waist. Jennifer did not open her eyes.

"I will place the first needles at pressure points on your shoulders and chest," Kathy said calmly, "and later in your third eye, which is the center of your forehead. You will experience some pain, as I mentioned, but it will pass. Also, you will feel that the needles are warm. That is because I am taking a ball of dried wormwood—it's an herb—and I'm placing it on top of the needle's handle. Then I light it when the needle is inserted. The warmth will aid in the stimulation of your memory cells."

"Tell me when you're about to begin," Jennifer asked.

"I've already begun."

Jennifer opened her eyes and saw two long needles protruding from her chest.

"Jesus," she whispered.

Kathy smiled sweetly and asked, "Do you want to watch?"

"I don't know. Do I?" She felt better now that she had actually seen the needles in her body. "Ouch! What happened?" Jennifer blinked back tears.

"Nothing. I stimulated your cells by twisting the needles, that's all." She reached across to select another needle, slipping it behind Jennifer's right ear.

"I don't feel a thing," Jennifer whispered. At that moment she felt wonderful, warm and comfortable.

"Of course not. You're doing just fine." She smiled down at Jennifer. "Soon you'll begin to see your lives unfold. Take another deep breath."

She did.

"This will help stimulate your memory."

"I'm getting excited," Jennifer said, smiling.

"I've turned on the tape recorder, so speak up when you notice anything. Sometimes it's only an odor or taste that comes back to us from another time. Anyway, speak up, talk to me, and we'll have all the memories recorded for you."

Jennifer waited, her eyes closed again. She felt Kathy's soft hands on her body, felt another fine needle pinch the skin between her breasts, but there was no pain. Then Kathy drew the sheet up over the tops of the half dozen needles, and when Jennifer opened her eyes, it looked as if she were enclosed inside a tent.

"Your spirits are arranging themselves, battling for position, so to speak," Kathy explained as Jennifer felt another wave of cold air. "Do you see anything?"

Jennifer shook her head. "No," she giggled. "I feel as if I'm waiting for my life to begin or something."

"Well, you are. But don't be afraid. You won't see anything that you don't want to see. Our bodies protect us in that way." She fell silent.

Jennifer felt herself drifting off, as if she were taking a morning nap. She started to resist the urge to lose consciousness but remembered that Kathy had told her to let her mind wander, to let it find its own place in the depths of her subconscious. She stopped thinking. She forgot about her body and focused her attention on trying not to think. Everything slipped away. She felt as if she were falling gently through the space of her memories, dropping and dropping without fear. Then she was floating free of her body, like the night she was attacked and was looking down at herself on the operating table.

"You're beginning to recall," Kathy said, speaking, it seemed, from across the room. "I see flashes of your life. I'm picking them up."

"What?" Jennifer stirred but did not open her eyes. She smelled eucalyptus.

"Are you getting any reactions? Any sensations?"

Jennifer nodded. "Yes," she whispered. "It seems I'm in a tropical jungle or something. I can smell fruit, figs particularly. I am high up, sitting in a tree, I think." She shook her head as the image faded, then quickly was replaced with a stronger, more vivid picture. "I'm seeing primitive people. Very primitive people. They are running, throwing spears at each other. It's so weird. I mean, I don't know." Jennifer smiled, amused by the images that floated to the surface of her memory.

"Keep talking," Kathy instructed. "What else do you see?"

"I don't know. I mean, I'm seeing lots of things. I see a little girl. I know it's me, somehow. I am pounding on an animal's skull. Someone is going for me. A woman. She's running fast. My father is there, I think. It's all whirling past me, out of control." Jennifer felt her body tense, opened her eyes. She saw that Kathy had pulled away the flannel sheet and was gently twisting a few of the gold needles.

"Don't open your eyes. Don't stir. Everything is fine, just as it should be. Talk to me, Jenny, and tell me whatever you can about these images."

"I see myself. I mean, I know it's me. I'm somewhere else, I think. I'm standing at the entrance of a cave. I'm bare breasted, and I'm wearing just a piece of leather around my waist. I am happy, very happy. And I am beautiful. An African, maybe. My skin is chocolate colored. I am carrying this bowl in my hands. I am a painter, I know. I hear something. I'm looking around, looking at this dense jungle, and I think I am hearing something. Then I see a crowd of people—cavemen!—they are coming towards me. I am frightened, but I don't know why."

Jennifer stopped speaking.

"Yes," Kathy whispered, leaning closer. She had taken out a pad and begun to scribble down notes.

"It's gone. Nothing."

"That's all right," Kathy instructed, "let the image go and wait for the next one. There's more. Your body is in tune. Your meridian points have been reached."

"I see Rome or somewhere like that. Greece!" Jennifer interrupted. "It's a building with a open courtyard. I see two men talking. They're talking about me. I'm a student here, at the palestra, a young boy. One of the men, the man on the left, will be my lover. I know that, looking at him. He's a poet."

Jennifer fell silent. The recollection stunned her.

"Don't try to evaluate anything," Kathy urged. "Just describe. We'll talk later."

"I see something else," Jennifer whispered, concentrating on the visions. Her eyes were closed, but the images that filled her mind were fully realized and brilliantly rendered.

"I see a ship. On the Nile, I believe—and it's extremely warm. Blistering hot, really. I am wishing for a breeze, any sort of breeze. The boat is moving with the tide, toward the sea. I'm a maid, a lady-in-waiting or something." Jennifer saw a man turn to her and ask a question. She did not hear the question, and the handsome Egyptian was someone she had seen before. It was the young reporter from the magazine. But before she could even describe the scene, explain it to Kathy, the scene faded, and dissolved. Then her mind was filled with another world.

"I'm walking down a cobblestone street. I'm wearing nun's clothes. A long black habit. There's a crowd of people. I'm being led to a square. I'm being punished for something, I think." Her body began to perspire on the massage table. The flannel sheet

suddenly was too warm. "Take it off," she begged, and Kathy Dart
reached over and pulled off the long sheet. Jennifer felt a cool breeze,
but her body was clammy with sweat.

"Go on," said Kathy.

"I'm to be burned to death for my sins." She felt herself being
pulled forward by black-hooded monks, saw herself going up onto
the great stage where the Grand Inquisitor stood. She glanced
around at the open square, crowded with peasants, then at the high
bleachers, filled with the aristocracy of the Italian town. She saw
Margit there, staring down at her. She kept turning and saw another
woman, dressed, as she was, in the habit of a nun. Then the Grand
Inquisitor stepped into her line of vision and began to read the
charges against her. He turned to the crowd as he recited the list
of her sins against God, and Jennifer realized it was Simon McCloud,
condemning her to death.

"Are you okay?" Kathy asked.

"I don't know." Jennifer realized she was crying.

"Perhaps we should stop." Kathy stood to remove the half dozen
acupuncture needles.

"No, please, let's continue." Jennifer wanted now to know the
secrets of her past. The Italian scene had slipped away to be replaced
by another image. Men were riding horses across open fields. She
could see snow-covered mountains in the far distance, saw, too, that
the men were being chased by Indians. Hundreds of warriors were
swooping down off the hillside, billowing dust across the landscape
as they galloped after the fleeing white men.

Behind them, in the distance, an overturned covered wagon
tipped into a rushing riverbed. She saw a child running from the
prairie schooner and realized that it was she. She saw the fright on
the little girl's face, the terror in her eyes, as she came running.
One of the Indian braves swept down on the fleeing child and lifted
her effortlessly into his arms. The child screamed in Jennifer's ears
as she was carried off into a cloud of dust, and she saw that the
Indian was Tom. Tom, as an Apache, was stealing the white child.

On the table, her legs jerked.

"I think we've had enough," Kathy whispered.

"No, no," Jennifer shook her head. She was naked and wet with
perspiration, but she was not cold. Her body felt aflame. "Please,
I want to know."

"All right," Kathy whispered, "but remember that you have
already lived these lives. Nothing can hurt you now. Lie quietly,"

she instructed. "We'll go on in a moment. Now, just calm yourself. Do you want me to explain anything of what you have seen?"

"Yes," Jennifer said at once. "Am I seeing a lot more than other people? Or less?"

"You are a very good subject, attuned to your previous lives. We say that such a person has 'clear antennae.' It isn't often that we receive such rich material on our first attempt. People often can only locate one or two such images from their past lives. I have to credit my spirits, too; they've guided my needles well."

"I was seeing people that I know today. What does that mean?"

"It's not surprising. We're all connected; what's important is the relationship. Who did you see?"

"Tom. Simon. And that young journalist who is doing that story about you."

"I wouldn't be surprised if we find out that Simon was once your husband. Or even that you were Tom's slave in a former life."

"And Margit was with me in one lifetime."

"The connection between you two is very strong. Perhaps she was your mother in another lifetime. What we have here is the intense bonding that is only possible in such maternal relationships. That is why Margit came to you after she was murdered. Are you ready to go on?"

"Yes."

Kathy Dart stood again and twisted the long gold needle that she had planted in Jennifer's third eye. "I'm going to stimulate your recollections." She pulled the flannel sheet up again over Jennifer's body.

"Have we been doing this long? I feel like I've been on this table for hours."

"Linear time means nothing to us, Jenny. Let your mind flow."

Jennifer kept her eyes closed and concentrated on relaxing, on keeping her mind free. She tried to keep herself from dwelling on what Kathy Dart had said about Tom, that he was such a dominant force in her life, her master.

Suddenly her mind was crowded with vivid pictures. They came swirling at her, and for an instant she panicked, worried that she would lose all this valuable information.

"I see a young girl, I think. I am a Chinese girl. I am being held, captured. People are after me. Chinese miners or something. They're going to kill me, kill the person who is holding me. I can't see his face."

"Relax, Jenny," Kathy instructed, touching her shoulder. "Let the images pass. They can not harm you. Don't concentrate too much. The images will find their way to the surface of your memory. Wait."

"I see a bedroom. An old-fashioned bedroom, you know, from the forties," Jennifer began again. "It's a little girl's room." She tried to scan the dark room. Though it was daylight, the blinds had been pulled, and the room was in shadow. A dozen dolls were stacked neatly on shelves, and there was a large dollhouse in the corner. "It's my bedroom, I just know!" she exclaimed.

"Is anyone there?" Kathy asked.

Jennifer shook her head. She was frowning, straining to see deep into her history. "There's a woman coming in," she said. And then, in her mind, the door opened and a shaft of light filled the dark bedroom.

"It's Margit!" Jennifer told Kathy. "She's my mother and she's come looking for me. I'm there, I know, somewhere in the room." Jennifer turned her head from side to side, trying to force the recollection, to pull the hidden memories to mind.

She saw herself then. She was just a teenager, not yet fifteen. She sat up in bed, just wakening, it seemed. She was naked. Then Jennifer saw the man, the young man beside the girl, saw him roll over in the bed. She knew even before she saw his face that it was Simon. And she knew, too, that these two were brother and sister. Her mother, Margit, screamed and brought her fists down on her daughter and son, striking them in blind rage.

Jennifer was shaking. She could not control her own body. She let Kathy tuck the warm flannel sheet more closely around her, then gently, expertly, Kathy began to massage Jennifer's temples. It took Jennifer several minutes to focus on what Kathy Dart was saying.

"You had an episode, Jenny, that's all. It happens sometimes. You pull up a past life that fills you with enormous guilt or remorse, and the realization has too much pain for you to handle now. But once it is uncovered, then the trauma is released. It won't haunt you. You have lived through the experience."

Jennifer was weeping quietly, and she kept crying, but her tears made her feel better. She was purging her body of the memory.

"I didn't know it would be this therapeutic," Jennifer whispered to Kathy, who was still ministering to her, arranging a small pillow beneath her head, wiping away her tears.

Kathy nodded. "At times, it is. We made tremendous progress

this morning, but I think it's time for you to let your body rest."
She smiled down at Jennifer. "I'll turn down the lights and leave
you for a while. You'll be able to sleep. Often such past life experiences completely knock you out."

"I'm just haunted by the thought of me and Simon. I mean, in
another life . . . brother and sister . . ."

"That's why you found him so attractive in this life," Kathy said.
"Brother or not, he's quite handsome."

"I have a lover."

"We all have many lovers, Jenny."

"Not me."

"Why?" Kathy asked. She waited patiently for Jennifer to respond.

Jennifer shrugged. She was suddenly uncomfortable talking
about her life in such detail.

"I think you would feel less stressful if you allowed your true
emotions to emerge."

"I don't think that the way to establish a permanent relationship
with Tom is to become involved with another man, with Simon,"
Jennifer replied. "You know we're living in the age of AIDS! Women
don't sleep around. Why do you want me to sleep with Simon,
anyway?"

Kathy nodded toward the stack of silver and gold acupuncture
needles.

"I can only do so much with my treatment. I think that a loving
encounter with Simon, where you share the pleasure of each other,
will enrich you. It will help break down the tensions you feel, the
rage you have against men."

"I don't have any rage against men," Jennifer said quietly.

"Eileen told me what happened in the motel."

"Okay, I was angry, but you would have been, too, if you had
seen him. Look, I'm not going to sleep with every man who hits on
me just to show that I don't have hidden hostility toward men. What
are you trying to say, anyway?"

"Look what happened to you when you saw Simon in that recall
from the forties," Kathy said patiently.

"Kathy, he was my brother! I was sleeping with my brother!"
Jennifer began to cry. Lying back on the massage table, she choked
on her own tears and had to lean up on one elbow, coughing and
sobbing.

Kathy waited until Jennifer had gained control of herself. She used the corner of the flannel sheet to wipe the tears away, then said softly, "I am not judging you, Jennifer, or prescribing a course of action. I am merely an instrument. The anger that you've been expressing, the conflict you have with your lover, Tom, are simply manifestations of a deeper and more profound unrest that is lodged within the cells of your body. Your spirit holds these memories and carries them forward, from one incarnation to the next. The body remembers everything, Jennifer. Everything! You have reached a critical moment in your life." She leaned back. "I don't know, Jenny, what is suddenly haunting you, driving you to such primitive rage. But I do want to help you discover its cause. Only by 'seeing' your past lives, by conversing with Habasha, by accepting who you were in other lifetimes will you find out who you are today. Jenny, you must accept your past."

"Am I to achieve this by fucking Simon McCloud?"

Kathy shrugged. "I only know that you two have a strong attraction to each other and that perhaps by sharing such an intimate moment, you'll learn something about yourself." For a moment she was silent. Then, slowly, she began to speak. "Our most intense experiences in life, Jenny, are with our family. Our lives are shaped from childhood. We're drawn to the kind of people we grew up with. I don't know yet what your parents are like, but I can guess."

Jennifer glanced over at Kathy Dart and waited for her explanation.

"You were born late in their lives, and I sense that you were an only child."

"I had a brother," Jennifer corrected.

"Yes, but he was much older, wasn't he?"

Jennifer nodded. "Eileen would have told you this much."

"I haven't discussed your family with Eileen."

"But she knew them. Eileen and I went to high school together. My parents are retired. They live in Florida."

"Yes, but you were never close to them. They were older. They were not pleased that you came along so late in their lives. From childhood, from infancy, really, you felt that you were unwanted. They did not give you the nurturing you needed. It was your brother—"

"Danny," Jennifer whispered.

"You lost Danny, didn't you?"

"Yes, in Vietnam. He never came home. They said he was killed in a bombing raid. They never found his body. I was only twelve when he died." She began to cry.

"You know, Jennifer, what you have to realize is that we choose our parents, choose our siblings. And we do this to resolve our experiences from previous lives."

"Why did Danny die and leave me?" Jennifer blurted out. "Was his death caused by something I did in another lifetime?"

Kathy shook her head. "I really don't know. Perhaps he had to fulfill another destiny. His destiny. But you were not really left, Jenny. You have seen him in your dreams, haven't you?"

"He's always with me," Jennifer acknowledged. "I feel him with me. He came to me when I almost died on the emergency-room table."

Kathy Dart reached out to touch Jennifer's arm. "Danny is with you, Jenny. Always. He is one of your spirits. And Margit Engle is another. They—and others from your oversoul—are here to guide and protect you. Just like myself, Habasha, Eileen, Simon. We're all part of your oversoul, members of your support system." Her pretty face was full of assurance.

"But I still don't know what is troubling me, or which life is the source of these rages."

Kathy Dart nodded sympathetically.

"Soon," she whispered, "soon." She nodded toward the row of needles. "I think with another session, we'll have the truth."

Now she stood and patted Jennifer on the shoulder. "Why don't you rest here for a while," she said. "I'll shut off the light and you can take a nap."

Jennifer smiled. "Thanks. I think I will. I do feel sleepy."

"Regressions are exhausting." Kathy went to the door and dimmed the lights. "I'll come back later to see if you're all right. You've had an exhausting morning, Jennifer, but I think we're very close to getting some answers."

"Yes," Jennifer whispered, closing her eyes. "I think we are, Kathy. Thank you."

"Thank Habasha, Jenny. He holds the eternal truths. I'm simply the messenger."

Kathy Dart closed the door, leaving Jennifer in the dark.

28

JENNIFER OPENED HER EYES in the dark clinic and saw that Simon had come into the room. Her heart beat against her chest. He must hear the wild pounding, she thought, and she took a deep breath in an effort to silence her body.

"Yes?" she asked, not moving.

"I spoke to Kathy. She said you were resting."

"Yes."

"Well, I came to see if you were okay." He was beside her. His face, inches away from hers, was silhouetted in the dark room.

"Yes, I'm okay. Thank you."

They were almost like lovers, Jennifer thought, whispering in the dark.

"Would you like me to give you a massage?" he asked. "I know that past-life recall is very tiring. You go through so many time frames."

"I've never had a massage," Jennifer admitted, "except when—" She stopped midsentence, remembering how in college her boyfriend had given her massages before they had made love. "What do you do? What types of massage, I mean."

"I know a lot of different methods, actually. There are the shiatsu and acupressure systems. They use finger and hand pressure on the body's energy meridians—the same principle as acupuncture, except without the needles. Or Swedish, which is body manipulation. I was taught that as a kid by my uncle. Then there's reflexology, you know, the kind that focuses on your feet and hands."

"They're all different?"

"Yes, and all are for different purposes. Hydrotherapy, for example, uses water and develops muscle tone, helps reduce swelling. Esthetic massage is a way to improve your looks."

"Good, I could use that one."

"No, you're already very beautiful," he said.

Jennifer smiled, afraid to say anything.

"And then there's myotherapy for the treatment of muscular pain." Simon went on. "And sports massage for runners, you know." He shrugged. "Whatever you want."

"And you know them all?"

"Kathy sent me to school."

"Of course." Jennifer pulled herself up on her right elbow and turned toward Simon. "What massage does Kathy have?" she asked.

"I always give her a Swedish massage."

"Then that's what I want."

"Good!" Simon smiled. He stood up and stepped across the small room, moving carefully in the darkness.

He was out of the wash of light, but still Jennifer could see him open the closet and take out a low, padded bench. He placed it on the floor, then returned to the table and handed her a folded white sheet.

"You'll need to put this on," he told her, and turned away.

She swung her legs over the side of the table and put on the sheet. "Oh, it's cold," she said.

"That's okay. I'll warm you up." Simon had knelt beside the table and was pulling several thick towels from the bottom drawer of the built-in wall cabinet.

"I'll be using oil on your body," he told her. "It's warm and it will keep your skin smooth." He was all business. Now that the early intimacy between them had passed, she felt curiously let down. He glanced around and saw that Jennifer had tucked the long sheet around her body. "Ready?"

"I guess." She felt foolish now and vulnerable.

"Here," he whispered, taking her hand and gently maneuvering her into position on the table. He slipped a thick, rolled-up towel beneath her ankles, and another under her head, then turned her head so she faced the corner of the room. Jennifer closed her eyes, aware only of his strong hands on her back.

"I want you to relax and keep your eyes closed," he whispered. "I'm not going to talk at all, and I want you to focus on your body. Your neck muscles are very tight. Let me begin there." Leaning forward, Simon placed his hands, wet with oil, on her back. She shivered at his touch, and he whispered, "Relax, Jenny, relax and enjoy."

He began slowly and steadily to stroke her neck and back muscles with his strong hands, sliding them evenly down her back and up again. Jennifer felt herself grow sleepy, and gradually she let go of her defenses and surrendered herself to the pleasure of the massage.

Simon moved to her legs, kneading the calf muscles. She moaned when his fingers tightened on her legs, and he whispered an apology.

"It's okay," she answered, tucking her arms around the thick towel. She could lie there forever, she thought. She loved the feel of his hands on her body. "You have wonderful fingers," she told him.

"Shhh," he whispered. Moving to the bottom of the table, Simon began to gently stroke one foot, then the other. He began at the ankle and stroked toward the toes. She felt the tension disappear from her leg.

"I want you to do this to me every day," she mumbled.

"My pleasure," Simon answered, smiling in the dark. Slowly, he stroked up her leg, across her calf, up her thigh to her buttocks.

The loose sheet had slipped off her back, but she didn't care. It was dark in the room; she could not see him and was aware only of his hands and what they were doing to her body.

"Do you do this with Kathy?" Jennifer asked.

"Yes," Simon whispered. He was close beside her now, and she could smell the warm, fragrant oil on his fingers. "And now I'm doing it to you."

Simon turned her body with his hands, exposing her breasts. She reached down and draped the end of the long sheet across her waist. Slowly, carefully, he used his fingers and the palms of both hands to stroke her shoulder muscles, to pinch away the tightness and pain. Then he moved down the length of her body, using his hands carefully on her abdomen, kneading her thighs and calves, returning to her feet and stroking her to the tips of her toes.

He was working steadily, breathing harder from his steady effort, but he did not stop, and Jennifer fell silent, following obediently his hand signals, turning her body the way he directed. By now she was naked on the low table, and in the dim light, she saw the crumpled shapes of the discarded sheets.

Then she felt his hands on her thighs, rapidly striking her with the palms of his hands. He stopped and kneaded her legs with his strong fingers, then slipped his hands between her legs. She gasped.

With her eyes closed, Jennifer could not see him. She felt only his breath as he leaned across her body, using his full weight to bring pressure to his strokes. His fingers were warm and oily and lovely. When he touched her breasts, she felt her breath catch in her throat. Then he moved his hands up to her neck and, with his fingertips, massaged the tender skin at the base of her throat.

"Am I hurting you?" he asked.

"No," she whispered, her eyes still closed.

Again, he moved down the length of her body, silently stroking her flesh, as if her body were nothing more than an instrument for his use. This was what true submission was, she realized as she lay there. This was what real emotional slavery meant.

Jennifer knew now that she would give her body to him. She would surrender simply and gladly. She wanted to be his lover, if only once. This had nothing to do with Tom, with her life in New York. This moment in the dark room had meaning only to the two of them. It did not matter that Simon was Kathy's lover. They were all of the same soul; Habasha had told them. They were all connected in another life.

She opened her eyes and lifted her arms to take him into her embrace, and he smiled and whispered, "No. Not yet." Then he leaned over and slowly, lovingly kissed her breasts, then gently pulled a warm blanket over her. "Lie here a moment," he whispered, and then he was gone.

She lay still, as he had instructed, stunned by his unexpected refusal. He wanted her to wait. Wait. She was alone in the small room, warm and close under the heavy blanket, with voices coming to her from deep in the house, and the sharp Minnesota wind whipping against the walls. She thought of his lips touching her breasts, his warm cheek brushing against her aroused nipples, then she came.

29

JENNIFER OPENED HER EYES. It was already evening, and she heard voices in the other rooms, laughing and talking. It must be time for predinner drinks in the living room. Later, Jennifer knew, Kathy Dart would be channeling Habasha.

Naked, Jennifer slipped off the table and quickly put her clothes on, pulling her thick navy blue turtleneck over her head and sliding into her leather pants. Her fear had made her jumpy, and as she left the small clinic, she glanced through the curtains of the windows, half expecting to see Simon's face there, watching her from the darkness. But there was only a vast expanse of frozen snow, glistening from the outside floodlights. She saw a car swing into the small lot. Its lights swept across the fields before it pulled in.

She was afraid of Simon now, afraid of his power over her. She remembered vividly the past-life regression, how he had condemned her to death as the Grand Inquisitor. She had to get away from him, from this farm, before something else happened to her, before Simon tried to make love to her.

In her bedroom, Jennifer grabbed her parka from the back of the chair, then quickly threw her clothes into her bag and hurried out of her room and down the hall and into the night. Only when she reached the cold did she realize she didn't know how she would escape the isolated farm.

She glanced around. No one had followed her from the house, and the yard was silent and dark. She ran at once onto the road and waved at a passing car, which slowed for a moment, then sped away. Just as well, Jennifer thought. The driver had been a man, and she didn't want to tempt fate.

Another car swung out of the farm's driveway, and for a moment she was pinned in the bright headlights. The car came straight at her, and she backed away from the highway, looked to see where she might run, but there was no shelter, no woods, only miles of farmland and open fields. The car slowed, and she saw the driver lean over and open the passenger door. When the interior light came on, she saw it was the reporter who was doing the article on Kathy Dart.

"Hi!" he said, grinning. "Car break down?"

"Yes, I'm afraid so." She smiled back. "A rental car. I need to get to the airport in St. Paul. Could you give me a lift in that direction?" She stared at him. Her heart was pounding, and she was suddenly afraid that he was lying, that he knew she was trying to get away and had been sent to get her. He was one of them, not a reporter at all.

"Sure, hop in." He reached over and moved a stack of audio tapes from the seat. "Where's your friend . . . ?"

"Eileen?"

"Yeah, that's the one. I met you in Washington, D.C., right?" He was watching her, still smiling.

Jennifer nodded as she tossed her bag in the back and slid in beside him.

"She's staying longer?" he asked, starting up the car.

"Yes. Yes, she is." Jennifer took a deep breath and glanced around. No one else had come out of the farm's parking lot. "I saw you at the Habasha channeling session the other night. Is the article done?"

"Yeah, just about. I've got all of my research done on Kathy Dart. You had some reaction to old Habasha last night, didn't you?" the reporter commented.

Jennifer glanced at him again. He wasn't quite as young as she had first thought. And she hadn't realized how good-looking he really was.

"Are you going as far as the airport?" she asked, avoiding the question.

"Yes, I'm going back to Chicago. My name, by the way, is Kirk Callahan."

"Yes, I remember."

"And I remember you didn't want to be interviewed." He kept smiling.

"I didn't have anything to say. I'm not into channeling."

"But you're here now." He gestured toward the farm.

"Well, I was." She kept staring ahead at the dark highway.

Each mile, she realized, was taking her away from the farm. What would Kathy do when she discovered that she had left? She glanced again at the dashboard, thankful that Kirk was driving so fast.

"Where are you going?" Kirk asked, and she jumped, startled by his voice.

"Hey, I'm sorry." He slowed the car.

"Oh, New York. I'm going to New York City." She glanced out the rear window.

"I've never been to New York," Kirk said. "I'd like to visit sometime, to see a Broadway show or something."

Jennifer had forgotten what clean-cut, Midwestern kids were like. It was as if he were from another planet.

"You live in Manhattan?" he asked.

"No, Brooklyn. Brooklyn Heights, actually. It's right across the river." Still no headlights behind her.

"No one is following," he said, frowning.

"I'm sorry. I just keep thinking . . . you know, you're driving so fast. I'm worried about cops."

"It's okay. I'm keeping an eye out. We have nothing to worry about."

Jennifer nodded. "That's a nice notion, saying we have nothing to worry about. I wish it were true." She forced a smile.

"You like some music or something?" Kirk asked.

"Sure."

"Here." He handed her a box of tapes.

"No, you pick something you like. Anything." Jennifer noted with satisfaction how her smile flustered him.

"Okay, how 'bout a little John Cougar Mellencamp?" He slipped in the tape and hit the play button.

"Great!" Jennifer said. She had no idea whom he meant.

They drove without speaking as they both listened to the music, and Jennifer began to relax. The music helped to distract her, but it was really the car, speeding throught the dark night, that did it. She was driving away from the farm with this attractive young man, and she took a perverse pleasure in the knowledge that no one— not Eileen, not Kathy Dart, not Simon, no one—knew where in the world she was.

She slipped down farther in the soft bucket seat. "This is a nice car," she said. "What is it?"

He grinned proudly. "It's brand new," he said. "An Audi 80. Five cylinders, a two-point-three–liter engine. And this is all leather!" He reached over and ran his hand lovingly across the upholstery.

"A present?"

"Yeah. I bought it for myself. I made some money in the market."

"Congratulations."

"Thanks. But I was just lucky. I got out when the market heated up. It's due for a crash."

"You play the market?"

"I did. Now I'm into CDs and cash."

Jennifer nodded but said nothing. When she was his age, she had only college loans and debt. She didn't know anything about stocks. She slid further down into the seat, curling up as best she could in the tight space. She saw Kirk reach over and lower the music, and she smiled at him. Then she closed her eyes and thought how nice he was to leave her alone. She fell asleep in the bucket seat of his new Audi, grateful that he was such a nice guy.

In the last moments of her troubled dreams, in the silent drifting fog before consciousness, Jennifer saw the hand coming at her throat, and she tossed and turned trying to escape. Then she was startled awake. Kirk Callahan's hand rested gently on her shoulder, and he was whispering to her.

"Hey, Jennifer? Hey, I'm sorry. We're getting close to St. Paul; it's time to wake up." He withdrew his hand as he slowed the car.

Jennifer saw overhead expressway signs slip past. They were in traffic, and she was aware of buildings, flashing billboards, the roar of trucks. She felt a wave of panic. The car's dashboard clock read 7:32.

Kirk looked older now. His face was more sharply defined, with a blunt chin, a large, generous mouth, and a straight nose. It was a strong, masculine face, and it was made more masculine by his forthright manner. Jennifer mused as she watched him. A farmer's son. A Minnesota lumberjack, perhaps. She remembered then that he had been in her Egyptian past life, and to keep herself from recalling anything more, she said, "Okay, Kirk, tell me about yourself?"

He blushed, as she knew he would, and shyly, hesitantly talked about growing up on a farm in the Midwest, about high school football and girlfriends, and going to college on a track scholarship. Jennifer listened attentively for a while, and then she realized she wasn't listening to him, but was watching the way his lips moved, and how he cocked his head to the side when he started a new story, and how his eyes brightened just before he came to the punch line of a joke.

"What about it?" he asked.

"Pardon me?" Jennifer sat up, taken aback.

"What about riding with me into Chicago?"

"Are you going to Chicago?" she asked.

"Well, yeah, I've got an interview tomorrow afternoon downtown in the Loop, then I'm headed home."

"But where do you live?"

"St. Louis. But I can drop you at O'Hare, that's no big deal." He kept glancing at her.

"I don't know. That's a long drive. We'll have to spend the night somewhere, right?" She thought of the guy she'd shoved into the ice machine on the drive out from the East. She wondered if there was a warrant out for her arrest.

"They're not going to get you, not if you're with me," he said softly, watching her.

"What do you mean?" Jennifer realized her hands were trembling. "Who's out to get me?"

Kirk shrugged. "Those people at the farm." Kirk held her gaze evenly. He was waiting her out.

She did not want to lie to him. She wanted to tell him what had happened to her, how she had gotten to the farm, and why she was now running for her life. It was true, she realized, how one would tell strangers the most intimate of secrets and hide the truth from friends. And so, there in the small car as they raced toward St. Paul, she told Kirk Callahan how she had met Kathy Dart and why she had come to the farm in the first place. All she withheld was her crimes.

What startled her most was that he didn't seem surprised by anything she said. As she talked, he kept glancing at her with his sober gray eyes, never once registering surprise or astonishment at her story.

When she was finished, she finally asked, "Are you a follower of Kathy Dart? Do you believe in this New Age stuff? Are you going to turn me in or what?"

He shook his head as he looked ahead and watched the road. "All this New Age stuff is just a mind fuck. You do it to yourself. I took this course—abnormal psych—last fall, and you know, you start reading these cases, and suddenly you begin to think, Hey, I'm like that. That's me! Or you know someone who's slightly off and you think, He must be a paranoid schizophrenic, or whatever."

"But you're writing an article about it?"

"That doesn't mean I believe in any of that shit."

"Maybe you're right," Jennifer said vaguely, now not knowing who or what to believe. She thought again of the session with Kathy Dart and the vividness of her past lives. Those were true, she told herself. Whatever else had happened to her, she had seen into her past, she thought, sighing, and she had killed people with her primitive strength.

They drove in silence, out of St. Paul on Route 94, and into Wisconsin, then south through more flat farmland. For a while, Kirk fed cassettes into the tape deck. He played tapes of George Harrison, Billy Idol, and more John Cougar Mellencamp. She wished he wouldn't play anything at all. She would have liked the silence, but it was his car, his drive, and she wouldn't be demanding. She wanted only to get back to New York.

30

"DO YOU MIND SHARING a room with me?" Jennifer asked when Kirk decided to stop driving for the night. She had made up her mind when they had started across Wisconsin that she couldn't spend a night alone in a motel room.

"Hey, sure." Kirk grinned.

"I don't mean anything by that," she said firmly.

"Yeah, you can trust me!" he said, grinning.

"I know that." She opened the car door.

"Wait!" he told her.

"What? Did you see someone?" She slipped down into the car seat.

"No, of course not. Hey, Winters, no one is going to find you out here in the middle of this farmland. The farm doesn't employ the KGB. Just wait here until I get the room, that's all."

"Oh! How are you going to sign us in?"

"Well, I thought I'd put down Mr. and Mrs. Kirk Callahan. Or is that being too pushy?"

She allowed herself to smile back. "Fine! But don't use my first name, okay?" She knew she was being paranoid, but still. . . . "Here!" She reached for her purse. "Let me give you some money."

He waved her off. "Buy me dinner." He opened the car door.

"Okay, but we're eating in our room. And make it the second floor, okay?"

He sighed. "Any other motel obsessions?"

"No." She smiled after him, thankful that he was handling all the details. Then she reached over and locked the car door.

"How's this, Mrs. Callahan?" Kirk asked, opening the door and letting Jennifer lead the way into the motel room.

"Good!" she said, taking in the dimly lit room. "There are two beds."

"Hey, I asked for them!" He sounded hurt.

Jennifer watched him for a moment, holding her small plastic bag of toilet articles. She knew he hadn't been told enough to know why she was so on edge, but at least he was willing to take a chance with her, to go along with her erratic behavior. How did he know that she wasn't some wacko from a mental hospital?

She stepped over to sit down on his bed and said softly, "Kirk, I'm not trying to order you around or treat you like a kid."

"Then stop doing it, okay?"

"We're in an awkward position, thrown together, and I'm grateful for what you've done for me. You've saved my life. I just don't want you to misunderstand, that's all."

"I'm not misunderstanding anything."

Jennifer stood up. A single room had been a big mistake, she realized now.

"I'm sorry," he said.

"It's all right."

"Jen, I just"—he looked off when he spoke—"I'm sorry, I . . ."

"Kirk, it's okay," she soothed. She kept herself from reaching out and touching his cheek. "I'd better take a shower," she finally said.

In the small bathroom, she turned on the shower, buried her head in a thick bath towel, and let herself cry, knowing that it would calm her down. She didn't bother to lock the door. She wasn't afraid of Kirk. Of all people, she knew she could trust him.

She took a long shower, washed her hair, then went ahead and washed her panties and bra and hung them on the curtain rod. When she returned to the bedroom, she had wrapped up her hair in a bath towel and was wearing her red flannel nightgown. She'd thought about putting on her shirt and jeans again but decided against it. There wouldn't be a problem. Besides, after dinner, she wanted to get into bed and go right to sleep.

"Dinner is being served," he told her, pointing to the tray.

"Thank you," she said. "Where did this come from?"

"I told the desk we were on our honeymoon and I wanted to serve you dinner in bed. And they sent up the tray." He lifted a bottle of champagne from a plastic ice bucket and held it up with a flourish. "And this," he added.

"Kirk, you've got class," she said, impressed.

"You think so?"

"I know so. You're an all-right guy."

"An all-right kid, you mean."

"We're friends, remember?"

"Right!" He sat down on the edge of his bed.

"Hey," she cocked her head, smiling out from under the towel turban, "come sit with me. Let's talk. I've told you about Tom. Now it's your turn. Tell me about your girlfriends."

"Which one?"

"Well, let's start with the most recent." She bit into her hamburger, then took a sip of the champagne while Kirk told her about Peggy. They had gone to school together, but that Christmas she had announced her engagement to someone in law school, a guy she had met the summer before.

"She was your great love?"

"Yeah, I guess. I didn't date much in high school. We lived outside of town; there were always too many chores to do. Then when I got to college, Peggy and I hit it off right away and went together pretty much all the time until last summer. When she came back after Labor Day, it was all over between us." He shrugged his shoulders and went back to his hamburger.

"Well, don't worry. You're a good-looking guy, and there'll be plenty of others."

"You think so?" he asked.

"Of course there will be."

"No, I mean, do you really think that I'm good-looking?"

Jennifer glanced at him as she drained her glass. The champagne had had an effect. She felt relaxed for the first time that day, warm, and even safe. Impulsively, she reached over and touched his cheek with her hand, drawing her fingers down the length of his jaw. Fleetingly, she imagined what it would be like to make love to him, and then she pulled her thoughts under control and simply said, "Yes, you are a good-looking man." She paused. "But I think you should let your hair grow out a little. And now I'm going to sleep."

Kirk picked up the tray, and Jennifer crawled under the blankets and put her head down on the pillow. Her hair was still wrapped up in the towel and she knew she should comb it out, but she was too tired to even move.

Kirk leaned over, tucked the blankets up to her neck, then reached out and shut off the bedside lamp. Before he stepped away, he leaned down and kissed her softly on her cheek.

Jennifer smiled and mumbled thank you, and then she was asleep.

* * *

Much later, she woke up and saw Kirk standing by the windows in his white boxer shorts. She thought what a great body he had and then fell asleep again.

When Jennifer woke next, it was daylight. She turned over and saw that Kirk's bed was empty and she was alone in the room. She jumped out of bed at once and went to the windows, peeking out from behind the heavy curtains. Kirk's Audi was still parked where they had left it.

Jennifer sighed. What had she thought? That he would leave her there in the middle of nowhere?

She spotted Kirk then, jogging across the lot. He had been out running, that was all. She sighed and watched him slow down and walk by a station wagon that had just pulled into the motel. It was only when the driver lowered the front window to speak to Kirk that Jennifer realized who it was. Kirk was telling him something, pointing across the parking lot, but Jennifer had fallen away from the second-floor windows, fully comprehending what had happened. Kirk Callahan, the young man she had allowed herself to trust, had led Simon McCord to her.

He ran. Clutching the fist-sized piece of quartzite in his hand, he scampered down the bank and headed for the muddy river. The others were close behind. They had found the body of the female, and now they were after him, following his scent through the underbrush, following his footsteps in the soft soil.

He ran for his life. They would kill him, just as he had killed the female. He did not know why he had killed her. She would not come with him. But other women in tribes near the river had not come with him, and he had not hurt them.

Yet her refusal had enraged him, and without thinking, he had swung the quartzite at her, its sharp point piercing her neck, spraying blood in his face. He could taste her blood on his lips, in his mouth.

He reached the river and dove into the deep water, letting the swift tide carry him farther downstream. There were rhinos in the water, and crocodiles, too, sleeping up on the banks and in the shade of acacia trees. The sleeping crocs frightened him, but he feared more the band of men running along the muddy riverbank.

If he didn't bother the animals, he was safe. The river widened at the next bend, then swept away to the horizon. He did not know where the river flowed, but once, when he was younger, his grandfather had stood on the high cliffs behind their campsite and told him of lands beyond the grassland where elephants were as plentiful as raindrops and where berry bushes and yarrow plants grew beyond one's dreams.

He would have to leave this valley, he thought, catching hold of a bamboo limb and swinging up to perch on it. There were too many others living together in the valley of the honeycombs. He would be killed if he returned; the males of the woman's clan knew him. They would kill another member of his family, sweep down into their camp that night and slaughter one of the women for what he had done to the clan.

He knew that her people thought of him and his kind as nothing more than monkeys to be killed, their heads smashed with rocks so the sweet-smelling meat of their skulls could be scooped out with fingers, their eyes sucked like shellfish; and then, later, her men would heat the thighs and arms of their enemies' dead bodies over the campsite fire and linger in the shade with no pain from hunger.

Her people kept his kind away from the grasslands, away from the berry bushes on the far side of the river. Still, he and his cousins crept across the river after sunset, slipping by the sleeping crocodiles to steal the honey or to find the patches of yarrow and take away the white flowers in the dead of night. Her people said these fruits and berries belonged to them, to all the cave people who lived high up on the steep cliffs, and they drove off his people, kept him and his cousins from the lush vegetables. They fought his people off from the water holes where the bushbucks lingered, where they could trap and snare a zebra or giraffe, kill it with blows from their axes.

He slipped his knife into his buckskin pouch as the swift river bore him away. It had taken him weeks to find the stone, then to shape it as he wanted, chipping away the slivers of quartz as his father had taught him. With it, he could kill. With it, he could defend himself against the cave people.

He thought of the woman he had killed. He had seen her first by the river's edge, then followed her to the crest of the hills. He had called to her then, but she had mocked him, jutting her chin out, pushing her breasts at him, slapping her thick upper lip with her tongue, and saying, "Maa-naa, Maa-naa," as she turned to show him her behind.

He had wanted to lure her from the track, to entice her into the deep gully beside the huge banana trees where the ground was soft and mossy, but she wouldn't budge from the clearing. He watched her prance in the bright sunlight, flicking at her pelvis as if to entice him. He rushed out from the safe patch of underbrush, and she scooted away, giggling. Enraged, he had grabbed his new quartzite ax and struck her.

He would stay with the river, clinging to the thick log of bamboo. His grandfather had told him tales, stories told to him by his grandfather, of hills beyond hills, of other people, tall and slim like running giraffes, who wore the skin of animals, and told tales of giant mountains where the rain was white and cold.

These were only tales, he knew, shared around warm fires on cold nights, when the old people huddled and sang stories of lands beyond the river, stories they said that came to them in dreams, when the body sleeps, and the spirits sail with the moon, and they painted such songs on their cave walls.

He did not believe the old men's stories. He knew only what he saw, only what he tasted in his mouth, only what had happened to him.

He had killed the woman, and the cave people would kill him. He did not want to leave his own woman, his children, or his mother and father, but he did not want to die from a flying spear and have his eyes sucked from his head.

He clung to the bamboo stump and was happy to be alive, happy, too, that he had killed her. She had laughed at him with her eyes and jutted out her sex as if it were the lush fruit of a berry bush, but would not mate with him. Yes, he was glad that he had killed her, and he kept sailing away on the tide of the wide river, heading toward the rising sun and the land of white cold rain and tall slim men.

31

JENNIFER BOLTED THE BATHROOM door and spun around to face herself in the mirror. Under the bright lights, she was amazed at how frightful she looked. It was as if she had stuck her finger in an electrical outlet.

She thought of Kirk, of how he had come out of the night and helped her get away from the farm, of how he had been so nice to her. Her mind whirled as she linked together all the strange coincidences that had brought this man into her life. She had been trapped and double-crossed by this innocent-looking guy.

"Oh God!" Jennifer exclaimed. The familiar rush of fear crippled her, and she slid to the bathroom floor, trembling.

It was so obvious. He had been sent out onto the lonely Minnesota road to pick her up when she ran away from the farm. He had been sent by Kathy Dart to keep an eye on her. No wonder he was so willing to indulge her whims, to go along with her scatter-brained theories about the farm and Habasha. He was one of them.

She curled herself into a tight fetal position, sobbing, but part of her mind had already begun to sort out what she must do to save herself.

Why did they want her? she kept asking herself. Who was she that they kept coming after her?

She forced herself to stop guessing and concentrated on how she was going to escape. Kirk would be returning soon, perhaps with Simon in tow.

She would call the police, tell them she was being kidnapped. She remembered reading stories about cult groups and how they always fled once the police became involved.

Jennifer pulled herself up from the floor and glanced around for a telephone. When she saw there wasn't one in the bathroom, she leaned against the door and listened for sounds of Kirk moving in the room.

Slowly, quietly, she pulled open the bathroom door and peeked into the bedroom. Kirk was standing in the door, filling the frame with his body. He was grinning at her, still sweating from his early-morning jog.

Jennifer jumped him.

"Jesus Christ, what's going on?" He ducked her swinging fists.

Jennifer tried to grab him by the hair, but it was too short. Frantically, she flailed out with her arms. Swearing, Kirk caught her arms in his hands and pinned them to her sides. She kept struggling, and he picked her up and dropped her on the bed. Then, with some effort, he turned her face toward him and forced her to look at him.

"Hey," he said softly, as Jennifer kept kicking. "Hey, what the hell is going on?"

Her nightgown had torn open and exposed one pale, milky breast.

"Christ," Kirk murmured, keeping her arms pinned to the pillow above her head.

"You! You're one of them!" She tried to keep fighting, but then, exhausted, she broke down into tears.

"What are you talking about?" he asked, holding her gently now.

"Simon . . . in the car . . ." She kept sobbing and explained how she had seen him talking to McCloud in the parking lot.

"Yeah, I know who he is. He wanted to know where the restaurant was, for chrissake!" He let go of her and stood up. "What are you talking, anyway?" He grabbed his sweatshirt and pulled it over his head.

"He's after me!" Jennifer said, sitting up. "Kathy Dart sent him after me."

"Jesus, you are paranoid." He glanced over at her, shaking his head.

"Why is he following me?" she shouted.

"He asked me where the restaurant was. He told me he was driving to Madison. He's giving a lecture or something," Kirk explained, returning to the bed. "And what else, he doesn't know you're even in this motel." He stared down at her.

"He'll ask at the desk!"

"And no Jennifer Winters is registered." Now he allowed himself to smile.

"I'm so scared," Jennifer whispered and, reaching over, touched Kirk. Her eyes were puffy from crying.

"It's okay," he answered softly. "It's okay." He pulled her into his arms.

"Let's get out of here," Jennifer pleaded.

He was shaking his head. "We've got time. He's having breakfast. Let him finish and get back on the highway."

"We can't stay on that road."

"Okay, we won't. We'll take another route. Don't worry, he won't find you. I won't let him. Okay?" He smiled at her.

Jennifer nodded, unable to speak, overwhelmed by his closeness and his strength. She realized that all she wanted at that moment was for Kirk to hold and comfort her.

He moved her then, gently eased her down onto the pillows. His eyes never left her, but his gaze moved from her face down to her breasts, then to her slender hips and thighs. He swallowed hard, and his gray eyes darkened. There was a long silence as they stared at each other.

"I'm sorry," she finally said. "I saw you, and . . . I started to get paranoid again."

"Hey, I said I'd get you to O'Hare."

"I can't go to O'Hare."

"Okay, come with me."

"And what?"

"I don't know! We'll figure something out."

Jennifer kept looking into his eyes. "You mean that, don't you?"

He nodded, and she saw him swallow hard again. He didn't take his eyes off her. She saw the blind, moonstruck look in his eyes. With a mixture of fear and desire, she waited for him to touch her.

"Is it okay if I kiss you?" he asked, sounding very young.

"I want you to kiss me," she told him.

He brushed her lips gently.

"Ouch," he said, backing off.

"What?" She looked up, concerned.

"My nose. Where you bashed me."

"Oh, I'm sorry, Kirk." She took his face in her hands and tenderly pulled him closer to kiss the tip of his nose. "I'm sorry," she whispered again. This time their kiss was more insistent.

Jennifer gasped as Kirk moved to stroke her breast. With his head still between her hands, she moved his face to her breast.

Sighing, she relaxed and let her young man make love to her in his own way.

He came quickly, and she was surprised that she was ready for him. She was sometimes slow to be aroused, but their battle had excited her. When he slipped inside her and came again, she had an orgasm of such power that for a moment she thought she might burst.

His body, too, was aflame as he lay by her side, his eyes wide. She turned and curled in against him like a matching spoon, and reaching back, took hold of his penis and smiled as it swelled to her gentle caress. This time, at her encouragement, he came at her from behind, kneeling on the soft mattress, and rode her until they were both panting with pain and pleasure. She pressed her palm flat against her abdomen, felt the length of his erection filling her, and then the sudden shudder of his orgasm.

Jennifer's body ached both from their fight and their sex, yet she could not sleep. She got out of bed and slipped into the bathroom for a quick shower, then dressed in jeans and a sweater.

When she reentered the dark room, he was still sleeping. She resisted the temptation to kiss him, though she did pull up the top sheet and blanket and tuck them around him. Then she carefully unlocked the door and slipped out into the hallway.

It was still early morning. She walked toward the front desk, thinking that she would pay their bill and check out.

The motel hallway was long, and when she reached the end, she stepped into a glassed-in stairwell. She took the stairs to the first floor and saw the parking lot was to one side and the empty swimming pool to the other. And then she spotted Simon.

He was standing behind the full-length glass doors in the lobby of the motel. Jennifer saw his foggy breath on the glass, saw him turn his head and speak to someone hidden by the curtains.

Simon spotted her. He waved, then pulled open the glass doors and ran across the snowy yard, circled the pool, and tried to catch her before she got away.

Jennifer took the steps two at a time, ran up to the second floor hallway and through the swinging doors. She stopped then and concentrated. Deliberately, she thought of Simon and how he was coming after her, coming to kidnap her. And as she had hoped, she felt the familiar surge of strength, felt her muscles bulge. Stepping into a supply closet, she stood there under the bright light, surrounded by rolls of paper towels and tiny pink bars of soap and an empty cleaning cart. She waited for Simon to burst through the door and see her.

Moments later the door swung wide, and Simon filled the frame, a smile spreading across his face when he saw her.

"Hi," she said. She stood with her fingers laced together, like a girl at a high school gym waiting to be asked to dance.

"Jenny, Jenny," he said with a sigh. "What happened to you? Why did you run away? Kathy was so worried. What are you doing in here?"

"Waiting for you," Jennifer said calmly, holding back the surge of adrenaline that swelled her strength. She wanted to wait until she was strong enough to kill with one swift blow. She wanted to wait until he was close enough for her to grab his throat.

"How did you get here, anyway?" he asked, frowning. He stepped inside the door. "Why are you so afraid?" he asked.

She grabbed him easily, with one sudden move. Her hands were around his neck before he could react, the scream in his throat sliced off by the pressure of her grasp. She felt the words die as she tightened her grip. She watched his face, saw his ice blue eyes pop out in his head, saw a bubble of blood squeeze from his mouth and drip down his lower lip. She lifted him up and flipped him over easily, dumping him headfirst into the empty cleaning cart.

Then she grabbed a clean bathroom towel and wiped his blood off her fingers. She threw the towel into the cart, turned off the light, and went back into the hall. It would be another hour before the maids finished the rooms on that floor and came back to the supply room and found him there, stuffed upside down in the cleaning cart.

"You killed him?" Kirk asked again. They were back in his Audi, speeding east on Route 80.

"No, I don't think so. He was alive when I left him."

"Jesus H. Christ."

"Kirk, I know this is more than you bargained for." Jennifer nodded toward the next exit sign. "Pull off there. You can drop me at the nearest car rental place." As she spoke, she rested her arm across his thigh. She could not keep herself from touching him. She needed the physical contact. If he did stop and put her out, she would truly be lost. She didn't think she had the strength or the courage to drive a car.

"I'm not going to ditch you," he told her.

She sighed, then leaned forward and briefly rested her head on his shoulder.

"I don't think anyone will be looking for us," he said next, taking charge.

Jennifer shrugged. "I don't know. I mean, he might call the police and tell them he was attacked."

"By a woman? Come on, no way." Kirk was shaking his head as he speeded.

In New York, Jennifer knew, she could get away with hurting, even killing, a person. It was done every day. But not in the heartland.

He reached across her and took several maps from the glove compartment. "But just in case," he said, handing them over to her as he kept his eyes on the road, "look at these and find some secondary roads that will get us across the state. Look south."

Jennifer stared down at the open maps, unable to focus. She couldn't go to St. Louis with him. Besides, he had a meeting in Chicago. No, running away with Kirk Callahan wasn't the answer. How long could she hide away there? Kathy Dart would find her; when she learned Simon had failed, she'd send others. She wanted Jennifer, and she would find her wherever she went.

"I can't go with you," she said, looking up from the maps. "I have to go to New York."

"I'll come with you."

"No, you have your work, that interview in Chicago."

"I'll do the interview, then catch a flight to New York." He glanced over and smiled. "Come on, you can show me Broadway."

"I would love it if you came to New York." She took hold of his hand again.

"But what about this boyfriend of yours?"

Jennifer shook her head. "I have to speak to Tom, tell him what has happened. The only one good thing out of this trip is I know now that it's all wrong, Tom and me."

"But what about me?" Kirk asked. "You met me on this trip!" He kept grinning.

Jennifer stared at him and studied his face, then she asked, "You do want to come see me in New York?"

"You're damn right!" And then, as if to prove himself, he pressed down on the accelerator and speeded up the car. "But I think you should stay with me in Chicago. Then we'll fly together."

"It will be all right, Kirk. In New York, I have help."

He glanced over at Jennifer. "You mean Tom?"

Jennifer shook her head. She was staring ahead at the long straight highway. "No. A woman. Another channeler." Jennifer could see Phoebe Fisher now, see her in the lovely basement apartment on Eighty-second Street, see her walking slowly with her silver cane, see the way the soft, orange sun warmed the brick walls of her living room. She saw Phoebe waiting, smiling, encouraging her. It would be all right, Jennifer told herself. She had Phoebe. She had someone to turn to for help.

BOOK FOUR

Know that if you become worse you will go to the worse souls, and if better, to the better souls; and in every succession of life and death you will do and suffer what like must fitly suffer at the hands of like.

—Plato
The Republic

And as Jesus passed by, he saw a man which was blind from his birth. And His disciples asked Him, saying, Master, who did sin, this man or his parents, that he was born blind?

—John 9:1–2

32

"YOU'RE SAFE NOW," PHOEBE told her, welcoming her into her basement apartment. "And where's this young lover of yours?" she asked next, smiling.

"But how could you know?" Jennifer stood back, startled by the channeler's question.

"Dance told me." She kept smiling, looking up at Jennifer. "I think it's wonderful!"

"Kirk saved my life, really. He came racing by in his little car and picked me up. God knows what would have happened to me if he hadn't stopped."

"He didn't just happen by, Jennifer, as you must realize by now. People don't meet by chance. It's all planned and ordained. It's your karma. Both of your karmas."

She had her thin arm linked into Jennifer's and was using Jennifer to support her as they walked into the living room, which on this cloudy afternoon was lit by a dozen small candles casting shadowy light.

"Where is your young friend now?" Phoebe asked offhandedly as she eased herself onto the small sofa.

"He's flying in later this afternoon. He had an appointment in Chicago."

"Good! Then you'll be together in a few hours." She seemed pleased.

"Why?" Jennifer asked, watching the small woman, wondering about the odd collection of questions.

Phoebe shrugged. "It's always better if you are with someone who understands you, especially now while you are having such intense past-life regressions."

"I have you," Jennifer whispered, wanting to show the woman how much she depended on her.

"Thank you." Phoebe smiled, nodding her thanks. "It is my privilege, really, to be so close to such a powerful source as yourself."

"Except no one knows who I am! Or who I really once was, I should say."

"I think it's time we did force this spirit into the open, Jenny. We need to identify it." She was not looking at Jennifer, but reaching down beside the sofa and pulling out a large box.

"Can Dance tell us?"

Phoebe shook her head. "Dance can't help us. He operates on another level of consciousness. He isn't a reincarnated spirit like Habasha. What I must do is contact directly the spirit that is using your body, trying to work through your consciousness."

The channeler leaned forward and lowered her voice. She held Jennifer's attention steady with the intenseness of her gaze, the look in her brown eyes. "The entity that wants to be channeled by you, Jenny, is also protecting you. He or she is waiting for the right moment, waiting for you to come into your full powers, so that you'll accept him. So far, however, this spirit has only been protecting you from physical attacks. It is also clear that there is another reincarnated spirit, Jennifer, that is trying to kill you before you realize your full spiritual power."

"But who is that person, or whatever. Is it Kathy Dart?" Jennifer had raised her voice. She was frightened again.

"I don't know," Phoebe said softly. "But this may help us." She held up a game box.

"A Ouija board! That's a children's game."

"Yes, unfortunately it is treated as a child's game, but it is a dangerous toy and should not be used by adults, either, without training and experience."

Phoebe set the board on the coffee table and opened it, continuing to talk as she took the board from the box.

"A Ouija board, or talking board, as it is sometimes called, is very old. In 540 B.C. Pythagoras used them in his seances. This board was reinvented in 1892 by a man named Fuld. It's very simple, really, just a semicircle of the letters of the alphabet, and the words 'YES,' 'NO,' and 'GOOD-BYE.' " She looked over at Jennifer. "Have you ever used one?"

Jennifer shook her head. "No, not even as a child. I seem to remember it was banned from our house—something to do with the devil."

Phoebe smiled. "Yes, that's the cultural superstition. And today among parapsychologists it is accepted that Ouija boards attract channel entities of the lower classes, unless handled by a channeler."

Phoebe picked up a small platform supported by three inch-long legs. "This is a planchette. See how it's shaped like a pointer? As I ask questions, the pointer will indicate letters to spell out a message." She handed Jennifer paper and a pencil. "I'll ask the questions, Jennifer, and would you please take notes."

Phoebe lifted the board off the coffee table and set it on her lap. "I need to have physical contact," she explained, placing her fingers lightly on the planchette.

"We'll begin slowly," Phoebe went on. "I'll ask the questions and summon up the spirit. It may take several minutes after I ask a question for the spirit to announce itself," she added. "You'll see the planchette move. When the planchette indicates a letter, just jot it down."

Jennifer nodded, but she was already tense.

"Relax, Jennifer," Phoebe advised, and then she placed her fingers lightly on the planchette and, closing her eyes, asked the Ouija board, "Do you wish to communicate with us?"

Jennifer glanced from Phoebe's hands to her soft, pale face, and then steadied her gaze again on the channeler's fingers. For several minutes nothing happened, and Jennifer realized she was holding her breath. She took a deep breath to calm herself and was about to speak, to tell Phoebe that she was too frightened and tense to go on with this, when the planchette suddenly moved and the pointed end of the plastic platform turned in the direction of the word "Yes."

"What are you called?" Phoebe asked.

Jennifer kept staring at Phoebe's hand as the instrument moved again and in rapid jerks pointed to more than a dozen letters.

Quickly, Jennifer scribbled down the letters as the planchette tracked across the smooth board, then read the words out loud: "I am one of many names."

"You say you are one of many names," Phoebe said, still with her eyes closed. "But what do you wish us to call you?"

PHARAOH

Next to the name "PHARAOH," Jennifer wrote "Egypt."
"Do you know Habasha?" Phoebe asked the board.

ETHIOP

"Yes, an Ethiopian. Have you and Habasha been reincarnated many times?" Phoebe questioned the spirit.

Again the planchette moved.

YES

"And our Jennifer?"

YES

"Is our friend Jennifer in danger?" Phoebe asked, softening her voice.

The planchette moved quickly under Phoebe's fingers. The heart-shaped instrument crossed the flat smooth surface on its own accord. It pulled back to the middle of the board, then sped again to the word "YES" and the symbol of the bright sun. Jennifer stared at Phoebe. The channeler's brown eyes had opened and widened.

Phoebe continued with her questioning. "Tell us, spirit," she asked calmly, "who wishes to harm our soulmate Jennifer?"

The planchette hesitated, spun freely under Phoebe's fingers with a life of its own and quickly spelled out a message. Jennifer read the letters aloud as the planchette rapidly moved across the board: "T-A-M-I-T."

Phoebe, her eyes closed again, paused a moment to frame her next question.

Her hands stopped moving. The heart-shaped planchette froze. Jennifer held her breath and watched Phoebe.

"Tell me, Pharaoh," Phoebe said to the Ouija board, "who in this lifetime is Tamit?"

K A T H Y

"No!" Jennifer whispered, and the breath went out of her.

Jennifer looked down at the board as the planchette, moving under Phoebe's touch, spelled out the story from the days of Ramses the Great, of how Amenhotep had fought a battle and killed the Ethiopian monarch to marry Roudidit. Then Tamit, the jealous daughter of Nenoferkaptak, had Roudidit murdered when Amenhotep was away at Memphis.

"And who is Amenhotep?" Phoebe asked.

KIRK

Phoebe Fisher pushed the Ouija board away and looked over at Jennifer. She looked worried now. The warm softness had slipped off her face. She seemed older in the winter light of the afternoon. "It is clear from what this 'Pharaoh' spirit is telling me," she said carefully to Jennifer, "that an ancient drama is being played out today."

"I just don't understand why *now*." Jennifer kept shaking her head. "It's an endless puzzle. We keep going around in circles. Everyone used to be someone else; no one is who they are. I'm not me!" She looked at Phoebe, her eyes showing her feeling of help-lessness.

Phoebe reached over to hold Jennifer's hand, telling her, "You are frightened, I know, Jennifer, and with good cause. Your spirit has been in revolt against your rational consciousness. Your friends appear to be your enemies. Your whole world has changed beyond recognition. But you cannot let your fear become your prison. You must not lose hope, or you will not transform your life."

Jennifer shook her head, still bewildered.

"To reach the light, you must endure the burning," Phoebe summed up.

"I've had the burning," Jennifer replied soberly. "And there is going to be more."

"Yes, you must face your enemy."

Jennifer nodded, then asked, "Will you help me?"

"I'll try," she whispered, her eyes not leaving Jennifer's face. Then she said, "You could be killed, Jennifer."

"Or I could kill again."

Phoebe nodded. "You have no choice." Then she stood up, saying, "I'll get your coat." The channeler stepped around the coffee table and limped into her bedroom, to where she had left Jennifer's fur coat and luggage.

Jennifer pulled a tissue from the pocket of her jeans and wiped her nose. She was staring down at the Ouija board that Phoebe had left on the coffee table. It looked so innocent, she thought, nothing more than a silly children's game.

She reached out and touched the smooth heart-shaped plan-chette, let her fingertips rest lightly for a moment on the plastic surface. Her hands trembled, and she felt a sudden bolt of energy rush into her fingers, up her arms. It took her breath away. She jerked her hand away from the planchette and sat back.

What are you? she thought, staring at the Ouija board.

The heart-shaped planchette moved then without the touch of her fingers. It traced across the smooth surface of the board spelling out an answer. But this time it was not "Pharaoh" who replied to Jennifer:

I AM YOUR SOUL

Jennifer sat very still as she watched the planchette spell out the answer. She was frightened again, holding her breath, but she was also thrilled, as if she were lifting up the edge of a forbidden universe.

Who am I? Jennifer thought next, concentrating on the board. Her eyes did not waver from the plastic planchette. Again it moved, responding to her silent thought, spelling out the words:

YOU ARE THE FIRST

Jennifer sat staring at the Ouija board, puzzled by the replies and not sure what to say. She heard Phoebe in the next room, heard her say something about the weather, the terrible winter New York was having, and Jennifer quickly directed her concentration to the board and asked: I am the first what?

The smooth marker slid across the flat board, spelling out one word:

HUMAN

Then Phoebe reached the living room, carrying Jennifer's heavy fur coat, and saw that the heart-shaped planchette was moving effortlessly under the power of Jennifer's spirit.

"What are you doing?" the channeler shouted, dropping the coat and stumbling forward, tripping on her deformed leg.

"Nothing! I'm not doing anything!" Jennifer exclaimed, jumping up and tipping over the Ouija board, terrified by the violence of Phoebe's reaction. "I'm sorry. I'm sorry. I didn't mean to do anything."

"What did it tell you? Didn't I tell you the board was dangerous?" The small woman had regained her balance and had pulled herself onto the arm of the sofa. She kept glaring at Jennifer, her eyes white with fright.

"I'm sorry, Phoebe. I didn't mean—"

"What did it tell you?"

"Nothing. I mean . . ." Jennifer kept shaking her head, still terrified and upset by the channeler's violent reaction. "I'm terribly sorry, but I didn't understand. I mean—" Jennifer took a deep breath and, recovering her composure, said forcefully, "Phoebe, I'm sorry I upset you, but you shouldn't have shouted at me! I'm a case of nerves as it is." Jennifer glanced down and was surprised to see her hands were not trembling.

"What did you learn?" Phoebe demanded.

"Nothing! I was just asking a question."

"You're not trained to use a talking board," Phoebe said again, watching Jennifer. Her face had lost all of its soft, smooth glow.

"I'm sorry," Jennifer said slowly, not looking at Phoebe. She was afraid to trade glances with the channeler.

Phoebe stood again, fully recovered. The softness returned to her voice and she said, "I'm sorry, Jennifer. I just don't want you to be misled. Ouija boards, as I mentioned, are often controlled by spirits of a lower order." She bent then to pick up Jennifer's coat, and Jennifer glanced at the board, directing her thoughts at the heart-shaped planchette, asking one last question of her hidden spirit: Who wants to kill me?

The plastic planchette began to move on the smooth surface when Phoebe jumped forward and swept the instrument off the board, knocking it across the room, where it skipped off the stone hearth of the fireplace and flew into the fire, sizzling at once in the heat of the flame.

"You must never—!" The channeler regained her stance and focused on Jennifer.

Phoebe was trembling, Jennifer realized. The channeler was the one who was truly frightened.

"I am trying to save your life, don't you see?" Phoebe shouted at her.

Jennifer nodded, reaching for her coat. "I'm sorry," she said again.

Phoebe reached out and touched Jennifer's hands.

"Jennifer, I'm sorry I shouted at you. It's just that you must be careful when you involve yourself in the spirit world." She had both her hands on Jennifer's arms and was looking up lovingly at her. "You will be careful, won't you?"

"Yes, I'll try."

"Good!" And she reached up and quickly kissed Jennifer good-bye. "Remember, I love you. I'll see that you are protected from your ancient lives," she said, speaking softly to Jennifer, but the channeler's lips were cold on her cheek.

33

JENNIFER GRABBED A TAXI on Columbus Avenue and told the
driver she wanted to go to LaGuardia. Kirk's flight was not due until
after seven, and though she had time to go home to her place first
and unpack, she was now afraid to go there by herself, especially
after witnessing what the Ouija board had done, how the planchette
had moved, spelling out her fate. What would it have told her if
Phoebe hadn't knocked the instrument off the board? Jennifer shuddered, recalling Phoebe's act of violence, her sudden strange reaction to what the Ouija board was telling her. Phoebe's behavior
had upset her, Jennifer realized, as much as what had happened to
her on the farm.

The taxi crossed Central Park at Eighty-sixth and paused at the
stoplight on Fifth Avenue. Jennifer glanced out the window at the
Metropolitan Museum of Art. The lights were on in the Sackler
Wing, and she could see part of the Temple of Dendur. The ancient
Egyptian temple glowed in the soft yellow light, casting shadows
the length of the immense wing.

Jennifer remembered how she had gone once to the museum
when she was a teenager. It had been a junior-high class trip and
she had got upset, wanted only to get out of the museum. Jennifer
tried to remember what it was about, why she had been so upset
by the Egyptian wing. It had been new then, built to house the
Temple of Dendur, the small temple that had been saved in Egypt
when the Aswan Dam was built. The temple had been removed
from lower Nubia in Egypt, stone by stone, and rebuilt in the Metropolitan Museum. There was a pool of water in front of the temple,
and a wall of windows overlooking Central Park.

It was a beautiful setting, Jennifer recalled, but when she had
first come into the wing it had frightened her, upsetting her for
some unknown reason.

Of course, Jennifer thought. Of course!

She leaned forward at once and tapped the glass partition of the taxi, telling the driver that she had changed her mind. She wasn't going to the airport. She was stopping first at the Metropolitan Museum. She was going back into the Temple of Dendur to learn what secret of her past was locked away in her memory. She was going to let the ancient stone tell her what had happened to her on the banks of the Nile.

The new wing was at the rear of the huge Metropolitan, behind long galleries of Egyptian art and artifacts. Jennifer didn't rush herself through the exhibition. She moved slowly, waiting for her memory to be triggered by the objects, waiting for some connection to her life in Egypt, to the earliest time of her existence. The Ouija board had told her she was the first human. Was this what it meant? Did all of her troubles begin here, in one of the great dynasties?

Jennifer kept moving slowly through the rooms, from the time of the New Kingdoms, back into the Middle Kingdoms and the Archaic Period. She glanced from object to object, scanned the artifacts that the Metropolitan had in its vast collection. She waited for some memory. It had happened to her at the Museum of Natural History. When she had seen the primitive hut, she knew that she had once lived in that prehistoric hut, slept under those mammoth bones and animal skins.

Jennifer pushed the door and went into a room of glass cases and burial objects. There were mummies sealed behind the cases, shelves of ancient linens and small Canopic jars.

She reached out and pressed her fingers against the cases holding the mummies. No sensation touched her. She felt only the cool glass. There were no memories of her past life here, she understood.

She kept moving through the deserted rooms. It was late, she realized. The museum would be closing soon. She glanced at her watch to see how much time she had left, then opened another door and stepped into the vast Sackler Wing with the reconstructed Temple of Dendur.

Now she felt something. Her attention was alerted. It was as if some memory was trying to reach her from her early lifetime on earth. She was suddenly not frightened. The recollection was comforting, as if she had finally solved her problem, found the missing piece in the puzzle of her life.

She moved forward, closer to the temple itself, keeping her eyes now on the huge stone structure.

There were few other people in the wing. A tour guide was speaking to a group of women sitting on a stone bench. She was aware, too, of two guides standing together by the windows, but she concentrated on the temple, focusing her attention and waiting for more memories to flood her mind.

She stepped up onto the level of the temple, walked around the small pool of water, and approached the front of the reconstructed temple. In the foreground was an archway, and behind that, the temple walls. The spirit called Pharaoh had told Phoebe that Kathy Dart, as Tamit, had killed her when she was Roudidit and married to Amenhotep. It was the days of Ramses, and Kirk had been Amenhotep, her husband.

Jennifer paused on her approach to the temple. If this was the first incarnation and she had been murdered, she thought, then why now, after all the other lives she had lived, would Kathy Dart still be seeking revenge? It was her spirit, not Kathy Dart's, that had been violated!

It couldn't be her first life on earth, Jennifer thought next. She remembered the images she had seen of herself when Kathy Dart had pierced her third eye. She had been a wild creature then, living in a jungle world. But what had the Ouija board planchette spelled out? That she was the first human.

Jennifer shook her head. No, Phoebe was wrong. Phoebe was hiding information. She had swept the planchette off the board. She hadn't wanted Jennifer to know. But to know what?

Jennifer stepped closer to the interior of the temple and closed her eyes, concentrating on the temple, on her stone surroundings. When she opened her eyes again, she saw the temple women who sang and shook the sistra and crotals during services. They lived in the innermost sanctuaries of the temple and were called God's handmaids. All of these virgins were daughters of the wealthy families, of kings and queens, and she was among the selected few.

Jennifer stood perfectly still watching herself, the other young women of the temple. They wore shifts under transparent white pleated robes that were gathered over their left breasts. Their right shoulder was uncovered. She watched herself as she moved in procession. She was wearing rings of solid gold and strings of gold beads. A black curled wig fell over her back and onto her shoulders. She had a tiara of turquoise and gold tied at the back with two tassel cords, and her head was crowned with a scented pomade.

She was a beautiful young woman in this lifetime, Jennifer saw, and she wondered how she knew it was even her. Yet she knew. And she saw, too, as she searched the faces of the other virgins that Phoebe Fisher was with her, another of the young women. She scanned the corps of singers. Kathy Dart's spirit was not part of this divine harem.

The scene faded from her sight. She reached out, as if to pull back the ancient memory, but saw only her hand reaching into the vast wing of the museum. Behind her she heard the museum guard make a point to the tourists, heard a child's happy voice echo off the high ceiling. She glanced around and saw that she was being watched by a museum guard. To mask her confusion and hide her bewilderment at what she had seen, she walked to the edge of the wall and sat down.

Her legs were weak and she was out of breath. She leaned over and dropped her head between her legs. She would faint, Jennifer realized, if she wasn't careful.

"Are you okay, lady?" the guard asked, stepping over to her.

Jennifer sat up and tossed her hair back off her shoulder. She forced a smiled. "Yes, thank you. I just felt a little funny." The man's face was swimming in her eyesight.

The man nodded and moved away, saying as he did, "Well, you looked a little odd there."

"I'm fine now, thank you." Jennifer took a tissue from her purse and wiped her eyes. She waited until the man had gone back to his post before she looked again at the temple. The gray stones of the small building looked the same. There were no young virgins, no divine harem. She had imagined it all, she thought. It was nothing more than a psychic episode.

She kept staring at the Temple of Dendur, the silent gray building, nothing more than a few ancient walls dug from the muddy banks of the Nile River.

She calmed down, pulled herself under control. She was all right, she realized. She didn't have a psychic episode, she realized. She had seen herself as she had been as a young woman in Egypt. She had married Amenhotep—Kirk, in this reincarnation. She had seen Phoebe Fisher but not Kathy Dart. Why was Phoebe in her Egyptian days and not Kathy? The spirit of the Pharaoh said Tamit had killed her when she was Roudidit and married to the warrior Amenhotep.

The guard moved toward her again and signaled that the museum was closing. Jennifer nodded and stood up, collected her bag.

She glanced over at the temple, half expecting to see more shadowy shades from her reincarnated life drifting through the vaulted arch, appearing like a whiff of memory. Nothing now surprised her. But there was no image, nothing but the empty gallery, the silent walls of the temple. Jennifer stood and followed the last of the tourists from the Sackler Wing, taking the exit doors and going through more long, low-ceilinged hallways and galleries filled with the artifacts from the Old Kingdom of Egypt, at the time of the First Dynasty, over twenty-five hundred years before Christ.

In the last gallery, Jennifer stopped momentarily to look at a huge map of Egypt. She wanted to see where the Temple of Dendur had been located on the Nile River, but what caught her attention immediately was the vast expanse of Lower Egypt and the names Kush and Ethiopia.

There had been great civilizations on the Nile River before the ancient Egyptians, and before those, man had traveled north out of the primitive jungles of Africa. She remembered what Kathy Dart had said in Washington, how her connection with Habasha had come from a piece of crystal found in Ethiopia. Habasha had been alive then, 4 million years ago, and his spirit was on earth even before that, over 23 million years ago.

Jennifer kept staring at the old map of Lower Egypt, at the vast expanse of the Sudan desert and the high plateaus of Ethiopia. It was here, deep in the the gorges of southern Ethiopia, where Habasha had lived, that man first stood upright and changed from a beast of the jungle to a creature possessing a spirit, having a soul, a reincarnated soul that he carried with him throughout time and filled with all the memories of all his lifetimes.

Phoebe Fisher had not told her the truth, Jennifer realized. The spirit of the Pharaoh was not her first moment in time. Her spirit, her oversoul, which had moved the heart-shaped planchette, had existed before the great civilizations of Egypt. It had said she was the first human!

She was like Habasha—that was the connection! She, too, like Kathy Dart, went back to the dawn of mankind, to the first moments of the human spirits, millions of years before the Temple of Dendur. She had been reincarnated as a member of the divine harem in the temple, had married Amenhotep, and died in Egypt. Her body, she was sure, had been mummified and ferried across the Nile to be entombed. But she now knew she had lived even before this great civilization of pharaonic Egypt. She had lived with Habasha. She had lived at the same time as Kathy Dart's first incarnation. And now, she realized, Phoebe Fisher had been there, too. That was why the channeler had kept her from learning more from the Ouija board. They had all been alive together in their first incarnations on earth. And something had happened to them, there at the dawn of time.

Jennifer glanced around, suddenly afraid, fearing that Phoebe had followed her to the museum. But the Egyptian gallery was empty. The Metropolitan was closing.

The answer, she realized, would not be found here in the great dynasties of Egypt and in the days of Ramses the Great. Yes, she had suffered and died, murdered by Tamit, but this was not her first life nor her first death. She had to return to the prehistoric exhibition at the Museum of Natural History, where she first realized she had lived in the primitive hut from the Ice Age.

She walked out through the front doors of the museum and stood at the top of the stone steps, looking down at Fifth Avenue, crowded now with rush hour traffic. The city skyline was already aglow with lights and bright flashing signs. She needed to hurry. Kirk's flight was due from Chicago, and she needed to be with him. But first she had to telephone Kathy Dart and Phoebe Fisher. She wanted both channels to meet her at the Museum of Natural History. She wanted them to walk with her through the Ice Age exhibition. It would be there, Jennifer knew now, in that prehistoric graveyard, that she'd remember what had happened to her spirit when they had evolved as humans and come down out of the trees to walk upright as man.

Jennifer smiled. For the first time in weeks, she knew exactly what to do. She knew how to solve the mystery of her past, of all her reincarnated lives, and she hurried down the stone steps, rushing to meet her lover, her great love, she realized, of all her lifetimes, and she smiled with anticipation, her face suddenly bright and shiny with hope.

34

THE FRONT DOOR OF her apartment had been replaced and the locks changed. Jennifer took the set of keys given to her by the superintendent and unlocked the door, but she didn't step across the threshold. The apartment was dark.

"What's next?" Kirk asked. He was standing beside her, still holding their luggage.

"I'm not sure. I thought perhaps Tom would be here. I called his apartment while I was waiting for your plane and just got his machine."

"Is he at work?"

Jennifer shook her head. "No, I called his office, too." She stepped into the room then and realized at once that something was wrong. She flipped on the entrance light and peered into the living room. Her furniture was in order, and what she could see of her small kitchen looked untouched. In the three days that she had been gone, the super had cleaned the entrance and the living room. There was no trace of the dog's blood.

"Do you want me to look around?" Kirk asked, edging past her to set down their bags.

"No," she said. She moved a few steps farther into the apartment and glanced to her right. "Do you smell anything?" she asked Kirk.

He sniffed the air and shook his head. "The place could use a little fresh air, though. Shall I open a window?" He stood with his legs apart and his hands deep in the pockets of his red jacket.

"No, don't do anything. Please." Jennifer was apprehensive, but she tried to keep her voice steady. She slipped off her coat and dropped it on the living room sofa, then turned toward her bedroom.

"Hey, Jen . . ."

"It's okay, Kirk. Everything is all right." She didn't look at him. The bedroom door was slightly ajar. Jennifer stepped over and pushed it with one finger. Light from the street filtered through the closed blinds and left dim streaks on the opposite wall. She could see the clutter on top of her dresser. Everything was just as she had left it. She moved farther into the room and looked at the bed. It hadn't been touched.

"Hey, Jen, what's going on?" Kirk's voice trembled slightly.

Jennifer didn't answer him, just held her hand up in a gesture for silence. There was someone here, she knew. She felt someone's presence. But who? And where?

All at once, a breeze blew the heavy window curtains out, scattering the loose papers on her desk. Tom was here, Jennifer realized. She could feel his presence. But why would he hide from her? Was he waiting for her? Did he want to kill her?

"Tom?" she asked, turning and scanning the room.

Kirk remained standing in the bedroom doorway. He was afraid to enter, she guessed.

Jennifer opened the door to the bathroom. It was empty. Her towels were as she had left them the morning after the pit bull attack, crumpled on the floor.

"Is he there?" Kirk asked.

Jennifer shook her head, then reached over and turned on the lamp beside the bed.

"Are you okay, Jen?" Kirk asked, stepping into the room.

She nodded. "I think so. I feel him, that's all."

"Tom?"

"Yes." She sat down in a chair and pulled off her boots. "It was so strong, I thought he was here."

"Maybe he's under the bed or something," Kirk joked, pulling off his jacket.

Jennifer sat back in the wing chair. "Would you look?" she asked.

"Under the bed?"

"Yes."

"Hey, Jen, quit kidding."

"I'm serious." She was smiling in spite of herself. "I get myself scared sometimes. . . . Please, I know he isn't, but I can't look."

Kirk grinned. "Sure!" He dropped to his knees and lifted the bed skirt, peeping underneath. "He'd have to be a goddamn midget."

"Kirk . . ."

"Okay! Okay! No, he's not there." He stood up.

"I'm going to call his apartment again." She reached over to her bedside phone and quickly dialed his number.

"How about a drink?"

"Good!" Jennifer said, smiling up at him as she listened to Tom's phone ring. At the third ring, his machine clicked on, and she heard his message. He wasn't home, but he'd call back as soon as possible. She waited for the beep, then left another message, asking him to telephone her. "It doesn't matter when," she said, "just call."

Jennifer hung up and went back to the kitchen, where Kirk had found the liquor.

"Hold me," she told him, and wrapped her arms around his waist, snuggling her face into his shoulder.

Kirk turned around and lifted her up, grabbed her bottom with both of his hands, and pressed her against him. She felt his erection at once.

"Let's go to bed," she said.

"No drink?"

"I want you, not a drink."

He kissed her and began to unbutton her blouse.

"We'd better lock the door," she told him, a little breathlessly.

When Kirk left her, Jennifer unzipped her jeans, pulled them off, and tossed them onto the back of a living room chair as she walked back into her bedroom. There she dipped her head to one side and took off first one earring, then the other, and set them both in a tray on her dresser. As she pulled her blouse up over her head, she thought she saw something move in the far corner of the room. With her blouse still tangled in her arms, Jennifer stepped to the wall and flipped on the light switch. There was nothing in the corner but a bookshelf, filled with her familiar night-time reading and a few framed photographs.

She could hear Kirk's sneakers squeaking on the hall floor as he returned to the bedroom. Jennifer turned off the light, unsnapped her bra, and slipped into the bed.

"The barn door is bolted," he announced, and paused at the doorway, surprised that Jennifer was already in bed.

"Come here," she told him. She longed for the warmth of his body, ached to make love with him, and when he smiled lazily at her and unbuttoned his jeans, the sweetness of anticipation excited her more. She lifted her arms toward him, and he slipped into bed, under the down coverlet, and pulled her into his strong arms.

Jennifer felt safe, protected by his broad shoulders, and dizzy with longing as he moved to touch her. His mouth and hands were everywhere, and his eagerness made her more excited. She had never been with such an ardent lover.

In the darkened bedroom, Kirk's face glowed with pleasure. Jennifer held his face close to hers and worked her tongue into his mouth. She wanted to consume him. She wanted him inside her. She wanted their flesh to be glued together. For a moment she was afraid that her passion would frighten him off.

With trembling hands, she reached down to guide him into her body. She liked leading the way, making her lover respond to her needs. Jennifer pushed Kirk back onto the pillows as she straddled him. He rose high and tight up inside of her, and she twisted her hips to create more friction.

She leaned down and licked his chest, then tossed her loose mane of blond hair across his face like a wide, soft brush.

"Do you like this?" she whispered, smiling down at him.

Kirk nodded, then reached up and pulled her down on top of him, probing her mouth with his tongue. Jennifer felt his erection swell as he came inside her. She let herself ride with him, waiting for her own orgasm, shifting slightly so that her right nipple was exposed, and she arched her back so that he could reach her swollen breast with his tongue. With a sudden shudder, she came, driving her body onto his. Her heart pumped wildly, driving her blood to the center of her body, where her muscles exploded in passion. She found that she had detached a part of her mind and was watching her body rock in its own selfish ecstasy.

Suddenly Jennifer grew teary. She turned her face into the pillows, then kissed Kirk tenderly in the hazy afterglow of her orgasm. She nestled closer to him, longing to stay this way forever, to hold him captive for her delight, and she shifted her legs so that his erection was pinned inside her.

Kirk was kissing her gently, nuzzling her ears, her closed eyes, the dampness on her throat. He was coming again; she marveled as his orgasm pulsed within her.

Jennifer wrapped her arms around him and kissed his hair. The only light in the room came from the street, filtered through the drawn curtains, but her eyes had adjusted to the dark and she could clearly see the shadowy figure emerge from the dark corner of the bedroom. It watched them, watched her, and then stepped over to the doorway and paused there. There was no hatred in the figure's eyes, nor anger, only an immense sorrow, as if he had lost everything, lost her, lost his whole world.

"Jenny, what's the matter?" Kirk asked, pulling back from her breasts. Her body had turned cold in his arms. "What's the matter?" he asked again, frightened by the look on her face. He turned to see what she was staring at. But there was only the open doorway, a dim slanting light beyond.

"What is it?" he demanded, grasping her by the shoulders.

"He's here," she whispered, keeping her eyes on the doorway.

"Who? What are you talking about?"

"Tom is here."

"Jesus Christ, Jenny, what are you saying?" Kirk sat up on his knees.

"I just saw him. He's dead. He was here, watching us make love."

"Hey," Kirk said gently. "No one is here, Jenny; you're driving yourself crazy." He moved to the doorway and turned on the overhead light. "No one is here, I promise." When he looked at his hands, he realized he was trembling. "Christ, Jenny, you frightened the hell out of me."

"He was here. I saw him. His spirit was here," Jennifer said calmly. She was no longer afraid.

"Look for yourself! We're all alone," Kirk insisted.

"You don't understand," Jennifer whispered, slipping out of bed. She knew he was frightened, but she had lost all of her fear.

"Jenny, come on! Where are you going?" He watched her as she got out of bed and moved toward her closet. He swallowed hard, watching her tall, slender body. "Let's go back to bed," he cajoled.

Jennifer pulled open the door to her walk-in closet and reached in to where she always hung her flannel nightgown. Before her mind could react, before she could scream out in horror, the tips of her fingers touched the soft film of his still-open eyes. She saw him fully then, saw that her kitchen knife had been plunged into his heart, saw his bloated, grayish tongue and his swollen white face, and saw that her dresses and blouses had been shoved aside. Tom was hanging from the metal bar by his own black belt, the one she had bought at Brooks Brothers and given to him for his thirty-sixth birthday. He had been dead for several days and he smelled of death.

And then she screamed.

35

JENNIFER LEFT KIRK ON the street, telling him only to wait for her, and entered the museum from West Eighty-first Street. It was after ten o'clock. They had spent most of the night and early morning with the police, at her apartment, and downtown at the office of the Justice Department, giving statements, explaining where she had been for three days.

They were due back at the Justice Department later that day for more questions, but Jennifer had told the police she had to meet someone at the museum, that it was important for her job. She didn't tell Kirk that she had arranged for Phoebe Fisher and Kathy Dart to meet her when the musuem opened.

She took the elevator to the third floor and followed the signs to the prehistoric exhibits. It was early, and the museum was virtually empty as she walked quickly through galleries, heading for the one where the prehistoric fossils were displayed. It wasn't until she approached the special exhibit that she grew frightened. Stopping between two life-size models of reptiles, she tried to decide what to do next. She realized then that she had no plan for the confrontation. Phoebe Fisher had told her that she couldn't trust her rational mind, but that was wrong. She had listened to Phoebe and to Kathy Dart; she had let her emotions dictate her response, and she hadn't used her common sense. Well, she would figure it out as she went along.

Reminding herself to keep calm, she pushed open the glass doors and resolutely stepped into the darkened room, filled with artifacts of prehistoric man. She moved slowly past the glass displays of mammoth bones, the enlarged photographs of cave drawings and primitive sculptures. She kept herself from glancing to either side, afraid that seeing some ancient engraving would trigger a past life. She had to be alert. She had to be ready. She had to keep her attention focused.

She watched the few other museum visitors—couples, mothers with babies in strollers, school kids scribbling notes for a class assignment. She kept away from the center aisle and moved toward the rebuilt hut that dominated the exhibit.

It was here that she had first experienced the strange vibrations, here that she had told Tom the Ukraine model was built wrong. He had looked at her as if she was crazy. Well, she thought wryly, she wasn't crazy. She was worse than crazy. She felt herself tense up, become more alert to her surroundings, to the other people in the gallery. She was an animal on the prowl. She kept walking, moving slowly toward the next gallery, the one built with the remains of man's first family, the fossils of "Lucy" and the other early *Australopithecus* found on the banks of the Hadar River in the Afar Triangle of Ethiopia.

In the dark passageway between the two rooms, she caught a scent. She paused and sniffed the stale air of the closed rooms. Yes, she realized, someone was ahead of her, hiding perhaps in the next gallery, the large diorama that had been been built to resemble an African water hole. Through the thick leafy underbrush, she spotted several giraffes and the hunchback of a black rhinoceros, wallowing in the muddy African waters. And beyond them, reaching into the fig bushes, was a cluster of male and female hominid models, constructed by the museum to show how the first family of *Australopithecus* lived with the beasts of the African jungle.

Jennifer raised her head and snorted, then kept moving closer, keeping to the wall and out of sight as she approached the water hole. She was ready. Her blood was pumping through her body. Her neck muscles swelled; her nipples hardened. She kept moving.

Jennifer caught Kathy Dart's distinct scent, then spotted her on the other side of the diorama, near a grassy plain that had been built into the horizon, as if one could step into the museum diorama and travel to the horizon. Kathy was looking away from her, searching the room. She was looking for her, Jennifer realized. She sniffed the air. She was downwind, and Kathy hadn't caught her scent, hadn't realized she had come into the exhibition from the rear exit.

Jennifer flattened herself against the wall. She watched Kathy Dart, waited for Habasha to stir, waited for Kathy to realize what she had finally understood at the Temple of Dendur, that all of them had lived together at the dawn of time.

Jennifer moved from the pocket of shadows and stepped closer. She was less than twenty yards from the jungle water hole when she spotted Phoebe. She was standing away from Kathy and also watching the main entrance of the gallery. They had expected her to come that way, she realized, and smiled, pleased that she had outsmarted them.

She knew she wanted to battle now, and this realization surprised her. She had been terrified before by her primitive strength; now, as she gazed around the strangely familiar diorama, she felt stirrings of recognition deep in the lymphatic system of her brain that stored and carried through time all of her emotional memories. Yes, she had been here before. Jennifer knew that now for certain. She had felt this earth beneath her webbed feet, she had once climbed down from those thick branches and reached with short and hairy fingers to pluck sweet figs from the low bushes. She snorted again and crouched low, creeping closer to her enemy, this tribe that shared with her family the muddy water hole, here by the edge of the great lake and in sight of the smoldering volcano.

She spotted a mother with a child in a stroller glance at her and scurry away, as the deer did in the forest, frightened by the mere sight of her and the others who slept together in trees and lived off the fresh sweet fruit of the forest.

Jennifer took a deep breath, thinking: I will draw Kathy Dart away from Phoebe. She will attack if it is me that she has been stalking.

Jennifer left the hidden protection of the museum wall, stepped into the center of the gallery and closer to the African diorama. Then she shouted and waved her arms to attract Kathy Dart's attention.

Kathy saw her, smiled, and mouthed a hello across the wide water-hole diorama. Kathy did not rush her. Jennifer stared back at Kathy; she waited, breathing harder now, her body coiled and ready to defend herself.

"Are you all right?" Kathy asked, mouthing the words across the silent gallery.

Jennifer cocked her head. She heard Kathy and understood what she had said, but Jennifer was remembering another morning in a distant time, when she had come out of the trees to find a mate among the males who had gathered to forage for fresh sweet fruit. She remembered now how she had been killed. And she screeched, recalling her anguish.

From the corner of her eye she saw the black museum guard looked alarmed and was coming at her. Jennifer knew that man. She had seen him once before on a paddleboat in the James River.

Jennifer moved at once, she jumped over the low railing surrounding the water hole diorama.

"Be careful!" Kathy shouted at her.

Jennifer stood up straight. She saw that the guard was talking on a portable phone. More guards were running toward the gallery, coming at her from the other exhibits. But Jennifer was in the middle of the African jungle now, standing in the underbrush, surrounded by thick, hanging vines, enormous mahogany tree trunks, and the posed figures of short, hairy hominids, dull eyed and dumb, who stared at her.

She hooted for their attention, to get them away from Kathy Dart, to let her fight this woman who also had stepped forward and come into the re-created ancient water hole.

"Jenny! Jenny, you don't understand!" Kathy was saying. She spoke softly, as if to reason with her voice.

The museum guard glanced back and forth between the two women.

"What the fuck," he swore, standing at the edge of the exhibit. "What in hell's going on here?"

Jennifer squatted in the green underbrush. She felt the heat of the day, the wet air, and smelled the pungent odors of tropical evergreens rotting in the steamy heat of the equatorial jungle, mixed with the sweet smells of fruit and flowers. She could hear the jungle, too, the incessant noise of birds, flying squirrels, and monkeys swinging through the heavy overhang of vines. She saw the hippos wallow in the deep water and a dozen crocodiles slip off the muddy bank and slap the mucky water as they disappeared from sight.

Jennifer was not frightened by the crocodiles or a small herd of woolly mammoths thrashing through the trees and down to the water. She sprang out of the dense wood and, running forward, screeched again at Kathy Dart, startling her.

"Jenny! Jenny!" Kathy screamed, holding out her hands with her palms down, gesturing, whispering, and trying to placate Jennifer. "It's not me. It's not me that you want."

Jennifer bared her teeth, hissed again.

"Jesus H. Christ!" The guard stepped over the low railing and reached for Jennifer.

"Get back!" Kathy Dart told him. "She's out of control. She doesn't know where she is."

"But I know where the fuck she's going," the big man mumbled, approaching.

Jennifer hit the guard with her right forearm, knocking the man off his legs and sending him tumbling. He fell backward, hitting one of the poised figures of an early *Australopithecus afarensis*, knocking the plaster-of-paris hominid into the plastic lake.

In that moment, as she hit him, Jennifer saw Phoebe coming at her from the early morning mist. She had been hurt in a fall from the cliffs and was using now the short branch of a tree to support herself as she dragged her lame leg across the ground. Jennifer spun around to face the other channeler.

"Jennifer, come with us," Kathy ordered. "We know about Phoebe. We've been trying to save you from her. Habasha was there. He knows."

"Her!" Jennifer thought to herself. "Her!" She did not at that moment remember how to talk, and her anger and anguish came screeching out in the terrified sound of an animal of the jungle. She leaped forward, to the edge of the diorama, and turned on Phoebe Fisher, hooting and screeching, frightened and enraged. Inside the prehistoric diorama, in the midst of the jungle heat, Jennifer recalled those moments of her very first life. She knew who she once was, realized, too, what had happened millions of years ago at the dawn of time.

Phoebe raised her steel-tipped cane above her head and rushed Jennifer.

"No!" Kathy Dart shouted, pushing forward and trying to stop Phoebe. The raised cane, like a primitive club, whistled as it cut through the air and struck Kathy Dart. The cane's sharp point sliced across Kathy's right cheek and dug itself deep into the thick muscles of her throat. The channeler, gasping for breath, grabbed her own neck in a stranglehold. The blood from her jugular squeezed through her fingers.

A woman screamed. Her screams kept coming and coming. They filled the gallery, echoing, gathering strength, as she ran in hysterical, blind bursts of speed, trying to escape, to flee the gallery like any frightened animal would.

Jennifer remembered. She had come scrambling out of her rubber tree, out of her high nest in the jungle, stirred by the needs of her swollen sex. She had come to mate on the forest floor, followed by the other females of her family, including the mother who had once nursed her from breastless teats, and her own child. She danced off from the first male who came after her, but watched over her shoulder while scrambling quickly on all fours. He kept advancing, screeching and waving his long arms. It was Habasha, Jennifer realized. It was Habasha in his first incarnation, and then, with a speed that she had not anticipated, Habasha mounted her from behind, entered, and ejaculated.

The other males were on her next, fighting with each other to be first. They were screaming, hooting, and dancing in a circle, sniffing her sex. The fig fruit was forgotten as the males kept after her. Pushing and shoving each other, they mounted her again and again, until, exhausted from their efforts, they slipped away into the heavy shade of the trees and slept. They had no fear. They were with their own kind.

None expected that one of their own would attack.

The old female had been chased away from their band for fighting with the others, and now suddenly she had returned. Screeching, she leapt from the tree and landed on all fours. Then, glancing around, she grabbed a mammoth bone and swung it, Jennifer saw again, at her. The bone glanced off her shoulder and hit her face. She howled in pain, and the other females, too, hooted and danced away.

The old female was white haired and smaller than her, less than two and a half feet tall, with a flat, hairy face, and a mouth misshapen by the swat of a saber-toothed tiger's paw. She kept after her, thumping the long bone on the earth, then raising it up with both arms and swinging wildly. Then without warning, the female turned aside, struck her mother, then killed her child.

She screeched when her child was struck down, and baring her teeth, she charged the cast-off female, knowing in the dimness of her brain that this predator was more dangerous than warthogs or two-tusked deer.

Phoebe Fisher raised her cane to strike. Jennifer screamed, leapt aside, and attacked with her ancient rage. She raked her nails across Phoebe's face, seized her hair, and jerked the head of the small woman back, exposing her pale white neck.

Her lost spirit possessed her now. She was living out her prehistoric revenge. She screeched and bared her teeth. She would rip out Phoebe's throat and kill this beast.

"Jenny, no!" Kirk screamed.

He came running through the gallery and lunged at Jennifer, knocking her to the floor. Phoebe Fisher scrambled to her feet, swinging her cane. She caught the black museum guard in the neck. The cane's sharp tip sliced him like a razor. Without a pause Phoebe stepped over Kathy Dart and lunged again at Jennifer, who was on the floor now and beyond the edge of the water hole diorama.

Kathy Dart stumbled to her feet. She was holding both hands to her cut throat, but the blood kept spreading between her fingers. She reached toward Phoebe, tried to keep her from killing Jennifer.

"Jenny!" she whispered, and her mouth bubbled up a mouthful of blood.

Phoebe struck again, swinging her cane down at both Jennifer and Kirk, who was down on the carpeted floor trying to shield Jennifer. The metal tip of Phoebe's cane jabbed Kirk's shoulder. He cried out and rolled away from Jennifer, leaving her momentarily helpless on the gallery floor.

Phoebe, raging, screeching, attacked again, aiming for Jennifer's face, trying to drive the ice-pick tip deep into her eyes.

Jennifer's ancient memory summoned their long-ago battle. It was at the African water hole that the first incarnated spirit of Phoebe had struck Jennifer with the mammoth bone, knocking her back into the deep water. She had tumbled and splashed, unable to swim, and then the crocodile had struck, seizing Jennifer's arm and pulling her deep into the jungle pool.

Jennifer smiled. She knew finally who it was that had been trying to kill her now, before she could remember, before she could gain all of her channeling powers. Jennifer jumped to her feet, avoided a wild swat by the small woman, and seized the cane from Phoebe Fisher, then raised it herself as a weapon. She saw the sudden terror in Phoebe Fisher's eyes. Jennifer knew that in one swift stroke she could kill her ancient enemy.

Jennifer stood poised, aiming for her mark. The old female had attacked her because she had mated with Habasha, attacked her because the other males had cast her aside. Now Jennifer would avenge the killing of her mother and first offspring.

"No, Jenny," Kirk pleaded from where he lay, clutching his wounded shoulder.

Jennifer swung the light cane at the channeler, aiming the steel point at the small woman's face, and as she did, Phoebe Fisher's face changed before her. The beautiful, bisque white skin exploded in blood, and Phoebe's small body jumped back, away from her. Jennifer missed her mark, and then she heard the sound of the museum guard's pistol shot.

Phoebe Fisher bounced off a plaster-of-paris model and slid

over the top of the plastic lake and disappeared into the grove of fig trees. She died in the mists of prehistoric time.

Deep in the heart of Africa, at the dawn of life, she had been the first hominid to kill another. She had come down out of the trees to kill the incarnated spirit of Jennifer Winters.

The death of the first human was murder.

EPILOGUE

JENNIFER DROVE SOUTH ON the New Jersey Turnpike. It was a month since the museum, and Kirk was still in pain, but she knew how desperately he wanted to get out of New York, at least for a while. She would never get him to live in New York, she thought, but so what? She wasn't sure she wanted to, either. Not in this lifetime anyway.

It was over. Phoebe was dead. Kathy Dart was in the hospital, as was Simon. She had not killed him, after all. She was thankful for that. But poor Tom. He had been just been an innocent victim, killed by Phoebe in her lust for revenge. But there was no innocent victim, Jennifer knew now. Whatever happened in life was simply the playing out of one's destiny.

At the dawn of time Phoebe had killed her, and in another life she had avenged that act. She had once been a poor black girl in the south who had jumped to her suicide, and Phoebe had been the white man. At every incarnation their spirits had returned to seek revenge on the other.

Spontaneously, she reached out and touched Kirk, let her right hand linger on the inside of his thigh.

"Happy?" she asked.

He nodded. "I'm happy you're with me, and I'm happy to be getting away from that place." Without turning around, he jerked his head back toward the city.

Jennifer glanced in the rearview mirror. She could see across the marshy industrial flatlands of New Jersey and the lower west side of the city. She saw the twin towers of the World Trade Center, and Battery Park City, both cast in the deep orange glow of the setting sun. It would be dark in another hour, but by then they'd be far from New York. Safe.

She touched him again to reassure herself. "Thank you," she said softly.

"Why?" he asked.

"You know why." She longed to kiss him, to be in his arms, and she almost suggested that they stop, that they find a motel right off the highway, but she knew he wanted more distance between them and the city.

Jennifer took a deep breath and kept her eyes trained on the expressway, at the rush of cars and trucks on the turnpike. Newark Airport was to their right and planes were landing and taking off, gliding onto distant runways, their colored landing lights flickering in the sunset. The air was warmer than it had been, and they were headed south, away from all her tragedies. Everything would be all right again.

She glanced again into the rearview mirror of the small rental car and saw Margit sitting quietly in the backseat, enjoying the drive. She caught Jennifer's eyes in the mirror and smiled.

"What?" Kirk asked again.

Jennifer shook her head. "Nothing. You wouldn't understand."

"Hey, come on, don't give me that!"

"I love you," she said instead, then weaved the car smoothly through the traffic.

"You don't really believe any of that stuff, do you?" he asked her.

"Of course not, darling, it's just a silly game, like reading your horoscope in the newspaper."

Kirk smiled and seemed to relax.

Jennifer reached over again and gently stroked the inside of his thigh, letting her fingers enjoy the touch of him. She could not see his eyes, but she knew they were the same beautiful sweet eyes of her Egyptian prince, the same eyes as her brother Danny. It was not necessary, she realized, for her to share her new knowledge with him. She would take care of him, now that he had come back into her life.

Someday, perhaps, when they were older, she might tell him how they had been together once in Egypt, and before that in other lifetimes. In some they had been lovers, and at other times a sister and brother.

It wasn't necessary to tell him everything now. They were together again, and soon, she knew, they would be husband and wife. Jennifer glanced around. Margit was gone from the backseat, but Jennifer knew the other woman's spirit would never leave her. Just as Kirk had returned, Margit, her lost mother, had returned in this life and would come again in future lifetimes.

Jennifer watched the traffic and the approaching darkness and let her thoughts wander. In the close warmth of the front seat, she smiled, happy and at peace. She wondered about the other lives she might have lived. So far she had remembered lives of retaliation and revenge, yet there must have been happy lives as well. She sat up and regripped the steering wheel of the car.

Perhaps in other incarnations she had been a woman of importance, a high priestess, even a princess or queen. Someday she would remember those lives, all those glorious lifetimes when she wasn't doing battle with the spirit of Phoebe Fisher.

At that thought, Jennifer's heart soared with anticipation. Her life was not over, but her days of anguish were.

"Why are you smiling?" Kirk asked, watching her.

Jennifer kept watching the expressway. She shook her head and said, "I'm just happy, that's all, and in love." The nightmares of her primitive past were over. Phoebe's spirit was gone from her life. Because the channeler's death had not come at her hands, she had finally escaped Phoebe's vengeful spirit.

Yes, Jennifer thought, she would ask Kathy Dart to help her. By making contact with her higher consciousness, with her unlimited soul, she would use the wisdom of her reincarnations to chart a long and happy life with this wonderful young man, her ancient lover.

It was all so obvious now, Jennifer thought. Her life was a perfect puzzle, and she had always been meant, from time eternity, to be on that cold highway in Minnesota so Kirk might find her. It was all God's plan.

No, she realized. It wasn't God. She had made the long journey herself. She had found her own way to salvation. She was, as Kathy Dart had said, her own god. They were all gods, she thought, with their own destinies. Everyone worked out his own karma.

Then Jennifer reached over and flipped on the headlights of the car. The high beams lit up the New Jersey Turnpike and cut a path of light into the dark night, and at that moment on the long dark expressway, Jennifer Winters knew she could see forever.